Jair knew, the moment that Ovard woke him in the pale light of early morning, that the time had come at last for them to run. The sun had scarcely begun to rise in the sky by the time Jair pulled himself out of his bed. He dressed in silence, pulling his long-sleeved roughspun shirt over his head and tucking it into his breeches. He pushed his feet into his thick leather boots and shrugged into his hooded wool cloak just as Ovard reentered the small room.

"Are you warm enough?" the aging man asked the boy, pulling the cloak tightly around Jair's shoulders.

"Yes. I'm all right." Jair kept his gaze on the floor, avoiding Ovard's eyes. Although he understood *why* they had to leave, he still did not like it, not in the slightest.

Ovard let out his breath in a sigh, and Jair finally looked up at him. Ovard's kind, bearded face was creased with the usual wrinkles brought on by age, but it was also creased with regret at having to pull them all away from their home. Jair managed to lift the corner of his mouth in an attempt to smile. He truly felt no anger toward Ovard, and he couldn't find it in his heart to make the man feel worse about the whole thing than he did already.

A familiar movement caught the corner of Jair's eye, and he looked toward the doorway, where Tassie stood, dressed for travel. With the leather bag she had slung over her shoulder, the wide strap crossing over her narrow chest, she looked to Jair just the way he imagined a traveling medic should look.

Ovard let his eyes pass from Tassie back to Jair. "Remember," he told him, putting a hand firmly on his shoulder. "We must do what we can to blend in with the traveling merchants who are getting an early start on the road. We can't draw any attention."

Jair nodded. "I remember."

Tassie took his hand and squeezed it reassuringly as the three of them left the house. Jair noticed, though, how Tassie's eyes nervously searched the shadows as they stepped through the streets of the sleepy villa toward the wide-open wooden gates. Under normal circumstances, Jair would have told Tassie that at the age of twelve he was too old for her to be holding his hand. At the moment, however, given the situation, he wasn't minding so much.

The road was crowded with merchants, even at such an early hour. Some went on foot, pulling small carts by hand, while others drove rickety wagons pulled by mules. None of them paid the small group of travelers any heed as they took to the wide, dusty road. Wooden wheels rimmed in steel rattled over the stony path, and the sound was loud in the otherwise quiet air of the early morning.

Jair kept his eyes fixed on the ground just ahead of his feet as they walked, feeling quite sullen. Not until they reached the crest of the hill did he look up. Pale golden sunlight was streaming across the valley, pushing back the last bit of gray shadows into the far-distant hills.

The world was a very big place, Jair realized. He had seen so little of it in his almost thirteen years. He turned then, for what he supposed would be his last look at the only place he'd ever known as home. The smooth, warm, brownstone wall surrounding the villa, the sleepy little houses, the faded and tattered yellow flag bearing the Lidden crest, the soaring eagle, only slightly stirred by a morning breeze—he tried to fix it all in his memory, until he felt Ovard's hand on his arm.

"Come, Jair," he said in a voice both gentle and firm. "We knew this day would come to us. Going back is no longer an option. You know that as well as I."

Jair nodded. "I do," he replied. "But I will still miss it."

Ovard understood completely how the boy felt in his heart, for he felt it as well, only much stronger, much deeper. He put an arm around Jair's shoulders.

"Keep the memory of it in your heart," he advised, "but leave plenty of room for the hope of something. ... so much better."

Jair nodded and leaned against Ovard, matching his stride as they walked with Tassie beside them, and left behind everything and everyone that they had ever known, ever loved.

The question, the fear, that hung over each of them was: had they been, or would they be, betrayed by the very ones in whom they had for so long placed their trust?

~1~

Brace frantically unlatched the large wooden trunk and threw open the lid. Without a pause, he grabbed at the clothing inside and flung it to the floor, not caring where it landed. He pushed aside long, thick candles and wooden spoons and bowls until he saw the only thing he cared about at that moment—his small leather pouch, full of gold and silver coins. He stared warily over his shoulder toward the old cabin door as he hastily tied the pouch to his belt, where it would not be easily seen under the cover of his long, dark gray cloak.

No one had found him—*yet.* He dared not waste another moment, however, to think about what else he might possibly want to keep. Pulling himself to his feet and hurrying to the window, he peered out just long enough to be sure that it was safe to leave the cabin. Then he burst out through the door and headed straight for the wilderness.

He knew that he would be hunted after, and the wild lands were just as likely a place to be searched as were the surrounding cities and villas. But if he could cross over into Danferron, the keepers of the law here in Dunya would have no authority over him, and they would have no choice but to give up the chase.

Brace's heart thudded in his chest as he clambered up the hillside, his feet slipping in the loose, sandy soil. Grabbing at weeds, bushes, and roots of trees, he managed to pull himself to the top, stopping a moment to lean his back against a tree and take a few breaths before hurrying on.

Brace was in more trouble now than he had ever known in his life. How could he have allowed himself to be seen? Had he truly become so careless as that? He had been a rogue and a thief nearly all of his years, a skill that he had honed into what he had come to believe was perfection. Admittedly, there were times when he'd been caught in an outright lie, or found cheating at chips in a country ale house, but in Brace's eyes, those times had been minor inconveniences, forcing him to move from one province to another, to a place where no one knew his face.

Very few ever learned his name.

But now—he had been seen robbing a wealthy man's cottage on the outskirts of Bale, where he'd been living these past two years, for the most part unknown to the inhabitants of the villa. They knew him only as "the man living out in the old Polattis cabin." As far as Brace knew, none of them had ever thought to associate him with the little things that had gone missing here and there throughout the villa.

But as soon as Brace overheard talk that morning about there being a price on his head, he had hurried back to the run-down little cabin, grabbed his treasures, and fled.

He was angry with himself now for having been discovered, and for having let fear take over, and flying into a panic. Fear was one emotion that he had long been fighting to keep under control. It prevented him from being able to think clearly, to keep his head and worm his way out of unpleasant situations. But, when he'd heard tell of the large sum of money that was being offered to anyone who could hand him over to the law, he'd felt his heart miss a beat.

It was still pounding now, though he'd slowed his run to a steady, even pace through the trees, tall and sparse, looming over him as if they, too, were watching him. Using his sleeve, he wiped the sweat from his face, then ran his fingers through his shoulder-length brown hair, pushing it away from his eyes. Looking around for a place to hide himself and take stock of the situation, he spotted a slope in the ground. He hurried toward it, his long cloak flapping out behind him, its tattered lower edge brushing against the backs of his loose-fitting trousers.

Brace lay flat on the far side of the sloping ground, his back pressed up against the dry, sandy soil. Fully aware that he had been leaving tracks in the dirt, which a well-trained eye would easily be able to follow, he allowed himself only a moment to close his eyes and breathe. The sun was high overhead, warm on his face. The ground was warm as well, and the heat rising from it absorbed through his worn cottagers' clothing, soothing his tense muscles. The sounds of bird calls echoed high in the trees, but there were no other sounds indicating that anyone was close on his heels. *Not yet.*

Brace let out a breath and closed his eyes. *So foolish!* He scolded himself. Foolish for getting caught, foolish for being so afraid! He recalled how his heart stopped cold when he'd overheard that he was wanted by the law. His mind clouded over now with the possible outcomes of the situation. He could escape, yes—but he could just as likely be caught. If the law keepers knew how much he'd stolen during his lifetime, they would probably want him put to death publicly.

Brace couldn't picture himself begging for mercy. He'd grown too cold for that, hadn't he? He would remain hard and defiant to the end, and no one would mourn him. Brace swallowed and pictured himself the way he would want to go out—staring boldly into the eyes of the man who would put the rope around his neck. He wouldn't show any hint of fear. *Fear.* The thought of it—of being hanged—made Brace's throat close up. *Staring boldly into his executioner's eyes?* He questioned himself. Or would he crumble and stand trembling as much on the outside as he would on the inside?

No! Brace told himself, so firmly that he almost spoke the word aloud. He pushed himself up and looked back over the sloping ground in the direction he'd come, then glanced around, noticing the position of the sun. South-southwest, that was the direction he needed to go in order to get to Danferron. *They won't be hanging me any time soon,* he thought. *I'm getting out of here for good.*

It would be a long walk, to say the least, across desertlike terrain. Brace knew how completely unprepared he was to make such a journey. He had no supplies—not even a flask to carry water in.

How ironic, Brace thought. He would have to steal what he needed to survive his way through the wilderness.

He stood, brushing the dirt from his palms. There was a small encampment of goat herders, he knew, about two miles east. He was sure that there he could manage to lift a canteen or a flask—maybe both.

With a quick glance over his shoulder, he hurried off, weaving his way through brush, rocks, and trees. Despite the heat, he continued wearing his heavy cloak, as it provided him cover, keeping out of sight his heavy coin pouch and the dagger he kept tucked away inside the boot on his right leg.

It was not long before Brace's hair began to stick to the sweat beading on his forehead. His eyes stung, and he glared up at the blazing sun, mentally scolding it for throwing so much heat down upon the earth.

Brace's mind was cluttered with unanswered questions, which he had begun to ask himself for the first time in his life. What would he do when he reached Danferron? During the eighteen years he'd been living as a thief, he had run from city to city, villa to villa, province to province. He had learned that the only person he could count on was himself. Stealing, conniving, hiding, running—these were the things he knew, the things he excelled at. Now he found himself filled with doubt. He had been all but caught in the act of theft, and his confidence was beginning to crumble.

How could he possibly give it all up? If he thought he would be able to make a new start in a new country, what honest work would he find? He was not skilled in any arts; he knew nothing of metal works or farming. He was twenty-six years old. Who in Danferron would believe that he had no training, had never apprenticed in anything?

He would likely end up shoveling out mule stables.

The ground was now quite overgrown with shoulder-high bramble bushes, and Brace pushed his way through them, straining to see over them and find the clearest possible path. His frustration grew as every turn he made led him into another sharp branch, jabbing into his arms and legs, even scratching at his face. He began snapping the brittle branches with his bare hands, pushing his way through toward what he hoped would soon become a clearing.

He growled in pain and anger when another sharp twig dug into his cheek. He snapped it off and threw it to the ground in front of him as he at last broke free of the brambles and stumbled into the open—face-to-face with trouble.

The snarling creature was knee-high to Brace, its four legs tight, ready either to run or attack. Brace jumped backward in alarm when he heard the ferocious growling and saw the sharp teeth, but what shocked him most was that the color of the fur on the animal's slender body was a vivid blue, like pure, deep lake water. The creature's large ears were pressed back against its head, and its black eyes flashed.

Brace collected his wits and quickly bent forward, just enough to pull out his concealed dagger. He gripped it firmly, holding it out in front of himself in a threatening manner.

"What are you going to do?" he spoke loudly. "I am armed as well as you are. Come at me, you, and I'll have you for dinner!"

The animal hissed and snarled, the hair along its back standing on end. Brace took a step toward it.

"Don't do that!" A female voice rang out through the trees, startling Brace so that he nearly dropped his blade. He looked around quickly from left to right until he spotted a tall, blonde woman standing nearby, in an authoritative posture.

Brace could see at once that she was no simple cottager. Her long, loose-fitting breeches, tucked into the tops of her dark brown leather boots, just below her knees, along with the heavy, embroidered cloth jerkin, a soft gray-green in color, which she wore over a long-sleeved tunic, it all spoke of a higher class, almost nobility.

"Leave him alone, please!"

"Do you mean me?" Brace asked. "Or that ... *thing*?"

The woman stepped closer, her azure eyes meeting Brace's dark brown ones with a piercing gaze.

"You only frightened him," she answered. "He isn't out to kill you. Leave him alone and he will do the same, I promise you."

The creature stared at Brace, less aggressively, but still bristling.

"Is it yours?" Brace asked, incredulous.

The fair-haired woman hesitated. She seemed unsure how to answer.

"He stays with me," she finally replied. "He is not a pet."

Brace blinked, and slowly lowered his dagger.

The woman moved through the brush toward him, keeping a wary gaze fixed in his direction. She seemed to be reading him—his face, his clothing, his body language.

"Who are you?" she asked, her voice heavy with suspicion.

"I'm no one," Brace replied. "Only a traveler."

"The wild lands are no place for travelers."

The blue-furred creature apparently no longer felt that Brace was a threat to him, and it moved away, toward the woman, who stood boldly nearby.

"You're here," Brace pointed out.

The woman's eyes registered a flicker of amusement, acknowledging Brace's remark.

"True, that," she replied. "Where are you headed?"

Brace chewed on the inside of his cheek as he debated whether to answer truthfully. "No place of consequence," he finally spoke.

The woman crossed her arms over her chest and squinted at him harshly.

"Look," he said, "I don't know you, and you don't know me. I have my business, and I'm sure that you have yours, so let us keep to ourselves. No harm was done here. Let me go on my way, and I promise you I'll let you go on yours. I don't want any trouble."

The woman tipped her head, considering Brace's words. She

looked down at the blue animal sitting at her feet, and it looked up toward her. Finally, she turned her attention back to Brace.

"Well enough. But you're bleeding."

Brace frowned. *Bleeding?*

Ever stoic, the woman pointed to her cheek, then toward Brace. He reached up instinctively to touch the side of his face, and when he looked at his hand, there was a bright red smear across his fingers.

He looked up in surprise.

"Let me help you," the fair-haired, blue-eyed stranger offered. "That wound needs tending to, from the look of it."

"Why would you do that?" Brace asked her abruptly.

The creature at the woman's feet growled deep in its throat, but she scolded it with a click of her tongue, turning away, gesturing for Brace to follow her.

Brace had mixed feelings. How could he be sure that this wasn't some sort of clever trap set by the authorities to ensnare him?

"You don't need to do anything for me," he called after her.

"Nonsense," she replied, without turning around. "We'll fix you up and send you on your way."

Brace tucked his dagger away, slipping it into the hidden sleeve inside his boot.

"*We?*"

The woman turned abruptly to face him.

"I am not alone out here." Her tone was heavy with a warning. She looked him up and down once more, as though she still wasn't sure what to make of him, as though she suspected the same of Brace that he did of her—that he was hiding something.

"But *you* are alone," she continued. "I can't in good judgment allow you to go on like that. The smell of your blood will draw curious beasts. Let us help you."

Brace hesitated, but knew she spoke the truth. He nodded in consent, and the woman turned once again, heading off through the trees. The blue creature walked by her side, the fur puffed up along the spine of its long, twitching tail. It turned its head several times to glare at Brace distastefully.

"What's the problem with your animal?" Brace finally asked.

"He doesn't trust you," the woman replied.

"Did he tell you that?" Brace asked in a snide tone.

The woman looked over at him as they walked. "You don't know much about lorrens, do you?"

"I don't know *anything* about them," Brace admitted.

"He can sense what others are feeling. You fear that I know something of your secrets."

Brace looked down at the blue animal, at its long tail and high, pointed ears. "It can't speak," he said. "How can it tell you what it's thinking?"

"He and I are bonded."

"Bonded?"

"We share one another's thoughts, feelings."

"How can it do that?"

"Stop calling him 'it'. His name is Zorix."

"My apologies." Brace's tone of voice did not match his words, but the woman shrugged it off, leading the way on in silence.

Brace was watchful, and fighting his conflicting feelings. On one hand, he wanted to get away from this uncomfortable encounter with this unusual woman and her strange creature. On the other hand, he knew that she was right about him drawing unwanted attention due to the bleeding wound on his face. He was well aware that the wild lands were home to all sorts of large, often hungry creatures, and he was in no mind to become anything's dinner.

Brace followed the woman down a long, gentle slope, and looked ahead as four people came into view, sitting or standing around a small camp. The blonde woman called out a greeting, and Brace felt everyone's eyes turn on him in surprise. A tall, well-muscled man stepped forward, looking quite forbidding with the scowl on his face, and the heavy brown leather jerkin he wore over his pale-colored woven shirt.

"Leandra, what is this?" he asked.

The woman gestured toward Brace. "He had a run-in with Zorix," she explained. "The wound on his face is bleeding. I offered him our help."

Brace immediately took note of this man's appearance—his hair was cut extremely short on the sides, and the top was kept long, reaching to halfway down his back, and tied securely at the base of his neck. By this Brace knew he was an archer. Trained archers in these parts always kept their hair in such a manner. It was even likely that this man worked for the law keepers.

"Did Zorix scratch him?" The man asked, turning an accusing stare on the blue-furred animal, who wrinkled his muzzle in a snarl.

"No," Leandra answered. "Zorix never touched him." She stood at the archer's side, mere inches shorter than her companion.

Brace stood twitching inwardly under their scrutiny. Glancing past them, he realized that the others in the camp were watching him as well, from a safe distance.

"What was it, then?" The archer demanded.

Brace met his gaze. "Brambles," he answered. "Sharp twigs on bramble bushes."

"Who are you?" This was the same question that the woman, evidently named Leandra, had asked him only moments ago. Brace swallowed and gave no answer.

"He tells me," Leandra spoke, crossing her arms over her chest, "that he is a traveler, nothing more." The expression she wore said that she was not certain whether she believed him. "I thought we could enlist Tassie's medic skills to clean him up before he goes on his way. If she's willing."

The two briefly exchanged some knowing glance, then the man gave a stiff nod, motioning for Brace to follow him into camp. Brace gave Leandra a questioning look as he stepped past her. The faintest hint of a smile touched her lips as she moved to follow after him.

Nervously, Brace kept his eyes alert for any sight of the creature

Zorix, but saw no trace of it … of *him*. Concerned, unsure of whether the animal intended to ambush him, he only vaguely overheard the archer explaining the situation to his companions. Brace felt the uneasy stares of an older man and a young boy, who wore the hood of his cape pulled up over his face. The fifth member of the group was a young woman of slender build, with long brown hair cascading in waves down over her shoulders. When the archer gestured toward Brace, the woman turned her green eyes in his direction.

"Tassie?" the archer asked, and she nodded, stepping closer to Brace and examining the bleeding gash on his face. Without a word, she turned and rifled through a deep leather bag until she pulled out a clay jar and a small wooden bowl. Finding a canteen as well, she unstopped it and poured a small amount of water into the bowl, which she had placed on the dirt at her feet.

Brace found that he enjoyed watching her work. Her long, thin fingers moved with ease and familiarity at her task. He was now quite disarmed, his concerns having been melted away by this woman's striking beauty. Brace had always had a weakness for beautiful women, and this Tassie was no exception.

She—*Tassie*—added a bit of fine powder to the bowl of water and dropped in a rag before returning to Brace's side.

"Sit down," she instructed, and Brace obeyed. "Sit still."

Her voice sounded a bit strange to Brace's ears. Was that some sort of foreign accent? He was intrigued.

The wet rag stung Brace's skin sharply when Tassie pressed it against his face, and he flinched involuntarily. Whatever she had put into the water was thoroughly cleaning the wound, he knew, and preventing any infection, so he kept still. Tassie wet the rag once more and wiped every trace of blood from his cheek. She examined the puncture again, and satisfied that it was no longer bleeding, she stepped back.

"You are fine," she said, then turned away abruptly. Brace stared after her until the large frame of the archer's body blocked his view.

"You heard her," he said gruffly. "You're fine. It's time you went on your way."

"Arden," Leandra scolded. "That was terribly rude. Look at him. He has nothing."

The tall archer looked Bracc up and down. Leandra was right. He had nothing but for the bag of coins hidden beneath his cloak.

"Traveling alone in the wilderness with no shelter, no food, no water?" Arden asked, his voice heavy with accusation. "How is that? What are you not telling us?"

Brace felt backed into a corner, but he was by no means helpless.

"My business is my business," he replied, rising to his feet only to find that Arden still towered over him. "I'm no threat to you. Believe me. You can keep your secrets, and let me keep my own."

Brace held Arden's stare, making the archer aware of his suspicions that their little group seemed to be hiding something.

"Fine then," Arden finally spoke. "Be on your way."

Leandra held up her hand, signaling for Brace to wait. "Let me at least find something for you to carry food and water in."

"I don't need anything else from you," Brace snapped.

"*Young man.*"

Brace turned with a jerk as the gray-haired man stepped toward him. Until now, he had not spoken a word, nor had he moved from where he'd been standing behind the hooded boy.

"What?"

"These are hard times. People tend to guard their secrets well. Please don't take personal offense."

Brace shrugged stiffly. "Whatever you say."

"Arden is only doing what he feels is best in order to protect us, as he has sworn to."

Brace glanced toward the archer, who stood close by, his arms crossed over his muscular chest.

"I see that," Brace acknowledged the older man. "You have him to help you protect your secrets. I have only myself. I've only *ever* had myself, and I've gotten by just fine."

"Have you?" Leandra stood in front of Brace, holding out a small leather canteen and a belt pouch, most likely containing dried meat. Brace only glanced down at what she offered him.

"I have," he replied defensively.

"And yet you have no water to wet your lips," she pointed out. "Please, accept what little I have to share."

Reluctantly, Brace reached out and took the gifts from Leandra's hands. He had to admit to himself that he needed them. He nodded his head in a slight gesture of thanks.

Leandra stepped back, once again at the archer's side.

"*Harbrost*, Arden," she told him quietly. "Isn't that always what you're saying?"

Arden regarded her with a bit of resignation in his eyes.

Harbrost. That word was completely foreign to Brace, but it was at that moment that he took notice of something quite familiar—the matching ornate lines of blue-black ink that wound their way across the backs of Arden and Leandra's hands, encircling their wrists. They were unquestionably husband and wife.

Brace cleared his throat. "I apologize for the disturbance I've caused," he addressed the group, realizing again that he was intruding. "Thank you for your help. I'll be on my way now, if it's all the same to you."

He turned to leave, but stopped short when he saw movement amid the brush. A four-legged, large-eared, red-furred animal came into view, blocking Brace's intended path.

"Zorix!" Leandra called out. "Leave him be."

"Zorix?" Brace asked in surprise. "Wasn't … Wasn't he blue?"

Leandra came forward, and Zorix pressed his side against her legs.

"He was blue," she answered. "You interrupted his hunt. He was angry."

"And now?"

"He is ... nervous."

Brace couldn't take his eyes off the strange animal. He nearly jumped out of his skin when he felt a hand on his shoulder, and he whirled around. It was the old man who stood behind him, stocky, and nearly a head shorter than Brace.

"Easy, son," he said, holding up his hands in a gesture of surrender. "Calm yourself. I only mean to ask—have you a safe place to stay the night? Darkness will be falling soon, fast and hard."

"I ..." Brace stammered, caught off guard. "I planned to find rest at the herders' camp."

The old man shook his head. "That is much too far. You'll never make it there on foot by nightfall."

"Oh, no?"

The man stared at Brace, his gray-green eyes searching.

"I am offering you some protection," he told him firmly. "And some company, if that is something you have a heart for."

Brace's jaw tightened at the reprimand.

"I've never had much need for company," he told him. "But thank you. I don't much favor the idea of being at the mercy of hungry beasts, so I will accept your offer. If it still stands."

The gray-haired man looked to the archer for approval, and did not receive much, only a slight tilt of his head.

Leandra spoke up for her husband. "You'll keep your own fire," she told Brace matter-of-factly. "And know that you'll be watched at all times, traveler. Trust must be earned."

Brace nodded, heeding her warning. The matter settled, he turned and marched several paces away from the odd group of strangers. Coming upon the crumbling remains of a fallen tree, Brace sat, still clutching the unexpected gift.

Food? Water? Safety? Even *company*? Brace had never been offered so much, certainly not all in the same day, by complete strangers, no less.

From this distance, Brace could observe the group as he pleased. The archer was ever watchful, as he stood facing the direction in which Brace had retreated. The tall man—Arden, was it?—allowed himself to be momentarily distracted when Leandra stood close to him, speaking quietly in his ear. He turned and faced her with a hint of a smile, and caressed her short, smooth hair. Leandra kissed her husband briefly before walking away. Brace turned his attention elsewhere. The hooded boy, ever still and silent, remained seated, but Brace could see that he had pulled back his hood just enough to get a better look at him—the intrusive loner. When the boy realized that Brace was watching him as well, he turned away.

Brace frowned in thought. He had his secrets, sure as day, but he still had the suspicion that these people were trying to hide something much bigger than being a wanted thief.

Darkness will be falling soon. Brace remembered the old man's words, and knew that if he wanted to have a fire to keep warm by, he needed to gather some wood. He stood, pulled the strap of the canteen over his head and shoulder, and tied the small food pouch to his belt, beside his hidden treasures.

Casting another glance at the neighboring camp, he turned and started off through the trees until he found one short enough to reach its branches. He snapped off an armful of smaller twigs and a few thicker branches, then walked on, his eyes scanning the ground for dry brush that would easily burn. He stopped when he came upon the unexpected sight of the young woman who had consented to clean his wound. Her back was to him, and she was kneeling in the dirt, pulling tiny leaves from the bush in front of her and stuffing them into a cloth bag.

Brace cleared his throat. "I want to thank you for helping me," he told her.

She gave him no response, but continued gathering.

Brace frowned. She was completely ignoring him. "I know it was an inconvenience, but I am grateful."

Still nothing. Did this woman despise him? He had never experienced this response from any woman. They usually fawned on him—his looks drew their attention, and Brace had learned well how to keep it. This complete disregard was foreign to him. He took a step closer to her, not knowing what to say or do next.

"Um, Miss?"

"She doesn't hear you."

The voice came from behind, and Brace turned in surprise to see the old man.

"What's that?" he asked.

"She doesn't hear you," he repeated. "She hears nothing."

Brace stood in bewildered silence as the gray-bearded man stepped around in a wide circle until he came into the young woman's line of sight.

She looked up abruptly. "Ovard!" she exclaimed. "You startled me."

"Forgive me," he replied, raising an arm to point in Brace's direction. "You have company."

She turned in alarm, pushing aside her long, brown curls. Brace glanced from Tassie to Ovard.

"You can speak to her," the old man informed him. "She can see what you're saying by the shape of your lips."

Brace shifted the bundle of twigs from one arm to the other. "I … I only wanted to thank you," he spoke slowly.

The young woman stood and stuffed the small bag of leaves into her large leather one. "No need," she replied, not unkindly. She turned toward Ovard. "I've finished," she told him. "I'll go back now."

Ovard nodded, and Tassie walked back toward camp, giving Brace a little bit of a smile as she passed him.

~ 2 ~

Sitting alone near his meager fire, Brace chewed on a piece of the dried meat he'd found inside the pouch Leandra had given to him. He watched the others as they sat close together around a fire of their own, not much larger than his. They were all quite familiar with one another, Brace could see from the way they interacted. They did seem ill at ease, however, and Brace was not sure if that was due to his unwanted presence, or if they had something much heavier weighing on their minds.

Leandra sat close to her husband, who from time to time cast his eyes toward Brace. Ovard was seated between Tassie and the boy. Zorix, now a light purple in color, lay on the ground a short distance away from the group.

The boy had removed his hood some time ago, after dark fell, and Brace could see, even from where he sat, alone, some sort of unusual markings on the side of his face. A crescent moon shape curved around the outside of his right eye, and there were lines, or writings, Brace wasn't certain which, on the inside of the shape, high on the boy's cheek.

Brace had never before seen anything like this. Surely, people commonly had themselves marked, as Arden and Leandra had, but not at such a young age, and generally not on the face.

Brace suspected that the image must represent something, as these markings usually did.

Who are these people? The question played over and over in Brace's mind.

Tassie noticed when he was looking at her in particular, and she gave him that same little smile that she had earlier in the day. Brace smiled slightly in return. Zorix lifted his head and looked toward Brace then, making a sound like a huffing bark. This aroused Leandra's attention, and soon Brace realized that everyone's eyes were on him. Odd—he hadn't seen any of them exchanging any words. Why were they eyeing him so suddenly? Recalling what Leandra had told him, that she and that creature, Zorix, could share one another's thoughts, Brace wondered what the furry little beast might have told her. That he was having inappropriate feelings about Tassie? Well, what if he was? He was not foolish enough to do anything about it, with a man like Arden keeping watch.

"Foul creature," Brace muttered under his breath. He turned his back on the neighboring camp, preferring to be surrounded by the darkness than to acknowledge their judgmental stares.

Brace left early the next morning, before anyone in the neighboring camp had a chance to stir. He'd had enough company, he decided. Still naggingly perplexed by Leandra's unexpected generosity, he knew all the same that he had to get out of Dunya. He had by no means forgotten the danger that threatened him if he stayed.

The wild lands were not by any means friendly to men traveling alone, even in daylight. Wild beasts lurked everywhere, from high in the trees to their hidden underground burrows. The weather was unpredictable—the full day's heat could get intense, but there was also the threat of windstorms, or sudden onslaughts of wind and rain so fierce, one could imagine that nature itself had turned on you personally in an attack.

Endless miles of enormous trees, all of which were beginning to look the same to Brace, went on all around him. Grains of soil and pebbles managed to work their way into Brace's boots, giving him pains. The first two times he began to feel the irritating lumps underneath his foot, he stopped, grumbling, to untie the leather straps and knock them out, back onto the ground where they belonged. As the morning stretched into midday, he did his best to try to ignore them. He would not cover as much distance if he kept stopping.

Now, his left heel in particular was giving him trouble. Begrudgingly, he allowed himself a moment to sit and rest. He pulled off his heavy wool cloak and draped it across the dirt, then sat on it, feeling suddenly very exposed. Instinctively, he looked around, but he was very much alone.

That was the way he preferred to be. No one could cause him trouble or pain if they were not around. Alone, he was safer. If he extended trust to no one, it could not be broken, and neither could his heart.

It had been broken once—no, *twice*—so many years ago. Brace had done everything he could to prevent it from happening again.

As he sat, Brace breathed in deeply. The heat of the sun's rays piercing through the trees caused the soil to emanate a sweet, spicy fragrance, stronger here where Brace's footsteps had disturbed it.

It had been scarcely a day since he had fled from his cabin in Bale. How far had the word been spread about his thieving? How many people had begun to suspect that *he* was the one responsible for all of the things that had gone missing? How many upstanding citizens were on the hunt now, greedy for the reward they would receive for his capture?

Upstanding citizens, Brace thought with a sneer. How many nights would they gather around the fire at the local ale house and regale one another with their tales of how they'd turned in that rogue thief? The stories would grow with each telling. He had seen it happen, although not once had Brace ever been part of the cheering crowd, raising their frothy glasses high. He was always hiding in the shadows, or drinking in secret behind the ale house alone, from glasses or bottles that he'd swiped and hidden beneath his cloak.

The tipsy laughter would come to him, muffled through the thick stone walls. It always sounded the same to Brace, and there were times when he wished that he could walk in to join the group, greeting a close friend with a handshake or a slap on the back. He would have a pint handed to him, and he would tap his mug against the mugs of the other men, declaring a toast to life, to health and to happiness.

He would know the songs and sing along with them. He would smile as he drank. He would laugh.

But—it had never been. And now Brace supposed that it never would. He ran his dusty hands through his shoulder-length hair, pushing it away from his face. *So be it.*

The air was still, and silent. *Very* silent.

Brace listened hard for signs of life stirring around him—birds, insects—but heard nothing. Not a leaf rustled. Despite the heat, Brace felt a chill run down his spine.

Looking toward the sky, at first he thought it appeared quite normal. Then Brace noticed the thick, gray mass along the horizon. *A storm*. He knew that sight. And not a rainstorm—no, that would be dust, carried along by a wildly swirling wind.

Brace looked around for some better vantage point. The land here was very flat, but close by Brace spotted a younger, smaller tree with thick limbs that he could easily reach. He pulled himself up high enough to where he could get a better view of the horizon and watched for several moments. The massive gray-brown cloud was most assuredly a dust storm, and it was coming his way.

Even as Brace climbed back down from the tree, he noticed that a breeze had already begun to pick up. Hurrying to where he'd left his cloak on the ground, he snatched it up and flung it over his shoulders, securing the clasp at the base of his throat.

He hadn't too often experienced a dust storm, but from the few times he had, he knew that there would not be much time before this one came on in full force. The herders' camp was still a long distance away, but he had to try to reach it. It was the only sort of shelter available to him for miles.

Brace broke into a run across the open brush, knowing full well that his effort was all but pointless. There was no possible way that he could reach the walled encampment before the storm came to swallow him up. The flat ground became more rugged as he traveled farther to the east, and now Brace had to be careful not to strike his feet against any of the large stones that lay scattered here and there.

By now, the wind had grown stronger, and it pulled at his hair and his long wool cloak. Flecks of dirt irritated his eyes, and he shut them as often as he could, stumbling along from one sturdy tree to another for support. Only a short time passed before the wind began to howl, and even with his eyes open, Brace could see only a few steps ahead. He found breathing difficult, as the air was now clogged with dirt. Pulling the edge of his cloak around his face, he huddled against the rough surface of the nearest tree.

He was just beginning to dwell on what a mess he'd gotten himself into, and wondering how on this earth he would manage to survive the storm, when he thought he heard voices. He lifted his head slightly. Could it be possible? Was he only hearing things? Was that odd group of traveling companions that he met the previous night really so close by that he could hear them?

Brace strained to listen past the wind that swirled all around him.

There! Again, there were the sounds of voices shouting to be heard over the constant high- and low-pitched roaring of the storm.

If there *were* other travelers nearby, whoever they might be, Brace had to make them aware of his dire straits.

"Hello!" he called out, but no sooner had he opened his mouth than it was filled with dust. He choked and coughed, pulling the hood of his cloak tightly around his face. It was no use, he realized, trying to call out while the wind swirled around him so fiercely. He slumped to the ground against the base of the tree, pulled his knees to his chest, and covered his face with his arms to wait out the storm as best he could.

Only a moment passed before Brace felt a hand squeeze his shoulder tightly, and he looked up in surprise to see a somewhat familiar face. It was the old man, Ovard, with a cloth tied across his nose and mouth to keep out the wildly flying dirt.

"Come with us!" Ovard shouted.

"What?"

"Come with us!" he repeated, pulling Brace to his feet. "We're making shelter. Help us, and you can take cover with us. We need your hands."

Brace nodded. "All right. I'll come."

Always having been self-reliant at any cost, Brace was in foreign territory, he felt, as he struggled to follow Ovard toward the others. They soon came into view, partially visible through the dust-filled air. Arden and Leandra, cloths tied across their faces, pulled at large pieces of hide, lacing them together with long strips of leather.

They were tents, Brace realized, as Ovard went to help them— one-man tents that they were joining into one large shelter. Tassie stood nearby, her long dark hair blowing wildly around her face. The boy was huddled against her, and she held him close. Zorix lay at their feet, his raccoonlike front feet pressed over his face, his long tail wrapped around his body. He was covered in brown dust, through which Brace could see that his fur had changed color once again, to a lighter blue.

"So that *was* you calling out through the storm," Arden addressed Brace in mild surprise. Brace only nodded.

"Here," said Leandra, raising her voice over the noise of the wind rushing through the trees. She held out a long leather strip, and Brace took it. She pointed.

"Help Ovard!"

Brace obeyed without hesitating. He wanted shelter from the storm as badly as the rest of them.

Weaving the leather through the preexisting holes in the hide was not the easiest task, for no matter how tightly Ovard held onto it, the strong wind continued to push and pull it in every direction. Brace was constantly having to shut his eyes against the dust blowing into them.

When all of the sides of the tents were secured together, Arden grabbed a long, smooth wooden pole, fitted at the top with a wide, flat disc, and dove under the side of the large tent. In a moment, the top raised up from underneath, and Ovard hurried to Tassie's side. He managed to get her attention, and she gave the boy a shove toward the tent. He disappeared inside, and she and Ovard began grabbing the bundles of their belongings and throwing them inside the tent. They didn't have much, and the work was finished quickly. Ovard pointed toward the shelter, and Tassie nodded, darting inside. Leandra gathered Zorix into her arms and followed her. Ovard grabbed Brace's shoulder and pushed him toward the tent. Brace dove for cover, with Ovard right behind him.

Inside the enclosure, Arden was kneeling in the center, tightly clutching the wooden pole to keep it upright. He instructed everyone to seat themselves on top of the lower edges of the fabric, to keep it firmly on the ground. Their belongings were scattered all around them.

Small clouds of dust managed to work their way through the seams, but conditions inside the tent were a vast improvement on the conditions outside.

Brace was coughing and wheezing uncontrollably, having been the only one in the group with nothing to adequately cover his face. As he struggled to catch his breath, Leandra leaned forward and offered him the wide strip of cloth that she'd been wearing. He had no opportunity to accept it, however. Tassie gently pushed Leandra's hand away, shaking her head. "That will do no good now," she told her, moving to sit close at Brace's side.

"Lean forward," she spoke into his ear, placing her hand on the back of his head. Still choking on the dust in his lungs, Brace surrendered once again to Tassie's directions. She pushed the hood of his cloak out of the way and pressed her fingertips firmly into the back of his neck. She squeezed his arm reassuringly.

"You'll be all right," she told him.

As the moments passed, Brace found it easier to breathe, and he gratefully gasped in lungs full of air.

"Thank you," he wheezed, being sure to face her.

"Don't talk," Tassie replied. "Just breathe."

~ 3 ~

T he dust storm seemed as though it would never end. While it lasted, not one of them bothered to speak. There was too much dirt in the air, even inside the enclosed tent, and the wind roared through the trees in every direction. Brace and the others still kept pieces of cloth pressed over their mouths. At least it helped keep their lungs free of any added grit. Arden had never let up his grip on the tent pole, fighting against the wind to keep a roof over their heads.

The boy—whose name Brace had not yet learned—again pushed back his hood, and was watching Brace with open curiosity. He smiled a little when Brace looked over at him, but he was in no mood for smiling in return. Dirt had gotten into his eyes, and they were scratchy and burned every time he blinked.

The unusual markings on the side of the boy's face were quite visible now, but for the moment, Brace had lost all interest in such things. He was feeling very trapped. He had never been comfortable in small, tight spaces, and the crowded tent seemed to be getting smaller and smaller.

He kept his gaze on his dusty leather boots and waited in silence.

When the storm finally cleared away, everyone emerged thankfully into the fading daylight, but none so thankful as Brace.

They were all cramped and covered with a layer of brown dirt from head to toe. The dirt had managed to find its way into every nook and cranny that it could, penetrating though the layers of their clothing, getting into their ears, their eyes, and their mouths. Brace could taste it, and feel it coating his teeth. Their hair was gritty with dirt. When they blew their noses into the wide strips of cloth, they came away brown.

Brace looked up when Tassie offered him a damp rag, holding it out to him. "To clean up with," she told him, managing to smile. He accepted it, struck by how much heart she and Leandra seemed to have toward him. He recalled how she had gripped his arm to comfort him when he was fighting for breath.

"How did you do that?" he asked her. When she did not answer him, he realized she hadn't been looking in his direction when he'd spoken to her. Tentatively, Brace reached out and touched her arm. She looked at him then, in mild surprise.

"How did you do that?" he asked again. "In the tent there—how did you stop my coughing?"

Tassie gave Brace a weary smile. "Our bodies have many ways to heal," she told him. "One only needs to learn what they are."

He nodded, understanding. "How ... Er, you speak very well. How is that, if you can't hear anything?"

"No more questions," Arden told him gruffly. Brace turned his face away from Tassie toward the archer, and she followed his gaze. "We need to find a water source," the tall, muscular man continued, wiping the dust from his hands. "All of our throats are dry. The day is half gone. If we're going to find water before dark, we need to start looking now."

Leandra, unable to rid her hair of any more dirt, tied it back to get it out of the way. "I agree," she told Arden, "but I'm afraid that any lakes or streams will be clogged with dirt for some time before they clear themselves enough to be suitable for drinking."

"What do you suggest we do?" Ovard asked, his short beard now more brown than gray.

Leandra turned her eyes onto Brace. "You said you were heading for the herders' camp," she told him. "They have a well there, yes?"

Brace nodded. "Yes."

"I say we head there ourselves, then. It's our best option given the circumstances."

"Will you permit us to journey there with you?" Ovard directed his question toward Brace, and he stopped in the middle of washing the dirt from his face.

"You're asking me to *let* you come with me?"

"That's what I'm asking."

Brace was incredulous. "What happened to your not trusting me?" he asked. "Your archer friend certainly doesn't want me around, even now."

Ovard and Arden exchanged glances.

"That's right," Brace continued. "I know he's an archer. Although I don't see you wearing your crest anywhere. Who are you hiding from?"

Arden stepped forward, a harsh look in his eyes. Zorix snarled and began pacing back and forth between Arden and Brace. Leandra stepped closer, her eyes glazed over.

"What is it, Leandra?" Ovard asked her. "What is he telling you?"

"He's feeling frustrated," she answered. "He says we know that *he's* hiding, and he knows that *we're* hiding. Zorix doesn't believe that the traveler poses any threat to us. He says … flaring tempers only lead to trouble, and we don't need any more trouble."

Brace stared wide-eyed at Zorix. That animal really *could* communicate with Leandra. Until now, he still hadn't been too sure that he believed it.

"Do you?" Arden was speaking to Brace.

He looked up. "Do I what?"

"Pose a threat."

Brace looked around him. Everyone was watching him, waiting for his answer. He quickly assessed the situation. Tassie and Leandra had been more than kind to him, and Ovard was welcoming enough. The boy seemed curious as ever. It was only Arden and the color-changing creature who gave Brace any reason to feel uncomfortable or unwelcome.

He preferred to be on his own. Life was much easier when he didn't have to concern himself with what others might do. Also, he did not want to stay long in the area. It would be a long trek to Danferron. The longer he waited, the more likely it was that he would be found. It was obvious that these people knew nothing about him. *Would they turn me in*, he wondered, *if they knew what I'd done*? If he agreed, and led the way to the herders' camp, he could easily leave at first light. He had done it before.

Brace finally answered Arden's question.

"I'm not out to make any trouble for you. I don't know who you are or what you're about. I don't really care to either. But I know you all need water to drink. You've done more for me than anyone I can remember in my life, so it's the least I can do, to show you the way to the camp."

"Many thanks!" Ovard replied, his voice genuine.

Brace let out a deep sigh. He was exhausted. His eyes felt sandy and irritated. What he wouldn't give for a lake—a fishing hole, even—that he could strip down to his skin and jump into. It would not be, he knew. Not this day. The nearest lake was far on the other side of Bale.

"*Traveler.*" Leandra's voice broke through Brace's daydreaming. "We'd best start off now. There's no sense wasting time."

Brace looked tiredly at the others. Taking the tents apart took much less time than putting them together, and was already bundled up. They all stood ready to leave.

Brace nodded, rising to his feet. He took a moment to look around and determine where they might be in relation to the herders' camp. The trees loomed over their heads, still and straight as stone towers. The ground was all wind-swept dirt, with an occasional shrub here and there. Large, craggy rocks pushed their way through to the surface of the earth. The air was still once again, and stiflingly warm. It was after midday, so the sun would be sinking to the west. The herders' camp lay to the east. They should still be able to reach it before it grew too dark for traveling.

"This way," Brace told the others, and with a wave of his hand, he started off, dragging his feet over the loose, sandy soil.

He led the way on in silence for some time before he noticed, out of the corner of his eye, the young boy hurry ahead of the others to walk beside him. Brace gave him a nod of recognition.

"Hello," the boy greeted him. "My … My name is Jair. What's yours?"

Brace cleared his throat and glanced back toward the others. They were only half paying attention, as they were all very tired, and focused on the path ahead of them. He turned back to the boy, and kept walking.

"Merron," he replied. It was a name he had used before, quite often, and it came to him easily.

"Where are you from?"

Brace gave a little snort. "Everywhere and nowhere," he replied.

"Where are you heading?" Jair's questions continued.

"Beyond the herders' camp, I am not certain," Brace lied.

"Why are you wandering?"

When Brace hesitated, Ovard spoke up, a short distance behind him. "Let's not bother our guide with too many questions, Jair. These are troubled times. Many people have secrets. He has made it clear that he is keeping his to himself."

Jair nodded in response to Ovard's instruction, then looked again at Brace. "Sorry."

Brace waved off the apology, and noted the rise in the ground on their right. He knew that the herders' camp was not far on the other side, in a flat, open stretch of land.

"The well is there," he called out, "over the other side of the ridge. It's not bad going up, but it's steeper going down the other side. We'll have to take it slowly, to keep our footing."

Ovard lengthened his stride to catch up to Brace.

"The herders will be able to clearly see us approaching, will they not?"

Brace nodded. "They certainly will."

"We are not herding goats," Ovard continued, pensively stroking his beard. "Will they give us any trouble about wanting to use the well?"

Brace thought a moment. He had seldom ever *asked* to get water from the camp; he had quite often waited until after dark and simply gone and taken it.

"I should think not too much trouble," he finally replied. "There are not many of us. We won't require a large amount of their water."

"And if we need to camp there for the night?" Arden asked, now carrying in plain sight his bow and large quiver full of arrows slung across his back. "What then?"

Brace stopped walking and turned back toward him. "We'll keep our distance," he answered, after taking a moment to think it over. "If you set up your tents well outside the wall, they won't have reason to feel threatened."

"Why would herders feel threatened by us?" Jair asked.

Brace considered his words carefully. "Sometimes, thieves work their way into the camp and make off with some of their goats. If we keep ourselves separate from them, we won't be as likely to put them on edge." Jair nodded, accepting the answer. Brace, however, did not very much like the look that passed between Arden and Ovard at that moment. He turned abruptly and continued walking up the ridge, and could hear the footsteps of the others following him. The soil on the ridge was loose and rocky, and as Brace picked his way toward the top, his boots knocked loose a cascading shower of pebbles.

He heard Leandra gasp slightly as she tumbled forward to keep her balance. Brace looked back to see Arden reach out to catch her and steady her. "You all right?" The archer asked, and she nodded. "I'm fine."

Zorix hurried to Leandra's side as well, and he seemed to be scowling up at Arden, who was still holding onto Leandra's arm.

"I'm all right, Zorix," she spoke to him aloud. Then she tipped her head toward him, and Brace assumed that she was once again, somehow, silently telling him something more. Zorix turned his head away, and continued forward up the sloping ground.

Ovard continued on while Leandra regained her footing. Brace's expression must have betrayed the question lingering in his mind, and the older man paused and cleared his throat. "Zorix is very ... possessive ... of Leandra." Ovard explained, laughing under his breath. "He was bonded to Leandra well before she even met Arden. He doesn't like the idea of having to share her affections."

Brace nodded. "I can understand that." Leandra was a woman of some beauty, tall, strong, with smooth golden hair and a kind but bold disposition. Brace, however, more often felt his eyes drawn toward Tassie—and not only for the reason that Leandra was spoken for. The younger woman had softer features and a smaller build, and her long brown curls were irresistible. He caught himself looking at her once again, and turned away before Ovard had a chance to notice.

"We're nearly there," he told the group, calling back over his shoulder. "Let's keep moving. We should get there just before night falls."

Dust billowed into the air as the six travelers half walked, half slid their way down the far side of the ridge toward the herders' camp. Zorix found his way much more easily, being smaller and lighter, and able to leap from place to place. But Brace noticed he looked back quite often. Most likely he was keeping watch on Arden and Leandra.

The herders' camp was surrounded by an old, crumbling stone wall, formed into a large circle, almost completely closed but for the entrance, which was simply an opening in the wall, with no gate. The wall itself stood more than thirty feet high in most places, where it remained intact, and formed a half-mile wide enclosure where at least a dozen goat herders had pitched their tents and gathered their animals into ramshackle wooden pens.

The camp had originally been built to provide simple shelter for the herders as they traveled through the wild lands to villas and cities where they would take their animals to market. But over the years it became considerably more. Herders had taken to using the camp as a place to breed their goats with others from other herds, keeping their bloodlines healthy. They also used the time for buying and selling, or trading one goat for another. It was often a very noisy place.

The travelers had been seen approaching the camp, as Brace was sure they would be. An elderly herder with a long, white beard and a slightly stooping back came slowly toward them, leaning heavily on a gnarled walking stick for support. His cotton shirt and leggings were patched and stained, and his cloak was hardly that—short and frayed along the edges.

He raised a tanned, wrinkled hand in greeting as the group neared him, who were now thankful to be on level ground. The sun had begun to set behind them, and the old herder held up his hand to keep the blinding golden light out of his eyes.

"Please," he said in a wavering voice. "What business have you here?"

Ovard spoke for the group. "We only ask for clean water to drink from your well, nothing more."

The old man watched them for a long moment. He seemed to be looking for their goats.

"Y'are not herders," he observed.

"No," Ovard replied, "only thirsty travelers. We were caught out in the dust storm."

"A bad one, that was," the old man agreed.

Brace stepped forward. "Will you help us?"

The elderly herder looked around the group a moment longer, studying each of them in turn. Brace was sure that he would not forget their faces, if in fact he could clearly see them.

He finally gave them a nod. "Come and have your fill," he invited.

"We give you our thanks," Ovard told him in the customary manner. "We would also like to be permitted to camp nearby. We will keep to ourselves, certainly, well outside the walls. But it is quite dark, as you can see."

The older man seemed less agreeable about this new request.

"So long as you keep to yourselves," he replied at last.

"You can be sure that we will," Brace answered first. He gave Ovard a slight push in the direction of the large, covered well, and they moved on. The old man began his slow, shuffling walk back toward the camp, keeping his eyes turned on the newcomers in unconcealed mistrust.

Brace lifted the edge of the hinged wooden slab that covered the old stone well. Arden reached out and took hold of the fraying end of the rope tightly in his fist.

"There's no bucket," he remarked bluntly.

"No," Brace replied. "Here, everyone generally brings their own."

Ovard stood at the edge of the well and peered down into it, although the sky had darkened considerably, and the interior of the well was black with shadows. "I have brought an old mug along," he said to no one in particular. "It will take longer than with a bucket to fill everyone's water flasks, but I'm afraid it will have to do."

Ovard looked over the old rope as though he did not fully trust it to hold together. Retrieving his mug from his small pack of belongings, he tied several knots around the handle. He had brought only the one drinking vessel, and he did not want it lost.

Brace found it tedious, standing by and watching Ovard struggle to pour water into the narrow openings of each canteen with the wide mouth of the carved wooden mug. Every drop that escaped was quickly absorbed by the dry, thirsty ground. Brace leaned back against the side of the well and began scanning the area for a suitable place to camp, knowing that he fully intended to strike out early, back up the ridge, and head for Danferron as he had planned.

"Merron?"

It took a moment for the word to seep into Brace's consciousness, to realize that Ovard was in fact speaking to him.

"What?" he asked, looking in the old man's direction.

Ovard held up the mug. "More water?"

Brace clutched the wide strap of his canteen, which fell across his chest. He'd almost forgotten it. He tested the weight of it, and knew that it was almost empty.

"Yes," he replied. "I could use more water."

He pulled the strap up and over his head and opened the canteen for Ovard to fill. It was a small vessel, and as the older man poured, cool water ran over Brace's hand, making him all the more eager to taste it.

Brace tipped his head in thanks when the canteen was filled, and took a good drink. He felt the water running all the way down his parched throat, and was instantly refreshed.

As Ovard untied all of the knots he'd made in the rope to retrieve his mug, Jair stood by silently, his hood covering his face once again, looking into the distance toward the walled encampment.

Odd, Brace found himself thinking. *The boy is the only one who really seems to be hiding himself.*

The loud scraping of wood against stone made both Jair and Brace flinch, as Arden lifted the heavy well cover back into place. Brace let out a breath and watched as Leandra poured some of the water from her larger flask into the palm of her hand for Zorix, who wasted no time in licking it up. She looked up and noticed that Brace was watching her. She smiled a little, grateful for his help. Brace allowed himself a crooked smile in return. He noticed that her attention shifted then to Arden. Her expression softened considerably, and this time when she smiled, Brace could see it in her eyes as well. Zorix stopped drinking and lifted his head to look at her, water dripping from the fur on his chin. Leandra turned back to Zorix and tugged playfully at his ear, securing the top of her canteen and wiping her hand on the side of her tunic.

Arden turned his back, facing the sloping ridge. "I think it would be best if we made our camp at the base of this," he said, pointing toward it. "We'll have some sort of cover."

Cover? Who were these people running from? And why?

Ovard agreed with Arden's suggestion, and everyone gathered their strength to pick up their things once again, and to walk the short distance back to the foot of the ridge.

Brace glanced back toward the herders' camp, considering what he could easily snatch and take with him early the next morning. Jair had stopped walking, and now stood looking at him.

"What is it?" Brace asked, somewhat irritated at having been distracted.

"Will you be camping out with us tonight?" The boy asked. He seemed hopeful that Brace's answer would be yes.

Brace turned toward the others, whose backs were already to him.

"I don't know," he replied. "I don't think I'm welcome."

"You are with me. You seem to have been so many places. I'd bet you have some interesting stories to tell." Jair tugged nervously at the shoulder of his cloak. "I ... I've never really been anywhere."

Brace was mildly amused with the boy's curiosity. "I don't think you'd like to hear any of my stories," he told him.

"Jair!" Ovard called from a distance. "Don't linger back! Stay with us."

"Right. I'm coming," Jair answered back. He turned briefly toward Brace before hurrying away. "I'm still inviting you to join us," he informed him.

Brace watched the boy go, kicking up sandy soil as he ran.

Strange folk, Brace thought. Never in all his days could he remember meeting anyone who sparked his interest the way these people did. He straightened up, away from the well, and with one more glance back toward the camp, he followed after them.

~4~

Brace's presence once again brought mixed reactions. Arden, though considerably more subdued, gave him a look that showed his irritation. Jair was smiling broadly, and Ovard seemed pleased that Brace had joined them. Leandra was busy setting up one of the small tents, and only slightly acknowledged him. Brace wasn't quite sure what Tassie might be thinking, as she stopped in the middle of unfolding the large fabric that would become her own shelter to stare at him momentarily, her face betraying no certain emotion. Zorix ignored him altogether.

"You are welcome here with us, Merron," Ovard greeted him. "You have so far shown yourself to be trustworthy. You may join us at our fire tonight, if you wish to."

Brace cleared his throat, hoping to cover up the surprise that he felt. The old man would not be so quick to welcome him if he knew what a rogue thief he was.

"We have no extra tents," Arden informed him. "And you have none of your own."

"I will do well enough without one," Brace told the archer, facing him. He would by no means allow Arden to believe that he was able to intimidate him, although he did somewhat, Brace had to admit, at least to himself.

Arden made no reply, but turned to help Leandra with her work.

Jair stepped up behind Ovard and timidly laid a hand on his

arm. "He could share mine," the boy offered. "I don't take up a lot of room."

Ovard affectionately rested his hand on the boy's head, then turned toward Brace. "I don't know if our guest is accustomed to such an offer. Well, Merron? What have you to say in response to Jair's kindness?"

Brace glanced toward Arden as he considered his response. "I appreciate your generosity," he began, "but just the same, I'll have to decline. I do prefer being out of doors."

His statement was true enough, but the fact of the matter was that he did not want to give the archer cause to make him feel that he was in any way beholden to them for anything. They'd already done plenty.

Jair nodded solemnly, and Ovard patted the boy's shoulder. "Why don't you go and get your tent put up. Perhaps, Merron, you would be kind enough to gather some dried brush to provide us with a bit of a warm fire before we turn in for the night?"

Brace nodded begrudgingly as he turned away from the others. *I'm getting too tied up with these people,* he grumbled to himself. *Come on, morning. Come quickly.*

He wandered slowly along the flat ground, but quickly realized that the goats had eaten everything they could reach. Only the rocks were left untouched. Looking along the edge of the sloping ridge, he could see scrub brush jutting up into the orange sunset sky. Breathing out in resignation, he began to climb his way toward them. Brace had to lean in toward the hillside to keep his balance as he wrestled with the tough brush. Small thorns dug into his calloused hands, and he grumbled under his breath. After managing to gather a small armload, he turned and stumbled back down the ridge.

By the time he returned to the camp, all of the tents were set up, and everyone sat, taking long, satisfying drinks of cool well water from their flasks. While Brace arranged the small heap of firewood, Ovard pulled a flint stone from a pocket hidden inside his outer garment. He produced a small knife as well, and after striking it against the smooth stone several times, he managed to create a small spark. A few breaths caused the dry brush to smoke, and soon a tiny flame leapt up, spreading quickly along the spindly twigs. Larger, more substantial pieces of wood were added until they had a small, dancing fire around which to gather.

Brace watched as everyone moved closer to the flames, stretching out their hands to warm them in the increasing chill of the early night air. Leandra laid her hand on Arden's arm and spoke to him quietly. The archer looked up, to where Brace stood opposite him.

"Thank you, traveler."

Brace crouched down and stared into the flickering blaze. Arden may only be thanking him at Leandra's request, but his voice had lost its harsh edge.

"It was nothing," Brace muttered.

Jair opened the pack that lay behind him on the dusty ground and took out a small bundle wrapped in cloth. Pulling the cloth away revealed two flat, hard pieces of bread. Jair stood and made his way around the campfire until he stood at Brace's side.

"You must be as hungry as I am," the boy told him. "You can have one, and I'll eat the other."

Brace found himself staring at the boy. With what little he had, he was willing to give him half? He shook his head slightly. "No. You don't have to do that."

"I want to." He held the bread out toward him. "Please take it."

Hesitantly, Brace reached out and accepted it. "Thanks."

Jair smiled, and returned to his seat.

Brace sat looking at the piece of bread in his hands. He had somehow managed to leave a small crack in the armor he'd built up around his heart, and this boy was beginning to work his way in through it. He couldn't let that happen. Whenever he left his heart open, someone always managed to sneak in and wound it. Brace rose slowly, turned away from the group, and wandered aimlessly toward the ridge, his eyes still fixed on the bread. He knew that he had to keep his distance from these people, in more ways than one. If he let them in any farther, leaving would hurt him.

Brace made his way up the side of the ridge a short distance, where he found a small outcropping of rock that formed a sort of natural seat, and he lowered himself onto it, tearing off small pieces of bread and chewing them slowly. The bread was nearly gone by the time Brace noticed Ovard's shape coming toward him. The older man's face was all shadows when he came and sat down beside him.

"You're planning to leave again, aren't you?"

Brace raised an eyebrow. "What's that?"

"You keep your distance because you're going to be gone again in the morning."

Brace swallowed the last of the bread in his mouth. "That is my plan. I'm used to being alone. It suits me." Ovard gazed thoughtfully out over the shadowy landscape.

"I believe that in life," the old man began slowly, "some things are meant to happen. Don't you?"

Brace remained silent.

"For whatever reason, young man, it seems to me that you were meant to find us."

"*Meant* to?"

Ovard turned toward him. "Meeting once would seem to be by chance. But twice? And in the middle of a wild dust storm? For us to have heard one another, to have found you—I could only see three steps ahead of myself. I could have walked right by you and never known it. It could be that our meeting was not by chance."

Brace considered Ovard's words for a few moments.

"Not by chance. Are you talking about *fate*?"

"You could put it that way. I firmly believe that not everything that happens in this world is an accident."

Brace flicked the breadcrumbs from his clothing. "I've never seen anything that would make me believe that," he replied brusquely. "If I've ever needed or wanted anything to happen, I had to be the one to make it happen."

Ovard sat quietly for a moment, seeming to gather his thoughts. "In my many years," he continued, "I have seen enough to come to believe that there is some ... master plan. It affects all of us. Sometimes, the unlikeliest of people have an important part to play."

Brace frowned. *Master plan.* If there had been a master plan laid out for his life, it was only misery.

"You don't even know who I am."

"No, that I don't. But Jair is quite taken with you."

Brace shook his head. "He only wants to hear tell of my 'adventures'."

"Do you have many?"

"I wouldn't call them adventures. The tales I have, I won't be telling anyone, not any time soon."

"Merron ..."

Brace sighed and stood. "My name is not Merron."

Ovard nodded slowly. "I suspected as much."

"I don't believe in fate, old man. My life is in my own hands. And I may not *mean* to bring trouble to you and your companions, but trouble may very well come to you if I stay. I'm ..." He shrugged inwardly. The old man seemed to know so much already, he might as well tell him more. "I'm a wanted man."

Ovard allowed Brace's words to settle. "Wanted for ...?"

"Thieving. My plan is to run to Danferron. The law keepers here will have no authority over me in Danferron."

"And what will you do there?" Ovard asked. "Go on stealing?"

"I don't know!" Brace snapped. "I haven't thought so far ahead."

Ovard was silent for a length of time. "What if ..." he began again, "what if there were another place, an unknown place? Better than Danferron. Would you go there?"

"What place is that?"

"The Haven."

Brace shook his head. "I don't know what you're talking about."

41

"The ancient city of our ancestors. It has been told of in prophecies, legends, and fireside tales for thousands of generations. You mean to tell me that you know nothing of it?"

"I've never had anyone around to tell me stories."

Ovard shook his head slowly, incredulous. "Well, we intend to find it."

"The ancient city?" Brace asked. "Why on this earth would I prefer some crumbling old city over Danferron? What could possibly make *that* a better place?"

"The Haven is said to be a city of light in this darkening world. It is a place of miracles."

"Darkening world?"

"Have you never asked yourself why the days are so short and the nights are so long?"

Brace shrugged his shoulders. "I assumed it has always been this way."

Ovard shook his head. "Not so, when I was young. The days were much longer, and the darkness ... not so dark." He stared ahead, as though his memories hovered like a cloud in front of him. "You say you have no adventures to tell of," he continued. "Come with us. Help us find the Haven. You will have a great adventure, one that will be well worth the telling."

"I'm not interested in adventures," Brace grumbled. "I'm interested only in keeping my hands—or my head!"

Ovard eyed him harshly. "What have you stolen?"

"What *haven't* I stolen?" Brace replied. "I've been a thief nearly all my life, and only recently I was caught at it. But if everyone realizes just how much I've taken ..." He shook his head. "At any rate, there is a price on my head. Trust me, old man. You don't want me as your traveling companion."

Ovard scratched the back of his head thoughtfully. "You asked once who we were hiding from," he told him.

"And?" Brace prodded.

Ovard pulled himself to his feet. "We are not the only ones who want to find the Haven. There are others: scholars, rulers, men of strength and authority, who know of its existence. They would take it by force as their own in order to use its miraculous powers against the people, to suppress them, force them into submission."

"What miraculous powers?"

"Truthfully, I don't fully know. There are only vague mentions of something in the tales I've heard or seen written down."

"So you're hiding from …?"

"Specifically, I'm not certain. But I have long studied the prophecies, and the time is right for the way into Haven to be revealed. If I am aware of this fact, others must be as well."

"What has all of this got to do with you?"

Ovard was silent. Brace glanced down toward the small camp, at the black shapes of the others, gathered close around the small blaze.

"The boy," Brace thought aloud. "This has something to do with that boy, with the markings on his face. Doesn't it?"

Ovard nodded. "It does. So, you see, we wish to avoid being found ourselves. You are in the same trouble that we are. Having you along would make no difference in that respect."

"But why would you want to include me? What good have I to offer you?"

"That isn't the question," Ovard replied. "The question is, what good have *we* to offer *you*."

Brace spread his hands, not having any idea what the old man could be getting at.

"If you truly prefer to be alone in life," Ovard began, his voice quickened in a reprimanding tone, "if you truly have no heart for friendship, and you want to go on to Danferron and pick up your life where you left off, by all means, go ahead. But if you want to take the chance, most likely the *only* chance, to truly be a part of something worth the doing, and to make a new start, a new life for yourself in an unspoiled place, to be a part of fulfilling prophecy and bringing light and hope to this world, then come with us. That's what I'm offering you. I won't ask again. The choice is yours."

Ovard turned and left, back down the side of the ridge, fading into the surrounding darkness. Brace stood and watched him go. He felt almost as though Ovard had physically struck him and left him alone to find his breath. A small flame of interest began to burn in Brace's thoughts. He had never of heard of such a place as this Haven, but if it truly did exist, could it be worth the risk, in order to have the chance to see it?

He battled against himself for some time. Part of him strongly desired to flee to Danferron. That certainly made much more sense. How did anyone even know how to find the ancient city? Once they discovered where it was, how long would it take them to get there? Then, if they were able to reach the city, what would they do after that? There would be a lot of work ahead of them. The other part of him considered the point that Ovard had made. If Brace ran away to Danferron, would he continue his life as a thief? This question he had already asked himself. He truly did not know what he would do, but he certainly wouldn't be blindly welcomed into the country, with no questions asked. He would have to sneak in over the border and lay low for a while. It would not be easy.

But nothing in his life had ever been easy. He'd never had anything handed to him; if he wanted something, he had to get it himself. Now the question he found himself asking was: *What did he want?*

He wasn't sure exactly what made him go back to the group, but go back he did. He stumbled over rocks in the darkness, and made his way to stand just inside the flickering circle of firelight. Everyone's eyes were on him.

"I think I'd like to come with you," he found himself telling them. "I'd like to help you find this 'Haven' you're looking for. I know that you don't all feel the same way about me, and I know that trust has to be earned. I can't promise you that I won't let you down, but if you'll let me, I'll do what I can to help."

In the dim firelight, Brace could not see everyone's faces to judge their reactions. Ovard, however, stood and held out his arm, welcoming Brace to come and sit among them. Hesitantly, Brace stepped forward and lowered himself to the ground between Ovard and Tassie.

"I believe you've made the right choice," Ovard told him, returning to his seat.

"Will you tell us your true name, then?"

Brace looked up at Ovard in surprise. "Did ... Did you tell everyone what I told you, up on the hill?"

"Not everything. Just enough."

Brace looked around at the others, and surprisingly, they did not seem to bear much harsher judgment toward him than they already had.

"Brace," he told them. "My name is Brace."

"Why did you tell us your name is Merron?" Jair appeared to have been let down hard.

"I'm sorry I lied to you, kid. I didn't know who I could trust. People might be after me, just like they might be after you. I've ... stolen things. I've made people angry. I had to run away, and I was only trying to protect myself. I hope you all will try to understand."

Leandra studied him for a moment, her head tilted to one side. Her smooth, fair hair was brushed clean, and fell softly around her face. "I can understand your wanting to hide," she told him.

"But not the stealing," Brace finished her unspoken thought.

"It is not my place to judge," she replied. "But it is never too late to change. To make things right."

Brace looked away, suddenly feeling too ashamed to look her in the eye. When he looked up once again, it was Jair's gaze that he met. The boy's face was clouded over with disappointment. Brace was somewhat grieved, but it was better, after all, that the boy learn the truth about him, *sooner* rather than later. Brace did not want Jair to hold him in high regard as someone he was not.

Ovard responded to the tension that was beginning to build up around what remained of the camp fire.

"It's late," he said, standing. "I think the herders will appreciate us getting an early start. Let's get some sleep."

Arden pulled himself to his feet and waited a moment for Leandra to join him. Together, they faded into the darkness. Ovard motioned for Tassie to move away, and to go to her own small tent. Without even a sideways glance toward Brace, she turned and left.

"You're certain you wouldn't like to have any shelter?" Ovard asked.

Brace shook his head. "I am fine out here."

Ovard nodded in response. "Sleep well then."

After Ovard departed into the shadows, Jair lingered a moment alone.

"You won't be gone in the morning?" he finally asked.

Brace considered the question. "Do you want me gone?"

The boy hesitated, chewing thoughtfully at his lower lip. "No," he replied at last.

Brace gave Jair a slight nod. "I will be here."

Jair moved away from the fire then, and Brace was once again alone, surrounded by heavy, solid darkness. The flames at his feet snapped weakly, and insects buzzed rhythmically in the distance. What made him decide to stay, he still wasn't certain. But this time, for the first time in so many years, Brace decided that he was going to keep his word. At least for the time being.

~5~

Arden was the second to emerge from his tent the next morning. Brace had already risen and stood pushing the cooled ash from last night's fire around with the toe of his boot, his long wool cloak billowing out behind him in a chill, early morning wind.

The tall archer stood watching him a moment. "Good day," he finally spoke.

"The same to you," Brace answered in a low voice.

Arden stepped toward him, away from the tent. "I'm surprised to see you're awake. I have grown accustomed to most often being the first to rise."

Brace shrugged slightly. "I sleep lightly."

Leandra stepped out into the morning air behind Arden, rubbing her arms against the cold.

"So you did stay after all," she greeted Brace.

"I did," he replied with a slight nod, avoiding her eyes.

A strained silence filled the camp as the three stood watching one another.

"Well," Leandra spoke at last. "Just see that you keep your nimble hands to yourself, won't you?"

Brace kept his gaze on the ground.

"He will give us no trouble." Arden's strong words filled the morning quiet, causing Brace to look up. Leandra rested her hand a moment on her husband's arm before she went aside to wake Tassie. The archer's steel blue eyes were set on Brace like stone.

"I will do my best to give you no cause for regret," Brace told him, "for allowing me to join you."

"Join us?" Arden asked. "You may be coming with us, stranger, but you are not yet one of us. You would do well to remember that."

"What must I do to earn your trust?" Brace challenged him. "Tell me, what must I do?"

Arden watched him in silence a moment. "We shall see," he replied before turning away.

That morning's meal was meager at best. It was not a pleasant way to start the day by any means. Brace found himself eyeing the herders' camp, wishing it were night once again. It would be easy enough to sneak in, wring a goat's neck, carry it back to camp, and cook it and eat it. He doubted that one goat would be missed. He preferred lamb over anything else, but goat's meat would fill his stomach just as well. Better than dried fruit and roasted grain.

Brace chewed disdainfully on his tough, bland meal and grimaced. Was he giving up a life in Danferron for this?

A heaviness fell over each member of the group. Brace could feel it. Ovard must have sensed it as well, for he tried to make light and cheer them. He succeeded only slightly, however. It was as though they had all come to the realization that their lives would never be the same. From this day on, they were leaving behind their pasts, for better or worse, and facing the unknown future head-on.

Zorix hovered nervously around the edge of the camp. From time to time, he made his way to Leandra's side and faced her intently.

"No, Zorix," she told him when he came to her once again.

"What is wrong?" Brace made himself bold enough to ask.

"He wants meat," Leandra replied, resting her hand on Zorix's furred head. The animal's wide black eyes stared unblinking at Brace, and he noticed that Leandra was watching him as well.

"What are your intentions?" she asked Brace abruptly.

"I don't know what you mean."

"You desire meat as well." She cut her eyes briefly toward the walled camp nearby.

Brace stood, offended. "I'm not going to try to steal a goat in broad daylight!" he exclaimed. "Do you think I would have gotten by for so many years if I were as foolish as that?"

"Come now," Ovard spoke up. "Let us not begin this day with such bickering. We must all be of one mind if we are to work together in this."

"Where are we even going?" Brace asked him. "Do you even know the way?"

Ovard sat a moment, his hand pressed to his bearded chin in thought. "For the most part," he replied. "We know that the path to Haven lies to the south, and then eventually to the west."

"How exactly do you know this?"

Ovard stood and studied Brace a moment. "Do you swear to me that you can be trusted?"

"As best I can," Brace answered, "for all that I am, and all I am not, I swear to you. I will betray you to no one."

A small hint of a smile tugged at the old man's mouth. He motioned for Jair to come to him, and the boy quickly obeyed, standing in front of Ovard. The top of his head reached just level to the older man's chin.

"These marks," Ovard began, pointing to Jair's face. "It is as you said. These marks show the way to Haven. I have studied them for some time, and I believe I understand them—or most of them."

Jair was in obvious discomfort, knowing that everyone's eyes were focused on him alone. Ovard patted the boy's shoulder.

"Thank you, Jair. You may sit down."

Gratefully, Jair hurried back to his seat beside Tassie, and she wrapped her arm around his shoulders.

"South, then?" Brace asked. "South from where? Do you know where to start?"

"The best I can tell," Ovard replied, taking his seat once more, "is that we have at least started in the right place—from Lidden."

"Lidden? So you've only just begun?"

"That is right," Leandra joined the conversation. "We very likely have a long, long way to travel."

Brace turned with a sigh and looked out over the valley and over the old stone wall surrounding the herders' camp. South. The way to this Haven was to the south, and Danferron also lay in that direction. Brace considered his options. If it seemed unlikely that the Haven could in fact be found, or if dealing with these people became too much to bear, he would not find it difficult to get back on track with his original plan.

He turned his attentions toward the group once more. "There is a long way to go yet? Then why are you all wasting time sitting here eating this so-called breakfast? We should be moving on!"

Jair looked up at Brace. He seemed to have regained a bit of the respect for him that he had lost the previous day. Zorix, however, Brace noticed, had narrowed his eyes in suspicion.

It would be near impossible, Brace realized, to hide his intentions from the group, with a creature such as Zorix in their midst. He knew that this animal would share anything that he felt was important with Leandra, and she in turn would keep no secrets. He would need to be very careful.

South. Quite a vague direction, but south they went. Brace kept to the rear of the group, as he felt it was his place. For a while, at least. He had made enough waves already. It was time to fade into the background for a time.

Everyone in the group seemed perfectly content to have Brace where he was, but for Jair. The boy hung back a bit at first, then eventually slowed so that Brace would catch up to him.

"Hello there," Brace greeted him, wiping the sweat from his brow with the back of his sleeve.

"Hello," the boy replied, walking beside him. Jair had long ago removed his heavy outer layers of clothing and packed them away, and the cloth bag he carried on his back now bulged around its metal buckles. Brace had held out as long as he could, but the cool of the morning quickly gave way to the full heat of the sun, and he had finally removed his own cloak, which he now carried draped over one arm.

Both Brace and Jair wore average cottagers' clothing—brown linen breeches and undyed roughspun shirts. Their leather boots were covered with dust, but Brace could see that the boy's footwear was considerably less worn than his own, as was his clothing. Brace had a small tear in the left elbow of his shirt that he had not gotten around to patching. He also wore his hair in a long, somewhat unkempt manner, while Jair's was cut much shorter, falling just over the tops of his ears.

"So, you really are a thief, then?" the boy worked up the courage to ask, knowing that Ovard was too far out of range to overhear and scold him for it.

Brace squinted through the heat and sunlight.

"I am," he told him. "Don't think too highly of me, young man. I'm not the sort of person you'd want to look up to."

"Why, though?"

"Why what?"

"Why did you start stealing things?"

Brace cleared his throat. "It's a long story."

Jair stepped wide around a large rock, then made his way back to Brace's side.

"You do have stories, then," he said with a bit of a smile. "They might not be adventures, but they're stories just the same."

Brace studied the boy's face. He must be older than Brace had first suspected. He had a bit of maturity in the way he carried himself, and in the way he spoke. He was certainly nowhere near the age, however, when he would be considered a man, and no longer a boy.

"You like stories, then?"

"Yes. I've read many of the old ones, the ones that are written down in history or legends. But I've not heard many told from our time, from people who have been to interesting places or had real adventures of their own." He smiled at Brace. "Ovard won't let me set foot in an ale house. I know there are many tales told around the tables there."

"That there are," Brace agreed. "But don't believe every tale you're told, boy. Many are exaggerated, or are altogether lies."

"Well?" Jair pressed.

"Well, what?"

"What is your story? Why did you become a thief?"

Brace shook his head. "You don't want to hear my story."

"Why not?"

"It's nothing grand. It's not a good one."

"Just because it might not be a happy story, doesn't mean it won't be a good one."

Brace was taken back a moment, and his stride faltered momentarily.

"Many stories don't start out well," Jair continued, "but anything can happen to turn them around, to make them worth the telling."

Brace let out a small laugh. "True enough, but mine has done no such thing. And all the same, I don't think that Ovard would approve of me telling you any of my tales. They're not fit for young ears."

Jair reluctantly shrugged it off, realizing that he would get nothing out of Brace. Not today.

"What about you?" Brace asked. "You must have a story?"

Jair shook his head. "I've never really been anywhere."

"What about ..." Brace paused. He had to choose his words carefully. "What about the markings on your face? Who put them there?"

"I don't know," Jair replied, shifting the weight of his pack. "They've been there as long as I can remember."

"Do you know anything about this Haven?"

"No more than Ovard. He has studied so much of our history and prophecies and legends and art and music. He has so many books back home. He had to leave all but a few of them behind. I think he brought only three of them. Or parts of them, maybe."

"You had to leave everything behind when you left?"

Jair nodded. "Everything. I knew we would leave someday. I've known for a long time. But it was still hard to leave home."

Brace could relate with having to leave a place, with leaving everything he owned behind. But no place had ever really felt like *home* to him.

"Well," Brace began, "you were lucky to have a place that you loved. I've lived in so many places I couldn't tell you how many, but none of them ever found their way into my heart, not so much as that."

Jair looked at Brace at that moment, as though he felt deeply sorry for him, and Brace was suddenly very uncomfortable. He cleared his throat and considered how to change the subject, but Ovard took care of that for him.

"Jair!" he called out. "Don't lag behind!"

"I wasn't lagging," Jair answered back. "I just wanted to ..."

"He wanted to keep me company," Brace finished.

Leandra had stopped walking and stood nearby, and as Brace and the boy caught up with the rest of the group, he noticed that familiar hint of humor in the woman's eyes.

"I thought you had no heart for company," she told him softly.

Brace stopped a moment, unsure how to respond, but Leandra quickly gestured with her head that he should walk on, staying closer to the others.

"You needn't hang back so far," she told him.

Jair reluctantly submitted to Ovard's request that he come to the front of the group and walk beside him.

Brace turned toward Leandra. "I thought you didn't trust me."

"I don't. But I'm willing to give you a chance."

"I can't say the same is true of your husband."

Leandra blinked in surprise. "Arden ... he is a man of honor. It's very important to him. Thieving, lying ... these are not honorable things. He doesn't understand at all how someone could choose that way of life. And ..."

"And what?" Brace asked, propping one foot on a large rock and leaning his arm across his knee.

Leandra turned and looked toward where Arden stood some distance away, watching them closely. "He has sworn to protect us all. He takes his duty very seriously."

"Is he a law keeper?"

Leandra turned back toward Brace sharply. "He is. He was ..."

"What is it?" Brace pressed her. "Was he, or is he?"

"He had to leave it behind. When we came to help Ovard, we were turning against the law. They would want to take Haven for themselves, in their greed. It is not meant for them. He and I: we are just as wanted as you are."

Leandra's words settled in Brace's mind. "One man," he commented. "If finding this Haven is truly as important as you all say, one man does not seem sufficient protection for everyone."

Leandra shook her head slightly. "No, it doesn't," she replied. In the next moment, everything happened so quickly, Brace wasn't quite sure at first what hit him. He felt his leg being kicked out from under him, and in a flash he was on the ground, flat on his back. Leandra was over him just as quickly, holding a large knife mere inches from his throat.

Brace flung out his hands in surrender, his eyes wide.

"How is that for sufficient protection?" she asked, smirking.

Brace swallowed. "Very effective."

Zorix began snarling from somewhere close by, and Arden came running.

"What happened?" he asked in alarm.

"Nothing," Leandra replied, rising to her feet. "He was only concerned for everyone's safety. I had to show him that we have things under control."

Zorix hissed at Brace as he moved to a sitting position.

"It's all right," Leandra told him. "Everything's fine. Calm yourself, friend."

The whole situation had Zorix completely confused, but Arden evidently found it rather amusing. His face only slightly revealed his feelings, but Brace noticed.

"Leandra is very capable," the archer informed him, crossing his arms over his chest and holding his head high.

"She is that," Brace agreed, rubbing his throat to be sure it hadn't been cut.

Leandra hid her knife away at her belt and offered Brace a hand. He accepted, and she pulled him to his feet. Standing once again, Brace caught sight of Tassie. She did not seem at all pleased. Apparently, she had seen the whole exchange, and, even from a distance, Brace could tell that she was looking him over to make sure he hadn't been injured.

"Come, Zorix." Leandra turned and walked away and Zorix followed, his long tail twitching uneasily. Arden kept his eyes on Brace a moment.

"Who taught her how to do that?" Brace wondered aloud.

Arden glanced at Leandra, and back to Brace.

"*I* did."

Brace recovered his heavy cloak, as well as what little dignity he had, and made his way through the brush to rejoin the group. Tassie stood staring at him, Ovard and Jair not far behind her. Brace couldn't tell, from the look in Tassie's eyes, if she was concerned for his safety or angry with him for causing a scene.

He decided to take a chance on his first assumption.

"I'm all right, really," he told her. "I think Leandra was just putting me in my place."

Tassie pressed her lips together, gave him a nod, and walked away abruptly.

"Well, so much for that," Brace muttered.

"She's a very strong-minded woman," Ovard commented.

"Who?" Brace asked. "Leandra, or Tassie?"

"The both of them, when you get down to it. But it was Tassie I was referring to."

"She's upset with me."

"It won't last. She has a soft heart."

Brace brushed the dirt from his cloak. "I wish I could say the same of Arden."

"Give him time, Brace," Ovard tried to encourage him. "You don't know the man."

"He's been very good to us," Jair agreed.

"Has he, now?"

"He's very brave."

Jair obviously held a high opinion of the taciturn archer, and Brace was not about to dispute the matter.

"Are you all right, then?" Ovard asked, giving Brace an amused smile.

"Oh," Brace answered, rubbing his neck once again. "I am. She never touched me with the blade."

"Of course not," Ovard replied. "She just wanted you to know that she *could* have."

When Ovard suggested that they all stop during the heat of the day, no one had any complaints. The afternoon meal they shared was no more substantial than the morning one had been—water from their flasks, and bits of dried meat.

Brace kept his distance yet again. He found himself aching for the slight breeze he felt on his face to grow stronger. He was drenched in sweat all the way down his back, and the feeling of his shirt clinging to his skin irritated him. Everyone else looked a bit wilted as well. Wide rows of shade stretching across the hot, dry ground provided them with a bit of relief, and Brace was grateful for the trees. Quite some time passed before Leandra surprised Brace by leaving the group to sit beside him.

"I hope I didn't scare you too badly?" she asked.

"What?" Brace responded. "Oh … right."

"Well, did I?"

He shook his head. "Not too badly. Although at the time I was afraid I may have nearly messed myself." A small laugh escaped from Brace's throat. "You took me by surprise, to say the least."

"I tend to have that effect on people."

Brace eyed her for a moment, then drank nonchalantly from his small flask. "I think you like having that effect on people."

Leandra studied him with her piercing blue eyes. "Well," she admitted, "one can't be too careful these days. It's hard to know who you can really trust."

The two sat in silence awhile, Leandra's words hanging over them. What she had said was very much the truth.

"So," Brace began again, "tell me more about this Haven city you're looking for."

"What has Ovard told you?"

"He said it's the city of our ancestors. That it has been told of in many tales, for generations. He said that it's supposed to be some place of miracles, of 'light in a dark world.'"

Leandra nodded.

"He also told me," Brace continued, "that it's been prophesied that the way to find it would be revealed. I'm not sure I understand. Was it lost? Forgotten? How does an entire city just get lost?"

"Forgotten." Leandra considered the question a moment. "It may have well been forgotten. But lost? No. I think *we* are the ones who have gotten lost. We abandoned the Haven thousands of years ago. It could be that our forefathers believed they no longer needed it. They left it behind."

"Our forefathers," Brace muttered. "I don't even know who my *father* was, let alone my forefathers."

Leandra seemed to be studying him once again. "We are the same race. We all belong to one another. We belong to the Haven, just as it belongs to us."

"What of the others who are seeking it?"

Leandra shook her head. "Many have been seeking, for many years. Those who understand the prophecies, who understand the times, know that there is now a key to be found."

"A key?"

"The way back. There is only one way to enter the ancient city."

"So you think those marks on Jair's face are the key?"

"Ovard believes so."

Brace reached down and picked up a small, rough stone. He turned it over in his hand several times, then tossed it aside.

"What if there really is no Haven?" he asked. "What if it's only a legend?"

Leandra took a breath. She gazed out across the wooded landscape, then shook her head slowly. "I can't believe that," she told him. "I have to believe in this place of goodness and light. The world is so dark. If there is darkness, there must be light as well."

"So those others, the ones who are also in search of the Haven: Ovard said they wanted to use its powers for their own selfish desires. Could they really use this city of goodness to further what is wrong?"

"I really don't know."

"You and Arden," Brace continued, "you are here to protect the boy, to keep him from falling into the wrong hands. To prevent them from finding the Haven before you all do."

Leandra responded with a nod.

"Who are the others? Ovard, Tassie? Where do they come into the picture?"

Leandra faced him again, and shook her head. "I'm sorry. If you want to know about Ovard, you'll have to ask him. It's not my place to talk about him."

"I just want to know who they are," Brace protested as Leandra rose to leave. "Is Ovard the boy's father?"

"I will tell you this much," she replied. "They are no blood relation. But he cares for Jair as though he were his own son, and Tassie as though she were his daughter. He will do all within his power to keep them safe. You would do well to remember that."

She was gone as suddenly as she'd come. The only remainders of her nearness were the aroma rising from the sand that had been crushed under her footsteps, and the unanswered questions that she left swirling in Brace's thoughts.

~ 6 ~

It's a compass," Brace announced, arriving back among the small group of travelers. He had been deep in thought ever since his brief conversation with Leandra.

"That mark on Jair's face is a compass."

Ovard looked up in surprise. "Yes. Yes, it is that."

"What about the rest of it?" Brace continued. "That moon shape, and the strange sort of writing. What do they tell you?"

The older man turned toward Jair for a moment, waiting to get a feel for how the boy felt about being the topic of conversation yet again.

"That I am not certain," Ovard finally answered. "Time will tell. If we follow what we already know, I believe that the rest will reveal itself."

Brace stepped in closer. "There is nothing there to mark any sort of distance. How far south do we travel before we go east? And why not go southeast? Why one direction, and then another?"

"There must be some sort of landmark—a city perhaps, that marks the point when we must turn to the east."

"But you don't even know what you're looking for," Brace pointed out. "You could go right past it and never know, or think you've come to it and turn too early. How do you even know that you started in the right place to begin with? You could be so far off track—"

"Are you *trying* to make trouble for us?" Arden spoke up. "We already know that this journey won't be easy. We will not be deterred by anyone, most certainly not by the likes of you, thief."

Ovard stood and spoke up forcefully. "That is enough, now!"

Arden averted his gaze, his face hard.

"The air is hot," Ovard continued, "and we're worn down. We don't need to stir up any tempers." The older man fixed his eyes on Brace. "If you intend to join us, to help us, as you have said, you would do well not to question things in this manner. Do not bring it up again. Am I being clear enough?"

Brace's jaw tightened. "*Very*. Forgive me. I was too bold. It must be the heat getting to me."

"It will be getting cooler soon enough," Ovard replied. "The days may be hot, but the nights are cold. If we are all going to work together in this important journey, we must be true to the cause, and to one another, at all times, and no matter *what* the weather."

Brace felt as though he was being scolded once again, and it made him bitter. He hated being made to look like a fool.

"Arden?" Ovard spoke through Brace's thoughts, and the archer looked up. "Come over to me, please."

The archer hesitated a moment, then pushed himself up, and made his way across the clearing, through the stripes of light and shadow, to stand beside Ovard.

"Brace," the old man spoke again. "Will you come as well?"

Uneasily, Brace obeyed.

"Now," Ovard continued, as the two younger men stood, avoiding one another's eyes. "Arden, Brace, I know that you have your differences, and you have your reasons for them. But I am asking that you make us all a promise, here and now. Will you lay aside these problems, for the good of us all? Search your hearts, men. This quest is bigger than any of our petty differences. You especially, Arden, know that full well."

Arden was the first to look up. "I do know this," he replied, then turned to look at Brace. "I am willing to bear with you," he told him, "if you are willing to bear with me."

Well, Brace found himself thinking. *This was unexpected, to say the least*. "All right, then. I am also willing. There can be a peace between us."

Arden nodded, and extended his hand toward Brace. He hesitated, then allowed himself to shake hands with the tall archer. Arden's grip was firm, but brief.

"*Harbrost*," he spoke, then turned away.

There was that word again. What on this earth could it mean? Brace wondered. He caught Tassie's eye for a moment. He noticed that she seemed to have softened toward him once again, and he felt relieved. Out of all the people in this odd little group, it was Tassie's approval that he wanted most of all.

Ovard had been right about the cold. This night seemed colder, in fact, than the previous one, despite the fact that they now had a more substantial fire around which to gather. Brace huddled inside his gray wool cloak, his hood pulled up over his head in an effort to warm himself. Eerie-sounding cries echoed through the darkness, making them all aware that there were strange creatures living in the wild lands, ones that they would likely never see in daylight.

The distant noises had unnerved most of them. Arden kept his longbow close at his side, along with several arrows. He stayed on the alert, always listening for sounds that might be coming any closer. Zorix twitched nervously, his large ears flicking to and fro as he sat pressed against Leandra's side.

Tassie was uneasy as well, though it had nothing to do with the strange cries echoing back and forth, which she could not hear. No, it seemed to be the darkness itself that distressed her. Brace noticed how she kept close to Ovard. She seemed to be reassured by his presence.

Brace was used to the dark. It had become his ally, a place he could hide. Nearly all of his thieving he did at night. No one could catch him if they couldn't see him.

Ovard, ever taking it upon himself to keep everyone's spirits up, reached into his outer shirt pocket and pulled out a small lyr flute. He began to play a slow, comforting tune, and it wasn't long before the group began to visibly relax. Tassie leaned against Ovard's side and rested her hand on his chest, feeling the vibrations of the notes that he played. Ovard appeared completely as ease with Tassie's gesture, as though she'd done the same so many times before that he no longer thought anything of it.

Brace watched them from deep inside the hood of his cloak. The strains of music from Ovard's flute made him feel sleepy, but the piercing cold kept him awake. He was still mentally berating himself for choosing to follow these peculiar people on their absurd, and likely impossible quest instead of going straight to Danferron.

It was for Jair's sake, mainly, that he found himself willing to stay. The boy's eagerness to befriend him came as a surprise. Leaving now would bring on feelings of guilt, which Brace suspected would not be easy to shake. Usually, such things did not concern him, as he had left people behind many times. Most often it was some woman who took a liking to him, but Brace preferred not to form emotional attachments. He always knew in the back of his mind that he couldn't stay long in one place. Better to leave early on, before he found himself in too deep.

This was different, though. There was no ale house tramp or lonely farmer's daughter here to draw his attention. This went deeper than that. And Tassie was attractive, he had to admit. But she was nothing like the women he was used to keeping company with. He was sure that she was out of reach for someone like himself.

The extreme cold had driven Brace to accept Ovard's persistent offers that he share his sleeping space inside the walls of the small tent. The older man laid awake for some time, Brace noticed, though neither of them spoke. When Ovard finally drifted off to sleep, he began to snore—not loudly, but enough to be a bother. Brace had tossed and turned—for how long, he had no idea—but eventually, shivering despite being wrapped in his heavy cloak, he drifted into a fitful sleep. The shrill cries of strange beasts infiltrated his dreams and gave him nightmares. So it was, when he felt himself being nudged awake in the morning, that his eyes snapped open in alarm, and he pulled away.

"It's all right," Ovard was telling him. "Morning has come. It's time to be up and about."

Brace let his eyes fall shut a moment, and he let out a long, wearied breath. "Morning already?"

"I'm sorry to say, yes. Did you sleep?"

"I think so. I don't feel very rested, though. Those creatures—did they keep it up all night?"

"It's likely they did. Fortunately, for myself at least, I've become quite the heavy sleeper. I heard nothing."

Brace shivered as he rose, the night's chill hanging over him. "I hope the day warms up soon," he muttered as he bent low to exit the tent. He stood tall and stretched his back, noticing that Tassie and Jair had already woken as well. Tassie had combed the tangles from her long, dark hair, and was working to secure it out of the way in a braid. Jair was rubbing the sleep from his eyes.

Ovard went to work gathering dry wood and brush for a morning fire. Looking around, he realized that neither Arden nor Leandra seemed to have yet risen.

"Odd," the older man thought aloud. "Arden is usually up long before any of the rest of us."

"It could be the cold kept them awake," Brace suggested.

"Perhaps so," Ovard replied. "Maybe I should go and wake them."

By now, Ovard had his arms quite full of sticks and brambles. He looked around, debating whether it would be wiser to first make the fire, to give everyone a chance to warm themselves.

Jair was in the middle of a yawn, and Tassie had turned to the side, unaware of anything that had been said. Brace groaned. "I'll do it," he grumbled. He stepped firmly across the hard-packed dirt to where the fourth tent was pitched. The tall archer already hated him; waking him up wouldn't make things any worse.

As he approached the weathered shelter, he spotted Zorix off to his right, sprawled on the ground at the base of a tree. The large-eared creature was staring hard at the tent, and didn't seem to notice Brace in the slightest. Brace stopped a few steps away from the tent and cleared his throat. He thought he could hear muffled voices coming from inside. "Arden?"

Brace heard a sudden rustling of blankets from inside the tent, and it was a moment before Arden pushed aside the door flap. He was clothed only in a linen sheet, tied around his waist, and he was scowling.

"What is it?" Leandra's voice drifted out. Brace suspected that he had interrupted something. He coughed.

"I'm sorry. I can come back." He turned to go, but Arden stopped him.

"What do you want?" he demanded.

"It's Ovard. He thought you would still be sleeping."

Arden let out a breath. "We are awake," he replied in a resentful tone.

"Right. Well, that's it. I only came to pass on what Ovard wanted, that you should be up. I'll leave you to your dressing." Brace turned and left as quickly as he could, grateful to get away. He sat down hard, not far from where Ovard was beginning to coax a small flame from the dried brush he'd piled on the ground in front of him. *Great,* Brace thought to himself. *A fine way to start the day off.*

Ovard paid no attention, but Jair drew aside from the growing fire and made his way to sit beside Brace. "I heard the way Arden spoke to you," he told him.

Brace grunted in response.

"He sounded angry."

"That's nothing new."

Jair glanced back toward the occupied tent before going on.

"Were they... pairing up?" he asked.

Brace looked at the boy, surprised at his question. "I think so," he answered. "Or something like it."

Jair smiled a little, then turned to look off into the distance.

Brace sighed, exasperated. He found himself willing to do his part to be at peace with Arden. He was sure that what had happened this morning was not going to help matters much.

Now, for the time being at least, it was Leandra who was unable to look Brace in the eye. She seemed bothered by the fact that he had come upon her and Arden's tent unexpectedly, at just the wrong moment. Embarrassed, she kept her distance.

Once again, the night's chill had quickly melted away, and the day grew very warm, to say the least. The soil at Brace's feet was dry and rocky, and the trees, though still rather enormous, grew farther apart, giving the travelers less shade, less refuge from the mercilessly blazing sun overhead. Ovard overheard Brace grumbling about it.

"Appreciate the light and the warmth while you still can," he advised.

"What do you mean by that?" Brace asked nonchalantly. "You talk like the sun's going to disappear."

When Ovard gave no answer, Brace stopped walking and looked at him. "The sun isn't going to disappear," he said, in an uncertain tone. "Is it?"

"Disappear? No. More like get swallowed up. The darkness is winning the battle."

Battle? What battle? Brace was gathering his thoughts and trying to formulate a reply when Leandra's voice called out from a distance ahead of them. Ovard turned in her direction.

"Look here," she told him.

Brace followed Ovard as he made his way to Leandra's side, where Arden, Jair, and Zorix had joined her.

The wide, flat stretch of land that lay before them had been almost completely cleared of trees. An ancient stone wall ran from east to west, with a vast array of small stone buildings and archways built up around and beyond it.

"Some sort of villa," Ovard remarked.

"I see no movement," Arden commented, scanning the area with his keen eyes.

"Strange," Ovard thought aloud.

"Where is everyone?" Jair asked innocently.

"It's been abandoned," Leandra surmised.

"But why?" Brace asked.

"No way of knowing," Ovard replied.

"Is it safe?" Leandra whispered. Zorix stepped forward, sniffing at the air. He sat perfectly still, only his ears turning slightly in different directions. At last, he turned to look up at Leandra's face.

"Not a hint of any death," Leandra reported. "No sounds either. Should be safe enough."

"Let's go in," Ovard suggested. "See if we can find anything that will tell us what happened here."

Arden hesitated, then readied his bow and nodded to Ovard. The group slowly approached the apparently empty villa.

When they came closer to the frontage wall, Brace could see that it rose in height to well over their heads, with several arched openings spaced evenly along its length. This must have at one time been quite a busy place.

"Hello!" Ovard called out, his voice reverberating across the landscape. There was no response.

"Is anyone here?" he continued. "We are only passing through, we pose no threat to you!"

Again, nothing.

Zorix stayed ahead of the group, his black nose twitching as he continued to sniff the air for any scent.

"What place is this?" Arden asked.

"I think it must be Bramson," Ovard replied. "From the maps I've studied, it's the only town or villa in these parts for many miles."

Leandra had gone a few paces ahead, through to the other side of the heavy stone wall.

"It hasn't been empty long," she said. "Look here." She pointed toward the nearest structure. Just inside the open doorway, a wooden table was visible, on top of which sat the remains of some kind of pie—slightly molded and half-eaten, by birds, from the look of it.

Farther in, the group discovered more signs of a hasty departure. Food, personal belongings, even a few items of clothing had been left behind in each of the stone buildings. Straw birds' nests could be seen peeking out from the tops of roof beams, and large spidery creatures had made thick webs in the corners of the stone walls. Tassie grabbed hold of Jair's sleeve and pulled him farther into the center of the hard-packed dirt roadway.

"Stay away from those things," she warned him. "They're dangerous."

"Right," Jair agreed.

The empty villa had an eerie feel to it. Brace found himself wondering what could have happened to cause hundreds of people to drop everything and leave so suddenly. He wandered from stone house to empty stone house, as did the others. Arden stood in a more open area, an arrow set to his bow, ready to fire. Tassie kept close to Jair, and Zorix stayed right at Leandra's feet.

A bird's cry could be heard from high overhead, piercing the silence. The hard-packed dirt under Brace's feet made no sound as he stepped cautiously across the ground. He felt a trickle of sweat sneak down the side of his face, and he wiped it away with his sleeve.

Ovard had gone inside one of the larger structures; he called out from just inside the shaded doorway.

"I've found something!"

Everyone gathered at once, joining Ovard in the welcome coolness just inside the stone building. The light was dimmer inside, but Brace could see that the walls were lined with shelf after shelf, all of them filled with books and scrolls. The table where Ovard stood was old and smooth, and two wooden chairs with seats of padded cloth sat empty on the far side.

One large book had been left open on the table, an inkwell and quill pen beside it. *A library?* Brace thought. He remembered what Jair had told him, about Ovard studying many different subjects, and having owned a lot of books himself. Fitting that *he* would have been the one to find this place.

"What have you found?" Leandra asked, peering over Ovard's shoulder at the dusty pages of the open book.

"Someone has been keeping records," Ovard replied. "This is indeed Bramson, as I suspected. There was much trading done here. Apparently, according to these ledgers, there are ore mines not far from here. The townspeople traded the raw ore they'd mined for things they needed—cloth and grain mostly, but they had a taste for luxuries as well. I found records of their having obtained exotic foods and dyes for clothing, among other things."

Brace looked around the dimly lit room. There was no sign of any richness left in the entire place. Had they taken their treasures with them, or had the villa been picked over by bands of herders or vagrants after everyone mysteriously vanished?

"But this," Ovard continued, "is what I found to be of more interest than anything else." He ran his palm along the smooth page before him, clearing it further of dust, making it easier to read.

"What is it?" Arden asked him.

Ovard leaned over the open book. "'The nights have become colder, darker,'" he read. "'The strange creatures have made their way closer and closer, daring now to appear within the villa itself. We have no means to fight them, for they move as quickly as the shadows in which they hide themselves. We have no peace, no rest. It has become too much to bear. I fear we may be forced to leave this place.'"

Ovard stopped and looked up, a look of dread on his face, which mirrored the feelings that had come over each of them.

"Is there no more?" Leandra asked him.

Ovard shook his head. "No more."

"What creatures?" Jair asked fretfully. "Could it have been the same ones we heard during the night?"

"There's no telling," Ovard replied. "It sounds like nothing I've ever heard of."

Jair glanced around nervously, as though he expected something to jump out from any shadowed corner.

"Come," Ovard addressed the group. "I don't like the feel of this place. Let's be moving on."

Making one last, quick search of the abandoned villa, they were able to come across one of the storehouses. Large barrels lined the far wall, and they were fortunate to find flour, sugar, grain, and a few potatoes. A few cloth sacks remained on the shelves, and everyone shared the load. Brace, finding a larger sack and a length of thin rope, rigged up a pack of sorts. He could carry his share as well.

Brace silently considered the idea that some items of value might have been left behind, and that it would be worth the time to search for them. The others, however, were more than ready to leave this place behind them, and moved out of the chill interior shadows, back out into the warm, welcoming sunlight.

Arden spotted the large main well in the center of the villa, and everyone filled their flasks before leaving. Clouds of gnats hovered in the air around the well, drawn to the water. Jair took a large drink from his own canteen and held it out for Ovard to refill it. Tassie seemed particularly bothered by the tiny gnats, which darted here and there around their faces. She continuously waved her hand in front of her face to keep them away, and although she looked perturbed, she uttered no complaints.

After being certain that everyone had gotten their fill, Ovard led the way south once again, through the outskirts of what remained of Bramson. Brace noticed that Arden looked back over his shoulder several times, to be sure they weren't being followed. Leandra was unnerved as well, and she stayed close to her husband's side as they walked on through the sparse, dry brush.

Brace only slightly felt the tension the others were experiencing. He was more surprised, more curious, than anything. All of the things that Ovard had been talking about, the increasing darkness, seemed like more of a reality now than it had. The people in Bramson had experienced it as well. And the strange creatures? What could they possibly be? Brace wasn't sure whether or not the idea frightened him. He was used to living on edge, never sure what would come next. It was as familiar to him as his own reflection.

Wanting to put as much distance between themselves and the empty villa as possible, none of them felt it necessary to stop for a meal. Their hard pieces of bread were easy enough to eat while they continued walking.

Leandra offered some of her bread to Zorix, but he wrinkled his nose at it.

"Not hungry?" Brace asked her.

She looked at him for the first time that day. "No, he's hungry," she replied. "But he'd rather have something more substantial. He is really a carnivore. Meat is what he prefers."

Leandra was silent a moment, then offered Zorix the bread once again. Reluctantly, he took it from her hand with his nimble, clawed fingers and gnawed on the hard bread. Leandra ran her hand down the fur on Zorix's back, which was now a very light blue color, as he had seen it once before. Brace watched Leandra as she stood straight and walked on. His gaze met Arden's, and he expected a scowl. Instead, Arden gave him a slight nod, and what Brace thought might have been the hint of a good-natured smile. He nodded in return.

~ T ~

Several hours passed, and Bramson was no longer visible on the northern horizon. The last time Brace turned to look, a long while ago, he had only seen waves of heat rising from the ground, distorting the landscape. No sign of any city. At one point, he poured a bit of water from his canteen over his face to cool himself. Even carrying his wool cloak, let alone wearing it, was becoming unbearable. If he didn't know how cold the nights could be, he would gladly have dropped it onto the dirt and left it.

The heavy coin pouch hanging from Brace's belt was easily visible now, without his cloak covering him, and he noticed Jair eyeing it. The boy was likely wondering who Brace had stolen that money from. The truth be told, Brace could not remember. One piece here, five pieces there. Smaller amounts, he had learned, were more likely to go unnoticed.

Two years ago, before fleeing to Bale, he had stopped over at an ale house known for being heavily frequented by trappers who would visit after returning from the wild lands and selling their piles of furs. Feeling quite wealthy, they tossed coins at the bar keepers and spent hours playing chips. Brace had made himself amiable, chatting with and buying drinks for one particularly boisterous trapper. The man invited him into the current round of chips, and Brace graciously accepted. Brace won several games, but the noisy trapper won considerably more. Congratulating him, Brace offered to buy another round of pints. The trapper had accepted, of course, and some time later, became quite inebriated.

Brace, ever the faithful companion, had helped the man walk—or stumble—to his room at the inn, where the trapper had passed out cold. Brace wasted no time in loosening the leather pouch from the man's belt. It had been quite heavy, much larger than the one Brace carried now. He remembered tying a piece of rope around the top and hanging it around his neck, where he could hide it under his shirt. It had been during the dark of night, and no one who might have seen him paid any attention to the drunkard weaving down the street and out of town.

Brace couldn't be sure now if any of the silver coins in his possession were left over from what he'd gained that night. He had been frugal with his money, but that was so long ago, and he had continued adding to his supply every chance he'd gotten.

"What's got you thinking?" he asked Jair.

The boy blinked in surprise. "Nothing," he replied quickly.

"You're wondering whether the money in my pouch was earned or stolen."

Jair hesitated. "I am."

"I'm not habitually a very honest man," Brace told him. "I have found it all too easy to connive my way through life."

"Finding it easy doesn't make it right."

"No," Brace admitted. "That it doesn't."

"Arden always says that it's better to live by *harbrost*," Jair continued.

"I've heard that word three times now," Brace replied, his curiosity aroused. "What does it mean?"

"Honor and courage," Jair answered. "Arden says that everyone should live with honor and courage. That way, no matter what others say about you, you'll know that you are choosing to do what's right, and take pride in that."

Brace chewed on Jair's words. Of course, he'd always *known* that thieving and lying weren't right. At first, he had felt very guilty. But his anger was stronger. No one cared for him, not one ounce. He had seen the way people looked at him. Some seemed to pity him when he had been a child, especially after he lost his mother. But more often, people had regarded him with scorn or indifference, if he'd been regarded at all. What had he ever done to those people, to see him as they did? He convinced himself early on that they deserved to lose what they did, and that he deserved to have it in their stead.

"Arrgh!" Arden's voice rang out suddenly through the trees. "Blasted creatures!"

Brace turned in time to see him push something from his sleeve and trample it into the dirt.

"What is it?" Leandra asked, rushing to Arden's side.

"One of those spiderlike beasts," Arden muttered, examining the two reddening punctures on his right hand.

Everyone quickly gathered in alarm. Tassie, having not heard Arden shouting, saw what was happening and followed the others. Pushing her way past Ovard, she noticed Arden's hand and grabbed it in alarm.

"What bit you?" she asked, her voice high with worry.

Arden pointed to the ground, to what remained of the large insect.

"*That* bit you? Are you certain?"

Arden nodded, sucking in air through his teeth as he winced against the pain.

"They are extremely poisonous!" Tassie exclaimed. Not hesitating for a moment, she quickly wrapped both hands around Arden's arm, just above his wrist.

"Keep still," she told him. "Keep your arm down." She turned and looked around until her eyes found Ovard.

"Help me!"

"What do you need?" he asked.

"In my pack—a strip of cloth. I can't let go of him." She turned to the side so that Ovard could easily reach into the leather bag she still had slung over her shoulder. He quickly reached inside and found the rolled piece of linen. "Tie it on tightly," Tassie instructed, and Ovard did so, as quickly as his aged hands allowed.

"Leandra!" Tassie called out, though she stood very close by.

"What can I do?"

"The wound needs to bleed," Tassie answered. "The blood flowing out will carry the poison with it, and keep it from flowing farther into his body. Your knife—"

Leandra had already pulled her blade from her belt, and held it ready.

"How, exactly?" she asked. "Where?"

Ovard finished tying the cloth snugly around Arden's arm, and Tassie hesitantly let go.

"Let me?" she asked, holding her hand out toward Leandra, who nodded gladly and surrendered the sharp blade.

"Just enough," Tassie said aloud, for Arden's benefit. "It won't need to be very deep."

Arden managed to nod, and shut his eyes tightly as Tassie pressed the knife point into his skin, directly over the swelling bite marks. A bead of red immediately appeared, and began dripping to the ground. Arden did not make a sound, Brace noted. He was certain that he would not have done so well.

Tassie took a moment to think, keeping her eyes fixed on Arden's palm.

"Will he be all right?" Jair voiced his concerns, but Tassie did not see him. Ovard gently placed his hand on Tassie's shoulder, and she looked up.

"How is it?"

"I don't know," Tassie replied. "The poison works quickly. This will help, but ..." She looked around. "Everyone, please give him room. Keep back a little."

Brace stepped back, and Ovard pulled Jair away. Leandra stayed, anxiously holding onto her husband's shoulder.

"Have him sit down," Tassie directed, and the two women gently lowered Arden to the ground, leaning his back against a tree.

"Keep your hand as low as you can," Tassie reminded him. The bleeding had slowed to less than a trickle, and Arden watched in pained silence as Tassie searched her medic bag for dressing, then pressed it over the open wound.

Arden let out the slightest hint of a groan, and leaned his head back against the wide tree.

"He must be still for a while," Tassie continued as she worked to secure the bandage. "He can't be moved."

"What more can we do for him?" Leandra asked.

"Nothing, really," Tassie answered. "All we can do now is take it as it comes."

"What will his symptoms be?" Ovard asked, after laying a hand on Tassie's shoulder to draw her attention.

"Uh ..." Tassie took a moment to search her memory. "Swelling, nausea, fever ..." She pushed her long hair away from her face. "We'll need to keep a close watch on him."

Leandra touched Arden's forehead, then pressed her hand against the side of his face.

"How are you feeling?" she asked.

Arden turned his head to look at her. "I've felt better," he replied weakly.

Ovard spoke up. "We'll stay here for the night. Jair, help me set up the tents."

Brace stood by for a moment as Tassie held Arden's canteen to his lips, giving him a long drink of water. He was feeling useless and out of place. He finally turned to follow Ovard. "Let me help you," he told him.

Brace felt in need of a distraction, and Ovard was grateful for the offer. He helped Ovard and Jair make quick work of getting each tent put up, while Tassie and Leandra kept close watch over Arden's condition.

When they were finished, Brace noticed that Arden had broken out in a sweat, and his breathing seemed labored.

"How is he holding up?" he asked, coming near. Leandra said

nothing, but her face was full of worry. Tassie remained focused on her patient. "He needs more water," she said at last. "He must keep drinking, and we need to keep him cool." She looked up, from Brace to Ovard, who came to stand beside him. "Is there any stream nearby?"

Ovard breathed in deeply, and shook his head. "There doesn't seem to be."

Tassie bit her lip nervously.

"Here," Leandra spoke up. "You have cloth rags in your bag, don't you?"

"Yes."

"Give me one of them?"

Tassie opened her bag and quickly placed a piece of cloth in Leandra's waiting hand. Leandra removed the top from her own water flask and thoroughly wet the cloth, then pressed it against Arden's face, letting the water run down onto his neck.

"You'll use up all of your water," Jair warned her.

"He needs it more than I do," Leandra replied, running the cloth over Arden's closed eyes and down the sides of his face.

Zorix had been watching from nearby, most likely his concern for Leandra's worries being stronger than for Arden's condition. He turned away suddenly, sniffing along the dusty ground, and at every bush. Finally, at the base of a large scrub brush, he stopped and began digging furiously, flinging the dirt out behind him.

"What is he doing?" Jair asked.

Brace watched as Zorix dug deeper and deeper. "He's looking for water," he finally answered. "It may not be good enough to drink, but it will help keep Arden's fever down. Ovard—your mug. Get it ready, will you?"

Zorix made a wide, round hole in the ground, and it was quite deep, so that now only his rump and long tail were visible. Ovard hurried to his pack and dumped his few belongings out onto the ground, not wasting any time. He grabbed the carved wooden mug and returned to where Zorix worked. In another moment, the creature came springing up out of the hole, his feet wet and dripping.

"He's done it!" Jair exclaimed. "Leandra, Zorix found water!"

Leandra had only a moment to feel cheered, for it was then that Arden leaned forward and vomited. Brace cringed. This crisis was not over, not by far.

Ovard got to his knees and reached into the deep hole to scoop out a mug full of the cool water. He took a small drink.

"It's good," he announced with surprise. "Everyone, bring your canteens. We'll fill them. Jair, Bring Tassie's."

"Right." Jair hurried to Tassie's side. "Give me your flask," he told her. "There's good water. We'll fill it."

Tassie took her attention away from Arden long enough to remove her small flask from her belt and hand it over to Jair. She turned back to Leandra. "Help me move him," she told her.

"Move him?" Leandra asked in alarm. "You said he shouldn't be moved."

"Not far," Tassie replied. "Only to the tent. He can lie down, it will be better for him."

Leandra nodded, and between the two of them, one on each side, they managed to support Arden long enough to get him into the nearest tent, where they spread out blankets for him to rest on. Leandra continued to soak the cloth rag, using it to cool Arden's face and neck. His breathing seemed to be getting worse.

When he was certain that Jair was out of earshot, Brace turned to Ovard. "He's going to pull through this, isn't he?" he asked quietly.

Ovard swallowed and took a deep breath. "He's very strong," he replied. "If anyone can, Arden will. And he's in good hands."

Brace nodded. He'd twice been under Tassie's care, and he knew that she was very thorough. She would leave nothing undone, if it was in her power to do it. He watched as Leandra wetted Arden's hair, then leaned over him and gently kissed his forehead.

"He's burning up," he heard her say. Tassie only nodded. Brace continued watching as Zorix slowly made his way toward the open tent, his wet feet collecting dirt as he went along. Hesitantly, he entered, his large ears tipped forward in concern. Leandra paid him no notice, but Zorix seemed to understand why. He stood back for a moment, then quietly, unobtrusively, made his way to where Arden lay on his back, wheezing. Zorix lay down on the bare ground beside him, resting his chin across the lower part of Arden's legs.

Brace was unexpectedly moved at the show of affection. Zorix always seemed to avoid Arden, to be constantly irritated at his very presence. Yet here he was now, doing what little he could to try to comfort him. Something stirred in Brace's heart, in his memory, and he felt tears form in his eyes. He cleared his throat to try and block the emotion, but it had come on so suddenly. Not wanting to be seen in this state, he quickly turned away.

He wasted no time putting distance between himself and the camp, until he came to a large rock, where he sat, his head in his hands. Only a moment passed before he heard someone speak to him.

"Are you all right?" It was Ovard, standing close behind him.

"Fine," Brace managed, not looking back. He wanted to be left alone, but if Brace knew anything about this man, he knew that Ovard would not leave it at that. It was no surprise to him, then, when Ovard came into view and sat beside him.

"What has you so troubled? I didn't think you cared so deeply for Arden's well-being."

Brace swallowed. "I hate to see anyone suffer that way," he replied.

"But?" Ovard pressed.

Brace avoided Ovard's gaze. He was glad that his hair was long enough to hang down around his face. He did not want the older man to see him in such a state, with his eyes damp with unshed tears.

"But," Brace answered, "seeing how everyone cares for Arden— even Zorix—it brought up memories I'd thought were good and buried."

"Memories of what, may I ask?" Ovard gently prodded.

"From so long ago. Of the only person who really cared for me."

"Your mother?" Ovard guessed.

Brace responded with a nod.

"Tell me about her."

"It was a long time ago. I was very young. I don't remember much, only feeling her arms around me. I felt ... loved. I felt safe. She was the whole world to me."

"What happened to her?"

Brace pushed the dampness from his eyes and swallowed before he continued.

"She became ill. I don't know what it was, but it happened so fast. It seemed that, in only days, she went from being this strong, beautiful woman, to lying in bed, unable to move or even eat. Then she was gone."

"What age were you?"

"Eight years, I think."

Ovard sat silently for a moment. "What became of you after she passed?" he asked gently.

"I had no other kin," Brace told him. "There was a man in our villa who had a farm, I remember. He took me in, and put me straight to work."

"You were so young."

"No matter," Brace replied. "He only wanted a farm hand. He wasn't looking for a *son*."

The bitterness in Brace's voice did not go unnoticed.

"He was not kind to you."

Brace shook his head. "No. It seemed that no amount of work was ever enough to satisfy him. He would tell me that I had to earn my keep. My meals, the bed I slept in. But I was small, and the work I did never met with his expectations. More often than not, it was a bruised face I would earn instead of a meal."

Ovard nodded, understanding.

"I grew weary of going to bed on an empty stomach," Brace continued. "So I started forcing myself to stay awake long after the man went to sleep. I would take just enough, so he wouldn't notice anything missing. A slice of bread, or a small piece of smoked meat. Just enough to keep me going."

"Surely someone must have noticed your bruises?"

Brace shrugged. "I was nothing to them. A worthless orphan, for all they knew. I never knew my father, or even who he was. I was likely born outside of marriage. They would have looked the other way."

"So," Ovard voiced his thoughts aloud. "That was when you began thieving."

"I had to," Brace defended himself. "The only way to get what I needed or wanted was to take it, and I became good at it quickly. Then, one evening, the farmer was especially angry, I remember. I feared a terrible beating, so I ran away. Far away. I didn't know how hard or how long he would search for me, but I knew that I wanted to be certain that he would never find me. I took to the trade roads at first. The merchants' wagons were easy targets, and I had my fill quite often, something I hadn't enjoyed for so long. A year, maybe."

Brace stopped and took a breath. He had never shared any of this, not with anyone. Surprisingly, it felt good to finally tell it.

"It became so easy," Brace continued. "The stealing began as something I had to do to survive, but I'd become so adept at it, that it was no longer a challenge. So I turned it into sort of a game. I would test myself, to see how much I could take at one time, or how long I could linger after my theft to see if anyone woke up.

"At first, it was only food. But I realized that since I was robbing traveling merchants, I could take whatever I wanted and be gone. They would never see me. That's when I started taking other things. Clothing, silver coins ..." Brace chuckled. "Once, I even managed to steal a pig."

"Noisy things," Ovard commented. Brace was surprised to hear not even a hint of disapproval in the man's voice.

"That they are," he agreed.

The silence of the fading daylight enveloped them. Brace had told his story after all. He'd always thought that he would take it to his grave. Jair would be disappointed that he hadn't been there to hear it.

At long last, Ovard spoke once again.

"I know what it is to suffer loss," he told him.

"Do you?" Brace asked softly.

Ovard answered with a nod. "It was many years ago for me as well. I was living just outside of Alaren. My sister's husband abandoned her and her child, and I invited them to come stay with me … with my family. I had a wife and a son. Despite my sister's troubles, life there and then was good. So good. We had everything we needed, and we had one another."

"What happened?" Now it was Brace's turn to ask to the questions.

"There was a fire," Ovard replied in a heavy voice. "I was away from the house that day, and my little niece had come with me. We went into town, to the market." He stopped, and smiled a little. "It was all the fruit that she liked—the sweet berries. We bought more than we needed. It was a good distance back home, and she was so young. We stayed the night at an inn. When … When we returned home the next day, we discovered that the cottage had burned to the ground. I still remember the faces of the people who bore the news. They hadn't made it out. My wife, my sister, my son: they were all gone."

Brace sat in silence. There were no words, he knew, that would be fitting to speak at that moment.

"Your niece?" he finally asked.

Ovard nodded. "Tassie. She was five years old at the time. She'd been born unable to hear. I taught her to use her eyes, to see what people were saying. She found so much hope in that, a way to feel not so cut off from the world around her. She wanted to go everywhere I did after that."

"Tassie is your niece?"

"She is."

"So, you raised her alone?"

"I wasn't alone. After the fire, I took her and we moved to Bale. I had help. Friends, others in the villa, women who could be there for Tassie in ways I couldn't, especially as she grew older."

"And Jair?" Brace asked. "When did you take in Jair?"

"Years later," Ovard replied, "when Tassie was nearly fourteen. The boy must have been three years old, no more."

"And he had already been marked?"

"He had."

"What happened to his parents? Were they killed? Did they give him up?"

Ovard seemed hesitant to answer. The sound of footsteps approaching from behind drew his attention.

Brace turned to see that it was Jair himself who'd come up behind them. Ovard stood and took a step toward the boy.

"How is Arden?" he asked.

"Well enough," Jair replied. "Not much has changed."

Brace could see that Jair was shaken, but trying to be strong. Ovard noticed as well, and wrapped his arms about him. Jair leaned gratefully against Ovard's chest.

"I'm so afraid for him," Brace heard the boy mutter.

"We all are," Ovard replied, holding him tightly. "We've done what we can. We'll pray for the best."

Jair nodded.

Ovard turned to look toward Brace. "How are you at hunting?" he asked. "We could use a good meal to end the day."

~ 8 ~

Between the two of them, Ovard and Brace managed to scare up a few small birds and a jackrabbit. Zorix watched them closely as they skinned and plucked and cooked the meat over a fire, and now he sat by, contentedly chewing on a strip of brown, juicy game bird. Zorix would have eaten it raw, but cooked was just as tasty. Also, Leandra never left Arden's side, so she was not available to be a voice for her furry companion.

Tassie brought Leandra a small plate, and returned with the news that Arden's condition was finally beginning to improve, much to the relief of everyone present. When he was at last able sit up, Leandra and Ovard helped him make his way to the fire, where he could warm himself before night fell. As Tassie removed the cloth that was tied around his arm and Leandra wrapped him in a blanket, Brace noticed how uncharacteristically small and mellow he seemed. He sat a bit hunched forward, his gaze kept low. Tassie heated some water over the fire and made some tea, which she poured into a small mug that she placed into Arden's hands.

"Try to drink it," she told him. "Slowly. It's hot still."

Arden breathed in the fragrant steam rising from the mug, and wrinkled his nose. "I don't know if I can," he muttered weakly.

"Try," Leandra encouraged, sitting close beside him, resting her hand lightly on his back.

Arden let out a shaky breath and took a very small sip of the hot tea.

"That's good," Tassie spoke up. "Just do that, a little at a time."

Everyone ate in a tired silence. Ovard offered Arden a small piece of what meat still remained, but he slowly, slightly, shook his head. "I know I wouldn't be able keep *that* in my stomach."

The archer's voice was low and strained, and even in the low light of evening, Brace could see that his face was quite pale. He wondered if Arden had any idea how he pitied him at this moment.

Arden managed to drink most of his tea by the time the sun faded over the horizon. He tired so quickly that he could hardly stay upright, so Ovard and Leandra supported him as they led him back to his tent to lie down once again.

"He's going to be all right," Jair said aloud, seated next to Brace.

"I think he will be," Brace agreed. "He's been through the worst of it, that's certain." He shivered involuntarily, beginning to feel the cold setting in.

Ovard returned and stood over the fire.

"I'm sure you're all as worn out from this day as I am," he said. "I don't know if we'll do any traveling tomorrow. Arden may not be strong enough."

Tassie had been watching Ovard closely through the low light of the fire, her long curls lit with orange and gold. Able to make out most of what he had said, she agreed with him.

"It would be best to give him at least one full day to rest. He'll need it."

"Right," Ovard replied. "Then I think I will be turning in for the night. Sleep long and well, everyone. No need to rise early in the morning. And keep watch. We don't need anyone else to be bitten by one of those long-legged pests."

Brace didn't need to be warned twice. When Jair offered to share his tent, Brace did not turn him down this time. The thought of those leggy creatures crawling all over him in his sleep gave him the chills.

Ovard's well-wishing for everyone to sleep long and well had been quite in vain, for none of them did. Worry plagued their minds far into the night, and although it was late in the morning by the time everyone got up, none of them looked or felt very rested.

Leandra in particular had a haggard look about her. Brace suspected that she'd likely gotten no sleep at all, keeping vigilant watch over her husband. Arden, however, had gotten most of the color back in his face, and even managed to eat a bit of dry bread while he drank another cup of Tassie's hot tea.

Ever diligent, Tassie examined the bite marks on Arden's hand, felt his throat for any signs of swelling, and rested her hand briefly against his face to be sure he was no longer feverish. Satisfied at his improving condition, she patted him on the shoulder and gave him one of her little smiles. Brace had received that smile once, though it seemed so long ago. *Did she reserve this gift for her patients?* he wondered. Just as much, he wondered how he could get her to see him as more than a thief, a troublemaker. He was well aware that she had many things weighing on her mind, but just the same, she seemed to be trying to avoid him.

Ovard pulled from his pack two narrow books and a small, thick roll of paper. Finding a convenient place to sit, he spread his things out around him and began to study them closely. Jair had found a long, thin branch and began to whittle the end of it to a fine, sharp point. Tassie and Leandra, using more of the water that Zorix had so cleverly provided them, took it upon themselves to wash some of their spare clothing as best they could, draping garments over low branches to dry. Arden began to make his way slowly around the camp, trying to work some strength back into his legs.

Brace watched him as he walked carefully back and forth, stopping often to rest. He turned once more and was walking away when he stopped suddenly. A feeling of alarm sweep over Brace, and he readied himself to get someone's attention, if need be. Arden took care of that for him, however.

"I can't see!" he exclaimed, reaching out for something to grab hold of, his hands finding nothing but air. Ovard dropped his papers into the dirt and hurried to his side, taking hold of his arm. Arden was visibly shaken.

"Ovard, I can't see *anything*!"

Brace watched, unmoving, as Tassie questioned Ovard about what was happening. He repeated Arden's words as Leandra stood back, watching helplessly, a damp piece of clothing hanging limply in her hands.

"Calm yourself, Arden," Tassie spoke. "It won't last."

Arden's breathing was ragged, edged with panic.

Tassie took hold of his arms and grasped them tightly. "It won't last," she repeated. "Close your eyes. Try not to think about it."

Arden obeyed, and Tassie led him to a nearby tree and helped him sit down at the base of it.

"You're certain it won't last?" he asked in an unsteady voice.

"Very certain. I have seen this before. It shouldn't last more than a day."

Arden breathed deeply to calm himself. Ovard stood by helplessly. Jair abandoned his carving. The entire camp was clouded over in an uneasy silence. Zorix had reacted as well, in his own way, his fur changing to a bright orange right before Brace's eyes.

"I'm sorry," Tassie spoke up once again. "I should have warned you that this might happen. I truly hoped it wouldn't. Can you forgive me?"

Arden nodded in reply, pulling the blanket that was still draped around his shoulders more tightly around him. "Of course."

Leandra approached at last, resting her hand briefly on Arden's knee to make him aware of her presence.

"Here," she told him. She found a wide, clean, dry strip of cloth, and held it over his eyes, tying it securely behind his head.

"Not too tight, is it?"

"No. It's fine."

Leandra sat on the dusty ground at Arden's side and leaned

against him, wrapping her arms around him. Arden held her close as Tassie stepped away.

"My favorite place to be in all the world," Brace heard Arden murmur in Leandra's ear.

"Where is that?" she asked him.

"Wherever *you* are."

Brace still found the archer to be quite enigmatic. His first impression of the man was that he was hard, firm, and unkind. He had seen early on, though, the effect that Leandra had on him. She seemed to be the only one for whom he had a soft place in his heart. Brace was still unsure what Arden's opinion of him was. The archer had been willing to back down in his opinion that Brace should leave them only when Leandra and Ovard had challenged him.

Brace knew the man was used to being the strong one, the brave one. The one who rose early in the morning before anyone else. He relied heavily on his archery training and his keen ability to tune into everything that he heard and saw. Now he was helpless—weak and unable to see. His hard shell seemed to have cracked, and Brace was seeing him in an entirely new light.

Was this all foolishness, Brace began to wonder once again, *trying to find some mysterious Haven?* He turned and noticed Jair standing nearby, looking very much in need of reassurance, but he had none to offer. Brace didn't belong with these people! He should be heading for Danferron. Frustration enveloped him, and he turned away.

Ovard called out to him. "Where are you running to now, young man?" His voice sounded harsh with reproach. "Will you run every time things become too difficult to bear?"

Brace stopped and turned back to face him across the camp.

"This is madness!" he exploded. "Look at us all! We are not heroes. We are not great men, mighty warriors. You think that this little group can possibly succeed? If the darkness, if the night itself, is truly working against us, what can we do to stop it? Think about it—we've got you and me—an old man and a wanted man—and

Arden, who can't see, Tassie, who can't hear, a woman, and her ...
creature ..."

Zorix snarled at Brace's comment, but he continued on, fully
realizing that he was not making himself appear favorable in their
eyes. "And the boy, who has a secret he cannot hide, and is being
hunted after by power-hungry overlords, if what you say is true.
How can we, so few in number, possibly win out with the odds so
strongly against us?"

"Arden will regain his sight," Ovard spoke firmly.

"Well, even so ..."

Brace was cut short, by Tassie, of all people, who rushed at him,
fury burning in her deep green eyes.

"How dare you!" she shouted. "How dare you treat us this way,
after all we've done for you. We've treated your wounds, given you
food, water, shelter, undeserved kindness, and you repay us with
this disrespect?"

Brace was taken aback. He didn't know that this fierce side of
Tassie even existed. She narrowed her eyes at him, and lowered
her voice. "We may succeed and we may not, but we have each
been willing to give up everything, to risk everything, not only
for ourselves, but for the good of the entire world. You may have
ever cared only for yourself, but now is your chance to care about
something more. Are you with us, or are you not?"

Brace pulled his gaze away from Tassie's iron stare, searching the
faces of the others for signs of how they were feeling—whether they
wanted him to go or stay. He saw nothing, however, but expectation,
waiting to hear his response.

"Well?" Tassie pressed, stepping so close to him that her chin
was only inches from his chest.

"Do *you* want me to stay?" Brace asked quietly, catching Tassie
off guard. "If you want me to stay, I will."

Tassie blinked and took a step back. She tipped her head to one
side in thought. "Only if you will be true to us," she finally answered.

"No going back and forth. If you can't be with us, for us, with every part of your mind and heart, then go. But if you can, then *stay*."

"Please stay," Jair spoke up. "I don't want you to go."

Brace looked up to acknowledge him, and Tassie only slightly turned her head. She kept her eyes fixed on Brace, waiting for him to answer. He took in a deep breath, then nodded, wondering what he was getting himself into.

"I'll stay. I would swear on my honor, but I'm afraid I have none."

Tassie regarded him closely for a moment longer. "Good," she said at last. "Help me, then."

"With what?"

"We'll be here at least another day," she replied. "I want to see what is growing here that might be useful. It is dry, but there may be something."

"How can I be of any help? I don't know what you'll be looking for."

"Arden's eyes are no good to him for the time being," she pointed out. "I won't wander off alone. I won't hear if trouble comes. I need someone to keep watch for me."

Surprised, Brace hesitated. "Do you trust me enough for that?"

"Almost," Tassie replied. "I am giving you a chance to prove yourself. Will you take it?"

Brace was encouraged by her willingness to include him once again. "I will," he told her.

Her face softened a bit as she stepped away from him. "Good. I am ready now. Are *you*?"

Leaning against the smooth, red-brown surface of a small tree, Brace watched as Tassie plucked a leaf from another bush and held it close to her face to smell it. She had pulled back her hair and tied it with a long, wide blue ribbon. Wisps of her long brown curls had escaped, and moved softly around her face in the warm afternoon breeze.

Ovard had been hesitant to allow Brace to accompany her, as though he questioned Tassie's judgment in the matter. But seeing that she had already made up her mind, he had relented.

The two of them walked on for a short distance, unspeaking, until they had found a sort of grove. The trees growing here were rather short and twisted, but quite heavy with long, narrow, papery leaves, creating sufficient shade for smaller plants, which were thriving. Tassie examined many of them closely, feeling the texture of the leaves and checking each one for its fragrance.

"Many of them have healing properties," she said, when Brace asked her why she smelled them. "They can be put into tea, or be crushed and mixed with water to make a paste. I recognize many of them by their smell as much as by their appearance."

Her temper had cooled considerably, a fact for which Brace was very grateful.

Brace had discovered snuff reeds growing in low bunches, and he had stuffed several of them into the small leather pouch on his belt. He had been chewing on the end of one of the reeds for some time, and was beginning to feel rather drowsy.

Tassie abandoned the brush she was examining, and made her way toward Brace, scanning the ground as she walked. Her long, loose-fitting green leggings were quite smudged with sandy brown dirt. It made no difference, Brace thought to himself. No matter the appearance of her clothing, she would always be beautiful. No amount of dirt would be able to change that fact.

"You've had enough of that, haven't you?" she asked, stopping in the shade at his side.

Brace pulled the reed from his mouth and tossed it lightly onto the ground. "How is it that you know so much about plant life?" he asked. "Did Ovard teach you?"

"No," she replied, shaking her head. "He did create in me a joy of learning, but from the time I was small, I knew I wanted to become a medic." Tassie pulled the wide strap of her leather bag over her head and gently rested it on the ground beside her. Brace realized that he had become very accustomed to the slight irregularity in her speech, so that he hardly noticed it.

"I studied every piece of writing I could get my hands on," she continued, after taking a long drink of water from her flask. "Plants with healing qualities, natural remedies. When I was older, I began my training with the medic in Bale. He taught me so much ..." Her voice drifted off.

"Then you had to leave."

She nodded.

"Do you regret it?"

Tassie crossed her arms over her long, fitted tunic. "Leaving? Yes, at times I do. But I tell myself that I haven't put my dreams away for good. They are only waiting for me until I can pick them up again. This is so much more important."

"Finding Haven?" Brace asked, and Tassie nodded.

"Of course."

Brace hesitated, unsure at first whether or not to voice his thoughts.

"I know that Ovard is your uncle," he told her.

She raised an eyebrow in surprise. "You do?"

"Yes. He told me about what happened to your family, to his family. About the fire, and how he's been raising you since you were small."

She smiled slightly in acceptance of the fact that Brace knew some things about her. "Did you ask about me?"

Brace was hesitant to answer. Would she be flattered that he'd wanted to know more of her, or would she think he was being intrusive?

"Actually," Brace replied, "I must admit that I did not, though I would have liked to. I ... confided some things to Ovard, and he did the same. I hope you're not offended."

Tassie shook her head gently. "No. I can tell, Brace, that there is more to you than one sees at first glance. You have the strength in you to be so much more than you are."

"More than a liar and a thief, you mean."

"Yes, more than a thief. Give yourself a chance; open up to this opportunity. Don't hold back. You keep your heart very closed. Don't be afraid to open up, to let others in."

Brace felt a brief wave of fear run down his spine. The very idea of leaving himself open to others made him want to run, to avoid the hurt that could inevitably follow. He had made a promise, though, to Jair and to Tassie, that he would stay. Promises had never meant much to him in the past, but he supposed he'd already opened up his heart enough that it would pain him now if he failed to keep his word.

Tassie must have seen the uncertainty that came over Brace, for she smiled and gently, briefly, touched his arm. Bending to pick up her leather bag, she suggested that they return to camp. She wanted to see how Arden was faring.

"So his sight really will return?" Brace asked. When Tassie gave him no answer, he realized that he'd begun to take for granted the fact that she could not hear him when he spoke. He decided to let it drop.

~ 9 ~

Unexpectedly, as far as Brace was concerned, Arden was quite apologetic that evening. He was ashamed of the way he had reacted to his eyesight fading to darkness so suddenly, and had been chastising himself for causing a scene.

"I frightened everyone," he continued, seated beside Leandra near the entrance to their tent. "I should have been better able to keep my head. I am truly sorry."

Ovard waved it off with a motion of his hand, which Arden could not see. "We're all right. I'm sure it was unnerving, to say the least. No one thinks any less of you. You're just as human as the rest of us."

Zorix was seated at Jair's feet, evidently realizing that Leandra's attentions were, at the moment, completely focused on her husband. Brace watched as Jair began to scratch behind the creature's large ears, and Zorix's color faded from a light purple to a much deeper shade. Brace found it oddly amusing. Maybe he was still being affected by the snuff reed he'd been chewing on earlier in the day.

Fortunately, Arden began to have an appetite once again. Now they had flour and sugar, which Leandra mixed with water in one of Tassie's wooden bowls to make sweet, hard biscuits. There were the potatoes as well, though they saved half of their limited supply for another day. It was by no means a luxurious meal, but along with some dried meat, it was enough at least to curb their hunger.

"I think you should tell us one of your stories," Jair suggested to

95

Ovard, after the meal ended and everyone sat in an almost contented silence.

Ovard interlaced his fingers and leaned forward in a relaxed manner. "What kind of story?" he asked.

"One of the old ones," Jair replied.

Ovard sat a moment, pensively stroking his short gray beard. Finally, he nodded. "Right," he said. Jair sat up expectantly.

"There was once in our land," Ovard began in a hushed tone, "a great, grand castle, at the edge of a very thick wood. It was during the rule of Lord Estan and Lady Maraya. When they had their first child, a girl, the Sprite of Blessing came to attend the infant's naming day celebration, to bring good fortune into the child's life."

Brace settled into his wool cloak. *Was this going to be a child's tale?* he wondered to himself. He had expected the man to tell something of a more historic-sounding nature.

"The child was very beautiful, with a joyful disposition, so they decided that she should be called Sola, for the bright summer sun. At the naming day celebration, however, what none of the guests knew was that a dark, angry, evil sprite had come, uninvited."

Brace looked around at the others. He had never heard this tale before in his life, and wondered if any of the rest of them had. Most likely Jair was familiar with it, but the boy was watching Ovard with expectation and unconcealed interest.

"Seen by the crowds as an old, old woman," the story went on, "the dark sprite asked to know the child's name. 'She is called Sola—little sunshine,' Lady Maraya replied.

"'And little sunshine she shall see,' the dark sprite exclaimed, 'for she shall sleep as long as the sun shines full in the sky!' After speaking her words, the dark sprite disappeared from sight.

"And so it would be, that little Sola would sleep every day and awake only at night, every day of her life, for there was no one in the entire kingdom who had the power to undo the dark sprite's spell. But all was not lost! For the sprite of blessing knew that there would be a way to put an end to what had been spoken over the child.

"For there would come a day, in twelve years' time, when the sun would not shine fully in the sky, for the moon would block out its light from the earth. The sprite's news brought a spark of joy to the Lord and Lady, and everyone present. For twelve years they clung to this hope, that the Sprite of Blessing was right, and that the spell on little Sola would be broken.

"It was a lonely life for Sola, being awake only at night, when all of the other children were at home asleep. But her parents shared their hope of the day when the spell would be broken at last, and she would again be free."

The only sound in Brace's ears, when Ovard paused in his story, was the sharp crackling of the fire. The sky began to dim, and he could see the orange glow of the flames reflected in the older man's eyes. Leandra, across the fire from Brace, tucked her arm through Arden's and sat close to him, leaning her cheek on his shoulder.

"The years passed slowly," Ovard continued, "but at long last, one summer day during Sola's twelfth year, the event that the Sprite of Blessing foretold came to pass! The sun was no longer full in the sky, for the moon completely blocked it out. Only a thin ring of light remained. Lord Estan and Lady Maraya waited in their daughter's room for her to awaken. They had just begun to lose hope that she would, when her eyes began to open gently, ever so gently.

"Seeing her parents' faces watching her so expectantly, Sola was concerned.

"'What is it?' She asked them, rising from the bed. 'What has happened?'

"'The sun,' her father told her. 'It is as the Sprite told us it would be! Will you come and see it with your own eyes?'

"And she did, that very day, for the moon continued on its path, and soon the sun was as bright and full as any clear summer's day. Never again would Sola be trapped in the darkness, for the sun was hers at last to behold."

The fire crackled in the silence, throwing a few golden sparks into the air. Brace was surprised, at the end of Ovard's tale, to discover that he had been so drawn into it that he was nearly holding his breath.

"Thank you," Leandra told him in a quiet voice, while Arden rested his head against hers, his eyes still bandaged over.

Ovard gave her a nod, then turned toward Jair. "Well, was that a satisfying story?"

Jair smiled. "Very much. Thank you."

Brace looked up, far beyond the trees, to the twilight sky. The stars were just beginning to be visible in the wide gray expanse overhead. Night was coming over them once again. He considered the words in Ovard's tale, describing how the young lady had never seen the sun.

He'd been told that here, now, the darkness was winning the battle, and that Haven was supposed to be a city of light, of miracles. If they were not successful in their attempt to find the ancient city, would it be for everyone the way it had been for Sola? To never again see the sun—and not because they were sleeping, but because its rays would never again pierce through the darkness?

The thought made Brace shiver.

Another night passed, and another morning came. Arden was standing tall once again, and he brought relief to the group when he removed the strip of cloth from his face and informed them that he was beginning to see light and shadow and some blurred shapes once again.

Brace found that he was relieved along with the rest of them. He was glad for Arden's sake, as well as for the fact that the archer's continued healing meant that they were that much closer to moving on. He was feeling stalled, and he was certain that the others, Ovard in particular, were feeling it as well, perhaps even more so.

Leandra, finally feeling that it would be acceptable to separate herself from her husband's side, left the camp to assist Tassie in her continued search of the area for anything that could be useful. Zorix went with them, leaving the men to stay in the camp.

Brace was in a contemplative mood. He couldn't get Ovard's story out of his mind. He watched as the older man once again pulled out his maps and papers and began to study them. Jair contented himself with sitting on a low, thick tree branch, his legs dangling, as he munched on pieces of dry, roasted grain. Arden sat nearby, a look of frustration on his face as he looked around, blinking, undoubtedly wishing he could once again see things more clearly.

"Ovard?" Brace spoke up.

"Yes?" Ovard asked, looking up from his worn and faded papers.

"That story you told yesterday. Is it true?"

Ovard smiled a little. "I can't tell you for certain if it actually happened," he told him. "It has stuck with you, though, hasn't it?"

"Yes," Brace admitted. "The light, the dark—you chose to tell that tale for a reason."

"I did."

Brace was silent for a moment. "So ..." He paused, trying to find the right words. "The darkness. You said that Haven is a city of light, of miracles."

"It is said to be those things, yes."

"Well, what I'm wondering is, in what way exactly is finding the Haven going to help dispel the darkness?"

Ovard shook his head. "I'm afraid I can't answer that question."

Arden sat by as quietly as ever, but Brace could see that he was listening, that his interest had been piqued.

"It could be," Ovard continued, "that the darkness can't be stopped. But it is possible that Haven will be the only place unaffected by the change. It could be the last place on this earth where the light will remain. I'm sorry, I really don't know. I can only make wise guesses, of sorts."

From his perch in the tree a short distance away, Jair had been listening as well. He hopped down now, and came to stand beside the place where Ovard sat with his maps.

"We're going to find Haven, aren't we?" he asked.

"We're going to do our very best," Ovard replied. "We won't give up easily."

Jair stood quietly for a moment. "I don't like the dark," he said at last, just above a whisper. "This dark that's coming—it doesn't feel right."

The expression on Ovard's face was quite serious as he patted the ground beside him. Jair sat, and Ovard put an arm around his shoulders and held him close.

"Don't get discouraged," he told him kindly. "We're doing everything we can."

There was a sudden ruckus as Zorix came bounding into camp, making a loud, huffing sort of barking sound, his large black eyes shining with joy. Leandra and Tassie were close behind him, smiling enthusiastically.

"What is going on?" Ovard asked, turning to face them.

"We found honey!" Tassie exclaimed.

"Quite a lot of it," Leandra agreed.

Tassie reached into her bag and pulled out a heavy glass jar full of the amber-colored substance. With the sunlight behind it, the honey seemed to shine like a pure, spotless jewel.

"Well," Ovard replied, "this is a fortunate discovery!"

"It was Zorix who smelled it out," Leandra told him. "We let him taste some of it first, and he said that it's absolutely mouth-watering."

Tassie handed the jar to Ovard, who held it up so that he and Jair could admire it. Leandra crossed to the other side of camp and sat beside Arden, taking his hand and kissing him on the cheek. Arden turned his head so that his lips met hers and kissed her again, briefly.

"Have you tasted it already?" Jair asked, inspecting the jar of honey.

"Only a little," Tassie admitted. "From the tips of our fingers. It is very good." Her eyes met Brace's gaze for a moment. His face must have betrayed his keen interest in her, for she smiled a bit, even as she blushed, then looked away. Brace was encouraged. Maybe she thought more of him than she let on.

They had biscuits again for dinner that evening, with honey this time, as well as a few more of the potatoes. Brace found himself oddly content, watching the others. Leandra was assisting Arden, who could not yet see clearly enough to spread the honey on his biscuits. Tassie and Jair shared a bit of laughter as they chose the same moment to lick their fingers clean of stickiness. Brace had no memory of ever having any such moments with anyone in his life. The deep care for and connection with one another that these people had was beginning to make him feel envious. Would he ever have this sort of relationship with anyone?

He shrugged inwardly, picking up his last piece of biscuit and taking a large bite. It may be, and it may not be. In the meantime, he was going to enjoy what little pleasure came his way. At that particular moment, it was the taste of fresh honey melting on his tongue.

Their travels began again the following morning, as Arden's eyesight had all but completely returned to normal. They kept on at a slow, steady pace across the sandy, rocky ground. Once or twice, Arden tripped over a larger stone that he failed to notice, and he grumbled under his breath. Brace suspected that he was more embarrassed than anything else. The man had had enough of people making a fuss over him for the last two days, and he very much wanted to once again be the strong, independent, confident archer that everyone was used to.

Maybe it was the fact that they had eaten honey with their

dinner last night, Brace wasn't sure, but for some reason Jair seemed to have forgotten about his fears of the increasing darkness. Maybe he was just still young enough to be resilient. At any rate, he was in a cheerful mood, talking lightheartedly with Tassie about memories they shared, of good times, and sharing humorous anecdotes.

The laughter in Jair's voice did much to ease any heaviness that the others might have been carrying, and Brace appreciated it as well. When he first woke up that day, it had been *very* dark. He felt the chill in the air, even through his clothing. A wind blew high in the trees, and he'd heard the eerie sound of thick, smooth branches rubbing against each other, creaking. He had found himself wishing for his tiny old shack in Bale, for a warm fire and a roof over his head, for a real bed to sleep in.

The weather was far from chilly now, as they traveled on across the unchanging landscape: Enormous trees, dry scrub brush, rocks. And dirt. Always, always endless miles of dry, sandy dirt. The muscles in Brace's legs were beginning to feel a constant, nagging ache. He was quite used to traveling on foot, but never day after day, with little rest. And he was not in the habit of having to keep up with anyone else. *How did the old man do it?* Brace wondered. Ovard didn't seem to be having any aches and pains. He certainly never let on, or complained.

The pack on Brace's shoulders was not heavy by any means, but the part of his back where the pack rested was quite damp with sweat. One positive thing that Brace was glad for was that he was able to tuck his long wool cloak over the top of the pack, so he no longer had to carry it. The bottom of the cloak almost dragged across the ground, and was quite dirty. Not that it mattered out here— none of them were very clean, not by any means. They had grown accustomed to the dirt and sweat that constantly clung to them.

Brace was surprised at how he'd begun to feel so at ease with the rest of the group, and they seemed to be comfortable with him as well. Brace had never before spent as much time with one small group of people as he had with these folks. Strange as it was, he was beginning to appreciate their company. Something seemed to be waking up inside of him that had been dormant for years. He wasn't sure if he could call them *friends*, not yet, but something like it. *Maybe* …

His thoughts were interrupted when Zorix, scampering just ahead of the group, stopped suddenly. His nose twitched, and he began to snarl, the fur along his back rising even as it turned from purple to red.

"What's going on?" Brace asked, but Leandra hushed him.

"There's something out there, in those bushes," she whispered, pointing to a place some thirty feet away.

"What is it?" Ovard asked quietly.

Leandra stood beside Zorix for a moment, then turned to look back.

"Wild pig," she said. "Just one, I think."

Wild pig. *Food*, Brace thought instantly, and he was sure the others thought the same.

"Can we …" Ovard began. He looked at Arden, who shook his head.

"I can't see well enough to use my bow, not yet. It's still much too fuzzy."

"I can try to take it," Leandra spoke up, pulling her broad knife from the sheaf at her belt.

"Let me help you," Brace told her, shrugging out of his pack and resting it on the ground.

She nodded, hesitating only briefly. She pointed again, and Brace caught sight of movement behind a large, sparse bush. He gave her a nod, and they were off just that quickly. The pig emerged from its cover, gave them a warning squeal, then turned and ran away from them. They got a bit of a head start on the animal, but it picked up speed fast. Brace forced himself to run as hard as he could. There was no way they could let that pig go without fighting for it!

He scarcely had time to think, for in a moment he found himself right behind the beast, and he lunged for it. Catching the pig by its back legs, he landed hard, holding onto it as tightly as he could as it kicked, wriggled, and squealed loudly, trying to get away.

In another second, Leandra was on top of it, and made quick work of silencing the creature. With one last twitch, it collapsed into the dirt. Brace released his grip and rolled onto his back, winded. He breathed in lungfuls of air, even as he smiled up at Leandra, quite satisfied.

She returned his smile, quite breathless herself. "Well done," she managed.

Brace nodded in reply as Jair hurried toward them.

"You got it!" he exclaimed. "You really got it! Ovard, did you see?"

"I did indeed," Ovard replied, coming near. "You two made that look easy."

Leandra laughed abruptly as she wiped her brow with her sleeve. "Easy? I don't know about that, but he did most of the work." She nodded toward Brace.

Ovard offered him a hand, and pulled him to his feet. "Nice work, the both of you. We'll eat well tonight, that's for certain."

~ 10 ~

S crub brush made for a very hot, fast-burning fire, and branches from the low-growing trees kept it going well, for hours on end. It was a larger fire that they had tonight, one sufficient for cooking the large slabs of meat they'd skewered.

Tassie had spared some of the herbs she kept in wooden jars in her large bag, and the meat was seasoned to near perfection, tender and juicy. They savored every bite, all but Zorix, who had started his meal by snapping it up as quickly as he could. He now lay on the ground nearby, licking his jaws contentedly, keeping his head up and his eyes alert, should anyone be gracious enough to toss him a bit more.

Brace was mildly surprised when Arden looked his way, pausing between bites. "Thank you for this," he told him, his voice heavy with deep appreciation.

Somewhat taken aback, Brace stopped in the middle of chewing. He swallowed, then nodded.

"My pleasure."

Leandra appeared quite encouraged, having taken note of the short exchange. She rested her hand on Arden's knee and gave Brace a quick smile, before looking into her husband's eyes. Arden realized that his wife was feeling proud of him for showing Brace the kindness that he had, and he shook his head slightly, a contrite smile on his face.

Jair pulled a thick piece of meat loose from what he had left, and held it out to Zorix, who sat up and, giving the boy a look of appreciation, took it deftly from his fingers and shoved it into his mouth, chewing ungracefully.

The creature's antics drew a bit of laughter from Tassie, which embarrassed him. He lowered his head, his large ears pressed out flat from the sides of his face, and he slunk to hide behind Leandra. This brought more laughter, however, as everyone had noticed him by now.

Brace found himself laughing along with the others. It was a good feeling, easing his nerves and bringing a lightness to his heart that he'd so seldom known. Their combined laughter rose into the night sky, where a spattering of stars gleamed faintly in the distance. For just that moment, they had been able to push their troubles aside, and the unknown dangers that awaited them. There was still a bit of joy left to be had in this world, and they allowed themselves to bask in it.

For two long days they went on, and nothing ever changed. The hot, dry days and the cold, dark nights. Trees and rocks and brush. The moment of levity they had shared around the blazing fire seemed so long ago now, though it had done its work in creating a deeper sense of unity among them, in particular where Brace was concerned. Small as it may have been, he had shared a moment with the rest of the group, and had created a memory.

The feeling stayed with them, though they were now quite exhausted. The meat was gone. The potatoes were gone. They still had most of the honey, and more than half of their supply of flour and sugar. But biscuits for every meal, for two days running, was beginning to be tiresome, as was the dry, dusty heat. They stopped as often as they could to drink water from their flasks and hide themselves in the shade of a tree.

As they pressed on, the land eventually began to rise and fall in gently sloping hills. Ascending higher, a light breeze ran across them, pulling at Brace's hair. There was something different about it. The air felt cooler. Was it possible? He looked back over his shoulder to see if anyone else had noticed.

"Do you smell that?" he asked.

Leandra looked up at him. "What is it?"

"The air. It smells fresh."

Leandra turned toward Zorix, and the two of them faced each other in silence for a moment, as they shared words that no one else could hear. Zorix turned to face the wind, lifting his head high as he sniffed at the breeze. Looking back momentarily in Leandra's direction, he turned and scampered on ahead.

"It *is* fresher," Leandra spoke, following Zorix. Arden wasted no time in going after her, and the rest of them were right behind him.

The ground continued rising in front of them as they hurried on. This was different, and different was good.

"What is it? *What is it?*" Jair asked expectantly.

"I don't know," Leandra replied. "It could be ..."

She reached the highest point in the rise and stopped, looking down into a sort of valley below. As Brace came up beside her, the others surrounded him on both sides. His eyes followed the slope of the land until he saw it—a river. A wide, quickly-flowing river, heading down to the southeast in the middle of a lush, green valley. The sight of it nearly took his breath away. Could he be dreaming?

Tassie let out a gasp of pleasure and surprise, stepping in front of the others for a better view. When she turned back, there were tears brimming in her eyes.

"Water!" she breathed. "Fresh, running water!" She gave Jair one of her easy smiles before she turned away again and started down the hill.

Jair let out a delighted laugh as he followed her.

"Be careful!" Arden called after them. "Wild creatures might be down there!" He carefully started off himself, and the rest of them followed.

Patches of grass pushed their way through the hard, rocky soil here and there, growing more and more profusely the closer they came to the river. Soon, Brace could hear the water flowing steadily downhill in its wide, curving path. Sunlight reflected off its surface like a thousand sparkling diamonds.

Arden readied his bow, knowing that there could be desert beasts in the area, just as needful of the fresh water as they were. Tassie stopped at the river's edge and stood looking down at it. Brace came to stand beside her as the others approached, admiring their surroundings.

"It's so clean," Tassie thought aloud.

Brace watched her for a moment, then crouched down and let the water run through his fingers.

"And cool," he added, but Tassie hadn't taken her eyes off the river's shining surface.

"I so hate being dirty like this."

Brace stood and gently laid a hand on her elbow so that she would face him.

"Well, you can get cleaned up now," he told her. She met his gaze for a moment, then looked away.

"We can all get cleaned up!" Brace called out to the rest of the group. "The water is fresh and cool!"

"That, my friend," Ovard replied, "is a *very* good idea."

Friend. The word lingered in Brace's ears as he watched Leandra take Tassie by the arm, smiling like a school girl. The two women headed farther downstream, away from the group, and Leandra called back to them over her shoulder.

"No men—or boys—permitted down beyond this tree!"

Each of them bathed thoroughly in the cold, clear water. They washed out their clothing as well, taking advantage of the remaining hours of warm sunlight, giving everything a chance to dry.

Brace lay on his back now in the soft, cool grass, clothed only in his loose-fitting cotton leggings. *As smooth as silk*, he thought, feeling the long blades of grass brushing against his feet. As if he'd ever even felt the touch of silk.

His hair was still damp, but the sun was warm on his face, and he felt completely at ease. The air had a sweet smell, quite unlike the scent of disturbed soil as it had been crushed beneath his boots. He closed his eyes and breathed it in. It smelled like blossoms. Brace felt as though he could fall asleep here, and go on sleeping peacefully for days on end. He thought that Ovard must be feeling the same, for he could hear him snoring faintly.

He smiled to himself, tucking his hands under his head, settling in for a good long nap, when he was startled by a shadow falling across his face. He opened his eyes wide and looked up to see Tassie's figure, outlined by the afternoon sunlight. She was quite a vision in a long, dark-colored dress of brushed cotton, with her damp hair falling in wavy curls around her face.

"Oh!" she exclaimed. "I'm sorry, I didn't know you were so close by. I came upon you suddenly; forgive me." She turned to walk away.

"Wait," Brace told her, sitting up. She saw him out of the corner of her eye and looked back.

"What … Where is Leandra?" he asked, wondering why she'd come back upstream alone.

"Back there still," she told him. "Arden was coming. He wanted to be alone with her, so …"

Brace smirked at her. "Good thing I've dressed myself. At least a little."

Tassie seemed uncomfortable, so Brace pulled himself to his feet and strode barefoot through the grass to where he'd hung his shirt to dry. It was only slightly damp, so he shrugged it on over his head and pulled at the leather laces to close it at the front.

"Where are Ovard and Jair?" Tassie asked him.

"Sleeping," Brace replied. "At least I know Ovard is. I can hear him snoring."

Tassie smiled at his comment and turned to face the wide open river.

"It's so beautiful, isn't it?" she asked.

Brace stepped up close beside her. When she looked over at him, he agreed with her. "It is that. I was starting to feel like that rocky desert was going to go on forever."

She nodded. "So was I."

"Do you feel cleaner now?"

Tassie smiled a bit. "I do."

"You look amazing," Brace told her, suddenly feeling clumsy. "I mean, what I want to tell you is that … I think you're beautiful. I hope you don't mind my saying so."

Tassie took a small step back, and leaned, half-sitting, against the low limb of a nearby tree.

"I'm flattered," she replied casually.

Brace cleared his throat. "Well, I … I always thought you were beautiful, even from the time I first saw you."

"You like beautiful women?" she asked him.

Brace nervously scratched at his elbow. "Well, why not?"

Tassie shook her head, smiling a wise smile. "I think you are a troublemaker. Aren't you?"

"I have been," Brace had to admit. "You don't like troublemakers. But you wouldn't. You're too good for that. Too smart for that."

Tassie sat in contemplative silence. "You have a past," she finally said. "Many people have a past to overcome. You are no different, I think."

"You have faith in me," Brace replied. "I hope you don't have too much. I'd hate to let you down."

"You haven't let me down yet," she told him. "But don't do what you know you must do for my sake. It is you who must live with the man you choose to become. You, and no one else."

Brace nodded. "I'm used to being alone with myself."

Tassie shook her head. "That is not my meaning. You have begun to let us into your life. I can see that. People will come and go through your years. But *you* will always remain. You can be true to others only when you know how to be true to yourself."

Brace considered Tassie's words, then gave her a nod. "Thank you for believing in me."

She breathed in, catching the scent of flowers on the breeze. "You were resting," she said. "I interrupted you."

"I don't mind at all," Brace replied.

"Still," she said, standing, "I think it's a good idea. This is a very peaceful place. I could use the rest as well."

Brace nodded.

"I ..." Tassie stammered. "I'll just go back this way a little," she said, gesturing downstream. "If Ovard wakes before I do, tell him where I am, will you?"

"I will."

Tassie murmured her thanks. Brace watched her as she turned and walked away, the sun in his eyes. *Beautiful, wise Tassie*, he thought. *Do you have any idea how much I've come to appreciate your honesty, your spirit? I'll never forget you, even if we have to part ways and I never see you again.*

"Though I hope," Brace said aloud to himself as he lay down on the grass once more, "I hope that won't happen any time soon." He let out a deep sigh and closed his eyes. "I see your face in my dreams, you know."

Traveling on through this new landscape was much more pleasant. Gone were the miles of bare dirt that blew into their faces, and though the air was still warm, they no longer felt the scorching heat of the midday sun. The trees were more plentiful here, where the river flowed freely, and the thick vegetation brought a coolness to the air they breathed.

Clean and well-rested, each member of the group felt a renewed sense of strength. And though they had by no means forgotten the reason for their journey, the sounds of birds singing, the smell of flowers blooming, and the feel of the soft grass beneath their feet all worked together to make each of them feel less serious, less heavy.

Zorix frolicked through the grass, leaping at small flying insects, and Jair followed close behind him, laughing at his playfulness. Ovard seemed to be admiring everything as a whole, while Tassie took notice of each individual plant. She would be on the lookout for anything with medicinal value, Brace knew. Arden and Leandra walked hand in hand, though the archer kept his bow ready, should they encounter any trouble.

They traveled on until they found a place where the river narrowed slightly and managed to cross over the shallow, fast-moving stretch of rocky riverbed without any mishaps. The chill water had gone up past the tops of Brace's boots, though, and even now his feet were still damp. He gave no thought to complaining, however. Having wet feet was a small inconvenience, a small price to pay for being allowed to enjoy the beauty and peace that surrounded him.

The view they now had of the horizon was no longer flat and barren, but they kept note of the sun's position even as it began to sink lower in the sky. Twilight was upon them just as quickly as it had ever been, even in this seemingly perfect place.

Using a small, tight group of trees as a sort of rear wall, they pitched their tents in close proximity to one another. A long, solid, fallen tree provided an ideal place for everyone to sit near their evening fire, which Ovard and Jair worked together to get going.

Brace seized an opportunity, while the others were busy, to go off alone a short distance and chew another bit of snuff reed. He lowered himself onto the soft grass, with tall, willowy ferns all around him. He could hear the inviting snap of the flames behind him, could hear the muffled voices of the others back at camp. He noticed when Ovard laughed once, a deep chuckle that reverberated through the trees. Crickets sang all around him, hidden in the brush. The gray sky overhead was filled with distant stars, and Brace watched them gleam and sparkle over everything.

Nothing in all the world is hidden from the stars. The words came back to Brace, softly and unexpectedly. He had heard them before, so long ago.

"Nothing in all the world," he said to himself, trying to remember. A story—he'd told Ovard that he'd never had anyone to tell him stories, but that wasn't completely true. His mother had told him a story once—about the stars, and how they saw everything. No one could keep secrets from them. Good deeds, bad deeds—the stars saw them all.

Brace watched as the darkness seemed to pour itself into the sky like ink spilled into a bowl of water. One by one, even the stars were blocked from sight. *Had it been a cloud?* Brace asked himself, pulling the snuff reed from his mouth, suddenly taken by a feeling of trepidation. He felt a chill. A cloud, or ...

The snap of a twig made him jump, and he looked back quickly over his shoulder.

"Jair," he breathed. "You spooked me."

"Sorry," Jair apologized. "I saw you come this way. I just wanted to ... What is that?" The boy asked nonchalantly, gesturing toward the snuff reed hanging loosely from Brace's fingers.

"Hmm? Oh ... This?" Brace chuckled. "Just a bad habit." He tossed it lightly into the grass. "What were you saying? Did you want to ask me something?"

"Oh. No, I came to tell you that there's something special going along with our meal tonight. It's ready, so they asked me to come and bring you back."

Curious, Brace rose to his feet. "What is it?"

Jair shook his head, smiling. "You'll have to come and see."

Brace gave Jair a nod and followed him back into camp. Everyone was seated along the fallen tree, the orange blaze snapping just in front of them. Brace looked around, puzzled. There didn't seem to be anything out of the ordinary, but for the way everyone had quieted down, and now sat in an almost reverent silence.

Jair left Brace standing alone and knelt in the grass near Ovard's feet. The older man nodded to him, then stood. Brace noticed that he held his carved wooden mug carefully in his hands as he spoke.

"This is truly a wonderful place we have come to," he began. "It has been quite a blessing, undeserved though it may be. It has made us temporarily forget our troubles."

Brace kept a watchful eye on Ovard as he stepped closer, slowly moving to sit on the ground opposite the others.

"I feel," Ovard continued, "that tonight is the right time for us to have a renewed sense of oneness, and of the importance of our quest, for that which we seek." He glanced down at the dark brown mug he held in his hands, and his voice took on a less formal tone.

"Traditionally, this should be something more substantial, like a good wine. But Tassie has provided us with some tea and honey, and this will serve its purpose." He paused and looked around, so that his eyes met each one's in turn, Brace's included. "We are all united in our desire to find Haven, to restore it to its proper place in the history of our land, and to keep alive the hope of all that is good and light, in the midst of this darkness. With this one glass, let us declare ourselves to be of one mind and heart."

Finally, Brace understood. He had seen this done before, a group of people all drinking from the same glass in order to signify that they were "all one" for a cause, or declaring themselves to be members of a particular group. He had seen it done, yes, but he had never been a participant.

Ovard carefully handed his mug down to Jair.

"You may drink first," he told him.

Jair nodded respectfully, reaching up to take the heavy mug from Ovard's hands. He held it a moment, took a sip, then handed it back to Ovard, who drank a bit himself, before he turned to the other side and passed the mug along to Leandra.

Brace watched as each of them in turn drank, fully immersed in the significance of the ceremony. The last of them in line was Tassie. After she had taken her turn, she rose and crossed over to stand in front of Brace. Cradling the mug in her hands, she held it out, offering it to him.

"Me?" Brace asked, hardly more than a whisper. Tassie nodded in approval, once again giving him that familiar hint of a smile.

Brace had never before sworn his loyalty to anyone, and as far as he could remember, no one had ever asked him to. It was with hesitation, then, that he reached out and accepted the warm mug from Tassie's hands. She stepped back to give the others a clear view of him, and they all watched him expectantly.

This felt to Brace like the point of no return. So many things had happened to him in the last few days. He'd had so many experiences that he had never even imagined he would have in his lifetime. He'd thrown caution to the wind, abandoning his plans to run straight to Danferron, and stuck with this group of people, despite the fact that he'd known nothing about them. But he found, sitting here now, holding onto Ovard's mug of tea, that he had no regrets. His life had always been one of unexpected twists and turns, and this was just another bend in the road.

A bend? Brace wondered. No—a fork, a split. His life had been going down a certain path, when suddenly there was another option, another way to travel. He had chosen the unknown path, and though he had no idea where it would continue to lead him, he had to admit that he was quite content with the choice he had made.

Lifting the mug to his lips, he took a long, slow drink. When he finished, Tassie was there in front of him once again. As she reached out to take the mug back to Ovard, she let her hands linger briefly over his.

"Welcome, Brace," she whispered. "You are one of us now."

~ 11 ~

Jair once again offered to share his sleeping tent with Brace, and this time he accepted. The boy had tried to stay awake and talk, but the day's travels had quite worn him out, and he quickly drifted off to sleep.

Brace had lain awake for some time, considering the events of the day, so he was not very surprised when he awoke later than usual the next morning and found that Jair had already risen. With a yawn, a stretch, and a moan, Brace pulled aside his covers and stepped out into the morning chill. The air was still, without the slightest hint of a breeze, and the smoke from the small fire billowed lazily into the air. Brace wandered, half-sleeping, to sit down on the fallen tree and gaze into the flames. He was aware, even in his drowsy state, of Arden's presence as he stood opposite him, sipping from a small wooden cup. More tea, Brace suspected.

Feeling as though Arden was watching him, he looked up.

"Morning," Arden greeted him.

"M–Morning," Brace stammered. He noted that the tall, well-muscled archer had regained, along with his physical strength, his hard-shell demeanor. But despite the taciturn air about him, he was actually being amiable. Brace decided to respond in kind.

"How are you feeling these days?"

Arden took another sip from his cup, then paused, evidently thrown off by Brace's unexpected question.

"Much better, thank you."

"You had everyone pretty worried for a while."

He gave Brace a half-smile, and nodded. "Myself included."

"Glad to see you're quite yourself again."

"Thank you," Arden replied, clearing his throat. "I … I apologize for the way I've behaved toward you. I'm afraid I've been letting my suspicions get the better of me."

Brace nodded, fully appreciating Arden's words. "No harm done."

He glanced aside, where Ovard stood, holding one of his old maps spread out in front of him. Jair was listening dutifully as the older man showed him where they'd been, and the place where he believed they were now camped.

"Where are Tassie and Leandra?" Brace asked.

"They've gone off for a bit of women talk," Arden replied.

Brace nodded in response. He'd only been somewhat curious as to Tassie's whereabouts; he had mainly asked in order to change the subject, as it had left an uncomfortable silence hanging over them.

Brace asked, "How long have you and Leandra been together?"

"In marriage?" Arden asked, and Brace nodded.

"Nearly two years," he replied.

"She seems to be …" Brace searched for the right words, "a very capable woman."

"She is that," Arden replied with a smile. "She is very bold as well. I think that one of the first things I truly loved about her, was the fact that she would stand up to me when she felt I was wrong. No woman I'd ever before met had ever done any such thing."

"She does that," Brace agreed, even as he realized that Arden had just spoken more words than he'd ever heard the man utter in all the days he'd been in his company. "Tassie can be just as bold," he added. "You have an eye for her, don't you?"

Brace swallowed. "You've noticed."

"It is not hard to see why. She is a beautiful girl."

Brace nodded. "What age is she?"

"Not certain. She must be past twenty." After a slight pause,

Arden continued. "You'd best watch yourself. She deserves to be treated with respect."

"I am aware of that, believe me. My feelings for Tassie are completely ..." What was that word, the one that Arden lived by? *Harbrost.* "Completely honorable."

Whether he believed him or not, Arden made no comment. The archer held his cup with one hand as he rubbed at the back of his head, then tugged at his long tail of pale blond hair, which he wore pulled back tightly, as always.

"You gave up quite a lot to come on this journey," Brace commented.

Arden acknowledged him with a bit of surprise. "I did." He sounded as though the thought had never crossed his mind.

"Well," Arden continued. "Whatever honor or respect I had, it would mean nothing if it meant the world would be lost to the darkness, or worse."

"Worse?"

Arden nodded. Then, glancing in Jair's direction, he lowered his voice. "If the city of Haven were to be taken by force, by men of evil intent, there would be no telling what horrors the people would have to face. It is imperative that we do all we can to prevent that from happening."

Brace thought a moment in silence. "Jair's markings," he began. "Does anyone else know about Jair's markings?"

Arden shook his head. "There's no way to be sure of that. But we cannot take any chances. Jair must not be seen, or as little as possible. He could fall into the wrong hands—of those who would care nothing for the boy's life."

The thought of Jair being hurt, or even killed, made Brace shudder.

Tassie and Leandra returned to the camp at just that moment, talking and laughing in a lighthearted manner. Small, white flowers had been tucked into Tassie's hair, and Brace thought that she looked positively angelic.

He and Arden exchanged a quick glance before Leandra stepped up beside her husband and kissed him firmly on the side of his face.

"You've been enjoying yourself," Arden told her, resting his hand on her cheek.

Brace rose to his feet. "I think I'll see what Ovard is talking to Jair about over there," he said nonchalantly. This time, as he walked away, he wanted Tassie to see that he was looking at her, admiring the sight of her. Unfortunately, her eyes were set on Zorix as she teased him good-naturedly with piece of dried meat, and she didn't notice Brace in the slightest.

"We've come a long way," Jair commented later in the day, hours after they had packed up the tents and continued on their southward journey.

"That we have, my boy," Ovard agreed, "but I'm afraid we may have a much longer way to go yet."

Jair accepted Ovard's words in silence. He smiled then, and laughed.

"Will we go as far as they did in the Fool's March?"

"Farther than that, I'm certain," Ovard replied, though he hadn't missed the humor in Jair's voice, and his mood was light.

Jair turned toward Brace. "Have you heard the story of the Fool's March?" he asked.

"No," Brace replied. "I'm sorry to say I haven't."

The story he had not heard, but he had lived for a time in the villa that had been named for the historical event. All of—how long had it been? Nearly three months, if Brace's memory served him. He'd been having a fling there with an official's daughter, and word about it had spread as fast as flames driven by the wind. Eyes bored into him every time he showed his face on the streets, and it got so he couldn't stand it. He had packed his few belongings and left in the dead of night.

"How long ago was that?" Brace heard Jair asking, and for a moment he was confused.

"Over two hundred years past," Ovard replied, and Brace remembered. The Fool's March. Yes, of course.

"What happened?" he asked.

"It was King Veryn," Jair told him. "He gathered together all of his ranks—eight thousand men—and led them on a march to attack the capital city in Danferron."

"It was said," Ovard joined in, "that he left only a hundred men to keep guard over the castle grounds."

"Yes," Jair agreed, "and while they were away, the castle was attacked by an army from Roshwan. One of the guardsmen escaped and rode hard after King Veryn, to tell him what happened. He had to turn the entire army around and go back."

"The place now called Fool's March is said to be where Veryn and his men received word of the attack, and turned around," Ovard explained. "Apparently, a few of the men in the king's ranks had been ailing, and stayed behind when the rest of them returned northward."

"Did King Veryn reclaim his throne?" Brace asked, in genuine interest.

"He did," Ovard told him. "But not without losses."

"Fool's March," Brace thought aloud.

"That's what everyone started to call it," Jair spoke up.

"That must have pleased the king," Brace laughed.

Ovard chuckled as well, but became distracted when Zorix came bounding toward the group, returning from where he'd run ahead. His tail was thrashing wildly as he made circles around Leandra's feet, making a deep purring sound in his throat.

"What is this about?" Arden asked, setting an arrow to his bow, his eyes on the surrounding brush. A moment passed before Leandra answered.

"There are eggs," she said at last. "Big ones!"

"Eggs?" Ovard questioned.

"Yes," she replied. "Zorix says he found them just up ahead, in a nest on the ground."

Eggs, Brace thought. That meant food! He said nothing, but he could see by the expressions on the others' faces that they were thinking the same thing.

"Zorix, show us!" Leandra said aloud, and he gladly scampered ahead. They all followed him, and after a short distance, Zorix stopped beside a cluster of tall ferns, looking back at them expectantly. Leandra stepped forward, pushing aside the tall leaves for a better look.

"There are six of them," she reported. "Zorix was right—they *are* big!"

"Are we going to take some of them to eat?" Jair asked.

Leandra looked at Ovard, as though asking his permission.

"Yes," he replied, looking around. "But only two. And make it fast! We're going to have to cover a lot of ground as quickly as we can with those eggs. Whatever sort of large creature laid them isn't likely to be very far away."

"Are you certain we can actually eat them?" Tassie questioned. "They may be too far along."

Zorix stepped into the large nest and placed his small, fingered paws on one of the eggs, sniffing at it.

"He says they should be fine for eating," Leandra told her.

With hardly a second thought, two of the eggs were chosen, each nearly the size of a man's head. Brace wrapped one in his cloak and placed it in his pack, and Leandra bundled the other just as carefully.

Then they were off at a fast pace, Arden keeping his bow ready, and Zorix bounding ahead of them. Their nerves were all on edge, fearful that at any moment they could be ambushed by a large, angry, female ... *what?* They couldn't imagine, nor did they particularly want to.

"Maybe it was just a huge bird," Jair suggested hopefully.

Whatever it could have been, they hurried on for a good three hours before stopping to rest. When they finally stopped, Brace pulled off his pack and lowered it gently to the ground, grateful to have a large stone to sit himself down on. He, like the rest of them, was breathing hard, and his legs were tired and sore.

"Have we come a safe distance?" Jair panted.

"I certainly hope so," Ovard replied. "At any rate, I don't think these old legs of mine can go any farther today."

"Neither can mine," Brace commented. "And mine aren't old."

His comment brought a smile to Ovard's face, while Arden remained serious, focused on listening for any signs that they might have been followed. Zorix scooted up beside Leandra, who was seated in the grass, and rested his furry chin on her leg, looking up at her with his large, black eyes. Leandra took a deep breath.

"I'm hungry too, Zorix," she said, stroking the top of his head between his wide, pointed ears. "We'll eat those eggs soon. Just give us a bit of a rest. Our two legs have to work twice as hard as the four of yours."

Zorix blinked in response, and placed his front paws on her leg as well. He watched Arden closely as the archer came to stand at Leandra's side, finally disarming his bow. Brace noticed that, though Zorix still eyed Arden closely whenever he came near to Leandra, the animal had seemed to mellow in his dislike of him. It could be that he still pitied him due to the terrible ordeal he'd been through after having been bitten.

Arden paid Zorix not the slightest bit of attention, however.

"Are you all right?" he asked Leandra, crouching beside her.

"I'm fine," she replied, smiling up at him. "Just a bit winded."

Arden reached out his left hand and touched Leandra's cheek, which was quite flushed from the long, hard walk. The ornate lines running across the back of Arden's hand and around his wrist stood out boldly, and Brace couldn't help but take note of them. That, and the way the two of them gazed into each other's eyes.

Two years, Brace thought. They'd been together two years. The longest he'd ever been true to one woman couldn't have been more than two months, if that. He looked down at his own hands. Would he ever bear the marriage symbols? *Not likely*, he thought, even as he glanced at Tassie, who sat drinking cool water from her canteen, her eyes closed against the afternoon sunlight shining onto her face. He scolded himself for even thinking that a woman like Tassie would ever stoop to committing herself to someone like him. She had said she thought he was a troublemaker. But hadn't she also said that he hadn't let her down, and that she had seen a strength in him, that he could be so much more than what he'd always been?

Stop your dreaming, he told himself, and was relieved when Ovard asked him to help gather wood for a fire. It was time to cook the eggs they'd stolen.

Being so very large, the eggs had taken quite a long time to cook all the way through. But they were delicious, and well worth the wait. The two of them had been more than enough to feed all six people, and Zorix as well. They'd actually each eaten more than their fair share, knowing that there was no way to preserve anything that could otherwise be left over for another meal.

So it was, later that afternoon, that each of them sat by the fire, quite satisfied as well as a bit lethargic. It took some time, then, for the faraway sound reverberating through the trees to register in their minds. By the second time they heard it, however, they had all scrambled to their feet, leaving Tassie staring up at them, bewildered.

"What is *that*?" Leandra voiced the thoughts that plagued each of them. There wasn't any time to respond, however, for at that moment, a large shadow fell across their camp. Brace spun around to look toward the sun and, shading his eyes, saw an enormous creature with a long, thin neck, wide, flat wings, and a long, thrashing tail hovering momentarily in the open sky far above them.

"Is that what I think it is?" he asked, even as he felt the blood drain from his face.

"It's a *dragon*," Arden breathed out in disbelief.

The creature dove out of sight, for the moment at least, uttering a loud cry of anger and frustration. Brace turned back toward the others. Tassie had seen the dragon, and she now stood, fearfully clinging to Ovard's sleeve.

"We've stolen a *dragon's* eggs," Leandra groaned.

There was no time for anyone to agree, for a loud, shrieking cry shook the ground as the enormous winged beast passed over them once again.

"Where are your arrows?" Brace shouted to Arden. "Shoot it!"

Arden's eyes widened as the dragon loomed into full view overhead. "They'll do no good," he replied. "It's too large. Run!"

He gave Leandra a push forward just as the creature let out a bellow and swooped toward them. Everyone scattered, diving low to the ground. Brace fervently hoped that the trees would be tall enough to keep that monster from being able to snatch them up and eat them.

"There!" Ovard shouted, pointing. "Up ahead there are larger rocks and an overhang—I think. Get there as quickly as you can. Take cover!"

The dragon had momentarily disappeared from view, but it rose to the sky once again. Everyone ran ahead, and Brace followed them. He took a quick glance back over his shoulder to get an idea of how much distance there was between him and the dragon's sharp claws, and noticed Jair far behind him, sitting in a heap. *What could the boy be thinking?*

There it was again, familiar but unwelcome, rising up in Brace's throat. *Fear.* Fear, not so much for himself this time, but more for Jair's safety. While everything in his head was screaming at him to run away, he hesitated. It must have been not more than two seconds. Two *long* seconds. With his head saying run away and his heart telling him to run back, Brace made a choice. Glancing up toward the sky once more, Brace turned and ran back to Jair, crouching on the ground at his side, his heart pounding.

"Are you all right?" he asked.

Jair seemed dazed, only half aware that Brace was speaking to him. He held his hand against the side of his face, where blood was seeping from a gash on his chin.

A loud, wailing roar filled the air, and Brace looked up to see the creature hovering in the air above them, beating its wings against the tops of the trees. Brace wasted no time. He thrust one arm under Jair's legs and the other around his back, and grabbed him roughly up from the ground. In a second, he was running as fast as he could, with the boy in his arms. He knew that almost no time at all had passed; the rest of the group, now safely hidden under a ceiling of thick rock, had just noticed that he and the boy were missing.

Arden flung his quiver across his back and emerged from the protective cover, an arrow ready on his bow, the string pulled back tightly. With a loud, threatening shout, he released the feathered shaft. Brace didn't wait to see if it hit its mark, however. He dove for cover, holding Jair tightly in his arms.

"What happened?" Ovard asked, but the dragon's loud, shrill cries filled the air, drowning out any answer anyone could have given. It flew in tight circles overhead, shrieking, as Arden fired arrow after arrow.

"I thought he said they'd do no good," Brace commented, crammed into the tight space with the rest of the group.

"They may frighten her, at least," Leandra suggested hopefully.

Arden ducked as the angry beast swooped low, clawing at the large outcropping of stone. Pebbles and larger rocks rained down, and Arden raised his arms over his head for cover, moving out of the open.

Raising its head in one last, loud, angry wail, the dragon pushed upward into the sky and soared overhead, casting a long shadow across the landscape as it returned the way it had come. Brace found himself able to breathe once again, when he realized the danger had passed. He also remembered that Jair had been injured.

"Tassie," he said, grabbing hold of her arm. He pointed toward

Jair, who sat blinking up at the sky, sitting on the ground beside him. "He's bleeding."

"What?" she gasped, crouching beside Jair and looking him over. Seeing that he was covering part of his face, she pulled his hand away.

"What happened?" she asked. "Did the creature do this?"

"No," Jair replied meekly, as Leandra and Ovard moved out from underneath the crowded space. "When I saw the dragon," Jair continued, "I started to run away, but I tripped and fell. I hit my face on one of the big rocks out there. I'm okay. I just got scared, that's all."

Arden was standing nearby, just outside the rock overhang, looking down at Jair and Tassie, still clutching his bow in one hand.

"We were all afraid," he said, as Tassie fumbled with her medic bag. She pulled out a bowl and the same jar of powder she'd used to help clean Brace's own small wound after he'd been scratched by bramble bushes. Jair looked up at Arden as Tassie poured water and a bit of the powder into the bowl. "I didn't think you ever got scared," he told him.

Arden smiled ruefully. "Well, I did today." Jair only blinked in response.

Tassie soaked one of her cloth rags in the bowl of water, and she looked over Jair's injury once again, shaking her head.

"The wound is deep," she said, picking up the bowl. "I'm going to have to pour this over it."

"Will it hurt?" Jair asked.

"Umm … Yes, Jair. I'm sorry, but it will."

"*Bad?*"

"Not too terribly bad, and only for a moment."

The look Jair gave Tassie said that he wasn't certain whether he believed her. Leandra reentered the cavern and held Jair's hand—the one not covered in blood.

"You can squeeze it as tight as you want," she told him. He gave her a slight nod and swallowed nervously. Tassie turned her eyes toward Brace. "Help keep his head still," she directed him. "Just hold it."

Brace nodded and did as he was told. Tassie held the wooden bowl in one hand and the wet cloth in the other.

"Try not to move," she told Jair as she tipped the bowl, letting its contents run over the gash on his chin.

"Ouch!" Jair groaned through clenched teeth, his eyes shut tightly. He pulled back, reacting to the pain, and Brace stopped him, gently but firmly. He knew that he was only doing what he'd been told, but he couldn't help feeling guilty.

"That's good," Tassie said, seemingly to herself. She lightly pressed the wet cloth over the wound. "You can hold this here now," she told Brace. "Just for a few moments."

Brace moved his hand down from the side of Jair's head to hold the rag in place. Tassie opened her flask once again and poured water onto Jair's hand, using another cloth to wipe away every trace of blood from between his fingers.

"I think that's it," she said as she sat back on her heels.

Jair finally opened his eyes. "Really?" he asked.

"Yes. But you need to sit still for a while, keeping your head up, until the bleeding stops."

"All right."

Leandra gave Jair's hand one last squeeze, then let go, affectionately brushing his hair away from his face with her fingers.

"Brave man," she told him, but Jair only sighed. Brace suspected that the boy was feeling drained after the whole ordeal. *He* certainly did, and there was no doubt about that.

~12~

The small covered area created by the outcropping of rock, though it made for rather cramped quarters, was decidedly the safest place to stay for the remainder of the evening. The deep gash on Jair's chin had been cleaned, allowed to dry, and properly bandaged. Now the boy sat forlornly on a heap of folded blankets at the back of the cavern.

Tassie checked on Jair's condition several times throughout the evening. The gash had stopped bleeding completely, and she gave him something to lessen the throbbing ache he'd said was spreading across the whole side of his face. Zorix remained faithfully at Jair's side while the rest of them busied themselves with gathering firewood, unpacking blankets, and preparing something to eat. Arden stood guard over the camp all the while, his eyes fixed on the empty sky.

The meal was ready—biscuits again—and Tassie started off to take one of them to Jair, along with some of the fruit she'd found growing nearby. Brace watched her a moment, then made a split-second decision and hurried to step in front of her, stopping her.

"Let me take it to him," he asked. "Please," he added, when Tassie frowned in response. "I'm sure he's fine. I—I'd like to help."

Tassie's frown faded and was replaced by a tired smile.

"You helped a lot today," she told him. "Thank you."

Brace nodded as Tassie handed him the bowl of fruit and bread. "See if he needs anything," she requested.

"I will."

TIA AUSTIN

Brace stood by a moment, watching as Tassie slowly turned away to join the rest of the group. He went on then, ducking his head slightly to enter the small rock cavern.

"Feel like eating?" he asked, sitting on the hard ground next to Jair.

"I think so."

"Here," he said, holding out the bowl. Jair took it and sat looking down at its contents.

"Tassie found the salmonberries growing nearby," Brace told him. "You'll find chewing them easier than you would the biscuit, I should think. You're lucky you didn't knock any teeth loose," he added with a chuckle.

"Well, but now I'm going to have *another* mark on my face," Jair sulked.

"This one will go away in time."

"I wish the other one would. I hate having to hide from people. I never had to hide when I was living in Lidden, and I don't remember any of the people there looking at me strangely."

"No?"

"No. Sometimes the merchants would, or people traveling through on the Royal Road. But the Liddeners never did. They knew me. They got used to it."

Brace thought a moment. "Don't you think your markings made them curious, even at first?"

"Probably," Jair admitted. "But I think Ovard told them that it was a family crest, or something."

"Well," Brace said as he leaned back against the wall of the cavern, "once we find Haven, none of that will matter."

"Do you really think we'll find it?" The slightest hint of hope had returned to Jair's voice. Brace stared out across the gathering darkness, as Jair tore a piece from his biscuit and carefully began chewing.

"We really have to, don't we?" he said, more to himself than to Jair. "We really have to."

That night was one of the worst Brace could ever remember passing in his life. He slept, but his sleep was plagued by dream after frightening dream. Looming before his face were dragons, heavy, swirling black clouds, and violent men with long blades threatening to steal Jair away. He tossed back and forth on the hard, cold ground and woke up twice in the dead of night with his blanket tangled around his legs.

When morning came, he was nowhere near ready for it. With a groan, he pressed his hands over his eyes, blocking out the light. Opening his eyes at last, he watched the others waking as well. Tassie was rubbing the sleep from her eyes and attempting to brush the tangles from her long hair. Arden and Leandra were already up, their blankets folded, and they stood a short distance away, talking quietly. Ovard was up as well, and he had apparently just woken Jair, who still lay under his covers. The boy must have been quite upset; Brace could hear Ovard trying to encourage him.

Brace wondered if the injury done to Jair's chin was giving him pains, or was he still feeling disheartened, as he had the previous day? Both, as like as not. But, it wasn't his place to listen in, so Brace reluctantly pushed aside his cover and sat for a moment before rising completely.

The grass was wet with morning dew, and darkened Brace's boots as he walked across it, stretching his aching muscles. He drew the attention of Arden and Leandra for a moment, and he raised a hand in greeting. Leandra gave him a flat smile and Arden nodded as Brace passed them, heading for the bushes to relieve his bladder.

When he returned to the camp, everyone was up. Ovard was folding and packing away the blankets while Tassie carefully removed Jair's bandages to see how his wound was healing. Zorix sat alone, staring at Brace with his wide, black eyes, his large ears pressed forward with interest. Or was it suspicion?

Brace glanced toward Leandra, but she and Arden were deep in conversation. He turned back toward Zorix, and for the first time, he spoke to him.

"I know you don't like me," he told him, feeling a bit foolish talking to an animal. He knew that Zorix could somehow understand him, though, so he continued on.

"I seem to have been accepted by the rest of them," he said, "though goodness knows I don't deserve it. You could give me a chance too, you know. I promise I won't do anything to hurt any of your friends. I know that you know all about me—what I'm thinking or feeling. So you must know that I'm telling you the truth. I'm one of *you* now. I'm on *your* side. You have to know that much, at least."

Zorix tipped his head to one side, listening. Having said his peace, Brace stood and waited, wondering if he would get any response from this strange, color-changing creature. Zorix tilted his head to the other side and studied Brace a moment before walking away.

Brace thought, however briefly, that Zorix was snubbing him, until he saw that he'd made his way over to sit directly in front of Leandra, looking up at her. Brace heard nothing, of course, but he knew that the two of them were conversing in their own secret manner.

Turning away slightly, Brace pulled his cloak tighter around his shoulders and sat himself down on a large rock nearby. His mood was beginning to sour when Leandra approached him and took her seat on yet another large stone.

The rising sun began to pierce its way through the trees. Its light made Leandra's hair shine like gold, and accentuated the design that was embroidered across the front of her pale gray-green jerkin.

"Zorix tells me," she began in a light tone of voice, "that you've been speaking to him."

"I have," Brace replied. "And?"

"And he says to tell you that he *does* believe you. He knows you are telling the truth, and that you are on our side, as he puts it. And, he wants to thank you for going back for Jair yesterday. As do I."

Brace shrugged. "I just happened to look back, and ..."

"Yes," Leandra said, cutting him off. "As the rest of us should have. As *I* should have."

Brace sighed heavily. "Don't make me out to be some kind of

hero," he told her. "Deep down, I'm still the same rogue thief I've always been."

Leandra gave him a slight nod. "Thank you, just the same. It was a brave thing you did. You showed that you have some *harbrost* in you as well."

Harbrost he may very well have—honor and courage—but Brace was still exhausted. His sleep had been fitful at best, and his back and neck ached from lying so long on the hard ground.

The air in this part of the wild lands was much cooler, though, and Brace was grateful for that much. The sun seemed to have lost its ability to scorch them, though there were few, and at times no clouds in the sky.

Brace realized that in all of his running from place to place, this was about as far south as he had ever been. To the north, he'd been as far as the capital city of Glendor's Keep, and to the east, as far as the borders of the neighboring country of Elfaras. He had been to Fool's March, of course, and in the hills just to the west of it. But now, he would be unable help to the others as he had been in leading them to the herders' camp. He was just as blind as they were as to what might lay ahead of them.

Tassie had changed out of her dress, and went back to wearing the same wide-leg woven breeches and slit overskirt she'd been wearing when Brace had first laid eyes on her. She held the wide leather strap of her medic bag securely over the front of her hand-stitched brown suede vest as she walked. Brace couldn't help noticing how her eyes darted to and fro as she nervously watched the trees for any sign of danger.

She flinched when Brace reached out to touch her lightly on the arm.

"I'm sorry," he apologized. "I just saw that you're a little frightened. I thought you might like someone close at your side."

"I'm all right," she told him, in as brave a voice as she could manage.

"I don't think that dragon will give us any more trouble. She still has four of her eggs to guard over."

"Really, I'm fine," Tassie asserted. "Please don't worry yourself over me."

Tassie widened her steps, putting distance between herself and Brace. He watched her go, making no attempt to keep up. There was that strong side of her showing again, the same as she first revealed the day she had confronted him about choosing whether or not to commit himself to their cause.

Brace was left wondering if Tassie was frightened, or just disconcerted. One thing was certain, he thought—she was not likely to be the lady-in-distress type, in need of comforting. The idea brought a smile to Brace's lips, which he tried to hide, feigning a cough.

He did his best to leave her be, and succeeded for the rest of the daylight hours. Fortunately, or unfortunately—Brace couldn't make up his mind which—Jair was right there beside him almost every time he turned around. The boy had gotten it into his head that Brace had saved his life, and his opinion of him had gone up at least two notches.

As evening approached, however, and they ended their travels for the day, Brace noticed Tassie standing alone, her back to the camp. That was quite unlike her, Brace thought. He paused for a quick glance to be sure that Zorix, more than any of the others, was occupied, then he quietly slipped away to join her.

She had wrapped her arms around herself, and was staring out at the gray early evening sky. She stood quite still, and Brace wondered for a moment if she had even seen him.

"Look at it," she finally spoke, just above a whisper, then turned to face him.

"At what?"

"The sky. It's so strange."

"Is it?"

"Can't you see the difference?" she pressed. "It's almost like I can touch it. And the dusk. It's coming too early."

Brace wanted desperately to say something to encourage her, to take her mind off the subject, but he couldn't bring himself to do it; he knew that she was right.

"I noticed it as well," he told her. "I thought I saw something the night we all shared Ovard's mug of tea. I thought it might be clouds moving in to block the stars. Or I *hoped* it might be clouds. It wasn't, though, was it?"

Tassie shook her head. "I don't think so."

"What is it, exactly?"

"I don't know," she replied, her expression grim. "It's just *darkness*."

"I know it worries you," Brace told her. "Earlier today, I know that you were just trying to be brave, to hide your fears. You don't have to do that, you know."

She shook her head. "I don't want people to feel like they need to take care of me. I never have. But it gets so dark now. I could always see everything. I have always relied on my eyes. I can't hear, and now I can hardly see. If it keeps getting darker—the thought frightens me."

"Well, I may not be an expert on the subject," Brace muttered, but Tassie interrupted him.

"I'm sorry, what were you saying?"

Brace cleared his throat, then spoke more clearly. "I know I'm not the wisest in these matters, but I think that caring *about* a person and taking care of a person are two very different things. Don't you?"

His comment brought a smile to Tassie's face.

"Very well put," she replied. "You're learning. I don't think you would have said anything like this only a few days ago."

"No, I suppose not."

Tassie's face grew pensive. "What has your life been like as a thief?" The question surprised Brace.

"Hmmm," he thought. "*Lonely.*" The word hung in the air, as

Brace realized that Tassie was the first person to whom he had ever admitted having such feelings.

"It was rewarding at first," he continued. "A challenge. It was a way to survive, the only way I knew how. And I was angry. I got pleasure out of getting back at the world for snubbing me."

In a flash, there he was, in his mind's eye. Young—ten years old, maybe. What city he'd been living in at the time, he couldn't recall. But he remembered, plain as day, hiding under the old broken porch of a busy inn. It was late, and cottagers and nobles alike poured in off the street for a table and a meal. Brace remembered smelling the food cooking, hearing the people talking and laughing. And there he was, right under their noses, cold and hungry and alone.

"But?" Tassie's gentle question brought him back to the moment at hand.

He took in a breath, and held it a moment. He wanted to turn away, but he knew he had to face her if he wanted to tell her more.

"But it's been hard," he told her. "There were times when I wanted to be different, but I didn't know where to start, what to do, or how to change. I didn't trust anyone, and they didn't trust me."

"You never let anyone know you?"

"No," Brace replied, shaking his head. "Not really." He laughed sarcastically. "I don't think I even know me."

"You will. I truly believe you will."

"How?"

Tassie paused, considering the question. "Just ask yourself what your heart wants, more than anything elsc."

"What my heart wants," Brace repeated. "That's good advice."

"You may not know for a long time, but it will come. When it does, you'll know."

"How did you come to have so much wisdom?" Brace asked in a lighter tone of voice.

Tassie only smiled at him. "Neither here nor there," she replied. "I think we ought to eat something, don't you?"

"What?" Brace asked. "More biscuits?"

Tassie looked for a moment as though she was about to put him in his place, not having heard the humor in his words. Looking into his eyes, however, she realized that he was joking. Or at least, *mostly* joking.

"It may be getting old," Tassie began, smiling again, "but I think I would rather eat dry biscuits every night for the rest of my days than ever again touch dragon's eggs, no matter *how* tasty they may be."

There were no more dragon eggs to tempt Zorix. Unfortunately, there was not much of anything; the farther south they traveled, the less green the landscape became. They had passed the last of the streams branching off the main river, and the sound of flowing water could no longer be heard among the trees. The lush green grasses dwindled as well, giving way to low-growing scrub brush. They were by no means in anything like a desert, nor was it as dry, hot, and sandy as the area around Bramson or the herders' camp, but they could not help but notice the change.

Jair's mood remained solemn, although not nearly as forlorn as he had been in the hours following his injury. Zorix kept his small black nose to the ground as he went along, constantly sniffing. There was nothing to be found, however. They had left it all behind them—all of the fresh water, cool grasses, ripe, sweet salmonberries and plentiful shade trees. Here there were only savage-looking thorny bushes and small outcroppings of rock, together with the all-too-familiar giant trees towering over their heads, few and far between once again. The only encouraging thing that remained was the cooler air, so much so that Brace had taken to wearing his hooded wool cloak, even at midday.

The sky had, in fact, clouded over, and there was dampness in the air, bordering on the threat of rain. Ovard commented that he was grateful at last for all of the long sleeves and outer layers that everyone brought with them. He, like all the others, had been loath to carry the extra burden while they had been traveling in the searing heat. They wore them gladly enough now.

137

Later that evening, the rain did come. A lazy rain, it was at first, but it picked up steadily over the course of an hour, and the drops now came down heavily on their backs and the hoods they'd pulled up to cover their heads. They continued on undaunted for nearly two hours before Ovard declared that he'd had enough, and was sure the rest of them had as well.

"Let's make our camp here tonight," he suggested.

The sky darkened rapidly as Brace pulled the folded tent from his pack. Since it had become understood that Jair's sleeping space was equally his own, he had insisted on carrying his own share of the load.

Zorix was quite a sight. He stood nearby, his large ears pressed out flat from the sides of his head, the fur along his back and down his long tail sticking together in wet, blue clumps. He clearly hated the rain, and the instant that Arden finished putting up his and Leandra's tent, Zorix dashed inside.

There were no casual good-nights that evening, no campfire, no dinner. Not even biscuits. Everyone was wet and chilled through, and in no mood for pleasantries. Once the tents were up, each of them disappeared from view, glad to take shelter at last.

Inside the walls of the tent they shared, Brace and Jair each pulled off their heavy, wet, hooded cloaks and traded them in for traveling blankets. The musty smell of damp wool quickly filled the small tent.

Jair lightly pressed his hand to the bandage on his chin. "It's wet," he complained. "Do you think I could take it off?"

"I don't really know," Brace told him. "I guess it wouldn't be too bad an idea, just for one night."

"It really bothers me," Jair insisted. "Can you help me? I can't see to do it right."

Brace nodded, but he was a bit reluctant. Tassie had secured the edges of the cloth bandage with some kind of adhesive substance, and Brace was not exactly proficient in handling such things. Much to his relief, however, the bandage came off quite easily after he began to pull gently at an upper corner.

"How does it look?" Jair asked, as Brace laid the bandage aside.

"Well enough, to my untrained eyes," Brace told him. "It's pink, at any rate. That's a good sign."

"So it shouldn't be infected?"

"No," Brace replied. "It doesn't look it."

"Good." Jair settled himself onto his sleeping mat and pulled his blanket tightly around his shoulders.

"Tassie has taken good care of you," Brace pointed out.

Jair smiled a little. "She always has. She studies medicine all the time. She wants to be a medic someday."

"She'll make a good one."

Jair nodded in agreement. "I think so too." He shifted his legs into a more comfortable position. "Ugh, it stung *so* badly when she poured that treated water over it to clean it!" His face scrunched up at the memory.

"I could tell as much," Brace told him. "I'm sorry I had to hold you there while she did it."

"I know you had to," Jair said in a small voice. "I knew you felt bad. Tassie did too. She doesn't like to make people hurt any more than she has to." He paused a moment, looking pensive. "She's just like a sister to me, you know."

Brace nodded. "I know."

Jair looked up at him, only a bit surprised. "You do? Well, Ovard took me in when I was small. I don't remember anything about my life before I was with him and Tassie. They aren't really my family, not by blood, but it seems just as though they are. They're the only family I can ever remember. I wouldn't have wanted to be raised up by anyone else."

"Not even your true parents?"

Jair shook his head. "I don't remember anything about them. Things could have been different," he admitted. "If I had stayed with them, I wouldn't know anything other than what I had. But

I'm glad I've been with Ovard and Tassie. They're good to me. I feel safe with them."

Brace sat by in silence for a moment. "I wished I could have stayed with my mother," he said quietly, looking straight ahead at the drab wall of the tent.

"Why couldn't you?" Jair asked.

Brace let out a breath. "She died when I was young. She was taken from me."

"I'm sorry."

Brace nodded. Silence filled the small space, and for some time, the only sound to be heard was heavy raindrops pattering on the cloth roof and running down the sides of the tent. Finally, Brace turned toward Jair and started to speak, but he was interrupted by an eerie screeching sound echoing through the trees. Jair's eyes widened.

"It's that sound again," the boy said in a fearful voice. "Those creatures—or something. I thought we'd left them behind!"

"I had hoped so as well," Brace agreed.

Again, a loud squalling pierced the night around them.

Jair let out a gasp. "Tassie's in a tent all by herself!" he exclaimed. "What if ..."

Brace shook his head. "No. She'll be all right. Don't worry. If those ... *things* ... get too close, Zorix will know. And Arden's a good shot with his bow. She'll be safe."

Jair nodded, though he still looked unsure.

Brace cleared his throat. "I have a blade myself," he admitted.

"You do?"

"Yes. It stays hidden in my boot. Even if I take off my boots when I sleep, I keep them right at my side, within easy reach."

"Are you good with it?"

"Good enough." Brace laughed a little. "Leandra is as well; you must know that. You saw, didn't you? When she showed me her defensive skills?"

Jair smiled. "I saw."

"Don't worry then. We can protect ourselves and each other when the time comes. Try to get some rest."

Jair nodded and lay on his side, curled his knees, and pulled the blanket over himself. Brace lay down as well, his back to Jair. He didn't want the boy to see the uneasiness on his face.

~ 13 ~

The days melted together, marked only by periods of rain and clearing, by day and night. Three of them passed, and Brace noticed the daylight hours seeming to grow shorter. *How could things be changing so quickly?* Undoubtedly, the rest of the world around them must be taking note of it as well. *The prophecies*, Brace recalled. Ovard had told him of prophecies that were coming to pass, about the Haven, and a way to get back to it. He had said that the time was right.

Brace felt isolated from the rest of the world, more than ever before. Surrounded by wild lands on all sides, he found himself wondering what was happening in cities, in villas, in Glendor's Keep even, all without any of them being aware of it. He had forgotten completely about being a wanted thief. The fear of being hunted after by law keepers had faded in his mind to almost nothing.

Finally, a night came when the rain stopped long enough for them to build a fire. Brace watched as Arden crouched low over a small heap of wet, smoking leaves and twigs, struggling to coax a flame from the faintly glowing embers. When he at last succeeded, Brace felt a strong sense of relief at the sight of the flickering orange flames. It was a comforting thing.

The darkness all around him was so heavy that Brace thought he could feel it pressing down on his shoulders. The very fire at their feet seemed to be fighting to keep the dark from putting it out altogether. Looking around, Brace could see nothing of what lay beyond the light of the small fire. He felt as though he was being watched in the night, as though hundreds of pairs of eyes were on him. The as yet unseen creatures of the night kept up their screeching in the distance.

The group sat huddled close around the flames to warm their hands and faces. Tassie stayed near her uncle, while Jair knelt between the older man and Brace. Leandra sat close by Arden's side, and leaned in to whisper into her husband's ear.

"This place scares me to the bone," Brace overheard her telling him. He knew what she was feeling; he was frightened as well. Despite having tried to comfort Jair on that first rainy night, he was still unnerved.

Zorix paced near Leandra's feet, his fur flickering in color from orange to red and back again. Even Ovard appeared ill at ease. Brace was certain that sleep would not come easily this night, not for any of them.

The rain started falling again by the following morning, but thankfully, for the time being it was only a drizzle. The group pressed on in an attentive silence, refraining from any complaints. Everyone, apparently, except Zorix.

"I know you're wet," Leandra said aloud, breaking the silence. "We're all wet. And cold, I know. *And* hungry."

Brace caught Arden's eye, and they both smirked.

"Doesn't keep his feelings to himself very well, does he?" Brace asked in a low voice, one that Leandra wouldn't overhear.

"Not at all," Arden agreed. "I never hear him, of course, but I do get the other half of their conversations. You're lucky," he commented. "You don't have to share a tent with him."

"Doesn't leave the two of you with much privacy," Brace commented, and instantly wished he could take his words back. Arden might find such conversation to be not very honorable.

"That it doesn't," was all the archer said in reply. He did not seem offended, though, and Brace inwardly breathed a sigh of relief.

The day was pleasant enough, despite the lingering rain, but Brace couldn't get his mind off of wondering about whatever sort of unusual creatures had been crying out so shrilly during the night. Before embarking on this trek with these people who had now become his companions, he had never heard anything like it. When everyone stopped to rest their sore, tired feet, Brace took the opportunity to question Ovard about them. The older man seemed to be the best person to speak to about such things, and other than Arden, the least likely to be disturbed at the mention of them.

"Ovard," Brace began, seizing the opportunity when the older man drew aside to sit on a damp rock, removing his boots and giving his stocking feet a chance to breathe.

"What is it?" Ovard asked, in a kind yet tired voice.

"There's something I've been wondering about," he told him. "Something I can't get out of my mind."

"Tell me."

"Those shrill cries we've been hearing at night—they give me the chills. What on this earth do you think they could be?"

Ovard's expression darkened. "I'm afraid I don't know," he replied. "I've never heard them until recently."

"Never? Not at all?"

Ovard shook his head. "I haven't done much traveling through the wild lands, though. It could be that whatever creatures are making those sounds have always been out there, and I've simply never been aware of them."

Brace hesitated a moment. "But you don't think that's truly the case, do you? You think it could be something more."

"In all fairness, I really can't say," Ovard replied. "My best advice is not to take for granted that they're out there, whatever they are. We must be ready for anything."

"I can agree with you there," Brace told him, "but ..."

"Ovard!" Arden spoke up from a short distance away, and Brace was unable to finish his thought.

"What is it?"

"You need to come and have a look at this."

With a sigh, Ovard forced his feet back into his boots and made his way across the soggy ground to stand beside Arden. Brace followed, keeping a fair distance between them, should this prove to be a private conversation.

"There," Arden told him, pointing farther south. "What do you suppose that is?" Ovard squinted into the distance.

"A lake?" he said, unsure.

"I think so as well," Arden agreed. "You've been studying quite a few maps. Do you know the name of it?"

Brace looked out at the southern horizon, at a wide, flat stretch of blue that went on for miles to both the east and the west. The rest of the group noticed the three of them standing aside, and came to join them. Leandra held her palm flat above her eyes to get a better look, a slight wind blowing through her pale, straight hair.

"It must be Wayside Lake," Ovard answered Arden's question. "Without any doubt."

"Are we going to cross it somehow?" Jair asked, straining for a better look. Tassie had placed a fresh, white bandage over what remained of the gash on his chin, though she was quite pleased with how quickly it was healing.

"There is a bridge," Ovard replied. "Wayside Lake is spanned by a bridge. But it leads straight into the city of Meriton."

"Into the city ..." Leandra thought aloud. She left the words unspoken, but Brace knew what they would be. A city full of people. They would be seen. *Jair* would be seen. It could be a dangerous situation.

"Can't we go around?" Brace asked. "How wide can the lake be?"

"Very wide," Ovard told him. "It would take us more than a week to travel all the way around, to one side or another. And ..."

"And what?" Leandra prompted.

"This could well be our turning point." A bit of hope had returned to Ovard's tired voice. "The city of Meriton could be where we need to turn westward."

"How can you be sure?" Brace questioned.

"I'm not sure of anything," he replied gruffly. "I am making an educated guess. We haven't come to anything yet, this whole way, that would stand out enough to be represented by Jair's markings as the point where we change directions. If Meriton is indeed our turning point, we need to get ourselves there."

"What if it isn't?" Arden spoke up, leaving Brace perplexed. This was the first time that he had ever heard the archer question Ovard's judgment.

Ovard only looked at him.

"We could be making a grave mistake," Arden pointed out.

Ovard stroked his short beard as he considered the best way to answer. Tassie and Leandra stood by silently, but Jair took a few steps ahead of them.

"What is that?" he asked, without turning back to face them.

"What, Jair?" Ovard responded. "Where?"

Jair pointed, far into the distance. "There. In the sky. Through the clouds."

Brace felt his breath catch in his throat. What could he be seeing?

Ovard stood directly behind Jair and followed his gaze. From a few steps farther back, Brace did the same, joined by the others.

The sky was overcast and gray with rain-bearing clouds, but a wind had picked up and was pushing the clouds across the sky rather quickly. Far above the tops of even the tallest trees, at a distance of what must have been at least a hundred miles away, Brace could see a shape in the break between the clouds.

"What is it?" he asked.

"A mountain," Ovard replied after a moment. "It must be."

"Are there mountains in this region on your map?" Arden asked.

"I'm afraid," Ovard began, turning toward him, "that the farthest point south on any of my maps is the city of Meriton itself. Beyond that, there is nothing of note but for the border we share with Danferron."

"It's a tall mountain, isn't it?" Jair interjected.

Ovard only looked at the boy a moment, then smiled and put an arm across his shoulders. "It is that," he replied. "A *very* tall mountain, from the look of it."

"You're thinking *this* is what we've been looking for?" Leandra asked. When Ovard gave her a nod, she turned once again to gaze at it. "Right there in front of us," she breathed.

"You sound as though you've found Haven itself," Brace told her.

"No," she admitted. "I know it isn't Haven. But *there*—that is where we turn westward. It must be. We may be halfway there!"

"Meriton," Arden muttered, his voice heavy. "It's a larger city, is it not?"

"It is," Ovard replied.

"Then we're likely to be getting near the Royal Road. Aren't we?"

"As like as not. What has you troubled, my friend? I know that we'll be wanting to make ourselves scarce, to get through the city as quickly as we can, but ..."

"You must understand," Arden told him, taking a few steps back, then pacing toward them. "When I joined you in the quest to find Haven, I abandoned my post! I am not only an archer, I am in the service of Glendor's Keep, and under the king's authority. Or, I *was*, at any rate. Word has likely spread of my unfaithfulness. It will have been seen as *treason*. If I'm spotted ... if I'm recognized as one of the Keep's own archers—" Arden paused and took a breath. "If I'm taken, it could mean my life."

Fear seeped into Leandra's eyes. "What can we do?" she asked, in her voice heavy with desperation. "He can't ..."

"We'll think of something," Ovard told her. "Don't despair."

Arden gazed out toward the horizon, then shook his head. "There's only one thing to do," he said after a moment. "The only way we can do this is if I'll not be recognized as a Keep's archer. I need to get rid of my hair."

"Your hair?" Leandra gasped. "Arden!"

"I know, Leandra, I know. But it's the only way. Without my tail of hair, I won't be seen as an archer by anyone in Meriton. I'll be a man, the same as any other."

Leandra's gaze fell to the ground. "You're certain?"

"I am. Leandra, please. You know this is the best option. The *only* option."

She nodded. "For so many years," she said softly. "Your hair—it's been your honor."

"Don't you think I know that?" Arden's voice was sorrowful as he stepped toward Leandra. "This is important, though. For all of us. We must do everything we can to go unnoticed if we're to get safely through the city."

Leandra nodded again as Arden rested his hands on her arms.

"You're certain you want to do this?" Ovard asked, with Jair standing nervously beside him.

"I am," Arden replied. He held out his hand to Leandra. "Your blade, please?"

Slowly, Leandra pulled her long knife from her belt and handed it to Arden, who held it a moment, looking down at it.

"I'm afraid I can't see the back of my own head," he addressed the group, a touch of humor in his voice. "I'll need someone else to do this."

"Let me," Leandra spoke up. "I will do it."

Without a word, Arden returned Leandra's knife to her. He briefly touched the side of her face before he found a large stone to lower himself onto. Leandra stood behind him, the top of Arden's head reaching just to her shoulders.

Brace continued watching everything in silence as Leandra ran her hand down Arden's long, straight hair. He could see her reluctance, could almost feel it, as she held the knife's sharp edge just above the place where Arden had tied back his hair. She hesitated, then pulled the knife away.

"Maybe it doesn't truly need to be cut," she said, her voice wavering. "Maybe the people won't recognize you as an archer."

"I did," Brace spoke up gently.

"Please, Leandra," Arden told her. "You can do this. It will grow again. It *will* grow again."

Leandra took a deep breath as she held the knife in one hand and Arden's hair in the other. She pulled upward on the blade, and it easily and cleanly sliced through every strand until it all came free. Leandra was left standing there, holding onto it, her eyes brimming with unshed tears. She acted as though she was unsure what to do with the bundle of hair, until Ovard stepped up and mercifully took it from her. Arden ran his fingers through the hair that remained at the top of his head, and it fell in uneven strands around his ears.

"I must look a mess," he said, trying to lighten the mood. When he turned and saw the emotion on Leandra's face, he rose to his feet and took her in his arms. "It's all right," he told her. "It's for the best. You're more upset about this than I am."

"I'm sorry," Leandra told him, leaning into Arden's embrace. "I just never thought it would come to this." She straightened up, taking another breath. "I'm all right."

Arden nodded, running his hand through his hair once again. "Can we clean this up a bit?" he asked. "I feel like a shaggy hound."

No longer looking quite so shaggy, Arden led the small group farther on toward the Royal Road. His hair was now short all over, but the top of it stuck out left and right as though it didn't know what to do, having been weighed down so many years by its own length. Brace couldn't help but feel pity for the man. There was no trace left of his former dignified appearance. He may not look like a shaggy hound, but Brace thought wryly that he reminded him of the way Zorix looked when he'd been out all day in the rain.

The farther on they traveled, the more clearly they could see the wide, blue-green surface of Wayside Lake as it stretched across the horizon. Arden stopped them when, only a few yards ahead, he spotted a long, flat area of land wide enough to drive three large wagons along the breadth of it, with room to spare.

"Is that the Road?" Jair asked.

"It must be," Ovard told him.

Tassie held tightly onto Jair's arm as though to prevent him from going on ahead too quickly. Zorix sniffed hesitantly at the air.

"It seems to be empty," Leandra spoke up, sharing Zorix's thoughts. "For the time being."

"We'd best cross quickly," Ovard advised.

After a quick glance around, Arden stepped out first, and the others followed him.

The Royal Road was indeed very wide, and very flat, and very open. The ground beneath their feet was bare dirt, muddy in places from the heavy rains they'd had over the past few days.

Brace felt suddenly very exposed, like a wild animal who'd fallen into a pit with the trapper staring down at him, armed with a spear. He was thankful that the Road was clear, but this was only the beginning of an entirely new set of dangers, he knew. The long, wide stone bridge began just on the other side of the road, and it ran the entire length of Wayside Lake, straight as an arrow.

Forbidding-looking creatures carved in stone lined the high walls of the bridge, and seemed to be staring down at them, ever watchful of anyone approaching the city, warning them not to bring any trouble there.

Brace was unnerved by them. He could see from the way that Jair allowed Tassie to cling to his sleeve that he was uneasy as well. The boy kept his eyes straight ahead as he walked, fixing them on the wide, gray floor of the bridge that stretched out before them. For the longest time, none of them spoke. Zorix kept his side pressed against Leandra's legs as she walked, so that she nearly tripped over him.

"Zorix," she scolded, her voice just above a whisper. "You're getting under my feet. Stop this, or I'll carry you."

Zorix stood still and looked up at her, his ears tipped forward. When Leandra continued on, he kept his distance—a little. Leandra's words served to break the tension that had been surrounding them. Halfway across the bridge, Ovard cleared his throat.

"We need to have a plan," he addressed the group. "Let us not go into this blindly."

"Agreed," Arden spoke up. He had already removed the string from his bow and bundled it inside one of the heavy blankets. Wearing it strapped across his back, with his supply of arrows tucked inside as well, it looked as though it could well be a long sword, which he had put away as a sign of good faith for the citizens of Meriton, that he meant them no harm.

"I think it would be best," Ovard continued, "that we find a place to stay inside the city for the night. We can rise early in the morning and make our way through during the busy hours of the day. We'll draw less attention. And Jair, you'd best keep your hood up."

No explanation was required there. Jair nodded and pulled the deep hood of his wool cloak up over his head so that only his bandaged chin was visible.

Leandra turned toward Brace. "You've wandered all over. Have you ever been to Meriton?"

"No, that I have not," he replied. "But if *I* can travel, so can others. I'd like to avoid being recognized as well."

"Well, we're in a fine state, aren't we?" Ovard found no humor in the situation, not this time. "Fully half of us have reason to hide! This is not going to be easy."

None of them had expected things to be easy, though, not in the slightest.

With their plans made, they continued on toward the city. Brace took advantage of the light rain that had picked up once again, and pulled his own hood up over his head, though not as much as Jair, who could now see only the ground just before his feet as he walked.

The rain pelted the surface of the lake as a steady afternoon wind churned across it.

As they neared the far end of the bridge, Meriton loomed large before them. The city walls were made of smooth gray stone, as were the buildings within. Just beyond the open gates, a large fortress jutted up into the cloudy sky, with the blue and red flag bearing Meriton's crest flapping boldly in the breeze. Two men in armor stood guard on each side of the bridge, which widened to accommodate them. A fifth man approached them from inside the gates, clad in a thick leather vest, tall boots, and a silver helmet with a feathered plume the color of a clear summer sky.

"What business have you here?" he asked them, in a tone that said he truly wasn't interested, but it was his duty to ask.

"We are just passing through," Ovard told him. "We journey south."

"South, is it?" The guard asked, scratching the side of his bearded face as he looked them over, one by one. Brace eyed the other guards, but they may as well have been made of stone, for all they had moved.

"Well, then," the city guard spoke once more. "Welcome to Meriton. What sort of creature have you got there?" he asked, nodding toward Zorix.

"He is a lorren," Leandra answered.

"Best keep him under control," the guard warned. "Wouldn't do to have him biting anyone."

"I assure you, he will do no such thing," Leandra replied as they passed through the open gates, with just enough boldness in her voice to cause the guard to smirk.

The sounds of city life reached Brace's ears as soon as he set foot inside the high stone walls. They were sounds that he was quite familiar with, but he had been so long in the wild lands, away from any settlements, that they almost sounded foreign to him now.

Bordering the nearest cobblestone road on both sides were shops of many varieties—bakeries, leathersmiths, butcher shops, and so on. It was by no means the busiest hour of the day, but still, several heavily-laden carts rumbled through the streets, and small swarms of people gathered here and there, particularly around one of the shops where Brace caught a whiff of freshly baked bread.

They all stayed together in a close group as they made their way down several busy streets. With Meriton being the southernmost city along the Royal Road, it was always crowded with traveling merchants and townsfolk from the nearby villages. The vast majority of the people appeared to be cottagers, dressed rather poorly and traveling on foot, though here and there Brace spotted a city guard in his leathers, a nobleman, or a Lord or land holder on horseback. He was passed by, rather too closely for his liking, by a stately young man seated on a large, heavily muscled black horse. The man's long sleeve crimson tunic, with a thick, ornate, silver chain draped across his chest and over his shoulders, gave him away in an instant as being nobility. No one, however, whether rich or poor, paid any of them any mind.

Ovard stopped when he came across an older man in a faded blue jerkin and stained beige undershirt. He was leaning his back against the outer wall of a fish market, his arms crossed confidently across his chest as he watched the throngs of people pass by him.

"Excuse me, sir," Ovard greeted him. "Might you be so kind as to direct us to where we might find a place to stay the night here?"

"Eh?" The man asked. "What's that?"

"A place to stay," Ovard repeated. "We're in need of a place to stay."

The grizzled old man glanced around at each of them, taking note of their damp and dirty appearances. They were not clothed as peasants would be, by any means, though Brace was sure he came close. He had stolen his boots and cloak from a well-to-do landowner several years back, and though well-made, they were quite worn by now.

"Ah," the man said as he stood up away from the wall. "It's the

Wolf and Dagger ye'll be wanting. Just down the road there." He pointed a bony finger down the street to his left. "Ye can't miss it."

"Thank you, sir," Ovard told him.

"Sir, sir," the man muttered. "Ain't been called sir too oft in my days."

"Thank you, just the same," Arden spoke up. The older man stared at him, apparently surprised at his stature, as he came closer, approaching from the rear of the group.

"Aye." His word was scarcely more than a whisper. Giving Ovard a stiff nod, he turned and hobbled toward the crowded fish market.

~14~

The Wolf and Dagger was not hard to find, just as the old man had told them. It was easily recognized by the square wooden sign hanging over the main door: A gray wolf leaping upward to the right, with a white-handled blade crossing over it, tilted toward the left. The paint was old, cracked, and faded, but it was yet as plain as day.

It appeared to be an inn of sorts, and quite crowded. Ovard stood and watched from the corner of the road for a moment, unsure what their next move should be. Between himself, Arden, and Leandra, they were certain they would have enough to pay for one room for one night, but *one room*, for six people? They had so long been spending their nights on the hard ground that sleeping on the floor would not be much different, if there were but one bed in the room. It would be crowded, however, and the innkeeper would no doubt find it strange. And people would talk. *Oh, yes, I remember. There were six of them. And that odd young lad—he never let down his hood, never let anyone see his face, as though he had something to hide.*

Brace stood by silently as Ovard pondered their dilemma, until he remembered the pouch full of silver coins that was tied firmly to his belt, hidden under his heavy cloak. He was struck by the realization that he had all but forgotten about it. Once, it had been all that had mattered to him. Had so much changed?

"I have a bit I can spare," Brace spoke up. Everyone turned

toward him. "It would be better to have two rooms, would it not? If there are two rooms to be had."

Ovard nodded. "That would be better." He looked around at each of them, considering how best to split the group. "Arden," he finally said.

"Yes?"

"How would it be if Tassie shared a room with you and Leandra? You have your gloves, do you not?"

"I do." Arden appeared a bit puzzled.

"I think," Ovard continued, "that you could pose as a sort of guardian over the women, while I take Jair and Brace with me in another room."

Arden considered the situation, then nodded. "That would be believable," he replied.

"Take Zorix with you," Ovard told him. Arden nodded as he removed the strap holding his well-hidden bow and shrugged out of his pack. As he searched for his leather archer's gloves to hide the unmistakable marriage symbols tattooed across his hands, Brace discreetly opened his pouch and pulled out several silver coins. He was by no means familiar with how much it cost to stay at an inn, but he could make a guess.

Jair stood by silently, hidden under the hood of his cloak, while Ovard repeated their plans to Tassie, to be sure there was nothing she had missed. When he finished, she nodded in agreement. Arden had pulled his yellow-brown leather gloves on over his hands, and took up his things once again.

"Zorix, stay close," Leandra said aloud as they stepped forward to enter the inn, and he gladly obeyed.

Once inside the door, Brace stood a moment to allow his eyes to adjust to the dim light. The interior space was quite large, with several black iron candelabras hanging on heavy chains from the wooden beams of the ceiling. There were tables everywhere. Apparently the Wolf and Dagger was more than an inn; it was also a place to get a good meal. The aromas of grilled meat, onions, and hearty ale hung heavy in the air. The establishment was rather busy, as the day had grown quite late. Attractive women in somewhat revealing dresses carried silver platters heaped with food around the room, from one full table to another. The din of voices filled the room, and Brace noticed when Zorix tried to hide himself between Leandra's legs. He had learned by now that the red color that had seeped into his fur meant that he was fearful. He could hardly blame him.

After a moment, Ovard waved them on ahead, toward a long wooden bar along the wall on their left. Behind the bar stood a man of middle age, of slender build, and an outgoing demeanor, who greeted them as they came closer.

"Welcome to my establishment," he said in a smooth voice, speaking loudly over the clatter of plates and clamor of voices. "What can I do for you?"

"We would like to have two rooms for the evening," Ovard told him, stepping forward.

"Ah," the man replied, "forgive me, but I'm afraid we only have one room available, and not a very good one at that. You see, we're quite full up." The man's eyes darted across them. "How many are you?"

"Six," Ovard replied, "and a small animal. He's well-behaved, I assure you."

"Well," the man said in an encouraging tone, "it is a large room. A bit chilly, though. It's just off the stables. Would you care to see it?"

Ovard looked back toward the group. "Only one room," he told them.

"We'll see it," Arden spoke up.

"Right," said the man behind the bar, clapping his hands together. He stooped to retrieve the key from below the bar and, stepping out into the room, gestured for them to follow him. Tassie was clutching her medic bag tightly, as though someone might try to steal it from her, and she was gazing uneasily around the crowded room. Brace stepped up close to her and rested his hand lightly on her back.

"Keep close," he told her. She nodded and followed after Ovard.

The owner of the Wolf and Dagger led them to the back, past all of the busy, crowded tables. In the far right corner, beyond the wooden staircase leading up to the main rooms, was an old, unimpressive wooden door. The tall, rather thin innkeeper, whom Brace noticed was well-dressed in a deep blue linen tunic with silver embroidering cascading down the long, loose-fitting sleeves, and a dark, almost black heavy vest, struggled a moment to turn the key in the door's rusty lock.

"Forgive me," he said smoothly as the door finally creaked open. "This room is generally used to house stable boys and the like. You have horses, mules ...?"

"None," Ovard replied. "We came on foot."

"Ah," the man replied, gracefully gesturing for them to enter.

The room was large enough, that was certain, but it was rather chilly and smelled faintly of a barnyard. Several small, dingy-looking cots lined the far wall. There was a fire pit, but it was cold and dark.

"I apologize that this is all I have to offer," the owner of the Wolf and Dagger continued. "Will you take it, or no?" Brace couldn't help but see the distaste in Arden's expression, but they hadn't much choice. "We'll take it," Ovard spoke up, rather reluctantly.

"Very good," the man replied in a pleasant voice. "Rune Fletcher, at your service. Welcome! Please make yourselves comfortable."

Slim chance of that, Brace thought glumly, eyeing the empty fireplace. "Can we get some wood?" he asked.

"Of course, of course," came the reply. "I'll have it here in a trice." He lowered his gaze slightly. "Pardon me, but who will be paying?"

"I will," Ovard told him, stepping forward.

"Very good," Rune told him with a smile. "If you'll kindly come this way, we can take care of business." Ovard nodded and left the room. Rune Fletcher followed him, gently closing the door as he went out.

"That man gives me the chills," Leandra muttered.

"You're right there," Brace grumbled.

"It's so cold," Tassie spoke up, rubbing her arms.

"We should have a fire soon," Arden told her, nudging at one of the beds with the toe of his boot, causing it to rock unevenly. "Perfect," he said under his breath.

Jair had made his way into one corner of the room and seated himself onto the farthest cot. "It's better than the floor," he said from underneath his hood.

Brace had to smile. "Now you sound like Ovard," he told him, and the boy smiled back. "Well," Brace continued, sighing, "at least we have our own blankets and things to cover them with. But there are only four beds."

"I doubt I could fit in one anyway," Arden pointed out.

Their conversation was cut short by a loud knocking at the door. Brace exchanged a quick glance with Arden, then moved to open it. A large, burly man stood before him, his arms full of roughly-cut logs.

"Wood for your fire," he said brusquely.

Brace stepped aside to let him enter. The man's heavy boots thumped across the bare wooden floor as he crossed to the fire pit, dropping the bundle of logs in a noisy heap on the stone hearth.

"Thank you kindly," Leandra told him, and he nodded in her direction.

"There's kindling for you as well," he replied. "Should be here momentarily." Without another word, the man turned and left.

"Where is Ovard?" Tassie asked anxiously.

Arden snorted. "That Rune Fletcher is likely buttering him up for honey," he commented sourly.

"I'll go and find him," Brace told her.

"Be careful," Tassie warned. "I don't like this place."

"I'll be fine," Brace told her, his hand on the open door.

"Go with him, will you?" Leandra asked, turning toward her husband.

"And leave you alone?" Arden was hesitant to say the least.

"We have Zorix," Leandra replied, stepping up beside him. "And you know very well what I'm capable of. We'll get the beds ready. You go and bring us something to eat. It's been far too long since we've had a good meal. We'll be all right here."

Arden looked from Leandra to Brace, then back again.

"All right," he told her at last. "You should be able to make a fire as soon as they bring the smaller pieces of wood in. You can warm yourselves. We'll be back as soon as we can."

Arden and Brace all but bumped into Ovard while they were crossing the main room of the Wolf and Dagger; he had paid Rune Fletcher for the room and had been on his way back to join them. Arden informed him that Leandra had suggested they order something to eat, and Ovard nodded in agreement. One of the serving women told them, after they managed to find an empty table, that there was roast pork, potato soup, and bread. Ovard discreetly asked after the price.

"For everything?" The young woman asked.

"Yes, for everything," Ovard replied. "Six helpings."

"Three silver each plate," the woman replied.

Ovard rubbed at his beard. Brace had no way of knowing how much he'd spent on the room, shabby though it was.

"I can help," he spoke up.

"As can I," Arden joined in.

Ovard smiled a tired smile and turned back to the server. "We'll take six plates, then. We'll take them to our room, if we may."

"Of course," the woman replied with a nod, then turned and left.

The three men sat in silence, taking in the busy scene going on all around them. Brace kept his hood pulled halfway up over his head, hoping against hope that he would not be recognized. Ovard gazed at the rough surface of the wooden table. He looked suddenly very tired, exhausted even, and older than Brace had ever seen him. Arden was just as steady as ever, his sharp blue eyes scanning the crowds, keeping watch for any signs of trouble.

"Your bread, sirs?"

A tiny voice drew Brace's attention. He turned to find a small girl with fair skin and long, unruly black hair holding a heaping basket of bread rolls in one arm and a bowl of melted butter in the other.

"Yes, thank you," Ovard spoke up, taking the basket and placing it on the table. The girl gently set down the bowl, being careful not to spill a drop.

"The rest of your meal is coming soon," she said politely. "Would you like anything to drink? Some ale?"

"Aren't you a little young to be serving us ale?" Ovard asked her.

The girl blinked repeatedly in surprise, as though she'd never before been asked that question.

"I ... I don't *drink* it, sir," she stammered. "Honestly I don't."

Ovard could see that he had upset the girl, and he reached out to pat her on the arm. "It's all right, child. Don't be afraid. We'll just have water, please."

Brace thought that he would indeed have liked to have a mug of ale, but kept his thoughts to himself.

"What is your name, child?" Ovard asked the girl kindly.

"Kendie, sir," she replied with a smile.

"Do you *work* here, Kendie?"

"Yes, sir, and I live here too. I help to serve the meals."

Arden leaned forward, at the other side of the table. "The owner ... Rune Fletcher," he asked, "is he your father?"

"Not my father, sir," Kendie replied. "He looks after me, is all. I wait on the tables to help earn my keep. I don't mind, really. It isn't hard."

Earn my keep. The words rung in Brace's mind. *Earn your keep. You have to earn your keep, boy.* He had heard those words before so many times as a child that he would never forget them.

"I see so many of the same people here most of the time," Kendie was saying. "This is one of the best places to eat in all of Meriton. The regulars all know me. I've never seen any of you before, though. Where have you come from?"

"North," Ovard replied. "A long way north of here."

"What made you want to come *here*?"

Before any of them could answer, Rune Fletcher himself appeared. He put a hand firmly on Kendie's shoulder, and she quickly looked down at the floor.

"Pardon me," Rune told them in his usual, courteous manner, smooth as oil. "Is the girl a bother to you? I know how she can prattle on."

"Not a bit," Ovard replied without hesitation. "She is quite charming, actually."

Rune gave Kendie's shoulder a squeeze. "Go and see about the soup," he told her.

"Yes, sir." Kendie turned away dejectedly. Brace watched her go, suddenly feeling a bit of anger rising in his throat. He averted his eyes, not wanting Rune Fletcher to get any glimpse of what he was feeling. He could see Arden looking at him out of the corner of his eye while the owner of the Wolf and Dagger flattered them, going on about how pleased he was to have them as his patrons, and telling them how much he hoped they would enjoy their stay.

When the man finally left, Arden squeezed Brace's arm. "What's wrong?" he asked.

"The girl," Brace told him quietly. "I've been in her shoes. Taken in by a man who is supposed to care for her, and made to work." He hesitated, looking off in the direction she'd gone. "I think he mistreats her."

"You can't be sure about that," Arden told him quietly.

"No." Brace shook his head. "I can't be sure. But I know that look about her. I've been there myself."

"You were mistreated as a child?" Arden asked.

Brace nodded. "I was. *Badly.*"

The table was silent a moment.

"I'm sorry," Arden finally spoke.

Brace nodded, looking down at his hands as he rested them on the table. "It's stuck with me all these years," he muttered. "The feeling of being so completely helpless."

Ovard sighed. "If that is the case, I'm afraid there isn't much we can do. We'll be gone in the morning."

"I know," Brace admitted. Suddenly, the room felt small. *Too* small.

"I need to get some air," he said abruptly.

"What?" Ovard asked sharply. "Where will you go?"

"Not far," Brace told him, pushing back his chair. "I'm just going out to walk and clear my head."

"Don't get lost," Arden warned him.

"I can find my way around," Brace told them, as he marched across the room and out the door into the cool air of the evening.

The cobblestone streets of Meriton had emptied considerably in the gathering darkness. Brace walked quickly at first, but soon slowed to a stroll as his frustration waned. A few of the last remaining merchants to pack up their wares had given him curious glances as he passed them. He was quite alone now, shadows from the high, square stone buildings creeping along the ground at the edges of the walks.

His anger had surprised him. After all these years, there it was, still burning beneath the surface. His brisk walk had cooled it to a simmer, but he could still feel it. The anger was old, but caring about others was something new. Brace had risked his neck to go back for Jair, despite his fears about the attacking dragon. And now, that little girl at the inn—this world was still a place where children were mistreated. Brace was familiar with the anger he'd always harbored about the way he'd been treated as a child. But *this* anger—this was something new.

Coming to the end of the street, he faced a high, ornately patterned iron gate standing shut before him. He came closer, wrapping his fingers tightly around the cold, hard metal. Leaning his head against its surface, he breathed deeply. *You're not that little boy anymore,* he told himself. *No one can hurt you like that any longer. You don't have to let them.*

"No," Brace said aloud to himself. "But there are still others who are hurting. What's to become of *them*?"

He closed his eyes for a moment, then heard a steady *clang, clang, clang* coming from just beyond the gate. *Clang, clang, clang.*

A blacksmith? he wondered. He looked around, then back at the gate. Giving it a firm push, it creaked open, just enough to allow him to pass through. With another glance over his shoulder, Brace slipped through the open gate and wandered down a narrow alley. He followed the rhythmic clanging, and it led him on, around the corner of the nearest building.

There it was, a familiar sight. The open flame of the hearth, the smooth stone of the anvil, and the smith himself, swinging his large hammer. Sweat glistened on the man's face and bare shoulders as he worked. Even from where he stood, on the far side of the alley, Brace could feel a touch of the heat that was pouring out of the workshop.

Brace stood watching the blacksmith, mesmerized by the steady motion of his arm as he worked. When the man stopped to wipe the sweat from his brow, he noticed Brace standing across the way.

"Evening," he breathed.

"Evening," Brace replied.

"Lost, are you?"

"No, thank you, I'm just clearing my head."

The smith nodded. "It's a nice night," he commented. "At least the rain has stopped."

Brace looked up at the twilight sky. "It has." He stood a moment, gazing back down the narrow stone-paved alley.

"Has something got you troubled?" The blacksmith asked, using a pair of metal tongs to pick up the horseshoe he'd been hammering.

"A little," Brace admitted. "Old memories." He watched as the blacksmith lowered the iron shoe into a barrel of water, releasing a cloud of steam with a long, loud hiss.

"Well, we've all got them," the man commented, turning toward the back wall of the workshop. Brace watched him, considering the fact that the blacksmith may well have lived and worked in Meriton all his life.

"Can I ask you a question?" He took a few steps closer.

The blacksmith eyed him curiously for a moment. "Sure enough."

"My friends and I are traveling through. We plan on heading west. Can you tell me what's out there?"

The man shook his head. "There is nothing," he told him. "Only a land more wild than anything we know in these parts."

"You're sure?"

"As far as I know. Just mountains, mountains, and more mountains. Why are you going west if you don't know what's out there?"

"We're ... searching."

"For?"

Brace hesitated. He had to be careful not to say too much. "A new start," he replied, then shrugged.

"Right," the smith replied. "None of my business, is it?"

"How far are the mountains from here?" Brace asked.

"Pretty far, I should think." He picked up another horseshoe, with his bare hand. "Do your animals need new shoes?"

"We have no animals," Brace told him. "We're on foot."

"On foot?" The surprise was clear and plain in the blacksmith's voice. "You're not going to have an easy time of it."

"We haven't yet," Brace told him.

"Come a long way, have you?"

"Quite."

"Tired out?"

Brace took a breath. "Exhausted."

The blacksmith glanced toward the far end of his workshop.

"What if I could be of some help?"

When Brace finally returned to the Wolf and Dagger, Arden was standing outside, watching for him.

"Where have you been?" he demanded, stepping toward him. "What's all this?"

Brace turned to look again at what he had brought back with him—a fair-sized wooden cart, pulled by a large, old mule.

"Not bad, is it?" he asked proudly.

Arden came closer, walking slowly all the way around the cart, which was warped and weathered, but the wheels were thick and sturdy, and rimmed with iron bands.

"Where did you get this?" Arden asked in surprise.

"From a blacksmith's shop," Brace replied, patting the mule's shoulder.

"It isn't ..."

"Stolen?" Brace finished Arden's question. "No. It isn't. It's fully paid for, with the silver from my own pouch."

Arden ran his hand along the mule's back. "I apologize," he told him. "This is so ... unexpected. Saying thank you doesn't seem like enough."

"You don't need to thank me," Brace told him. "This will make traveling easier for all of us."

Arden nodded. "That it will. How much did you pay for this?"

Brace took hold of the mule's lead rope and gave it a firm tug, leading it toward the stables adjacent to the far side of the inn.

"All I had."

~ 15 ~

It was not long after Brace took the mule into the stables when he rounded the corner and found himself facing Ovard and the dark-haired little girl, who was carrying a small basket filled with carrots and apples. Brace looked down at her in surprise, then back up at Ovard.

"Arden tells us you've brought something back with you," the older man greeted him.

"He said you have a mule," the girl joined in. "I brought something for him to cat."

Brace couldn't help smiling at the girl. "He's in there," he told her, nodding toward the stables. The girl smiled and went inside, past the empty cart that had been left outside of the old wooden doors.

Brace's smile faded when Ovard crossed his arms over his chest. He couldn't read the expression on the man's bearded face, but he wondered for a moment if he was going to chastise him for making a decision without consulting him beforehand. He averted his eyes, the muscles in his jaw tightening in frustration.

"You are quite a mystery to me, Brace," Ovard spoke again at last. "I never would have expected this from you."

When Brace looked up, he couldn't help but see the glint of respect shining in Ovard's eyes.

"Well done."

Brace looked aside, uncomfortable with receiving such praise from Ovard.

"It just sort of fell into my lap, so to speak," Brace told him. "We've all had to walk so far, for so long. I figured we could use a little bit of a rest."

"I can't disagree with you there," Ovard replied, giving Brace a friendly slap on the shoulder. Brace could hear at that moment the girl with the long dark hair approaching, humming a cheery tune as she came back toward them. The empty basket bumped against the hem of her faded blue dress with each step.

"Your mule was hungry," she said when Brace turned in her direction. "He really liked the apples. I left the carrots, so he can eat them later."

"I'm sure he appreciates that," Brace told her.

She nodded, smiling, the flickering light from the lamp outside the Wolf and Dagger falling across her fair, slender face in the gray dusk.

"What did you say your name is?" Brace asked.

"Kendie," she replied.

"Are you cold at all, Kendie?"

Brace couldn't help but notice how thin the fabric of her dress was; so little against the evening chill.

"A bit," she replied, trying her hardest not to sound as though she was complaining.

A quick glance in Ovard's direction was all Brace had to give him, and the older man was of the same mind.

"Why don't you come back to our room for a time?" he suggested. "There's a fire lit, so it's getting quite warm by now."

Kendie hesitated.

"No need to worry," Brace told her. "We have some of our friends there, two of them ladies. Tassie and Leandra. You'll like them, I'm sure."

"Well," Kendie replied slowly. Brace could see that she truly did want to accept their invitation, but she was a bit reluctant at the same time. "I suppose I could—just for a moment or two."

"Of course," Brace replied. "We don't want to get you in any trouble. Does the inn by any chance have a few extra cushions? There are six of us, and only four cots. Could you bring us two more, if you can find them?"

Kendie smiled broadly. "Of course. I'll go and see what I can find."

When Brace reentered the drab room at the back of the inn, he was glad to find that a fire had indeed been lit, and the warmth was very welcoming, as was the smell of food; their plates had been served and brought back to the room, and though much of it had already been eaten, the spicy aroma of grilled pork still hung in the air.

Leandra stood beside Arden to the right of the fire, and she smiled at Brace when he stepped inside, with Ovard right behind him. Tassie sat on a drooping cot at the other side of the room, and she too gave Brace a nod and a smile of appreciation. Her eyes shone, tired though she was, as if to tell him, *See? I knew you could be more than a thief.* Jair peeked warily out from underneath his deep hood.

"You really bought a wagon?" he asked.

"I did," Brace replied. He was suddenly eager to kick off his boots and curl up near the fire to sleep, cot or no cot, it made no difference.

"And a mule to pull it," Ovard added.

"Please, please," Brace spoke up, shaking his head. "It's nothing any of you wouldn't have done, if you'd had the opportunity. Can we just let it go?"

A gentle knocking at the door drew everyone's attention.

"That must be Kendie," Ovard commented.

"Who is Kendie?" Leandra asked.

"A child," Ovard replied. "She lives and works here. We told her that she could warm herself by our fire for a bit, in exchange for her bringing us something more to sleep on."

Leandra glanced at Arden while Ovard pulled open the door. Kendie stood hesitantly, looking in, her arms quite full with a rolled sleeping mat.

"I could only find one," she said, her tone apologetic.

"Well, that's most assuredly better than none at all," Ovard told her, waving her inside.

She smiled appreciatively as she came into the room. Ovard gently closed the door behind her.

"Kendie," he began, "I'd like you to meet everyone. My name is Ovard. This," he said, gesturing, "is Brace."

"Good to meet you, sir."

"And standing by the fire are Arden and Leandra, his wife."

Kendie nodded. "Good to meet you," she repeated.

"And here," Ovard continued, "is Tassie, my niece, and the boy is Jair."

Brace heard a soft huffing sound coming from underneath Jair's cot, and looked to see a pair of round, black eyes shining in a furry red face.

"Ah, and Zorix," Ovard finished.

"Hello, everyone," Kendie greeted them, struggling to hold the long, bulky cushion.

"Why don't I take that?" Brace asked her, holding out his hands.

"Thank you," Kendie replied, pressing it into his arms. Brace found a convenient place for it along the front wall, and unfurled it onto the floor. Kendie stood near the door, uncertain of herself.

"Don't be afraid," he told her. "You can stand closer to the fire, if you want to."

"I do," she said quietly, stepping gingerly across the room.

Arden gave the girl a friendly nod, and moved away, sitting down carefully on one of the beds.

"Hello, Kendie," Leandra said as the girl came to stand near her.

"Hello."

As Brace lowered himself onto the mat, Ovard handed him a plate, heavy with grilled pork and a thick-crusted bread trencher full of potato soup.

"Thank you," he told him, starting in on it without hesitation.

"Are all of you from up north?" Kendie asked, holding her hands in front of the fire pit.

Leandra gave her a curious look. "We are," she told her. "How did you know that?"

"He told me," she said, looking toward Ovard. "He said you've all come a long, long way."

"We have at that," Leandra agreed.

"Where are you on your way to?"

"West," Ovard replied. "We're striking out toward the west."

"Did you cross the wild lands?"

"Yes, we did."

"That must have been exciting," Kendie replied. "I would like to go places and see different things someday."

Brace swallowed the mouthful of pork he'd been chewing. "It's not all it's made out to be," he told her. "You would probably get frightened."

"I would like to, just the same." The girl was undaunted. She ran her pale hands along her long, black hair, trying to smooth it. "I don't get frightened easily."

Leandra smiled at the girl. "I'm sure you don't."

"Well," Kendie spoke up again, "thank you for letting me stand near your fire. I should be getting back to work, I think."

"You are quite welcome," Ovard told her, opening the door for her like a gentleman suitor.

Kendie smiled at him as she stepped toward the door. She turned around, looking briefly around the room, at each of them. "I hope I'll see you all at breakfast tomorrow morning."

"Well, miss," Ovard told her, "we may be up and gone too early to stop in for breakfast. We may yet have a long road ahead of us."

"Oh," she breathed, sounding rather disappointed. "Well, I hope you have a good rest."

Several expressions of thanks followed Kendie as the stepped out into the main dining hall, leaving Ovard to close the door behind her.

"Poor thing," Leandra muttered.

Brace stared at the scuffed wooden floor, the plate on his lap momentarily forgotten.

"She's too thin," he heard Tassie remark.

Brace's gaze shifted back to the food that remained on his plate. He felt suddenly quite fortunate. He was warm and well fed, with a bed to sleep on, such as it was, and a cloak to cover himself against the rain and wind. More than that, he was surrounded by people he'd begun to consider friends. So many things that he'd wanted for so many years, and now he had them. Who knew what conditions little Kendie had to return to every night? Her dress was close to threadbare. Was she cold? Did she have a pillow for her head, a blanket to cover herself with? Was Rune Fletcher ever kind to her? Had she no one to comb her hair, to tell her stories?

Hungry though he was, Brace managed only a few spoonfuls of soup before setting the plate on the floor near his feet.

"I think I'm more tired than hungry," he muttered.

"I'm sure the girl is all right," Arden spoke up, from where he sat across the room.

Brace nodded halfheartedly, though he appreciated Arden's words.

"I'm sure she is."

Not much discussion had been necessary to determine who was to sleep where. Tassie and Jair had taken the cots along the left wall, while Leandra and Ovard were given the ones at the right. Brace was grateful to have the mattress along the wall near the door, while Arden folded two of the tents to form a mattress of his own, taking up much of the remaining floor space to the right of the fire pit. With full stomachs and warm bodies, it hadn't taken long for everyone to fall asleep, Brace included. He awoke once during the night, and in the low light of the remaining embers glowing from the hearth, he could see that Leandra had abandoned her cot and lay snugly at Arden's side, with a wide, heavy blanket spread across both of them. Zorix had gladly curled himself up on the small bed in her absence, and Ovard was snoring deeply.

The last thing that Brace remembered before falling back to sleep was the warm, comforting light of the fire fading before his eyes, and the feeling of peace that surrounded him.

"Let tomorrow wait," he whispered. "We may have a long way to go, but this ..." He sighed. "This is near to perfect." Brace rolled onto his side before letting his eyes drift closed. "I could stay here and be content."

~ 16 ~

Morning came on hard and cold, an unwelcome intruder. The fire in the stone hearth had long since turned to ashes. Gone were the warmth and the gold light that had bathed the walls of the sparse, shabby room. Gone was the aroma of grilled pork.

Brace thought, as he pulled on his cold leather boots, that he could smell bread baking. He did not consider it likely that he and his new friends would be eating any of it, though. He'd spent every silver he had on the cart and the mule, and he had no idea whatsoever how much Ovard and Arden still had between them. No, the meal they'd enjoyed the night before would have to hold them over for a while, he was sure.

When they left the Wolf and Dagger through the dining hall, Brace caught a glimpse of Kendie among the serving women, wearing the same blue dress she'd had on the day before. She was standing with her back to them, on the far side of the room, and did not see them leaving. *Just as well*, Brace thought. He'd grown fond of the small, disheveled girl. He did not want to see the disappointment on her face when she realized they'd gone, knowing how much she had seemed to enjoy their company.

Everyone was quite glad to have a place to store their packs in the back of the cart. No longer having to carry everything on their backs was a welcome relief. Tassie, reluctant to part with her medic bag, decided that she would rather continue wearing it, and no one could find any fault with that, knowing how precious its contents were.

Brace, along with Arden in particular, hoped to leave the inn without having to speak to Rune Fletcher, but the man seemed to have eyes everywhere. He spotted them just as they were going out the door, and had gone on in his gushing manner about how glad he was to have had them as his guests, and he hoped they had enjoyed their stay, and he would be glad to have them come again, should they pass through Meriton in the future, and most likely he would have better rooms for them to stay in.

Ovard had taken it all very patiently, then thanked him in return for his hospitality, though Brace could hear a slight edge of frustration in his voice.

"Are you leaving the city, then?" Rune asked them.

"I think we'll stop at the marketplace first," Ovard told him. "Now that we have a place to put things, we could use some dried meat and such to take with us on the way."

"Yes, of course," Rune replied. "But your things—I wouldn't trust them to be kept safe, unattended as they would be. Would you like me to have one of my servers keep an eye on your cart for you?"

Out of the corner of his eye, Brace caught sight of Arden and Leandra exchange worried glances.

"Yes," Ovard replied, surprisingly. "That would be very kind. If everything is here and accounted for when we return," he added, "I'll have a silver coin to give the one who guards it for us."

"Very well, very well," the innkeeper crooned.

Brace was all too glad to leave the inn and its owner behind, as he weaved his way through the busy streets toward the market. Jair was close behind him, keeping a tight grip on his hood, which he still wore pulled over his face. Brace was aware as well of Tassie, Arden, and Leandra close around him, while Ovard led the way, a few steps ahead of the rest.

The marketplace in Meriton was crowded and busy, as the whole city seemed to be. Unable to help with the purchases, Brace could only watch as Ovard paid for more dried, smoked meat, root vegetables, a small sack of black beans and another of barley, and even some fresh fruit—pears and raspberries. There was still some of the flour and sugar left in the back of the newly acquired cart, as well as the jar of honey which Tassie kept in her leather bag. They would be eating fairly well, at least for the next few days.

It was a surprise to find, when they had returned to the Wolf and Dagger, that their mule and cart had apparently been left unattended. Brace watched as Arden's face clouded over with worry, then anger.

"What is this?" he snarled. "I'd have taken that Rune Fletcher for a lot of things, but not an outright *liar*."

Ovard quickly looked over their belongings, which were quite exposed to the throngs of people passing by. The tents, which Arden had used as a mattress the night before, were piled up along the side, and their packs, blankets, and bags of sugar and flour were there, along with the wrapped bundle hiding Arden's bow and arrows.

"It's all here," Ovard announced in surprise. "Nothing was taken."

"That man had better consider himself fortunate," Leandra remarked. "If anything had gone missing ..."

Ovard laid a hand on her arm. "But it hasn't, and *we* are the fortunate ones. I suggest we leave Meriton. I don't know about the rest of you, but I'd just as soon not hear any more words from Rune Fletcher's mouth. And with no one here to watch the cart, it'll save me the silver."

The mule lived up to the reputation given to its kind, stubbornly refusing at first to budge from his place in front of the inn. Ovard pulled and Arden pushed, getting nowhere, until Zorix stepped in and quickly nipped at the animal's leg.

Once they got moving, they had very little trouble. At Ovard's direction, Tassie, Leandra and Jair rode in the back of the cart with their belongings, while he, Arden and Brace walked alongside. Zorix had taken it upon himself to scurry along behind the mule, to be sure the stubborn beast didn't get it into his head that he could stop in the middle of any of the crowded streets.

It was a long, confusing road they took out of the city, with many dead-end alleyways, forcing them to turn to the right or left more times than Brace cared to count. Finally, after several hours of noisy travel, the high stone walls at the far end of the city could be seen rising ahead of them, just beyond the guard tower. A single armored guard stood watch, his eyes fixed on the stony road beneath them, the long blue feathers on his silver helmet blowing in the gusting side wind.

Many other guards lined the walls inside and outside the southern gates of Meriton, and Brace kept his gaze on the ground at his feet as he passed by them. They were almost in the clear—he did not want to risk anyone recognizing his face, not now. The mule prodded on, its head hanging low. Despite the difficulty they had getting the animal moving, it seemed that once it got started, it did not have the slightest notion of stopping. It was not until the gray city walls were far behind them that Brace heard Arden breathe a sigh of relief. He ran his hand through his hair, then looked a bit surprised until he remembered that it had been cut short.

"I'm glad that's all over," Tassie remarked, from the back of the cart.

"So am I," Jair agreed. "Can I take my hood off now?"

Ovard grinned. "Yes, son. Of course you can."

Gratefully, Jair pulled back the hood of the heavy wool cloak, wiping a bit of sweat from his forehead with the back of his arm.

"Thank you! I thought we'd never get out of there!"

"Well, we're not going to stop just yet," Ovard told him as they continued on. The Royal Road was nowhere in sight; it snaked its way along the edge of the wild lands from the east, across the far side of Wayside Lake, and continued as far west as Erast. None of that wide, flat stretch of land could be seen from where they had traveled; all around them was open land, dotted here and there with trees and brush, though it was nothing like what they had grown familiar with seeing in the wild lands. It was not particularly grassy—tufts sprouted up randomly through the soft soil. To the right, in the distance, Brace saw a low grove of trees that he was certain must be an orchard. Ahead of them, to the south, the tall rocky face of the narrow mountain loomed high in the sky, visible in patches whenever the clouds broke, allowing the sunlight to pierce through. After some time, Arden stepped up and took hold of the mule's lead rope.

"Why don't you ride awhile, Ovard? You do look like you could use a bit of a rest."

Ovard sighed and nodded. "I could, truthfully. Thank you."

Arden pulled the mule to a stop, and the animal bent its head closer to the ground and began munching at the grass. Ovard climbed into the back of the cart, with a bit of help from Leandra. Brace nearly stepped on Zorix as the creature wound his way under the cart and out the other side, sniffing at the air.

"Settled?" Arden asked, after Ovard found a seat. "Shall we go on?"

Ovard started to reply, but Leandra stopped him, holding up a hand in a gesture that meant *wait*.

"What is it?" Brace asked, feeling a bit alarmed.

Leandra held a finger to her lips. "It's Zorix. We have company," she whispered.

"Where?" Ovard asked in a low voice.

Silently, Leandra pointed to the opposite side of the cart, where the tents had been piled. She put her hand on the hilt of her blade, ready to pull her knife from her belt. Tassie grabbed Jair and pulled him back into the corner. Slowly, Ovard crept forward. When Leandra gave him a nod, he grabbed a fistful of the heavy fabric and quickly pulled it back toward him. A sudden squeal of surprise revealed who had been hiding in the cart—a young girl with long, unruly dark hair.

"Kendie!" Ovard exclaimed. "What on this earth are you doing here?"

"I'm sorry, I'm sorry!" she replied in a hurry, as she sat up. "I just wanted to get away, and I saw the cart, and the mule, and the things in the back, and it was an easy place to hide, and ..." She looked around, at each of them. "You're not going to make me go back, are you?"

Ovard sighed and sat down. "You know that Rune is going to be looking for you," he told her. "What if he thinks we've taken you? That won't be good news for us, now, will it?"

"No, I suppose not." Kendie's voice was very small.

Arden stood closely at the side of the cart, where he had been watching the whole ordeal. "Did Rune Fletcher ask you to watch our cart while we were at the market?" he asked.

Kendie nodded. "Yes. And I *did* watch it! For a while. And then I hid. Please don't send me back. I don't want to go back."

"You made it seem as though you liked it there at the inn," Arden spoke up.

"Sometimes it wasn't so bad. But I'm not going back! You don't have to keep me with you if you don't want to. I'll just run on. I'll find the Road and go to Larkswell, or maybe Fool's March. I can make it alone."

"We're not going to let you go off by yourself," Leandra told her. "It's far too dangerous out there."

"I won't go back," the girl asserted, still half-covered with the pile of folded tents.

"Rune Fletcher," Brace finally spoke up, his arms resting on the side of the cart near where Kendie's feet would be. "Does he hit you?"

The question hung heavy in the air. Everyone seemed to be holding their breath, waiting for the answer. Kendie looked at Brace timidly for a moment, then down at her hands. "Sometimes."

The muscles in Brace's jaw tightened as he turned abruptly toward Ovard. "Don't send her back."

Ovard sighed, rubbing at his beard. "I know, it's a bad situation, but we can't just *take* her. She isn't a puppy, she's a girl. She doesn't belong to us."

"If you send her back," Brace replied, "I don't care what promise

I made to you before, I'll leave as well. Danferron isn't far from here. I'll just do what I had planned before I ever met any of you."

Brace saw Tassie shake her head, out of the corner of his eye. Leandra's expression was troubled, and Jair appeared fearful that Brace would actually leave them. Arden only stared at him, his blue eyes sharp, full of something surprisingly very like respect.

"She's sure to have been missed by now," Ovard mused.

There was silence again, for a long moment. Only the sounds of wind in the trees and the buzzing of insects reached Brace's ears.

"Well then," Arden spoke up at last. "Don't you think we should be getting on again? And quickly. The farther we get from Meriton, the less likely anyone will be able to find her."

Leandra tried unsuccessfully to hide a smile.

"Do you mean I can come with you?" Kendie asked, her voice full of hope.

Ovard could be a firm sort, Brace knew, but he was by no means heartless. It came as no great surprise, then, when he relented.

"You may come with us," he told the girl. "But I warn you now, we are not taking a holiday. Our travels have not been easy, and I don't expect that they will be any time soon."

"Oh, I'm very strong!" Kendie replied. "I'll be all right. And I don't eat very much."

"True, that," Arden spoke up. "You look as though you should eat a bit more than you're used to."

Kendie gazed dejectedly at the wooden floor of the cart. "I am skinny," she admitted.

"Well, this will help fix that, at least a bit." Tassie pulled a pear from one of the baskets, and offered it to Kendie, along with a small pouch of dried meat. Kendie gazed at the food reluctantly.

"Aren't you hungry?" Tassie asked her.

"I am."

Tassie smiled. "Here, then."

Kendie returned the smile as she accepted the gifts from Tassie's hands. She quickly bit into the pear, the juice of it running down her chin. Ovard chuckled at the sight, and Brace felt his frustration ease considerably.

"Well, I don't know about you all," Arden commented, "But I think we'd best be getting on. This mule is not a racing stallion, that's for certain, and we're not yet half a day from Meriton. Let's put that place some farther distance behind us, shall we?"

~17~

By the time the afternoon began to fade into evening, Kendie had already begun to work her way into Brace's heart, and everyone else's heart as well. She was a talkative child, to say the least, gladly answering every question asked of her.

"What age are you, Kendie?" Leandra questioned.

"Ten years."

"What happened to your parents?"

"They're gone."

"Dead?"

"I don't really know. They left close to three years ago."

"*Left*? They left you?"

"Yes. We had nothing. No food, no money, no home. We came to Meriton from the farmlands. My father—he snuck us into the stables at the Wolf and Dagger late at night. I fell asleep in a corner, I remember, on a pile of musty old straw. When I woke up in the morning, they were both gone."

"Just like that?"

"Yes," Kendie replied. "I thought at first that maybe they had just gone out. But they never came back."

"Kendie, I'm so sorry."

Leandra in particular had warmed up to the girl very quickly, and remained close beside her during the hours since they found her hiding beneath the tents.

"I did miss them," Kendie told her. "For a long time, I did. Sometimes I still do, but it's been so long."

Zorix was a bit leery of the girl at first. But she won him over in a heartbeat when she offered him a palm-sized piece of dried meat, and after he swallowed the last of it, she began scratching him behind his large, furry ears. Kendie reacted in surprise when, before her very eyes, Zorix turned a deep shade of purple, purring softly.

"I think Zorix has made a new friend," Tassie commented.

"What is he?" Kendie asked with a smile.

"A lorren," Leandra told her. "He changes color when his mood changes. Right now he's very happy."

"Where did you find him?"

"In the woods near Lidden. He was very ill. I looked after him, and Tassie helped me. I stayed by his side night and day until he was well, and by then we had bonded to one another."

"What does that mean?"

"He tells me his thoughts and feelings," Leandra replied. "He can hear mine as well. Zorix is the one who told me where you were hiding. He has a very keen sense of smell."

Kendie smiled sheepishly. "I *am* sorry for hiding myself in your cart. It's just that you were all so nice to me, and I thought ..." She shrugged. "I thought this might be my best chance to get away. I hope you're not angry with me."

"No, child," Ovard told her.

"We understand," Arden joined in. "We were eager to get away from Rune Fletcher ourselves."

Kendie smiled again. "Where are you all going?" she asked.

"It's a long story," Jair spoke up.

Brace noticed the way Kendie looked at Jair then, just long enough to get a good look at his markings without being rude.

"That's okay," she replied at last. "I like long stories."

"We're trying to find a place called Haven," Brace joined the conversation as he walked alongside the slowly moving cart.

"Haven," Kendie repeated thoughtfully.

"Ever heard of it?"

"No, I haven't. It sounds nice. What is it?"

"A safe place," Ovard told her. "An ancient city, long forgotten."

"Is it a long way off?"

"We're not quite certain," Ovard admitted. "We have come a long way, so we're much closer now than we were when we started."

"How do you know how to find it?"

A moment of silence passed before Jair answered.

"From me," he told her. "The marks on my face are kind of a map."

"Wow."

"Doesn't seem real, does it?" Brace asked, drawing the girl's attention. "That's what I thought when I first got myself involved in all of this."

"But it *is* real?"

"It *must* be real," Ovard replied. "We've all given up so much to try to find it."

"What is it like?"

"A city of light," Ovard told her. "Light, and safety, and unexplained miraculous power."

"Really?"

"Yes," Leandra agreed. "And it's very important that we find it before any bad sorts of people do."

Kendie nodded, seeming to understand completely. "I ... I think I heard some men talking about it once."

Arden stopped in his tracks, pulling back on the mule's lead rope to halt it. "Did you?"

"Yes. They said something about a key. A key to the 'city of ancestors.' I think that's what they said. They were talking about prophecies, and light and dark—things like that."

"What did these men look like?" Ovard asked, leaning forward in interest.

"Well, they weren't cottagers," Kendie replied. "They had on sort of rich-looking clothes. People talk around me all the time, and don't pay me any mind. I find out people's secrets all the time." Kendie suddenly turned quiet. "You don't think Rune will send anyone after me?" she asked softly. "You don't think they'll find me, do you?"

Brace thought a moment. *What had he told the man?* They were going west. Or was that the blacksmith he had been talking to?

"I don't think Rune Fletcher has the slightest idea where to look for you," he told the girl. "I don't think you'll have any trouble with him."

Kendie smiled appreciatively, though she still wore a nervous expression.

"A key," Ovard muttered to himself. "A key into Haven. Jair, my boy, I don't suppose you have ever thought of yourself as a *key* before?"

Jair smiled a little. "No, I haven't."

"Well," Ovard addressed Kendie once more. "It looks like we've got the key right here in our cart. Jair is not only a friend to all of us here, he is a living, breathing map, and a key, leading us to a better future than any of us have ever dreamed possible, I dare say. We've all got to do our part to make sure he is kept safe. We don't want any men such as the ones you overheard talking at the inn to take him away from us. Will you promise to do your part, child?"

Kendie nodded solemnly. "I will, I promise!"

"Good, then," Ovard replied. "Let's travel on just a bit more today. It will be getting dark very soon, and we won't be able to get anywhere then. We'll stop and find a place to camp. Are you all right, Arden, Brace? Would you like me to give you a rest, and I'll walk?"

Ovard's question was met with protest, insisting he remain in the cart for the remainder of the day.

"We're fine here," Arden told him, tugging fruitlessly at the mule's lead rope. "If we can just get this blasted animal moving!"

Arden eventually succeeded in getting the mule moving forward, and they traveled on until the air grew chill and pale with twilight. They set up camp had with ease, as it had become a familiar process. Each of them had taken on a customary task, from getting the tents up to gathering wood for a fire, and preparing something to eat. This evening, they enjoyed the berries, some of the dried pork, and a few of the roots, cooked over the open flames.

Brace eyed the sky apprehensively while Tassie sat fixing Kendie's hair into two long braids. Ovard had pulled out his small flute and was playing a restful tune. Arden had removed his leather gloves, and he and Leandra sat close, their fingers intertwined.

There are no stars tonight, Brace noted. He gave up his vigil and allowed himself to enjoy Ovard's music for a bit. The notes rose and fell softly, reminding Brace of the way the wind ran down a mountain, or water over rocks. Jair sat beside Brace, once again carving at the end of a narrow stick. Brace suspected it was one way for the boy to release some of his tensions, his worries about what might lie ahead.

It was not long after the last note from Ovard's flute faded into the silence of the night that everyone began retiring to their tents to get some sleep. Tassie offered to let Kendie share her own tent, and Kendie, of course, graciously accepted. By now, Ovard had told the girl of Tassie's inability to hear, and she was fascinated by the fact that Tassie could speak, as well as *see* what the others were saying.

Brace remained seated near the fire while everyone else went off to sleep, and Jair stayed by his side. When they were alone at last, Brace could see that Jair had something on his mind.

"Anything you want to talk about?" he asked.

Jair shrugged, feigning deep interest in the quality of the point he'd carved on the end of the stick. "Well, I was just thinking ..."

"I can see that," Brace prodded gently. "What of?"

"What you said earlier today," Jair replied. "About leaving. If Ovard had made Kendie go back to Meriton, would you really have left?"

Brace considered the question in silence. "I'm not really certain," he told him at last. "I think, deep inside, I knew Ovard wouldn't make the girl go back to Rune Fletcher. I think he just needed a little nudge to help him make up his mind."

"But why did you threaten to leave?"

"Jair," Brace began, "you've grown up well cared for and protected. You don't have any idea of what it's like to live every day with the fear of being beaten, or the ache of knowing that you're not loved. *I do.* I couldn't just stand by and let Kendie get sent back to that kind of situation. No one deserves that."

Jair nodded, gazing at what was left of the fire. "I didn't know," he said quietly.

"Well, it isn't something I make a habit of talking about," Brace replied. "It was a long time ago."

"But you really won't leave, will you? Not now. We've come so far."

Brace studied Jair's expression. "Does it mean that much to you? Do *I* mean that much? I'm no one important, Jair. It really doesn't matter in all of this if I stay or if I go."

"It does matter to me. And to everyone else. I know they don't really say it, but none of us wants you to leave." Jair dropped the pointed stick and stood. "You promised you'd stay. You did!"

Brace reached up and grabbed Jair's sleeve, pulling him to his seat. "Hush, you'll wake the others." Brace shook his head. "I'm not leaving. I did promise. But I'm not used to keeping promises, you know. I'm new at all of this."

"All of what?" Jair asked him.

"Loyalty," Brace replied. "Friendship."

"You've never had friends before?"

Brace shook his head. "Not really. Not like this. I never would have thought ..." His voice trailed off, and he left his thought unfinished.

Jair nodded, though, understanding. "I'm glad you're my friend," he told him. "Please don't leave."

Brace had to smile. "I won't leave, Jair. I promise you, I won't leave."

~18~

"That mountain doesn't seem to be getting any closer, does it?" Arden stood eyeing the horizon as though by willing it, he could bring them nearer to their destination.

"Not just yet," Ovard replied, standing beside him.

Brace watched them from where he sat atop a smooth, flat rock. It was a fine day; the rain had stopped after last night's wetting, and sunlight glittered on each leaf and blade of grass. Small birds darted from tree to tree, chattering and cooing. Brace could hear laughter as Jair and Kendie stood knee-deep in the small lake they'd come upon, not yet an hour ago. He looked back to see Zorix watching the children from a safe distance, while Leandra stood at the lake's edge and pointed at the surface of the water. Tassie sat alone, on the ground near the back of the cart. The grass was still damp, so she had spread out her cloak and rested on top of it, her eyes closed and her face lifted to the sunlight.

A loud splashing caught Brace's attention, and Ovard's and Arden's as well. He looked to see Jair, just as he was standing, immersed in the clear blue water of the lake all the way up to his chest. Water was flinging everywhere, and Kendie giggled and squealed as she held her hands up to block it. It was a fish—a good-sized one at that—which Jair held, thrashing, in his hands.

"I did it!" Jair called out, his voice carrying easily in the still, quiet air. "Leandra taught me how to catch a fish with my bare hands!"

191

"Well done!" Ovard called back, cupping his hands around his mouth. "That will be our supper tonight!"

Jair laughed as he emerged from the water, dripping, followed by Kendie in her faded blue dress, wet from the knees down.

"That girl has been good company for Jair," Ovard quietly remarked. "He's been far too troubled for such a long while. Her light heart is good medicine, I think."

Brace nodded in agreement. *For all of us*, he thought.

Arden, though, appeared to be in a cloudy mood, even on such a bright day. It did not come as much of a surprise to Brace, however, as such moods were common to the tall, blue-eyed archer. Ovard startled the man a bit when he reached up to give his shoulder a friendly squeeze.

"Don't worry, my friend," he told him. "We'll get to that mountain soon enough."

Arden nodded in response. "Of course."

"Take the time to enjoy yourself a bit," Ovard encouraged him. "Goodness knows when we'll have another day like today."

Arden forced a bit of a smile before Ovard left him to sit beside Tassie on the grass.

"What's wrong?" Brace asked him.

"*Ewwww!*" He heard Kendie from a distance, commenting on the quick work Leandra was making of cleaning Jair's fish.

Arden shook his head. "It's nothing," he muttered, though Brace did not believe him. "I just want this to be over. I want us to find the Haven—a safe place, where we won't need to fear, and we can put our travels behind us. I'll rest then," he added. "Not before. I may not look it, but I am still an archer. I'm still sworn to protect everyone."

"Honor and courage," Brace muttered under his breath.

"You sound as though it's a bad thing to live by."

"Bad?" Brace asked. "No. But I think sometimes a person's mindset about rules can get in the way when it comes to actually living."

"I don't know what you mean."

Brace sighed and scratched the back of his neck. His hair was starting to get longer, he noticed. Now, it almost touched his shoulders.

"Well," Brace replied thoughtfully, "take me, for example. For so long a time, my focus has been on keeping myself unknown, as much as possible. Unseen. The world has treated me harshly, so I've kept myself separate from it, as much as I could."

Arden nodded in understanding.

"But," Brace continued, "I'm starting to realize that I've been wrong about a lot of things, like shutting everyone out. Keeping my heart closed. I've started to open it up again," he admitted, looking Arden straight in the eye. "It doesn't always feel comfortable, or safe, even. But it feels right somehow."

Arden turned his gaze toward the grassy area at the edge of the small lake, where Jair and Kendie had begun to arrange fist-sized rocks around a pile of sticks and branches. Leandra stood nearby, holding in one hand the long end of a thin piece of rope she'd strung through the fish's mouth, and a small flint stone in the other.

"I know I'm not the best person to be giving advice," Brace continued, "but I guess what I'm trying to say is, don't let honor and courage get in the way of the time you have to spend with people who care about you." He shrugged. "Just be there."

Arden managed an uneven grin. "Your arrow's hit the center mark," he told Brace. "When did you become so wise?"

Brace smirked. "I think Ovard must be rubbing off on me a bit."

Arden shook his head. "Well, whatever the case, it *is* good advice. I'll do what I can to keep it in mind."

Brace watched as Arden slowly made his way across the grass. Leandra had gotten a small fire going, and Jair was attentively keeping watch over his catch, turning it on the spit that had been rigged up over the open flames.

Brace let his gaze fall on Tassie, but she was quietly conversing with Ovard. Turning to look back over his shoulder, he could see the tall, gray, rocky mountain jutting up through the clouds. Who knew how much farther they had to go? The mountain did not mark the end of their journey, only the place where they would turn westward. Brace wanted to follow his own advice, as well as Ovard's. It was true, there was no way of knowing when they would have another sunny, peaceful day. Brace, however, felt more comfortable sitting back and watching the others enjoy themselves—Tassie feeling the warm sunlight on her face, Jair and Kendie talking and laughing, and Arden, who now stood beside Leandra, tenderly stroking her hair. Someday, maybe, he would be able to join them. For now, he had to be who he was, which was not the same person he had been only a month ago. Exactly how all of this was going to end, he had no way of knowing. He had no well-laid plan to follow now. He could only take each day as it came, just like the rest of them.

"Wow, it's so sharp!" Kendie admired the metal tip of one of Arden's arrows, which he had retrieved from the tightly rolled blanket along with his bow. There was no longer any reason to keep them hidden, now that they were all well enough away from Meriton and the risk of prying eyes. Jair's fish had been a nice change for the afternoon meal, and Brace now lay on his back, gazing up at the overcast sky.

"It *is* sharp," Arden told the girl. "Be careful."

Arden had restrung his long wooden bow, and was testing its strength. Kendie, who seemed to be curious about everything, had noticed right away and came over to investigate. Holding the bow parallel to his body, Arden pulled back expertly on the string, then slowly eased up on it.

"Did you make your bow yourself?" Kendie asked him.

Arden smiled down at her. "No," he replied. "But I did make the arrows."

"How?"

Arden gently set down the bow and picked up an arrow. "The shaft is made of wood," he explained. "It's lightweight, but very strong. The feathers at the end give it stability in flight."

"And the tip?" Kendie asked. "Is it made of silver?"

Arden chuckled. "Silver? No, not silver. *Steel*. Silver is much too soft."

"Can I hold it for a moment?"

"Yes, but just for a moment," Arden replied. "And be careful." He gently laid the arrow across Kendie's open palms.

"It feels heavy," she commented.

"It's the steel tip," Arden told her, taking back the arrow and putting it away with the others.

"Maybe some day I'll learn how to shoot."

Arden looked back at her. "I'm sure you will."

"But not today," Leandra spoke up. "Today, little thing, I think you need something to keep warm in. That dress of yours is far too thin, just as you are."

Leandra held up a gray-blue wool blanket, draping it across Kendie's shoulders.

"I am going to make you a cloak," she told her.

"It's your blanket," Kendie said in surprise. "If you use your blanket, how will you stay warm at night?"

"I can use my cloak for a blanket," Leandra replied. Then she smiled. "Or I'll share Arden's."

"He is your husband, isn't he?" Kendie asked.

"Yes, he is. Now, I am by no means a seamstress," Leandra continued, "but I think I can make this work."

"Thank you."

"It's my pleasure."

Leandra turned away, holding the blanket where she had folded it to be just Kendie's height. Brace watched her go, then, with a sigh, went back to gazing at the clouds.

"Ummm." Brace heard a small voice, and turned his head to see Kendie standing nearby.

"What is it?"

"I'm sorry, I don't remember your name."

"Brace."

"Oh, yes, Brace. Well, I just wanted to say thank you for being so kind to me."

"It's all right," he told her. "I was just doing what I would have wanted someone to do for me."

She smiled. "Sometimes," she continued, "I thought I'd never be able to get away. If you all hadn't been so nice to me, I never would have thought about hiding in the back of your cart."

Brace pulled himself up to sit with his elbows propped up on his knees. "I'm glad you did."

"Really?"

"Yes. I ... Well, I had the feeling that Rune Fletcher was treating you badly. I'm glad you don't have to stay in that situation." His voice grew quieter. "I've been there too."

Kendie sat down on the grass beside him. "People treated you badly too?"

"They did," Brace replied. "And I did pretty much what you did. I ran away."

"And things turned out all right for you?"

"Well, I don't know about that," he admitted. "Things have been tough, but I have to tell you truthfully, most of that was my own doing."

"Really?"

Brace nodded. "This, believe it or not, this is just about as good as I've ever had it. I don't have one piece of silver to my name, but ..." He paused, pushing his hair back away from his face. "I don't know. The people here, they're the closest I've ever had to friends in my life."

Kendie looked over her shoulder, where Leandra sat working a thin strip of leather into the wool blanket, turning it into a makeshift cloak.

"I'd like them to be my friends too," she told him.

Brace nodded again. "I think they already are, Kendie."

~ 19 ~

The nights were cold, dark, and filled with the all-too-familiar sound of screeching wild animals. The noise had upset Kendie on the first night. Brace could see her trying to be brave as they all sat around the fire eating bean and barley soup. Ovard told the girl that they had often times heard the squalling creatures, but had never once laid eyes on them. She was relieved to hear it. Now Brace wondered, every night as he lay in the small tent beside Jair, trying to sleep through the shrill, distant cries, if the sound still unnerved Kendie as much as it did himself.

Three full days passed before they finally stood near the craggy base of the tall, narrow mountain. A chill wind gusted across the land, thrashing the branches of low-growing trees and scattering leaves along the ground.

"This is it, then," Ovard said as he looked up at the cloud-covered sky. "This is where we go west."

"We really *are* going the right way, aren't we?" Jair seemed suddenly filled with doubt. Leandra wrapped her arm around his shoulders, surprising him a little.

"Have faith," she encouraged him. "You are the one who showed us this mountain when we were unsure of where to go next. I believe you've led us to the right place."

"I hope so."

There was no way for any of them to be completely certain, of course, but no one had any desire or need to bring up that fact. All they could do was go on, with the wind at their backs, as they turned westward.

Brace's long, tattered cloak pressed against the back of his legs as he walked, as though urging him to move faster. Tassie sat huddled in the back of the cart with Jair, Kendie, and Arden, who had at last been convinced that he had earned a chance to rest his legs for a while. Ovard led the mule onward, keeping his eyes fixed as far into the distance as he could see. Brace knew, without having to look, that Arden would be scanning the area around them, with his bow at his side. He also noted, with a bit of jealousy, that Arden had, for whatever reason, refrained from shaving and was beginning to grow a beard, something Brace had never been able to do.

Once again, it was Kendie's singing that broke the silence. The girl was fond of music, and a day hadn't gone by since she'd joined them that she hadn't been singing some tune or another.

"I once had a sweetheart," she sang now, full and clear, over the whistling of the wind through the trees, "but now I have none. She's gone and she's left me, I care not for one. Since she's gone and left me, contented I'll be, for she loves another one better than me."

Brace was unfamiliar with the tune, but Ovard began humming along as Kendie sang.

I passed my love's window, both early and late.
The look that she gave me, it makes my heart ache;
Oh, the look that she gave me was painful to see,
for she loves another one better than me.

I wrote my love letters in rosy red lines,
She sent me an answer all twisted and twined;
Saying, "Keep your love letters and I will keep mine.
Just you write to your love and I'll write to mine."

Brace smiled to himself as Kendie finished up her song, repeating the opening lines.

I once had a sweetheart, but now I have none.
She's gone and she's left me, I care not for one.
Since she's gone and left me, contented I'll be,
for she loves another one better than me.

"That's kind of a sad song," Jair commented when she'd finished.

"It is, a little," Kendie admitted. "But I like the way it sounds. I think Jax likes it too."

"Jax?" Arden questioned. "Who is Jax?"

"The mule," Kendie replied, blushing. "I named him Jax."

"It's a good name," Ovard said, grinning.

"You know so many songs," Leandra told her with a smile. "How do you remember them all?"

"I hear them all the time," Kendie told her. "And I really listen, and I sing them over and over again to myself when I'm working, so I don't get lonely."

Kendie blinked, struck with the realization that she would never again need to wait tables at the Wolf and Dagger, or shy away from Rune Fletcher's heavy hand.

"Or, that's what I used to do," she added, smiling a little. "I'm not lonely now. I just wish that Tassie could hear my songs. It must be sad, not being able to hear *anything*."

"I've never been able to hear," Tassie told her. "I don't know any different. Please don't feel bad for me," she added, seeing the look on Kendie's face. "It's all right, really it is."

"Will you sing another one?" Jair asked. "A happy one?"

Kendie smiled. "Of course," she replied. "There was a jolly miller once ..."

"Stop!" Arden interrupted suddenly, grabbing Kendie's arm.

"What?" Kendie cried out, looking at though she had done something wrong.

"Do you hear that?" Arden asked. Everyone had fallen silent, and Brace could hear the unmistakable sound of a galloping horse.

"Someone is coming this way, and fast!"

"What should we do?" Jair asked, his eyes wide.

"Don't panic," Arden told him, jumping down from the cart with ease. "There is no main road here," he said as Ovard halted the mule and came closer. "I don't think we're being followed. Get down, though, everyone," he added, holding out his hands to help Kendie out of the cart. "Better to be prepared."

"Prepared for what?" Jair asked in alarm as Arden gave him a hand down.

"Having to run," he replied.

"There is only one horse," Brace spoke up. "You could take him if you had to."

"One, yes," Arden agreed, after everyone had hidden themselves behind the far side of the wooden cart. "But the rider may be followed from a ways back. Anyone who knows better would not be out alone if he could help it."

The mule flicked its long ears nervously as the rest of them waited in silence. The hoofbeats grew closer, louder, coming on just as quickly as when they'd first heard them. In a moment, Brace could see, some distance away, a single rider on a lean black steed hurrying through the trees. The man was armored, though not heavily, and was holding tightly to a long, thin lance bearing a narrow flag in the red and blue of Meriton's crest.

The rider did not look to either side as he hurried past, his dark-colored half cape flapping behind him, and Brace thought it likely that he did not even see the mule and cart. If he had, he paid it no mind.

"Where is he going?" Jair whispered as the sound of hoofbeats retreated into the distance.

"I think he's delivering a message," Kendie replied.

"Where to?" Leandra wondered aloud.

"I don't know," Kendie told her. "I don't know if there are any villas out here. I only know there are farmholds to the east of Meriton. I've never gone this way before."

"Well, one thing is certain," Ovard spoke up, "we're going to have to be more careful. He's not likely going very far. We're not alone out here." He turned toward Jair. "No one could have gotten a look at your face back in Meriton, could they have?"

"No," Jair told him. "I wore my hood up the whole time, even when I was asleep."

"Right," Ovard agreed with a nod. "That rider is headed west," he said, almost to himself. "We're not likely to catch up to him, but he may pass us on his way back to Meriton, today, tomorrow, or the day after."

"What should we do?" Leandra asked him, holding Zorix close at her side.

"Just be cautious," Ovard answered. "Kendie, I'm afraid you're going to have to put your songs to rest for a while, or at least make them quiet ones."

Kendie nodded. "Of course."

Arden stated firmly that they should hold their position a while longer, to be sure no other riders were coming through. Ovard turned toward Kendie and bent low to speak into her ear.

"You said he might have been delivering a message," he said in a quiet voice.

"That's right," Kendie replied. "He was carrying Meriton's banner. There are so many guards and soldiers in Meriton who are in service to King Oden. They carry messages all the time; I've seen them."

"What message could he be carrying?" Leandra wondered aloud.

"It could be that someone may have recognized me," Brace spoke up.

Arden turned toward him in surprise. "Would anyone be looking for you this far south?"

"I've been all over," Brace reminded him. "And word spreads quickly."

"Let's not jump to conclusions," Ovard admonished. "This could very well have nothing to do with any of us. We'll just have to be on our guard, that's all."

Finally, enough time passed to satisfy Arden that no other riders would be following the first one. Brace led the stubborn old mule while Arden and Leandra walked, one on each side of the cart. Hours passed, and they saw no one, heard no signs of any approaching horses. As the daylight began to fade into the gray of evening, Brace pulled the mule aside, partially concealing the cart behind a small bunch of low, full trees. The tents were set up with ease, and were soon flapping sharply in the strong, steady breeze.

Kendie had shown an interest in learning about Tassie's medical supplies, and the two of them sat closely side by side while Tassie explained the uses for the contents of one of her clay jars. While Ovard poured water into a large bowl for Jax to have a drink, Arden stood at the far side of camp, bow in hand, his eyes and ears alert.

Brace noticed that Jair seemed to be almost sulking, keeping his distance from the rest of the group. It was quite unlike him, even more so since Kendie had been in their company. Her cheerful nature, along with the fact that her presence meant that Jair was no longer the only youngster, had raised the boy's spirits considerably. He seemed melancholy at the moment, however, as he wandered back into camp carrying a shingle-sized piece of tree bark. He stopped when he stood in front of Brace, where he sat leaning his back against the base of a tree.

"Can I ask you something?" he said in a serious voice.

"Sure you can."

Jair held out the flat piece of tree bark. "Are you very good with a knife? I mean, how are you at carving designs?" Brace sat forward and looked up into Jair's eyes.

"What sort of design?" he asked.

"This one," Jair replied, tapping his cheek with his forefinger.

"Why?" Brace asked. "What are you getting at?"

With a sigh, Jair sat cross-legged on the ground in front of Brace, resting the slab of bark in his lap. He shrugged. "Something might happen to me," he began. "That rider ... the messenger. You all should have a copy of the markings on my face in case I get taken away, so you can still find Haven, even if I'm not here."

Brace leaned forward and firmly took hold of Jair's wrist. "You know we're not going to let anyone take you away," he told him sharply. "You *know* that, Jair."

"I know you wouldn't *let* them," Jair replied. "But I don't want anyone to get hurt trying to protect me. Hurt or worse. Maybe it *would* be better for everyone, if people do try to take me away, to just let them. I can't stand thinking about anyone getting killed because of me."

Brace shook his head. "Don't think about that."

"But this *is* a good idea," Jair continued, holding up the piece of tree bark. "Having a copy is still a good idea, don't you think?"

Brace sighed deeply, releasing his grip on Jair's arm. He leaned back against the base of the gnarled old tree as a gust of wind rustled the boy's hair.

"Well, it's not a bad idea," Brace had to admit. "But I don't think I'm the best person to ask. I'm sure Leandra would be more skilled at this sort of thing."

"I thought that," Jair replied in a quiet voice. "But I knew that what I wanted to say would upset people. They've all known me longer than you have, so ..."

"So I wouldn't be as hurt by it," Brace finished.

Jair nodded. "Will you, then?"

"I will do my best," he told him, pulling his dagger from his boot. "Someone is bound to notice what we're doing," Brace commented as Jair handed him the wide strip of bark, smooth side up. "They are going to know."

Jair glanced back over his shoulder. "Well, I guess it can't be helped. I still think it needs to be done."

Brace nodded and pressed his blade into the flat wooden surface. The lines of the compass-of-sorts were easy enough to cut, but the crescent moon shape was filled with all sorts of curved lines and shapes, like some sort of ancient writing. Brace doubted his ability to accurately carve the figures into the wood.

"My blade is going to need sharpening after this," he commented, with a hint of humor in his voice.

"Sorry," Jair replied.

"Just keep your head still," Brace told him. "This isn't easy." Jair silently obeyed.

"These markings," Brace said softly as he tried his hardest to carve the first of them into the wood, "I have never seen anything like them anywhere else. Have you?"

"No," Jair answered. "I haven't, not even in any of Ovard's books."

"What do you think they could be? Some kind of language?"

"Maybe. I don't really know."

"And you have no memory of being marked?"

Jair started to shake his head, then stopped himself. "No," he replied. "None at all. It must mean something, though. It must be important, just like the lines. I hope we've been following them the right way."

"So do I," Brace agreed.

"What is this you two are doing?" Ovard's voice startled Brace, and he looked up. Jair kept his eyes on the ground. One glance at the carving that Brace had made in the tree bark gave Ovard his answer.

"Making a copy, I see?"

"It was my idea," Jair spoke up. "I thought it would be good to have one ... in case ..."

Ovard shook his head. "Don't fret, son. I'm not angry with you."

"No?"

"No," he replied. "But you don't need to trouble yourself, Brace. Not with that piece of wood." Ovard knelt down and rested a hand on Jair's shoulder. "After all these years," he said gently, "don't you think I would have made a copy myself?"

Jair's eyes widened a little. "You've never shown me," he told him. "Why?"

"It did not seem important until recently," Ovard replied. "And when you were younger ..." He shook his head. "You would not have understood. I'm sorry I never told you."

After a moment, Jair nodded. "I understand. Do you have it with you?"

"I do," Ovard told him. "In with what I have left of my library." He smiled ruefully as Brace tossed aside the piece of bark and brushed his hands off on his breeches.

"I thought you might be upset about it," Jair muttered.

"Why is that?"

"Because I thought we would need a copy of it ... if ... something happened to me."

Ovard gave Jair's shoulder a squeeze. "Nothing is going to happen to you."

"You can't know that for sure," Jair challenged. "You can't."

Ovard sighed. "No, I can't. But we can all do our part to keep you safe. To keep each other safe. We have all made it this far. I know we've had our share of troubles, but we've each gotten stronger for having been through them." Ovard smiled as he pulled himself to his feet. "You're hardly a boy any longer, do you know that? You'll be a man soon enough."

Jair tipped his head and gave a little shrug. "I don't feel like a man. I'm not as smart as you are, not as brave as Arden, not as cunning as Brace."

"Cunning," Brace said with a laugh. "You think I'm cunning?"

"You are," Jair said firmly.

"I would have said sneaky," Brace told him.

"Don't you try to be me," Ovard spoke up. "Don't try to be Arden, or Brace. You'll be your own man someday. Be such a one as you're not ashamed to face in a mirror, and you'll do well enough."

Jair nodded. "You won't tell anyone, will you?"

"Tell them what?" Ovard asked.

"That I'm afraid."

"No shame in being afraid," Ovard replied. "But no, I won't tell them. There is no need for that. We are all afraid, Jair. We're all equal in that respect."

It was true, they were all afraid, and their fears increased tenfold that night. Brace began to feel unsettled when he noticed the inky black clouds swirling in over them just after dusk. Arden saw it as well, and he stood watching the sky anxiously.

"What is that?" Leandra asked, standing beside her husband.

"I haven't the slightest idea," Arden told her, slowly shaking his head.

"I've seen it before," Brace spoke up from where he was seated near the camp fire.

Arden looked back at him. "When?" he asked. "Where?"

"The night we all shared a drink from Ovard's mug," he replied. "I went off a bit on my own, away from the fire, and I could see it pouring in, blocking out the stars."

"You never said anything," Leandra scolded.

"What good would it have done?" Brace argued.

Leandra pressed her lips together and went back to watching the sky.

"I'm scared," Kendie said in a small voice, and Jair moved to sit close beside her.

"It's all right," he told her, trying to sound more brave than he felt. Zorix sniffed at the air and uttered a low, snarling moan. Brace felt the hairs on the back of his neck rising at the sound.

"Now, let's not all get stirred up," Ovard urged. "This is the sort of thing we should all have come to expect. Until we find Haven, the darkness will be increasing quickly. Let's all keep our heads."

Brace was sure he had heard Ovard say those same words before, or something very like them. As the entire stretch of sky above them was swallowed up in blackness, Brace kept his seat, and fully intended to keep his head as well. It wasn't long before the nighttime screeching began once again, very close this time, judging from the sheer volume of it. He rose quickly to his feet then, looking around quickly in every direction. He did not enjoy the idea of his back being exposed to ... *whatever* they were. Arden drew his bow and readied an arrow to the string, while Leandra pulled her heavy blade from her belt. Kendie pressed her hands over her ears and huddled against Jair's side.

"What are they?" she cried out in alarm. "I wish they'd go away!"

"What is it?" Tassie asked Ovard, who seemed at a loss for what he should do to help the situation. "What is it?" she repeated, getting no answer.

"Noisy creatures," Ovard finally told her. "The ones we've been hearing nearly every night, but they're much closer now."

Tassie's eyes widened as she stared into the surrounding darkness. "Do you see them?"

"No," Ovard replied.

"What should we do?"

"Stir up the fire," Brace suggested. "Most wild things won't come near a fire." His eyes scanned the ground until he found a larger branch that had not yet been added to the flames. He snatched it up and jabbed at the fire, sending up a flurry of orange sparks. "Add more wood!" he shouted.

Jair leapt up from his seat and quickly loaded his arms with unused twigs and branches, quickly spreading them evenly around the blaze. The snapping of burning wood added itself to the chorus of shrill cries echoing all around them. Jax's eyes had gone wide, and he shifted uneasily, tugging at his rope.

Tassie moved to Kendie's side and wrapped her arms around her, but Brace could see the fear in the young woman's eyes. A thick, heavy fog swirled in around them. Arden and Leandra stood ready to defend the camp, should anything come at them out of the blackness. Zorix snarled as looked out, his long blue tail puffed up and thrashing.

"Zorix, no!" Leandra warned. "You stay here! I don't want you chasing after those creatures. They are not wild dogs. I don't know *what* they are."

The spine-chilling noises seemed to go on forever, late into the night, but none of them saw anything but thick blackness all around them, beyond the light of the fire. They hardly dared, for the longest time, to move away from the comfort and safety of the blazing fire, but after hours passed and their eyes grew heavy, they began to disperse. It was hard to convince Kendie to leave the fire.

"But Tassie can't hear them!" she whimpered. "What if they come, and ..."

"I'll not be turning in tonight," Arden told her, standing near the flames with his bow. "I'm keeping watch."

"All night?"

"Yes. All night."

"I'll be up as well," Leandra added. She glanced to the side, where Zorix sat plaintively at her feet. "Would you feel safer if Zorix was in the tent with you?" she asked.

"Um ... yes," Kendie replied meekly.

"Tassie?" Leandra asked. "Would that be all right with you, having Zorix in your tent?"

Tassie managed a nervous smile. "Yes, that would be quite all right with me."

Leandra looked down at Zorix, silently, though Brace knew she was speaking to him. Zorix's large ears twitched in response, and he scurried over to where Kendie sat beside Tassie. He looked up at the girl for a moment, before turning and leading the way toward Tassie's empty tent.

"Thank you," Kendie managed as Tassie walked with her, following what little they could see of Zorix at the edge of the firelight.

"I think I've had enough for today," Brace muttered as he rose to leave the fire as well.

"I'll come with you," Jair spoke up quickly.

High-pitched screeching continued to echo through the trees. Tired though he was, Brace found sleep difficult. He removed his tattered cloak before lying down and covering himself with a blanket. He grabbed it now, wadded it in a ball, and pressed it down over his head in a half-hearted attempt to cover his ears.

"Will those blasted creatures ever *stop*?" he complained, making use of Arden's preferred oath.

"Please, please," Jair begged, hiding under his own wool blanket. "You're only making it worse."

Brace groaned. "I'm sorry. I just can't stand that noise!"

"Neither can I."

"I'm exhausted," Brace muttered. "Even so, I don't think I can sleep."

"You'll be able to," Jair said quietly. "You have before."

Brace sighed. "I know, you're right. It's just that ... it's been a trying day."

Jair was silent, but Brace could see just enough to know that he had nodded in agreement. "I know," he whispered. "But ..."

"But what?"

"Well, I'm glad you're here. I'm glad you didn't leave."

Brace pushed his rolled-up cloak away from his head. He was still very aware that he could be, at this very moment, living in Danferron—but as what? A stable hand? A miner, a gravedigger, a *thief*? And what was he here, now?

"Cunning," Jair had said. And Kendie—he saw the way she looked at him from time to time, as though he had saved her from some terrible fate, worse than death. He was no hero though, not in the slightest. *What am I?* Brace asked himself.

A friend, an inner voice seemed to tell him. *You're a friend, Brace. Isn't that something you have wanted for so many years? Would you give it up now?*

No. No, he wouldn't.

"I'm glad too," he told Jair. "I'm glad I stayed."

~ 20 ~

Brace stood alone in the darkness, his back pressed against the wide trunk of a tree, his dagger in his hand. All around him, those strange creatures yowled and screamed, but he saw no sign of them. But—there! A pair of eyes, glowing white, reflecting the light from the small fire. He hardly had any time to think before the creature leapt at him, baring its long, white fangs.

Brace's eyes flew open, his heart racing. He was lying on his back, a wool blanket covering his legs. The roof of the tent filled his vision, a pale brown in the morning sunlight. Jair sat beside him, rubbing the sleep from his eyes.

"What?" Brace asked, confused.

"I think you were dreaming," Jair told him. "You move around a lot when you're dreaming."

Brace took a breath. "Do I?"

Jair nodded. "Was it a bad one?"

He had to think for a moment to recall; the dream had begun to slip away. "Yes," he replied. "Those noisy beasts. I can't get away from them, even when I'm asleep."

"Well, it's morning. They're gone now."

"Thankfully," Brace replied, sitting up and pushing the blanket away. He was slowly becoming more fully alert, his mind waking up to reality. He breathed out a heavy sigh. "I'm sorry about last night," he told Jair. "I should have held my tongue."

"What about?"

"Oh, just complaining about those wild animals, all the noise. I could have handled it better."

Jair shook his head, standing. "It's all right. I understand. Everyone is up, I think. I'm going to see how Kendie is doing." He pulled loose the leather ties holding down the entrance flap and stepped out, leaving Brace alone in the tent.

"No, I'm not so great, am I?" Brace muttered, looking over his dirty hands, his chipped and broken fingernails. He had upset the boy, he knew. Jair had been curt with him; Brace heard the edge in his voice. Well, who could blame him? Brace was the adult here, after all. He was supposed to be the brave one, the strong one, the one who would keep his head and say that things would be all right.

"Well," Brace said to himself, "if he wants someone to look up to, it shouldn't be me." He remembered, though, what Jair had said to him before falling asleep: He was glad that he'd stayed. Part of Brace wanted to lie back down, pull the wool blanket up over his head and stay there all day. Friendship was a complicated thing, he was beginning to realize. A thoughtless word so easily leads to injured feelings. It would not be wise to let it go, Brace knew that much.

When he stepped out into the pale light of early morning, Brace could see that the rest of them were indeed awake and had gathered close around a small, weak fire. Most of them looked as tired as Brace felt, Arden in particular. It was likely that he had gotten no sleep at all, given how serious he was about keeping watch. Jair stood beside Kendie, who was snugly dressed in her new wool cloak, and though she looked a bit weary, she had not let last night's events dampen her spirits. She was chatting away to Jair about the things Tassie had been teaching her, while Ovard watched, grinning.

"It seems as though we've got another medic-in-training," he commented.

Kendie smiled a shy smile as Brace plodded his way toward the small fire.

"Did you sleep?" Leandra asked him, running her hand along Zorix's back.

"I did," he replied. "Eventually." He glanced up, and caught sight of Jair's expression—a bit of a smile, almost apologetic. Only he knew how Brace had complained the night before, how he had let his fear and frustration show. He did not appear to be resentful, though, despite how he had sounded only a few moments ago.

Is he so quick to forgive? Brace wondered. Well, one thing was sure, it would not be easy to find time to talk it over with the boy, not without getting unwanted attention. This was something that Brace preferred to discuss privately, though it would likely have to wait until night fell once again.

Tassie moved aside, making room for Brace to sit at the fire.

"Thank you," he told her, sitting between her and Arden, who sat with his head propped in one hand, staring at the flames through heavy eyelids.

"You look like you could use some rest," Brace commented.

"Mmmm," Arden muttered. "I could, but ..."

"He *will* get some rest today," Leandra said firmly. "I will see to that myself, if I must."

Arden gave her a bit of a smile. "Yes, my love. As you say."

When Brace glanced sideways at Tassie, he could not help but notice the tired look in her eyes as well. *Had she slept?* he wondered. She hadn't heard the screaming creatures. What could have kept her up? Kendie had not seemed to be too terribly afraid when they went off together to the tent to sleep—Zorix had been with them, after all.

Tassie soon realized that Brace was watching her, and she looked up hesitantly, smiling, but he could see that she was only trying to stop him from worrying about her. He knew how she hated for anyone to make a fuss over her.

"I'm all right," she said, answering his unspoken question. "I'm only tired."

Brace nodded, understanding. "Not one of us had it easy last night."

He looked over at Ovard, but the older man appeared to be

deep in thought, gazing at the low flames. *He always seems to know something,* Brace thought to himself. *I'd say he knows much more about what's going on around us than he lets on.*

"True, it was a hard night," Ovard commented, looking up. "But we need to press on. We are getting closer to Haven, I'm sure of it. And ..." He hesitated, glancing toward Kendie. "And I don't think that I'm the only one who knows it. I think we're being watched."

"Right now?" Arden asked, sitting up straight in alarm.

"Now, I can't say. Perhaps not. But ..." He spread his hands wide and shrugged.

"What should we do?" Leandra asked him, sounding very weary.

Ovard stood. "We should move on," he told her. "The closer we get to Haven, the harder our journey could become. We can't afford to waste any time. Not now."

While everyone worked to strike the tents, Brace noticed that Kendie was constantly glancing around, toward the woodland surrounding them. She seemed to think that someone could be lurking there, hiding among the trees, watching them. Ovard voicing his worries that someone may be watching had obviously stuck with her. Brace felt some of her unease, and found himself watching the trees as well.

They cleared out, though, without any trouble, and continued on their westward journey. There were no roads here, in this part of the world. The civilizations of Dunya lay north of them, and the country of Danferron to the south, out of sight beyond the horizon. The mule-drawn cart clattered over stones as Brace led the way, with Jair beside him. The boy surprised Brace a bit when he insisted on walking with him, while the rest of them rode, seated haphazardly around their belongings and half-empty sacks of food.

Jair gave Brace a bit of a smile when they started off. He seemed to be telling him that he wanted no hard feelings between the two of them. Brace smiled in return, and gave him a friendly pat on the back, a wordless exchange of forgiveness and acceptance.

Arden had been hard to convince that he should ride rather than walk, but Leandra could be stubborn. The archer sat beside his wife on the left of the cart for nearly an hour, but the steady motion and the creaking of the wheels made his eyelids heavy. He was lying down now, cushioned from the hard, splintered wood by a folded tent. When Brace last looked back at him, Arden was trying hard to stay awake. But Leandra had been running her fingers through his short, unruly blond hair, he soon fell asleep, smiling contentedly.

The day was nearly half gone when Brace thought he spotted something unexpected, and pulled the mule to a stop. Ovard looked up with sleepy eyes.

"Is something wrong?" he asked.

"I'm not sure," Brace replied, as Jax began tearing at the grass near his feet. "The sky," he continued. "It looks ... hazy or something. Smoke?"

Ovard carefully stood in the back of the cart for a better view.

"Campfires?" he wondered aloud. "Or chimneys?"

"That messenger," Leandra added, as Arden slowly woke beside her. "He was heading somewhere. There could be a town or a villa."

"Right," Brace agreed. "So, what's our plan?"

"What it has always been," Ovard replied. "Be cautious. Jair?"

"Yes?"

"I want you to be in the cart now, son. And keep covered."

Jair's face showed the disappointment he felt at the thought of wearing that hood over his face once again. Brace gave his shoulder a squeeze.

"It shouldn't be for very long," he said, hoping that he might somehow encourage the boy.

Jair smiled as much as he could manage before he turned and climbed into the back of the cart. Arden swung easily over one of the high wooden sides and stood in the grass.

"I think I've slept long enough," he said, running his fingers through his hair. Leandra watched him closely as he made his way to stand next to Brace, in front of Jax, who was busy chewing a mouthful of grass. Arden rubbed the heels of his hands against his eyes. "I need to be moving around," he muttered.

"Would you like to take a rest, Brace?" Ovard asked him. "I can take over for you."

Brace shook his head. "No, I'm all right here. I'm used to being on foot." He looked around at the back of the cart.

They still had several sacks of food among their belongings, and with Ovard, Jair, Tassie, Leandra, and Kendie—not to mention Zorix—seated around the edges, it was more than a little crowded. *Too crowded for my liking*, Brace thought.

Tassie favored him with one of her coy little smiles, and he gave her a nod and a grin in return, his heart skipping a beat. As he pulled the mule's rope to get him moving again, he noticed the look that Arden gave him. The archer must have seen that little exchange with Tassie. His expression was not a harsh one, however, as it once would have been. He seemed to have surrendered to the idea that Brace had feelings for Tassie, which might very well be reciprocated. The tired archer even managed a knowing smirk. Brace dipped his head self-consciously, then looked up and nodded in the direction of their intended travels.

"My thoughts are really on only one thing right now," he said softly as he walked beside the mule, for Arden's ears only.

"What's that?"

"I never thought, after all that time we spent traveling through the wasteland, that I would be so reluctant to enter any city or villa." He shook his head. "I hope this new place isn't anything like Meriton."

Arden nodded in agreement. "Likely it won't be. If it were a large place, it would have been on one of Ovard's maps."

"True, that," Brace responded, feeling only slightly more at ease. "We're going into this blindly." Brace walked on in silence, recalling the day that Arden's vision had left him. Though the blindness had not lasted, he was certain that the tall archer would still feel the sting of the memory. Arden gave no hint of a reaction, however.

Brace glanced back toward the cart, where everyone sat still and silent. Each of them seemed to be wrapped up tightly in their own thoughts and fears. He turned back to Arden, whose eyes were scanning the trees.

"What is it that you hope to find in Haven?" Brace asked him.

Arden fixed a thoughtful gaze on Brace. "Hope to find?" he asked. "I haven't gotten around to thinking about all of that. I've had to stay focused on the reason why I'm here. Keeping everyone safe from harm has been foremost in my mind."

Brace nodded. "Even from the likes of me," he commented lightly.

Arden shook his head. "I was wrong to judge you so harshly."

Brace waved him off. "We've already been here," he told him. "It's forgotten."

Arden nodded in his familiar solemn way. "What of yourself?" he asked. "What are you searching for?"

Brace walked on, not having the slightest idea how to answer. "I can't say either," he finally spoke. "Everything has happened so quickly since I ran into all of you. Everything I ever planned for in my life has been thrown out of the window, so to speak. So many things I thought I wanted—they don't seem so important now. And what I do have, I never thought I would, not in all my life." He shook his head. "I don't want to lose it. Any of it."

Arden nodded again. "I can see that. There are some things to be had in life that are worth so much more than silver."

"I'm learning that." Brace was suddenly struck by the friendship that had begun between Arden and himself. He never would have expected it, this feeling of kinship toward the man. With all of them, really. Brace supposed that there were places in his heart that had not been completely closed off, as he had believed them to be. How much room must he have there, to fit seven people into it? *Seven*, he told himself, *and one color-changing creature.*

As they went on, Brace could see more clearly the columns of gray smoke rising into the air above the trees. Soon, he could smell it as well, a sweet, warm smell that touched his senses so that he could almost taste it.

When the trees began to thin out, Brace noticed that they were approaching what was clearly a farming community. It was not long until the land stretched out wide and open before them, criss-crossed with fields of various crops, and dotted here and there with sturdy wood-and-pitch homes. Just beyond the farmland, gray stone mountains jutted sharply into the blue of the sky.

Here, there were no stone walls, no guard towers, nor any cobbled streets. Nothing at all like Meriton. Brace felt a bit of relief. As they stopped at the peak of a slight rise and looked out across the open land, a chill swept across them. Brace felt the hairs on his arms raise, and he shivered briefly.

"Do you know this place, Kendie?" he heard Tassie asking.

"No," the girl replied. "I don't think I've ever seen it. But, this doesn't look to me like a place that a messenger from Meriton would come to. It's only farms."

"Very well put, Kendie," Ovard told her. "My thoughts exactly."

Brace turned back toward Ovard. "If he didn't come here, where would he have gone?"

Ovard slowly shook his head. "I'm afraid I haven't the slightest. He may very well *have* come here. Keep your eyes open, everyone. Stay alert."

Brace gave Ovard a nod, then tugged at the mule's lead rope to get him moving. "Come on, Jax," he grumbled when the animal pulled back stubbornly. Arden got him going with a firm slap on the rump, jolting the cart and nearly tumbling Tassie from her seat.

"Sorry about that," Arden told her as the cart rumbled past him.

"I'm all right," Tassie replied flatly, holding tightly to her leather medic bag. She sounded either very worried or very exhausted.

Brace's worn leather boots scuffed against thick bunches of grass as he picked his way down the hillside toward the wide, flat farmland. Jair had begrudgingly pulled his wide woolen hood up over his face, and sat hunched at the back of the cart, his knees drawn up to his chest. Leandra sat forward, watchful, a stiff breeze pushing back her smooth, fair hair.

As the land leveled out before them, the crops growing in the nearest field towered above their heads. The wide, flat leaves brushed together, blown by the wind, creating a constant whisper.

"It's so quiet here," Kendie voiced her thoughts.

True enough, Brace told himself. If he weren't so focused on staying alert, the warm sunlight, stiff breeze, and continuous soft sounds would have sent him right to sleep.

"Not *too* quiet, though, is it?" Jair asked. "It is a farmhold, after all. I mean, it isn't abandoned like Bramson was."

"I would say not," Ovard agreed. "Everything that is growing here is strong and healthy."

"Not abandoned," Arden repeated. "Farmhold or no, it would be wise not to take the people here by surprise. We should not make ourselves seem a threat to them."

"Quite so," Leandra spoke up, swinging her leg over the side of the cart and climbing to the ground. "Ovard?" she asked. "Permission to make us known?"

Ovard's eyes darted here and there across the still, open land, then he nodded. Leandra turned toward the nearest rough wooden building, cupped her hands around her mouth, and called out.

"*Helllllooooooo!*" Her voice flew out over the fields and seemed to go on forever. Several small, plain-feathered birds took flight, stiff wings flapping loudly as they retreated, but there was no answer. Leandra took a deep breath. "Hello!" she called again. "Is anyone there? We are travelers, passing through! We want no trouble, and we pledge not to bring any to you ourselves!"

She slowly let her hands fall to her sides and waited, the wind playing at her hair as she turned to face Ovard and gave a small shrug. Brace was startled when at last a man's voice suddenly called out to them.

"Hello there! We hear you."

Looking around, Brace could see only land and crops, no approaching figures that he could match the voice to. "Do you *see* us?" he demanded.

"Sure as day," the voice replied.

Brace leaned in toward Arden. "Do you see anyone?" he whispered.

Arden shook his head. "That I don't, but I'm sure that is his intention."

"We mean you no harm!" Ovard called out. "All we ask is safe passage."

There was silence once again, and Brace noticed when Arden's muscles tensed, as though he were readying himself for trouble. Momentarily, a head came into view, eyes peering through the wide green leaves. The man's shaggy red-brown hair blew in every direction around his lean, sun-browned face. In a moment, he was joined by another younger, leaner man, nearly as brown as the first.

"Safe passage?" The taller man repeated, coming slowly toward them. "I can promise you that only so far as our master's land is concerned. Can't promise for what any of the others might do."

"Well enough," Ovard replied. "That's all we ask."

"Where is it y'are going?" The younger man asked, a note of curiosity playing at his voice.

"West," Ovard answered.

"Toward them mountains?" The first asked, gesturing, his gray eyes wide. "What be out there, that draws you?"

Brace exchanged a quick, uneasy glance with Arden. These men were farmers, simple folk. Surely they would pose no threat, surely they knew nothing of Haven, of the prophecies. But ... Out of the corner of his eye, Brace saw Ovard step up beside him.

"Our new home, or that is our hope, at the least," Ovard told the man.

"Out *there*?" the younger man asked, pushing his ash-blonde hair away from his face.

"Here, now," the tall stranger said, laying his hand on the other's shoulder. "If these folks want to go to them mountains, who is we to trouble them for it?" He turned to face them once again. "I'd just as soon keep myself here, all the same."

Ovard gave the man a chuckle. "That is very wise, my friend. You have good land here. I might be tempted to stay myself, if …"

The taller man responded with an understanding nod.

"Well," he said, tipping his head back toward the rough wood-frame house, "I've got to let the lady know you've come and all."

"The lady?" Ovard asked. "The lady of the house?"

"S'right," the younger man replied gruffly. "This is her land y'are on. Don't you be thinkin' …"

The tall farmhand stopped him, firmly grasping his arm. "Get off'a that," he scolded. "They said they want no trouble, now, didn't they?" He looked back, first at Ovard, then at Brace, and Arden. "They don't want no trouble, they'll cause no trouble. Right?"

"Very much so," Arden told him.

"Besides," the farmhand told his young companion, "Ya know how the master is about havin' visitors. She don't want anyone to pass by without she gets a chance to show them some kindness."

Brace let out a long, slow breath. This was a fortunate thing, the news of the landowner being a friendly sort. The taller man turned toward the house, gesturing for the rest of them to follow him between the fields.

Arden pressed his hand against the small of Leandra's back, tipping his head toward the cart. Seeing that he wanted her to ride, she obediently pulled herself up over the rough wooden side of the cart, seating herself beside Tassie, who was struggling to gather her hair into a braid while the wind tossed it.

Brace walked beside Arden, leading Jax, while Ovard went ahead of them, following the farmhands. They were very lean men, Brace noted, but not *thin*, not as though they lacked food. Their faded brown clothing was rough and tattered here and there, but clean, and had been mended in places. They were well cared for, these workers. The people here did not seem to be lacking, at least at this farmhold.

The cart's thick, heavy wheels clattered over the rough dirt pathway leading toward the stout wooden home. A stream of gray smoke poured out of the stone chimney, and was snatched away by the steady wind.

The tall farmhand gave out a shrill whistle as they neared, and in a moment, a woman's figure stepped outside the house, shading her eyes from the sunlight.

"What's all this, Nav?" she called out, stepping toward them. The woman's hair shone silver under the bright light of the sun, almost like metal, Brace thought.

"Visitors of sorts," the tall, lean man replied. "They're askin' us for safe passage."

Coming closer, the woman eyed them all with a bit of hesitancy: Arden and Brace standing beside the old mule; Ovard, with his short gray scruff of a beard; Tassie, Leandra, Jair and Kendie, along with Zorix, in the back of the cart. The woman's long, heavy, woven dress blew in the dirt at her feet. Once, it may have been red, but it had faded to a drab brick, and though it was quite worn, it was clean and well-mended.

"Are those children you have there?" The woman asked, her voice wavering with age.

"Yes, my lady," Ovard replied. "Two."

In the back of the cart, Kendie leaned in toward Tassie, nervously clutching her arm, as though she feared this elderly woman could possibly know that she was a runaway.

The woman smiled. "My lady? You honor me too much. Please, call me Milena. That is my name, always has been."

Ovard tipped his head respectfully. "Milena."

The woman smiled. "Are any of you in need of rest, something to eat?"

"We carry our own supplies," Arden told her, nodding toward the cart. "We don't want to take away from your larders."

"Are you thirsty, then?" she asked. "Will you stay and enjoy some freshly-made apricot juice?"

Apricots! Brace could almost smell them, almost taste the sweetness. How long it had been?

Ovard smiled courteously. "It sounds enticing," he said. "We would be honored, if you're certain you're of a mind to share with the lot of us, as many as we are."

"Oh, there is plenty," Milena interrupted. "I would be well pleased if you would allow me to show you this courtesy, however small it may be."

Only then did Kendie release her grasp on Tassie's arm.

"You are very kind," Leandra spoke up. Milena stood smiling, as she took note of the ornate pattern stitched into the front of Leandra's light gray-green vest. One that looked nothing like the ones worn in Meriton.

"You've met the lads, then?" The older woman asked, referring to the two farmhands, who were now standing beside her.

Lads? Brace thought. He would never have thought of them as lads, most certainly not the taller of the two, who had lines creasing his face at the corners of his browned face.

"We have," Ovard told her. "Though we don't have the pleasure of their names."

"Forgive us," Milena said, resting her hand on the arm of the man nearest her, the one with the shaggy red-brown hair. "This is Nav," she told them, "and the other is Dursen. They're good men, I assure you, though they may seem a bit churlish at the first. One finds it hard to know who can be trusted in these dark times."

"You have the truth of that," Ovard agreed. "Please know that you can trust us, each of us. We'll cause no trouble."

"Oh, I'm certain of that," Milena replied, in a warm, kind voice, waving them on toward the house.

~ 21 ~

The sun was warm on Brace's shoulders, and the sweet fruit juice was cool as it ran down his throat. Dappled sunlight filtered through the leaves of the trees above him, where he sat leisurely in the grass. He had even removed his heavy boots, allowing his feet time to breathe and his toes to move freely. Milena was quite the welcoming hostess, pouring each of them a generous serving of apricot juice, and surprising them with wedges of soft, spiced bread. She particularly seemed to favor Jair and Kendie, lavishing them with kind words, pats on the head, and extra helpings of bread. Jair put up with it all gracefully, while Kendie reveled in it. She was happy to have another opportunity to sing a handful of her songs, and the woman never seemed to tire of the girl's continuous chatter.

The farmhands, Nav and Dursen, warmed considerably as well, once they became fully convinced that none of them intended to cause any trouble. Ovard relaxed enough to join in with one of Kendie's songs, playing his lyr flute, and Dursen joined in on a small reed pipe. Brace enjoyed seeing Tassie smile while the music drifted through the air, content once again, though she couldn't hear it. She'd had little cause for joy these past days. He recalled the first time she smiled at him, after she had cared for the slight injury he'd gotten forcing his way through the sharp brambles. It had seemed almost a smirk, hinting at some playfulness, even flirtatiousness. His relationship with her—if he could call it that—had been neglected of late. When was the last time he really spoke to her? Before Meriton?

227

This was something Brace hoped to change, as soon as he could find the opportunity.

Tassie brought a spark of encouragement into his life, more so than any of the others, even Leandra. What she saw in him, Brace still couldn't be sure, but he enjoyed hearing her say that she believed in him. And he her blush when she realized that Brace noticed her looking at him. What she felt for him, he could not say exactly, but he fully intended to find out, somehow.

Milena smiled as Kendie finished her song, a cheerful tune about a rushing river and the secret lovers who had stolen away to cross it.

"You have a beautiful voice, sweet one."

Kendie smiled shyly and bowed her head. "Thank you."

"What is your name, child?"

"Kendie, ma'am."

"Kendie," Milena repeated. "How sweet." The old woman's eyes clouded over with consternation as she looked around the group. "How rude of me," she said. "I have not asked any of you to introduce yourselves."

"Please, don't worry yourself," Leandra told her. "You've done us no terrible offense. My name is Leandra. And Arden," she said, resting her hand on his arm, "is my husband."

Milena was all smiles and nods as Tassie, Jair, and Ovard introduced themselves to her in turn. When her kind eyes turned toward Brace, he hesitated instinctively. He found himself thinking that a name was not just a name, he knew. A reputation follows it. Even so far south, he had no assurance of being beyond recognition.

"Merron," Brace heard Jair saying from beneath his hood. "His name is Merron."

Milena only smiled in response. She had no reason to doubt Jair, or any of them, Brace realized. Just as well. He looked up at the woman, and gave her a bit of a smile.

"Yes," he said at last. "It's Merron."

"Well," Milena said as she turned toward Ovard, who had stood out as the head of the group, "I am so glad to have the honor of your company. The times are few and far between when I am visited by folk so gracious as yourselves. Would you please be so kind as to stay and share a meal with the lads and me?"

Arden discreetly looked toward Ovard. Brace knew little of social graces, but he was aware what a slight it would be if they refused her offer. Brace noticed the look in Tassie's eyes as she faced Ovard as well, hoping against hope that he would accept.

"Well," Ovard began, "we have no idea how much farther our travels will take us, or how difficult the journey will be."

Brace eyed him, frowning. Ovard sounded as though he were giving her reasons why they shouldn't stay.

"So then," Ovard continued, "a good meal would be a very welcome thing. I can't say when we're likely to have such an opportunity again. Thank you. We accept."

Milena's eyes shone with delight. "Splendid. I'll go and get right to it."

"Let us help you," Tassie spoke up, rising to her feet. "It isn't right, one person having to prepare a meal for so many others. Please, let me help you."

Milena hesitated a moment, but Brace suspected that she could no more refuse Tassie's help than Ovard could her offer of a meal.

"All right, my dear," the old woman replied. "I would be glad of the help, and the company as well."

Leandra also offered her hands, and Kendie followed. Brace could hear the laughter from the open window some time later, as he accompanied the young farmhand Dursen on his walk through the rows of crops, searching for any sign of disease among the tall, broad leaves.

"You're an unlikely lot," Dursen told him as they walked. "But you've made her very happy."

"I'm glad of that," Brace replied, though it was Tassie's happiness that concerned him more. "They all sound happy enough. Tassie, I know, appreciates all of it. I think she's missed being in the company of townsfolk more than she likes to let on."

"Tassie?" Dursen asked. "Which one is she?"

"With the long brown hair," Brace answered abruptly. He was not keen on the idea of any other young men paying her any extra attention. He wanted to keep that for himself alone.

"Ah," Dursen commented, whacking a thick, discolored stalk away from the main shoot with a wide, heavy blade. "There seems to be something a bit off about her. Is there?"

"She can't hear, is all," Brace told him. "She makes do, more than well enough. She's training to be a medic." He found himself defending Tassie. He couldn't stomach the idea of anyone thinking of her as somehow impaired, defective.

"A medic? Truly?"

"Yes."

"Well," the farmhand continued nonchalantly. "Can't have too many medics, now, can we?"

"I suppose not," Brace replied. "She's helped me out plenty."

"That boy," Dursen said after a moment, as they continued through the field. "Why does he remain hooded?"

Brace was silent for a time. This question was not so easily answered.

"It's the wind," he finally told the farmhand. "He takes sick easily. He needs to stay protected against the chill."

Dursen squinted at him a moment. "Fair enough," he replied.

Whether the younger farmhand believed him or not, he pried no further. Brace wandered up and down the rows of crops, now and again lending Dursen a hand cutting stalks or plucking leaves, and all the while watching as the sky filled in with a pale gray haze. The sun's rays were unable to penetrate through, and the warmth in the air had soon surrendered to the cool wind that continued to gust across the open land.

Dursen caught him looking at the sky and the haze as they turned down yet another row of hard-packed, yet somehow spongy dirt.

"It's been doing that more and more lately," he commented. "The sky. Those … clouds, or some such thing. Earlier, too. Gets so dark and cold so fast, Nav and me can't hardly get all the work done we used to in a day's time, but the master can't afford to hire no one else."

Brace considered Dursen's words. "Have you ever wondered *why* the sky is changing?" he asked him.

The farmhand only shrugged. "Can't say at all. I'm not studied in such things. Would … would you be? Knowing why, I mean?"

Brace shook his head. "No, not me. Ovard. He knows about more things than I ever knew existed."

"What does he know about the sky?" Dursen pressed.

Brace was beginning to feel as though he'd said too much. "Times are changing," he said simply. "Not just the sky. Everything. But you'll have to ask him about it. It's more his business than mine."

The young man eyed him suspiciously, as though he was beginning to wonder if Ovard could actually have something to do with *causing* these perplexing changes, and not just being knowledgeable of them.

The work finished, Brace followed Dursen as he sauntered leisurely back toward the rough-cut wooden building that was Milena's home. The brown wood had faded to gray in most places, and the wind had torn tiles away from the roof, leaving behind empty patches, like scales missing from a dragon's back. Despite its rough appearance, Brace felt drawn to the small, square cottage. Varying aromas from the fresh-cooked meal lingered on the breeze, and the sounds of talking and laughter came from within as well.

Tassie stepped outside as Dursen was showing Brace where the water pump was located, where they could draw water to wash the dirt and sweat from their hands and faces. The young farmhand was bent low, with cool streams of water running over his palms, while Brace stood and watched Tassie approaching. Coming straight toward them, she seemed to have been watching for their return. Her long, wavy hair had been pulled back into a loose braid, but a few strands had escaped and fluttered around her face. The legs of her long, loose-fitting trousers hugged her legs as she came toward them, moving against the wind. Her emerald green eyes shone more brightly than Brace remembered ever having seen them.

"Hello there," she said, when she'd come near enough to be heard. Dursen was slightly startled, and looked up from washing. "The meal is ready," she told them. "You've come back just at the right time."

Brace could manage only a bit of a grin in response. *Why did she have to be so beautiful?*

"What is it?" Tassie asked. "Why are you staring at me that way? Do I have flour on my face?" She ran her fingertips across the bridge of her slender nose and inspected them.

"No," Brace told her, trying to appear nonchalant as he turned toward the water pump. "You're fine."

Tassie was aware that Brace had feelings for her; there was no need to pretend otherwise, not where she was concerned. But Dursen—that was another matter. If the farmhand had not been standing there, Brace would have let his gaze linger a moment longer, perhaps even let her believe that she *did* have white powder streaked across her cheek, giving himself an opportunity to lightly brush his fingers against her skin, to wipe it away.

Brace made a quick task of washing his face and hands, then turned, using his long, rough sleeve as a towel. Tassie stood there still, her eyes fixed on him. Brace felt cool water dripping from his chin onto his neck and chest, but he momentarily stopped drying himself as he returned her gaze. She smiled then, a knowing smile that lit her whole face. After a moment, she turned to face Dursen, who stood just behind Brace's left shoulder.

"You must be hungry, the both of you," she said in a carefree tone of voice. "Why don't we all go in for the meal?"

"Thank you, miss," Dursen replied as he stepped forward. Brace followed him, with Tassie walking at his side.

She caught him off guard when she lightly took hold of his arm with one hand, draping the other across the crook of his elbow. When Brace looked at her in surprise, she was smirking.

"Let's hope that your stomach is as hungry as your eyes are."

The meal was mouth-watering. Heaps of steamed vegetables, boiled potatoes, stewed rabbit, and more fresh bread filled the long, heavy wooden table where everyone gathered inside Milena's cottage. There were by no means enough chairs for all of them, but they brought stools and such in from the barn, and swept the floor clean. Jair seated himself beside Nav and Dursen, under the window. The rest of them sat on this or that around the table, Milena at one end, Ovard and Kendie at the other. Leandra was seated across from Arden, and Tassie across from Brace, a fact for which he was silently grateful.

The mood during the meal was light and easy, filled with conversation. Milena and her farmhands asked very few questions, Brace noted, but Jair nonetheless recounted tales of their journey— Arden's illness resulting from the insect bite, finding the large eggs and running away from the angry dragon, and such. Nav listened with interest, smiling his uneven gap-toothed smile from time to time, particularly when conversation turned to Zorix and his antics. Brace was sure Ovard was relieved that Jair mentioned nothing of Haven, or the increasing darkness, and that he remained hidden beneath his hood, even indoors. This would have been considered a terrible insult to their hosts, if they had not been made to believe that Jair became ill so easily, and needed to keep warm.

When the meal was over, Milena encouraged Kendie to sing another of her songs. The girl agreed, smiling, then thought long and hard, searching for what she felt would be the perfect choice for the moment.

"I ask not for ease and riches," she sang at last, "nor earth's jewels for my part. But I have the best of wishes for a pure and honest heart.

Oh, pure heart so true and tender, fairer than the lilies white,
The pure heart alone can render songs of joy both day and night.
Should I cherish earthly treasure, it would fly on speedy wings.
The pure heart a plenteous measure of true pleasure daily brings."

"Thank you again, you dear thing," Milena told her.

When Kendie smiled, it was a tired smile. The day had worn on, and the light coming through Milena's window was faint and dim, though the hour was by no means late. Nav stood, stretched his long legs, and peered outside.

"Dark again, Milena," he said, "earlier still."

Kendie suddenly looked fearful. "Do we have to go on again, even in the dark?" she asked. "Those screaming creatures ..."

"Creatures?" Dursen asked. "What's this now?"

"We hear them all the time, but we've never seen them," Kendie answered. "I try not to be afraid, but ..."

"Well, it wouldn't be any trouble for you to rest here for the night," Milena spoke up. Seeing the look in her eyes, Brace realized just how lonely the old woman must be, with only her farmhands for daily company. Ovard cast an uncertain glance around the room.

"But believe me now," Milena added, "I had no intention of inviting you in for the meal just so you'd be unable to go on, with it getting dark so soon. The thought never crossed my mind."

Ovard shook his head. "No, of course not. I could never suspect you of such craftiness. I know all too well about the increasing darkness."

"That's right," Dursen spoke up. "Merron here said you knew so much about it. Tell us?"

Brace ducked his head, casually scratching his forehead and trying not to appear as guilty as he felt.

"He said so, did he?" Arden's voice was low and strained. "What all did he tell you?"

Dursen shrugged. "Just that. That Ovard knows a lot of things about why the sky gets so dark so fast and all. He said that things were changing, but if I wanted to know more, I'd have to ask *him*."

"Is that all he told you?" Leandra asked.

Dursen nodded, looking quite perplexed. "Yes, that's all he said. Should … should I not have asked about it?"

"No," Ovard said after a tense moment of silence. "No, it's all right that you asked. The whole world has noticed the changes, I'm sure. It would certainly not have escaped you, son."

Dursen appeared relieved at Ovard's words, but Brace was sure he was not so relieved as *he* was. Ovard breathed out a long, heavy sigh before he continued. "The darkness is increasing," he began. "Darkness in the sky, and in men's hearts, I'm afraid. The whole world is in danger of being swallowed up in it."

Milena's eyes went wide, while Nav swallowed in dismay.

"But," Ovard continued, "there may be hope out there, for all of us. A city of light—a haven. And we intend to find it." Ovard seemed relieved in having said the words once again, as though the longer he carried the burden of his secret, the heavier it became, the harder to bear.

"A haven?" Milena asked. "A place of safety?"

"Yes," Ovard replied.

"And what?" Nav spoke up, his voice heavy. "Is everyone in the world supposed to pull up roots and go to this place? Hide behind its walls? Just how many folks will it hold?"

Ovard shook his head, as Brace picked up on the unease in Tassie's eyes, the way Leandra gazed unseeing at the table, and the tension in Arden's face.

"I don't know all there is to know," Ovard told Milena and her farmhands. "I only believe that Haven is our last hope. I don't know how many can live there, but please know that I don't intend to keep the place for myself, or for just our little group. I know that Haven is to be a refuge for all who seek it with a pure heart. I don't know exactly how it will bring relief, but I can discover the answers to all of my questions, and yours, only if we just can start by *finding* it."

~22~

B race noticed the relief in Tassie's face when they went out to put up the tents behind Milena's farmhouse. Kendie's face as well. Nav had confided in them that he thought he'd heard the screams of the wild animals that they'd mentioned—from afar, but he'd heard them nonetheless. As he gazed out into the darkness beyond the light of Milena's lanterns, the tall, weathered farmhand's gray eyes were filled with worry and questions, so many questions—but not one of them did he ask. When the work of getting the tents up was finished, and Jax had been well fed and watered and unhitched from the cart to rest, Nav simply left without a word, disappearing into the heavy darkness.

Milena had kindly provided them with firewood from her own shed, and they sat close around it now, watching the movement of the flames—all but Ovard, who had lingered at the house to properly thank Milena for her generosity.

Leandra sat close beside Arden, leaning her head on his shoulder and holding his hand, their fingers intertwined much like the ornate lines tattooed across around their wrists. Jair had finally removed his hood and was running his hands through his hair, while Tassie kept her eyes fixed on their small fire. She seemed to be lost in her own thoughts. Brace wanted so badly to move closer to her, to take her hand in his, to breathe in the smell of her hair, to have her smile at him the way she so seldom did. But, of course, he did no such thing.

Zorix wandered in lazy circles around the fire, his long tail twitching, his large ears shifting this way and that, reacting to all of the new sounds and smells. He seemed to be trying to sort through them, searching for the ones that were familiar to him, whether they told him of food or of danger. He stopped when he came to Leandra, whimpering from deep in his throat, so softly that Brace barely heard him. Leandra ran her free hand across his back, smoothing his fur.

"It's all right," she said quietly. Zorix pressed his face against Leandra's knee before he turned to Kendie, curling up beside her. The girl smiled and reached out to scratch behind his ears.

The sound of dry grass crunching underfoot told them of Ovard's return from Milena's home, some small distance away, yet unseen beyond the reach of the light from their fire.

"Well," Ovard groaned as he lowered himself to sit on the ground, "this has been a pleasant turn, has it not?" he was smiling broadly from behind his coarse gray whiskers.

"Very," Leandra replied.

Such mirth, Brace thought. After all the old man had been through—losing his sister, his wife, his son—how did he keep such a positive view of life?

Zorix yawned a wide yawn, baring his small yet sharply pointed teeth.

"I can agree with that, little one," Arden commented, drawing a sleepy gaze from Zorix.

"Will we be leaving early in the morning?" Jair asked, sounding clearly as if he hoped the answer would be no.

Ovard hesitated. "Not too early," he replied.

"I'm glad of that," Jair commented. "I'm so tired out."

Brace kept his eyes on Ovard. Something did not seem quite right about the way he'd answered so simply. It would have been more like him to explain what he had planned. None of the others seemed to think anything was out of sorts, however. Arden had eyes only for Leandra at the moment, and Kendie was busy scratching the fur behind Zorix's ears. Tassie appeared to be fighting off sleep, her eyelids heavy.

"We can rest easy here tonight, I think." Ovard looked up at the black cover of sky. The wind had softened, and the night was quiet. No eerie screeching sounds echoed through the air, but no insects chirped either, which Brace found unusual given the miles of surrounding farmland.

Brace blinked at the orange glow of firelight. *Rest easy.* When had he ever been able to rest easy? All throughout his life, there had always been the fear of some threat or another clinging to him like a chill that no fire could chase away.

When morning came, the air was cold and heavy, settling over the land with the dampness of the dew that covered everything—the canvas of the tents, every blade of grass, every broad leaf in Milena's fields. A gray haze hung over everything as well, lingering along every horizon, as though daring the sunlight to try to chase it away.

Brace wrapped his tattered cloak close around his shoulders, breathing warmth into his hands. Leandra's breath clouded in front of her face as she worked at folding up the tent she shared with Arden. Zorix sat close by, watching as though he were keeping guard over her. Arden had gone off with Ovard to speak with Milena, and Brace knew that the small, furry creature must feel that responsibility for Leandra's safety now rested on his shoulders alone.

Brace looked aside, where Tassie, Jair, and Kendie sat close to the newly lit fire. Jair had pulled out his small knife and was whittling down the end of yet another twig, but slowly this time, talking as he worked. Kendie watched him closely, nodding every so often. *He's teaching her how to do it*, Brace realized, and found himself smiling. Shrugging deeper into his cloak, he turned back toward Leandra, where she had begun to roll one end of the folded tent inward. Brace leaned down and held the side in place.

"Thank you," Leandra breathed. Her shoulder-length blonde hair hung down around her face, which was slightly flushed. She wore her knife at her belt, as always, as well as her heavy leather boots and her embroidered vest. Brace recalled with amusement the day she'd held that knife to his throat. He must have been smirking now, because Leandra stopped and looked up at him.

"What?" she asked suspiciously.

"Oh," Brace replied, shaking his head. "I was just thinking back. My first impressions of you were that you are such a strong, independent woman."

Leandra grinned, continuing her task of tightly rolling the tent. "And what do you think of me now?"

"Much the same," Brace told her casually. "You are a woman who speaks her mind, and it seems to me you're always in the right. And you're more independent than most of the women I've known."

Leandra was silent a moment as she pulled the leather ties tightly around the canvas. "Not completely," she said quietly. "I'm not completely independent. I do *need*, like any other woman."

Brace looked back over his shoulder when he heard Arden and Ovard approaching, accompanied by Milena, her silver hair reflecting the sunlight.

"Sometimes, I think Arden needs you more than you need him," Brace confessed.

Leandra smiled at his words, watching her husband walk toward them.

"Sometimes," she agreed.

Brace lifted the tightly-rolled tent.

"I'll take this to the cart for you," he offered.

Leandra shook her head. "No, not in the cart," she told him. "It's going in Arden's pack."

"In his pack?" Brace asked, alarmed. "Why? He can't be leaving us?"

"No," Leandra replied quickly. "Not Arden."

"What?" Brace began, but Leandra shook her head. She looked aside, and when Brace turned, he saw that Ovard, Arden, and Milena stood close by. The older man wore a heavy expression, as though he was the bearer of some unfortunate news. Brace felt his heart skip a beat. Someone was leaving? Ovard? No, impossible. They needed him!

Ovard cleared his throat, drawing Jair's attention. The boy tapped Tassie's arm lightly, and she followed his gaze, eyeing Ovard with apprehension. Kendie had been trying out Jair's knife on a narrow twig, but she relinquished it to him when he held out his hand.

"What is going on here?" Brace demanded, lowering the tent to the ground. "Ovard?"

The man held up his hand, signaling Brace to wait. "Kendie," he called out gently. "Come over here to me, child."

Kendie obeyed silently, casting nervous glances around the group. "What is it?" she asked in a strained voice, despite Milena's pleasant smile.

"We're going to be heading out soon," Ovard told her, taking her gently by the shoulders.

"I know we are," Kendie began, but Ovard shook his head.

"Not all of us," he continued. "I … Milena and I … have decided that you should stay here."

Brace felt a wave of relief. Ovard was not leaving.

Kendie's eyes widened in alarm. "What? No! I want to come with you, please!"

"We've got to cross the mountains, Kendie. It's going to be hard and dangerous."

"But I'm brave and strong, you know I am!"

Ovard nodded. "I know that you are. Even so, I fear it may be too difficult. None of us knows what to expect. You'll be much safer here."

Tears filled Kendie's eyes as she looked up at Ovard's face. "But

I won't see you anymore, not any of you. And I want to see Haven, too. You said I could come to Haven."

Ovard rested his hand on Kendie's braided black hair.

"We will come back for you, child. I promise you that. You will see Haven. We'll come back after we've found it, and we'll bring you there safely. I promise you."

"Truly?"

"Truly."

Kendie blinked, and tears streamed down her face before she could brush them away. "As long as you promise."

Leandra stepped forward and bent to pull Kendie close. "We will come back for you, sweet one," she said as Kendie wrapped her arms around her neck and hid her face against her shoulder. "Please don't cry."

Kendie stepped back, wiping her palms across her cheeks. "I'm sorry," she said. "I'm just going to miss you all so much."

Leandra affectionately touched Kendie's face. "And don't you think we'll miss you?" she asked. "We'll miss you terribly." Leandra coughed to clear the emotion from her voice. "You are brave, Kendie," she continued. "And you can show us how brave you are by waiting here for us, and taking care of Jax. We can't take him with us, either. Will you do that for us?"

Kendie sniffed and nodded, drying her eyes on the threadbare sleeve of her dress. "I'll take good care of him," she answered. "I'll do the very best I can."

"I'm sure you will," Ovard told her.

"And I will be here to help you, child," Milena spoke up. "And Nav and Dursen as well."

Kendie managed a bit of a smile, for a short moment. "When are you leaving?" she asked, facing Ovard.

"Very soon," he replied. "We are running out of time, I'm afraid."

Kendie nodded solemnly. "I know." She looked around at each of them, studying their faces as though she desperately wanted to remember them, for fear that she may never see them again. She turned then, toward Milena, who stepped forward and put her arms around Kendie's shoulders.

"You really want me to stay with you?" Kendie asked her.

"I do, of course I do," she replied. "You are very welcome here. I'm glad to have you, and I hope you'll be glad to stay with me."

Kendie nodded. "I'm sorry I cried. I didn't mean that I don't want to be here, I only wanted to go on with them."

Milena smiled. "I understand, child."

Brace watched as Tassie and Jair came forward to embrace Kendie one last time before their departure. *There is no guarantee*, Brace thought to himself, *that we will ever see the girl again.* She would be safe enough here, he was certain, but as for the rest of them ... there was no way to know what they would face in the days ahead.

Tassie's eyes were damp as she stepped away. Arden coughed lightly as he crouched beside Kendie. "I'll miss you too, little one," he told her.

"So will I." Kendie eased out of Milena's arms and pulled Arden into a tight embrace. The archer reacted in surprise for a moment before putting his arms around her, lightly. A quick moment later, Arden released her and stood. "Be a brave girl," he told her.

"I will," she said with a smile. "I'll have *harbrost.*"

Arden smiled in response, and then Kendie turned toward Brace. She hesitated only a moment before she hurried to him, hugging him tightly.

"Thank you," she told him, her voice muffled against his cloak.

Brace swallowed. "What for?" he asked.

"For wanting to help me," she replied, looking up at him. "For caring about what happens to me."

Brace nodded as he looked into her young, innocent eyes. *I had eyes like that once,* he thought. *I'm sure I must have.*

"You have a chance now," he told her. "A chance to make something good out of your life." He smiled regretfully. "Don't do what I've done."

"Stealing?" Kendie whispered as she stepped back.

Now, how did she know about that? Brace wondered.

"No, I won't," Kendie told him. "But you have a chance to make something good of your life, too. You will, won't you?"

Wise little thing, Brace thought. "I'll do the best I can," be promised her.

Milena took Kendie back to the house with her before they left. They'd all had a chance to say their goodbyes, after all, and leaving had been easier that way. Not much, but a bit. No one doubted Ovard's decision to leave Kendie at the farmhold. Jagged, windy mountains were no place to take a small girl in a threadbare dress. The cart and the mule would do them no good either, once they passed beyond the sprawling farmland. Once again, they were resigned to carry their belongings, sharing the weight of tents, blankets, extra clothing, and food among themselves as equally as they could.

The mood was heavy as they went forward on foot, with the sun at their backs. Brace had never paid much attention to Kendie's songs, but now he found that he missed them.

Some of the food they had carried in the cart they left with Milena; there was too much to carry. Still, among their various packs, they had dried meat, black beans, and barley, as well as small amounts of sugar, flour, and honey. Milena had insisted that they accept her gifts of butter and vine peas, so they added them to their supplies. Their flasks were now filled with fresh, cool water from the farm's well—enough, Brace hoped, to last them for two days.

Passing other farms brought mixed reactions. Many stared, either out of curiosity or hostility. Dogs barked; children ran to hide indoors. From time to time, Ovard raised his hand in a friendly greeting, but he so seldom got any response that he soon gave it up.

Jair found a long, broken tree limb, and he dragged it through the dirt as he walked, leaving a snaking trail behind him. Zorix stopped to sniff at the air quite often, and more often than not, Leandra called out to him to keep up with her.

Brace let out a long breath when finally, several hours later, they left the last of the fields behind them. Spire's Gate, or so Milena had told them, had known its share of trouble, and for the most part, the farmholders did not welcome outsiders. The old woman had shared memories from years past, when traders going between Dunya and Danferron passed through regularly, and she'd always considered it a pleasure to open her home to them. She'd often been repaid for her kindness with fur pelts, rolls of cloth, and songs or stories. Once or twice, she told them, she'd even heard legends of the Haven itself.

"But that was so long ago," she had said, her face sorrowful, knowing that there may never come such a time again, not while she yet lived. "Men's hearts seem to have grown cold," Milena had commented.

True enough, Brace thought, though most of the hearts he had encountered in his life had been cold ones.

Now the wind blowing over the mountains was cold as well, colder than Brace had felt in so many years that he'd almost forgotten what it felt like. Staring up through the trees at the enormous gray crags, Tassie shivered. "Uncle." Her voice was quiet and full of dread as she turned to look at Ovard. "Is this really the way, Uncle? Do we need to cross these mountains?"

Ovard slowly stepped toward her. "We must," he told her. "I believe we must. The markings. We've been following what the markings show us. South, then west. The stony mountain tower. Now we must keep going west."

Brace looked back at Jair. The compass lines did point south and west, but then there was the large crescent moon shape, with the strange sort of writing inside the hollow shape.

"What about the rest of it?" Brace asked. "What could the curved moon represent? This range of mountains isn't curved at all."

Ovard shook his head. "It could be that the answer lies beyond these mountains. Nav told me that there is a pass. He said it should be easy enough to find."

"Are we going to start up it today?" Jair asked. "It's going to get dark again soon!"

"No," Ovard answered. "I just want to try to find the way, so we can start early tomorrow."

"Let's get searching then," Arden spoke up. "A pass shouldn't be too difficult to spot." Adjusting his bow, which he carried strapped on his back, he turned aside and began walking through the trees. His heavy boots crunched over loose rocks as he went along, searching the mountains for an easy way to cross.

Leandra stood, smiling proudly as she watched her husband go. "Come on, everyone!" she called out, marching away in the other direction. Jair hurried after Arden, and Tassie followed him, admonishing him to be careful of where he was walking. Brace joined Ovard as Zorix scurried ahead of them to catch up with Leandra.

The mountain range that loomed before them was rocky and jagged against the cloudy afternoon sky as Brace searched for any signs of a pass.

I certainly hope this Haven is everything they expect it to be, Brace thought. *We've been searching long and hard enough.*

"Look there!" Leandra cried out, pointing upward. Brace flinched, startled, then hurried toward her with Ovard right beside him. The horizon line of the craggy row of mountains curved and dipped slightly, rising sharply again on the right, where it continued on its rugged path.

"Could that be the way?" Leandra asked, her voice full of hope. Ovard stared at it so long that Brace began to wonder if he'd even heard the question.

"I think it must be," he said at last, his voice low. Brace studied the sky line. The slight dip in the rocky peaks was very narrow, and only scarcely smoother than the cliffs on either side of it. He shook his head slowly.

"You call that a pass?"

"It's as much of a pass as we're going to find, I'm afraid," Ovard replied. Turning aside, he cupped his hands around his mouth and called out to the others.

"Here! We've found it!"

The heavy, dense range of stone seemed to throw Ovard's voice back at him. Leandra let out a shrill whistle, and in a moment, another was heard in reply.

By the time Arden, Tassie, and Jair rejoined them, they had already found a suitable site for making camp, and unpacked the tents. Arden gazed at the pass for a long a time, and Brace wondered what the archer thought of it. Was it a place that they would actually be able to climb, to cross the mountains? Brace was grateful, at the moment, that Ovard had thought to leave Kendie with Milena. Determined though the girl was, this was not going to be an easy thing, not by any means. Finally, Arden turned his back on the mountains and unloaded his bow, quiver of arrows, and heavy pack onto the ground at his feet.

Jair couldn't seem to take his eyes off the meager pass, even as he helped Brace to get their tent raised. "Are we really going to cross there?" he asked quietly, peering at Brace over the roof of the tent.

Brace nodded in response. "It seems we are." He tried to sound nonchalant about the whole thing, not wanting Jair to pick up on the trepidation he felt.

"Ovard thinks that is the way across that Nav told him about?"

"He does."

"Well," Jair continued, turning once again to gaze at the mountains, "if Ovard says that's the way, then it must be the way."

Brace managed a grin. "Such confidence."

"Don't you trust him as much?" Jair was defensive.

"I do, Jair. Believe me, I do."

Jair's eyes softened. "I wouldn't want to have anyone else leading us," he said softly.

Brace remembered how he felt, back at Milena's farm, when he'd thought Ovard might be leaving them.

"I wouldn't either," he replied.

~ 23 ~

Loud, high-pitched screams filled Brace's ears, echoing off the sloping crags of stone. *It's only a dream*, he told himself in his half-awake state. He rolled over onto his side and opened his eyes to see Jair sitting up, staring out into the darkness, tightly clutching the rough blanket bunched at his waist.

Brace sat up quickly in alarm. "I'm not dreaming, am I?" he asked. "You hear them too."

Jair nodded wordlessly, his eyes wide. Again, screeching filled the air. The sounds were closer, so much closer than they'd ever been.

"What should we do?" Jair asked him in a strained whisper.

"I don't know," Brace replied. "But keep your head, all right?"

Jair nodded as Brace slid his dagger from his boot. Slowly, full of uncertainty, he crawled to the tent flap and pushed it aside. The night was black as pitch, but all the same, Brace thought he could see movement. "Arden?" he asked, his voice catching in his throat. He coughed, then called out again. "Arden? Are you out there?"

No response came, but the screeching sounds of the unknown creatures continued and grew louder still. Brace knew that if he and Jair had been awakened, the others must have as well. A flash of gray came and went, from what distance, Brace could not say. A high, warbling cry filled the air, almost like laughter.

Brace swallowed back his fear. "Arden!" he called out, louder this time.

"Yes, Brace!" came the reply. "I hear it too. I'm keeping watch."

"I think I can see something," Brace told him.

"I can as well."

"Don't you dare set foot outside this tent!" Leandra's voice was firm, almost a little desperate. "Don't you dare!"

"I'm not going anywhere," Arden's voice came through the darkness.

"I'm here too," Ovard's voice joined the others. "How is Jair?"

Brace looked back over his shoulder. The boy was scarcely visible.

"I'm all right," Jair whispered, his voice shaking.

"He's fine," Brace called out. "Tassie—she's all alone!"

"She won't likely waken," he heard Ovard tell him. "She can't hear them. She'll be safe if she stays in her tent.

Will she? Brace certainly hoped so. Swirls of what seemed to be gray fog hovered through the camp, accompanied by ear-piercing howls. Zorix snarled, and Leandra hushed him sharply.

"They're right here, right in our camp!" Brace called out. "I know it," Ovard replied.

"What can we do to chase them away?" Jair asked frantically.

"I don't know," Brace told him. "I don't even know what they are."

"Can't you see them?"

"I see *something.*"

"Can we make a fire?" Ovard asked. "I can think of nothing else that might frighten them." His voice was drowned out by a loud, shrill shrieking.

"Do you have a flint?" Brace asked.

"I do."

Brace swallowed and nervously licked his dry lips, still clutching his knife. "I think I remember how far it was to the campfire. We had some extra wood left, didn't we?"

"We did."

"Is it wise to go out there?" Leandra asked hesitantly.

No one answered for some time, while the screeching sounds grew louder and gray whorls of fog churned through the black night.

"I think we've got to," Brace said at last. "Ovard! Have your flint ready. I've got my dagger. I'm going after the wood. Arden, as soon as you can see me, cover me, will you?"

"I will."

"I'm going now!" Without another moment's hesitation, not allowing himself to have second thoughts, Brace flung himself headlong out of the tent and into the darkness, scrambling along the ground with his free hand, desperately searching for the pile of unburned branches. Ovard was beside him in an instant; Brace could not see him, but he could hear his quick breathing, and soon felt his hand grasp his shoulder. Screams of complaint filled the air as Brace continued blindly running his hands along the stony ground until he felt the roughness of tree bark. Closing his fingers around it, he held it tightly.

"Grass!" he exclaimed. "Or moss. Something! Ovard, we need something to get the fire started." In a heartbeat, Ovard answered him. "Here it is. Give me your knife. I'll try to get a spark going."

Slowly, carefully, Brace surrendered his dagger and listened through the screeching as Ovard struck the blade against his flint. Gusts of wind rushed past his head, as if stirred by the wings of low-flying bats.

"Come on, come on," Brace urged as tiny sparks jumped from the stone and disappeared.

"If I can just get one spark to catch," Ovard muttered.

"What are you doing out there?" Leandra called to them. "Light a fire!"

"We're trying!" Brace shouted back, ducking his head as a puff of cold gray fog rushed at him.

"There!" Ovard cried out in relief. Looking up, Brace could see a tiny hint of orange glow working its way through a bunch of dried moss.

"That's it, that's it!" Brace held the end of the narrow branch just above the embers and blew softly. *Gently, gently,* he told himself, fighting against the feeling of panic that had taken hold of him. *It won't do to put the fire out. Blow gently.*

Finally, a flame took hold of the twig, creating a small circle of light. Brace turned, slowly moving the branch until he could see more of the firewood. Snatching up two pieces, he thrust one into Ovard's hands and took the other himself. In another moment, three dancing flames pierced the thick blackness that surrounded them.

Brace stood, lifting the branches high overhead while Ovard hurried to build a substantial fire. The high-pitched shrieking took on a distraught edge as arcs of gray, swirling fog retreated from the light. As the flames grew, Brace looked around until he spotted the dimly lit figure of Arden standing in the entrance to his tent, his bow drawn.

The eerie sounds quickly faded into the distance, and soon Brace heard only the snapping of burning wood and his own heavy breathing. He crouched low, placing the burning twigs onto the strong, steady blaze, then turned to look back at the tent where only moments ago he'd been asleep. Jair was peering out anxiously.

"Are they gone?" he asked in a timid voice.

Brace looked around, and Ovard did the same.

"I think so," Brace replied, pressing his palm against his forehead and pushing back his hair. "I can't hear them now."

"Neither can I," Ovard added as Arden slowly lowered his bow.

"What were they?"

Brace took a deep breath before turning again to face Jair. "I don't know. I couldn't really see anything."

"Whatever they were," Ovard spoke in an exhausted voice, "the fire did the work of chasing them off. Your knife, Brace," he added, holding it out to him hilt first. "Thank you."

"Of course." Brace retrieved his blade and slipped it into his boot, then took another breath. "Maybe someone should go and check on Tassie?"

"I'll do it." Leandra pushed her way past Arden, stepping into the open night air with a posture that showed her wariness, yet determination. The three men stood in silence. What was there to be said? None of them had any idea what they were up against.

Only a moment passed before Leandra returned. "Tassie is still asleep," she reported. "She's all right."

Arden took Leandra's arm and pulled her close as though shielding her from danger.

"I don't think Tassie should sleep alone out here," Leandra told him. "If those creatures can get into tents, she needs protection."

Arden swallowed wordlessly, then nodded. "You'd have to be the one to do it." Resignation was heavy in his voice. He knew that Leandra was right once again, but Brace could easily see that he did not like the idea of spending the nights without his wife safely by his side.

Brace heard the entrance flap to his tent rustle, and he turned to look.

"No, Jair," Ovard called out firmly. "You stay in there!"

"But they're gone," Jair argued, halfway out of the tent.

"They are gone," Ovard agreed. "So we can go back to our beds. Try to get some more sleep." Turning to Arden, he rubbed the side of his bearded face. "We're going to have to be prepared," he told him. "I think we're going to need to keep a fire burning every night. We'll need to stay awake in turns to watch over it as well."

Arden nodded in agreement. "I'll take the first watch tonight. Leandra, you should go and stay with Tassie."

"You'll be all right?" Leandra asked.

"I will."

Leandra gazed at the flames a moment, then at Tassie's hide tent. Finally, she turned back toward Arden. "I will go to her, then. But my knife—it's still in our tent. I'll go and get it. I'll tell Zorix to stay with you."

Arden shook his head. "He'll want to be at your side. That's where I would want to be."

Leandra ran her hand along Arden's unshaven face, then pulled him toward her, kissing him gently on the cheek, then his lips. Arden let his bow drop to the ground as he gathered Leandra in his arms, holding her tightly as though he feared he would lose her if he let her go.

Brace stood close to the fire with his arms wrapped around himself under his wool cloak. He was shivering still, but not only from the cold mountain air. He didn't think he had ever been so frightened in his life as he had been tonight, not since he had been a child and the first time his guardian had come rushing at him threatening to beat him.

Glancing back over his shoulder, he could see Jair sitting in the entrance to their tent. Choosing obedience to Ovard, he had not come to join them at the fire, but he had not crawled back under his blanket either.

Gazing again at the snapping yellow-orange bursts of flame, Brace flinched when he felt a hand on his arm.

"You should try to get more rest," Ovard told him, his own face lined with exhaustion and worry.

Brace took a steadying breath. "Sleep?" he asked with a melancholy smirk. "I don't think I could sleep, after all of that."

"You must try, just the same. We're all of us going to be needed, keeping watch in turns at night. We need to be well-rested for the journey through the mountains."

Brace nodded in response. His fear was starting to melt away, and a heavy tiredness was replacing it. He turned to face Arden, who now stood alone near the edge of the fire. "Wake me if you need me to take your place?"

"I will," Arden replied. "Thank you."

Giving Ovard a nod, Brace turned away and scuffed the short distance back to Jair's tent in silence. *Strange*, he thought. He seemed to have gone so much farther, scrambling through the dark. He'd been in a panic; reaching the stack of firewood seemed to take an eternity. Those creatures, or whatever they might be ... There was only one thing Brace was left asking himself.

What have I gotten myself into?

It was not difficult for Tassie to pick up on everyone's frayed nerves in the morning, and she wasted no time in pulling Ovard aside to question him about it. Leandra had risen early, so as not to alarm Tassie with the unexpected sight of her there in the tent beside her.

Tassie stood silently absorbing everything Ovard told her of the previous night, her green eyes wide. "Those same creatures you've been hearing?" she asked in alarm. "They were right here, in our camp?"

"They were," Ovard replied. "But fire scares them away. We're going to have to keep one burning every night. And we're going to rearrange where everyone sleeps. Tassie, Leandra will share your tent with you. I don't want you sleeping alone any longer." Tassie nodded at his instruction, and though she didn't say a word, Brace could see that she was not keen to spend the night alone either, not with those strange, shrieking beasts coming out after dark. "Brace will stay with Jair," Ovard continued, "and I will move into Arden's tent. One less tent means less work, and less weight to carry."

"Right," Tassie agreed.

An icy wind whipped across the camp while the small group sat huddled together for a meal before starting off. They pulled extra layers of clothing from their packs as well, and everyone piled on all of the clothes that they possibly could in order to stay warm. Brace had only what he wore, though, and nothing else. Arden had to have noticed, Brace realized, when he came to him offering the use of his gloves. Surprised, he accepted. The honey colored leather was thick, but very soft and smooth.

"They aren't winter gloves by any means," Arden told him. "But they should help keep off the chill, just the same."

"Thank you." Simple words, Brace thought. These were his archer's gloves, he could see from the crest that had been burned into the leather. Costly things.

"It's no trouble, my friend."

As Arden walked away, Brace slipped his hands into the soft leather. The gloves were a bit too large, but they would most assuredly help to keep him that much warmer. An unexpected gift, as much as Arden's friendship itself. Turning, Brace looked up at the rugged stone mountains they would be crossing soon enough. His brown shoulder-length hair swirled around his face in the mountain winds. There it was—the pass, if one could call it that.

When Ovard silently stepped up beside him, Brace was not at all surprised. He'd come to expect that from him.

"Are you going on with us?" Ovard asked him.

"What?" Brace replied, incredulous.

"Are you going on with us, all the way?"

Brace looked back at the high, jagged cliffs, heard the wind howling as it swept over the ridge, and felt the cold all through his body. If there had ever been a time to turn back, it was now.

"I am going all the way," Brace answered. "I made a promise."

Ovard smiled wisely, as only he could.

"When do thieves start keeping promises?"

Brace looked away, staring down at the stony ground. "I don't know," he replied, suddenly feeling ashamed.

"When they are no longer thieves, but honest men."

Brace looked up. "Do you think I'm an honest man?"

Ovard nodded his gray head. "Yes, I do. And I *am* glad to have you with us."

"Do you still believe that it was fated for us to meet?"

"One can never be certain about such things," Ovard said thoughtfully. "But you have truly become a part of us all, Brace. Part of you now lives within each of our hearts, as I am sure part of each of us lives in yours." He smiled again. "Some of us have taken up larger parts than others, I think."

Brace tried to speak, but his voice caught in his throat. "Wh—what?"

"Don't you think I would have noticed the way you look at Tassie?"

Brace tipped his head slightly. "I admit, I do have feelings for her, but ..."

Ovard interrupted, waving his hand. "No, no, it's all right. I approve, truly I do." Ovard was smiling when he laid his hand on Brace's shoulder. "So long as you go about things the right way."

"I don't even know what Tassie feels for me," Brace pointed out.

"She's taken a liking to you as well," Ovard told him. "I have not had much opportunity to speak with her, but I do know my niece. I know that look in her eyes."

Brace was glad to hear him say it, but he shook his head. "None of us knows what we're facing, crossing the mountains, and going on after that for who knows how long. What if we can't find the Haven? This isn't the time for thinking about such things."

The joy left Ovard's eyes at his words. "You are right, now may not be the best of times. Things are difficult. But your life is now, Brace, and so is Tassie's. Some things simply cannot be put aside until later. We don't know what tomorrow holds, that is true. Just as much of a reason not to wait."

Brace nodded in agreement. "I don't know how ready I am."

Ovard smiled once again. "I'm not necessarily talking about marriage, my friend. All I am saying is: tell her. Tell her how you feel about her. See where things will go from there. Will you?"

Brace swallowed, hesitating. "I will."

The stony ground sloped upward toward the foothills as they all went on at last, fighting against the wind blowing in their faces and the cold in their fingers and toes. Loose rocks slipped under Brace's boots so that he stumbled several times, until he learned how to spot them. He hung back a little, keeping Jair and Tassie in his sight. Zorix scurried ahead of Leandra, his claws giving him a good hold as he went, though he stopped often to look back. It was a slow journey until the ground eventually leveled out. Brace was grateful, as he easily made his way across the flat, rocky ground, with small, hearty shrubs pushing their way through cracks all around him. He knew that the way would become harder still, and this easy stretch of rock was a welcome relief.

Ovard suggested that they all stop when they reached a point where the craggy stone jutted high into the air. Glad for the break, they huddled against the wall where the wind was not quite as strong or as cold. Jair leaned against Ovard's side, all but hidden under his own cloak. There was no need to tell the boy to wear his hood, not this day.

"Water," Arden told everyone. "Be sure and drink plenty of water! In this cold, you may not feel your thirst so strongly, but it is there."

Brace watched Tassie as she lifted her flask to her lips. She did not look so encumbered now, with her medic bag worn on her back. They had made good use of the tent that they no longer needed. They transformed Tassie's leather bag into a pack, and each of them now carried with them a rain cloak that covered their heads and their backs. Some of what was left they cut into small pieces and stored among Tassie's jars of herbs and other supplies. The rest they left behind.

As Tassie closed her flask and let it hang from her belt, Brace kept his gaze in her direction. Her eyes eventually met his, and she seemed to be blushing, though the rosy glow on her cheeks could very well be from the cold. It was her coy little smile that Brace wanted to see, but instead, Tassie's face was a mixture of confused emotions. Gritty persistence, longing, and self-doubt could be seen in her eyes and in the set of her mouth. Recalling the words that Ovard had spoken to him, Brace was sorely tempted to go to her now, hold her close, and tell her that he would be there to watch over her, protect her, that she could rely on him—to tell her that he loved her, hoping with all of his heart that she would say the same. But Tassie, he knew all too well, was not the kind of girl who would simply melt into his arms. No, she was strong—much too strong for that.

"I hope we find Haven soon," Jair complained, drawing Brace's attention. "It's so cold here. Do you think it will be cold inside the Haven?"

"Let us hope not," Ovard told him, rubbing the boy's arms, creating warmth. "We can hope that the ancient city remains. There will be walls, and pits for making blazing fires. Try not to think about our troubles. Keep your thoughts on Haven, and what miraculous things we'll find there, things we can't even imagine."

Much more easily said than done, Brace thought as he leaned his head against hard stone. When he closed his eyes, all he could see was thick, heavy darkness, with strange, gray, swirling creatures darting in every direction, and he could almost hear the shrieking. Despite everything he had been through with these people, there were moments when Brace couldn't help but think he'd been crazy to stay with them. There would be no leaving now, that much he knew, but he couldn't shake the doubts and fears that they might not survive the rest of the way to Haven. He was always trying to distract himself from such thoughts, but there they were, chasing him at every turn, leaving him feeling completely exhausted.

~24~

The climbing was slow and difficult, with the icy wind swirling around them, howling through cracks in the high, jagged rock. Although the sun had risen, its light seemed dull and distant. It was all beginning to feel so much more real to Brace than it had—the darkness, the battle of wickedness winning over good—he had long ago come to believe it all, but now he was seeing it for himself. And the night screamers, as Jair had taken to calling them: they were more than just wild beasts. Could it be that they *wanted* the darkness to win? Were they trying to stop anyone from finding Haven?

They were each of them tired and irritable, but Jair was the one most often heard voicing his complaints. The air was too cold, it was too windy, and the way was too hard.

"Whatever happened to you trying to be strong and brave?" Brace challenged him when he complained of his aching legs. "Don't you think the rest of us are aching as well?"

Jair's face was downcast. "I'm not being very brave," he admitted. "I'm just so tired."

Brace softened. "I know you're tired. So am I. Maybe we can share what little strength we have left, and help each other on?"

Jair managed a bit of a smile, pulling tight the scar that had begun forming on his chin. "That sounds good to me. Thank you."

By the time the darkness began to increase around them, they had made their way down the first ridge and found themselves in a narrow, rocky valley. It was small, but provided enough room to put up the tents and make a fire using smooth, gnarled branches from the low, scraggy brush growing among the rocks. Finally able to rest, they were beginning to take notice of the scrapes and bruises they'd incurred while picking their way across the rocky pass. Tassie doled out whatever bandages or ointments had been needed, and Brace rubbed a pungent liquid over a large purple mark on his right shin while he watched Arden tend to a gash on Leandra's elbow.

Brace let his eyes fall on Tassie, who was busy wrapping the fingers on her left hand with narrow cloth bandages. His mind wandered back to what Ovard had told him, that relationships were not to be put off for a future that no one was certain would ever come. He knew that he wanted to pursue a relationship with Tassie, but what had he always done in his past flings? Quite a lot of flirting, that was certain. Stealing away together when no one was watching. And the gifts—he had always lavished his women with gifts, usually something he had stolen. But there were no fancy jeweled hair combs here, no baskets of fresh pears or bunches of exotic flowers. What could he possibly give her? All around them were only bare rocks and sparse bushes. He wasn't skilled in any craft, but Brace thought that just maybe he could make something for her. From what, though?

Brace looked around. Boots, cloak, belt. What did he have that he was not making use of? He ran his hands along his belt until he felt the small leather pouch. Empty. Was this all he had? So be it, then. He pulled at the leather cord and loosed the pouch from his belt, then sat thinking, rubbing his thumb along the smooth, worn leather. What would Tassie truly like? A flower? Recalling the day he'd tried to carve the image of Jair's markings into a piece of wood, Brace thought he might be able to manage cutting through the thin leather pouch.

He slid his dagger from the sheath inside his boot and tested the blade on his thumb. It was quite dull compared to what it could be, but the tip was sharper. Maybe he could make it work.

Eventually, Brace held in his hands an acceptable representation of a seven-pointed star- flower. Looking up, he saw that Tassie was still sitting alone near the fire. *Now is just as good a time as any*, he told himself as he rose and made his way toward her.

When he stood directly beside her, she looked up at him, her eyes tired but curious. Brace tried to smile, but it came on unevenly. *Why am I so anxious?* he wondered as he sat beside her, clutching his gift. But he really did know the reason. Tassie was more than just a fling, some woman he'd seen in passing. She really had taken up a part of his heart, a piece that would be crushed if she should turn him away.

"How are you feeling?" he asked her.

"All right," she replied with a shrug, holding up her bandaged fingers. "Just a little sore. How are you?"

"The same." Brace hesitated, wondering if he was losing his nerve. Feeling a gentle touch on his arm, he looked up.

"Is something wrong?" Tassie asked.

"No. Nothing's wrong. I … just … wanted to give you something." Without another word, Brace held his palm open before Tassie, revealing the leather star-flower, flat but a bit crumpled.

"Where did you get this?" she asked, picking it up gently. "Did you make this yourself?"

"I did," Brace replied with a shrug. "It may not be the best, but I put my heart into it. I wanted you to have something special."

Tassie sat quietly rubbing the surface of the leather with her fingertips. Brace swallowed. Why did she not say anything?

"Do you like it?" he managed, after lightly touching her arm.

Tassie smiled. "I do. I like it very much. Thank you."

Brace spread his hands in a slight shrug. "I thought you could wear it in your hair, or on your cloak, or something."

Tassie nodded slightly.

That's it? Brace thought. No embrace, no quick kiss? He opened his mouth to say more, but stopped when he heard the same familiar shrieking in the distance.

"Not again," he heard himself saying as he felt a chill run down his back and along his arms.

"What is it?" Tassie asked in alarm.

"Those things again," he told her.

Everyone moved closer to the fire then, as though directed by some unheard command. Arden was not the only one who kept his eyes fixed on the darkness.

"I see them!" Tassie exclaimed, grabbing hold of Brace's arm.

"I do as well," Arden spoke. "But the fire should keep them away, if it's large enough. Everyone stay close to the flames."

No need to tell us that, Brace thought. Far into the darkness—how far he couldn't say—he could see pairs of glowing yellow eyes appearing all around them, like so many tainted stars. He hoped against hope, as he was sure the rest of them did, that their fire would be enough to prevent them from coming into camp.

Fortunately, they were given a reprieve that night. Though the creatures wailed and howled, they did not venture near the flames. When he was certain that they would have no trouble, Ovard told everyone to go and get what sleep they could, that he would keep the first watch. Leandra offered to take the second, volunteering Zorix to stay with Tassie in the tent. Her large-eared furry companion stared plaintively at her for some time, until she drew him close, and in their own silent way, she must have been able to find just the right words to put his mind at ease. Zorix followed Tassie willingly enough as she went into her tent, holding the door flap aside for him to enter. Brace hoped that she would give him one last look before she let it fall into place, but she disappeared without so much as a glance, he and his gift apparently forgotten.

Maybe he was only fooling himself. Tassie could very well be fond of him, and have faith in him, but it seemed that she did not love him, at least not as much as Brace was beginning to love her. *Well, so be it*, he told himself. *At least now I know.*

More wind and more cold greeted them the next day. What sunlight they had was very dim as well, as though blocked by a thick fog. Moisture in the air became a light but steady rain, and it wasn't long before their wool cloaks were wet through, and heavy on their backs. Everyone seemed equally miserable now, and Ovard was trying in vain to cheer them and speed them on.

"We are so very close now, I am sure of it," he told them. "The resistance against us is getting stronger. We can't let up now, let's keep our pace up."

There was not much of a pass left, however, and the way was very rocky. They were more climbing than walking now, up and over large boulders, through winding cracks that served as trails.

"Haven will be there when we get to it, Ovard," Leandra spoke up through the wind and rain as she picked her way between two large, uneven stones. "Whether it is soon or late, it *will* be there. Let up a little, please."

"You've always been one of our strongest," Ovard admonished her. "Don't hold back on us now. I know you can keep a quicker pace. I've seen you do it."

"Leave her be, Ovard!" Arden spoke up gruffly, surprising the older man, and the rest of them as well.

He came and knelt beside Leandra, where she had gotten her boot wedged between the rocks. "Are you all right?" he asked gently. Leandra simply nodded, not looking up, the wind sweeping her pale hair across her reddened face.

"What's wrong?" Ovard asked, his tone mild now. Leandra leaned against the rock as Arden pulled her foot free. She did not answer. Brace thought she seemed to be looking at her husband, a questioning look in her eyes. "Leandra, what *is* wrong?"

Arden nodded, a very slight movement, and it was only then that Leandra looked up.

"I ... I am *pregnant*, Ovard."

The older man was visibly taken back by her words. Brace was quite shocked as well, and as he glanced around at the others, he could see surprise on every face, all but Tassie's. She had to have known. She was likely the one who had verified Leandra's pregnancy. No one dared speak as they waited for Ovard's response. Slowly, laboriously, he climbed his way back to where Leandra half-sat against the side of the rocky peak. Ovard braced himself for balance and leaned toward her.

"Why did you not tell me?" he asked.

"I didn't want to burden you," she replied. "I didn't want everyone to feel like they have to go more slowly on account of me."

Ovard took a breath and rubbed at his beard. "How far along are you?"

"I'm not sure, exactly. Not far, but far enough."

"Arden, you knew this?"

"I did," he admitted.

"You should have told me," Ovard scolded them. "I would have understood."

"Forgive us, please," Arden replied. "There has been so much going on, so many things we've all had to struggle with. There never seemed to be the right time to say it."

Brace noticed tears running down Leandra's face, though she made not a sound.

Ovard let out a sigh. "It's all right now," he said more gently. "It's done. We know now. Believe me, Leandra, I would have shown more understanding if I'd known."

Leandra nodded, pushing away her tears. Ovard looked around, seeing that everyone stood watching him. "Let's ..." he began, then paused. "Let's just see how far we can get today. Let's just keep an even pace, shall we?"

"Thank you," Leandra told him.

Ovard smiled, nodded, then turned and picked his way along the rocks, searching for the best path. Arden took Leandra's arm and guided her through a few difficult steps over rocks jutting from the side of the cliff.

"I'm all right, I truly am," Leandra said, her voice raised to carry through the wind, so that everyone could hear. Brace gave her a smile as she and Arden neared him.

"Congratulations," he told them. "It's good news ..." His voice drifted off when he saw their somber faces. "It *is* good news, isn't it?"

"It is," Arden told him. "It's only that ..."

"We don't know what's going to happen," Leandra finished for him. "If we find the Haven soon, and it's all we hope it to be, things will be all right. But, if we don't ..."

Arden shook his head. "This dark world is not a safe place for a newborn baby."

"What will you do then?" Brace asked.

"We'll have to try to make do the best we can," Leandra replied, running her hand along her stomach. She had not yet began to show, but knowing that she carried a child within her drew a tender touch.

Jair made his way across the rocks toward them. "You're going to have a baby, then? I'm happy for you," he said, smiling again at last.

Leandra smiled back and mussed his hair.

"I hope you'll want to be our child's good-uncle," she told him.

"Me?" Jair asked, his eyes widening. "You want *me* to be the good-uncle?"

"Yes, we do," Arden spoke up, finally beginning to show signs of relaxing. "One of them." Brace noticed when Arden and Leandra both turned their faces toward him as one. For a moment, he thought he would choke on his own breath.

"You and Ovard as well," Leandra told him softly. "Our child will have three good-uncles, and one good-aunt. He—or she—will be very well looked after."

Brace was so full of emotion that he thought he might burst. "What can I say?" he managed. "I never thought anyone would ever ask me anything like this."

"Say yes," Arden suggested, grinning.

Brace let out a quick breath of laughter. "Yes, I will. Of course I will."

Tassie came forward, held Leandra in a tight embrace, then gave Arden a kiss on his scruffy cheek.

"I'm so glad that's not a secret any longer," she said, smiling. "Now come on. We had better get going again. It's cold and wet, but moving around makes me feel warmer, and I'm sure it's the same for the rest of you."

What she said was true, of course, so move on they did. Ovard did not push them nearly so hard now that he was aware of the tiny life growing inside of Leandra's womb. By the time the darkness began to close in around them, they had already stopped in an area of slightly sloping rock flat enough to put up their tents. The scrub brush was sparse there, so they had to wander long and far to find enough dry wood to make the fire they so desperately needed. It would be a small one, though, Brace realized when everyone combined what little wood they'd been able to gather. If they wanted the fire to last through the night—which they most certainly did—they would need to use it sparingly.

As the early dusk faded farther into the black of night, the flames snapping at the meager heap of firewood barely illuminated past the tops of Brace's boots while he stood gazing down at it, as though by sheer will he could make it grow larger. When the high-pitched cries could at last be heard in the distance, Brace could see fear in Ovard's gray-green eyes.

"Will it be enough?" Brace asked him quietly. "Will the fire be enough to keep those things away?"

Ovard looked at him, doubt written heavily across his lined face. "I truly hope so."

They got their answer much sooner than any of them expected it.

No. Moist, cold, gray wisps of fog came arching around them, over their heads, while the creatures causing the wake wailed in shrill, ear-piercing cries. Everyone dove lower to the ground, trying to keep out of their path. Zorix snarled, baring his teeth, and Leandra pulled him close.

"Stay with me!" she told him firmly.

The creatures—they had no bats' wings, Brace could see, but still they moved with ease through the night air, leaving trails of smoky fog in their wake.

"Battle stance!" he heard Arden shout, grabbing a long, flaming branch from beside the fire and clutching it in both hands.

Battle stance?

Leandra understood his meaning well enough. She moved to stand behind him, her back to him. She drew her heavy knife. Its large blade flashed, reflecting light from their small fire.

Of course!

"Ovard!" Brace called out, taking another branch, lighting the end in the flames, and swinging it about him. "Here! We'll guard one another's backs!"

With a quick nod of understanding, the older man moved into position, waving a fiery branch at an approaching night screamer.

Jair was squirming where he crouched low, caught in Tassie's firm grasp.

"Let me help you!" he called out. "I can fight them off too!"

"No, Jair!" Ovard replied, his voice loud and full of fear. "You stay safe. Get into one of the tents with Tassie and stay there!"

"Please!" Jair begged. "I want to help!"

"No!" Came Ovard's firm reply. "Get to safety—now!" He swung as another creature zipped past him. "Watch over Tassie," he added. "That is how you can help us."

Jair resigned himself to Ovard's directions, but Brace could see the disappointment on his face as he pulled Tassie into the nearest tent. All too quickly, they were surrounded by night screamers on all sides. They came on, unafraid and shrieking so loudly that Brace could feel their cries piercing through his skull. The flaming branches answered back with swooshing sounds of their own as Arden, Brace, and Ovard swung them at the creatures.

"Ouch!" Brace cried out when he felt the heat of fire on his hands. The twig he'd been using to defend himself had burned down so far that he had no choice but to drop it to the stony ground. Without a moment's hesitation, he reached down and pulled his dagger from his boot. When the next puff of gray came near, he swung his blade, but it passed right through—it was only air!

Brace ducked as the creature careened unhindered past his head. Leandra was having no better a time with her wide, heavy blade. She brought her left arm up over her face and was waving her knife through the air, hoping it would be enough to at least hinder the approaching screamers. Despite seeming to be made of air, one of them had somehow been able to draw blood, either clawing or biting at her hand. Zorix, meanwhile, sat hunched at her feet, bristling and snarling.

Brace cast a quick glance at the dying flames beside him. "It's no good!" he told Ovard, keeping his back to him. "We need more to burn."

"We haven't got more to burn!" Ovard replied.

"Not wood, no," Brace agreed, looking around. "But something—we must have something here that will burn. We need to make the flames bigger. We have no other choice!"

"Right," Ovard agreed, swinging what remained of his burning branch before adding to the fire. "Arden! Leandra!" he called out. "Give us cover!"

"What can we burn?" Brace asked frantically as he and Ovard rushed across the camp toward their half-empty packs. "One of the tents?"

"No," Ovard answered quickly. "They're too thick, they will take too long to catch. Here!" He pulled one of the large woolen blankets from inside. "Cut it into strips. Quickly!"

Brace forced the blade of his dagger through the fabric, and Ovard pulled at it, tearing along its length until it came free.

"Another!" he instructed, and Brace obeyed, again and again, until they had a heap of long, narrow strips piled at their feet.

"Add one at a time," Ovard shouted over the cries of night screamers. "Carefully; don't smother the flames."

Brace watched as Ovard coiled a piece of the wool blanket around the pile of burning twigs. The cloth began to smoke, then burst into flames.

"Yes!" Brace cried out in relief. "It's working!"

"Keep adding to it," Ovard told him. "One at a time."

As the flames began to grow and the brightness increased, the attacking creatures began shrieking in dismay, retreating farther into the darkness. Suddenly, a loud yowling filled the air. Leandra gasped and collapsed to the ground, falling onto her hands and knees, her knife grating sharply on the rocks. Arden was at her side in an instant.

"What happened?" he asked, quickly looking her over to see if she had been injured. "Leandra, what happened?"

"Zorix!" she exclaimed. "Where is he?"

Arden glanced around. "I don't see him."

"Find him!" Her voice was pained and full of desperation.

Arden obeyed in a hurry, grabbing up one of the larger branches, lighting the end, and rushing into the dark night, his heavy boots pounding the rocks at his feet. "Zorix!" Brace could hear Arden's voice calling out across the mountains, while he and Ovard stood guard over the fire, breathing heavily from exertion. "*Zorix!*" Arden's voice sounded so far away, and Leandra still knelt on the cold, hard rock, her eyes shut tightly.

Ovard moved to kneel by her side, resting his hand on her back. "Arden will find him."

Leandra opened her eyes and took a steadying breath, leaving her knife on the ground and pushing her hair away from her face.

"He's been hurt," she said, her voice strained. "I can feel it."

"He can't have gone very far," Brace told her. "Arden will find him. He won't stop looking until he does. None of us will."

Leandra looked up and nodded. "I can't hear him," she muttered.

Zorix? Brace wondered. *Or Arden?* He couldn't hear anything either. The night had become completely quiet.

"I'll go and help him look," Brace decided suddenly. He turned to find a branch that would make a sufficient torch to light his way, but stopped when he saw Arden returning to camp, Zorix creeping along slowly beside him.

"There now, he's come back," Ovard said joyfully. "The both of them."

Leandra sucked in a breath as she pulled herself up from the ground and stumbled toward them. When she reached Arden, she leaned against him for a moment.

"I tried to carry him back," Arden told her. "He wouldn't let me."

Leandra slowly went to her knees and reached toward Zorix, her hands shaking. She took his small face in her hands and looked into his eyes. After a long moment of silence, she pulled him into her arms.

"I told you not to wander off," she said, burying her face in his fur.

Zorix only moaned.

Brace stood helplessly beside Ovard, the snapping flames at their feet. "Do you think he'll be all right?"

"Hard to say," Ovard replied. "Leandra will know better than I would."

"They are gone now, aren't they?" Jair's voice called out.

"They are," Ovard told him.

"Can we please come out there?"

"It should be safe enough," Brace told Ovard when he hesitated.

Ovard nodded. "You can come out now. Come close to the fire."

Jair turned back toward the tent and spoke quietly to Tassie, who followed him outside when he came toward them. She was hesitant and fearful though, Brace could see that clearly enough. She looked around anxiously at the surrounding darkness, her hands curled up under her chin, and she was shivering, either from the cold or from fear.

"Go to her," Brace heard a quiet voice telling him. He turned and looked questioningly at Ovard. "You should go to her," he repeated.

Brace swallowed. "I don't know if she'll want me," he told him. "Maybe you should."

But Ovard shook his head. "I've been there to comfort her all her life. Now it's your turn."

"All right," Brace replied with a nod.

Ovard gave Brace an encouraging pat on his back as he left his place beside the fire, slowly making his way toward Tassie.

"Are you all right?" he asked her.

When she didn't answer, he realized that she hadn't seen his face. He took a step closer and repeated his question.

"I ... I don't know," she said quietly. "Those *things*. I could see their eyes glowing. I saw their teeth, their claws." She stopped, wrapping her arms around herself. "They were so close, Brace. I could almost feel them."

"I know, I know. So could I."

"How are we supposed to keep fighting them off, night after night?" she shook her head. "And Zorix," she continued. "What's wrong with Zorix?"

"I'm not sure," Brace replied hesitantly. "I think one of the screamers might have bitten him."

Tassie pressed her hand over her mouth in alarm. "Brace, I ... I don't know anything about those creatures or how to treat wounds made by them. If anything happens to Zorix—Leandra ... she ..." She started to turn away, but Brace caught her arm and pulled her into his embrace.

"It's going to be all right," he told her, knowing full well that she couldn't hear him, or see his face, leaning her head against his shoulder, crying quietly. But he needed to hear the words himself, though he was not quite certain that he believed them.

~ 25 ~

Night settled deeply around them, but tired though they were, for a long time none of them slept. Zorix had indeed been attacked by at least one of the night screamers. The wound on his back left leg was bleeding into his red-orange fur, and Tassie did what she could, pouring water mixed with her cleansing powder over his leg, causing him to yowl. Then she had wrapped the leg tightly with several layers of bandages. She instructed Leandra to keep Zorix still, but there was no need to fear him moving about. What kind of pain the poor creature must be feeling, Brace couldn't begin to imagine, but Zorix made it clear that he had no intention of moving from his place in Leandra's arms. His round, black eyes were shut, and his large ears drooped limply.

Eventually, Jair, sitting near the fire, grew so tired that he sank down to the ground and lay sleeping on his side, with only the edge of his cloak for bedding. Ovard woke him gently, just long enough to lead him, half-stumbling, back to the shelter of his hide tent. Arden did all he could to try and comfort Leandra, and although she graciously accepted his efforts, it had not been enough to erase the lines of worry from her face, as she sat stroking Zorix's head.

From where he now sat beside Tassie, Brace could see worry and exhaustion on every face, just as he was certain that they could see the same on his own. One thing, at least, Brace found to be a blessing. He and Tassie sat on the opposite side of the now healthy blaze from Ovard, Arden, and Leandra, and with the sound of the crackling flames, he was able to speak quietly to her, without anyone overhearing. He was in quite a state of confusion concerning where he stood with Tassie. She didn't react the way he had hoped she would when he gave her his gift. At the same time, it was fresh in Brace's mind that she didn't pull away when he'd held her for the first time, to comfort her. In fact, she had leaned into his arms, as though it were the most natural thing she could do. Had it only been because she was distraught? Or did she truly care for him? He had to know.

Gently placing his hand over hers where it rested in her lap, he drew her tired gaze.

"Tassie?" he began, unsure.

"What is it?"

"There is something I've been thinking about. Something I'd like to ask you."

Is this foolishness? Brace wondered to himself.

"All right." Tassie seemed wary, not knowing what his question might demand of her, as though she doubted that she had the strength to face it.

"When I gave you the leather flower," Brace went on before he lost his nerve, "I was hoping—or expecting ... well, I was hoping you would truly like it."

"I do like it," she told him, confused.

"But do you know why I gave it to you?" Brace kept his hand over hers, and squeezed it a little. "I meant for it to be more than just a gift of friendship. I was hoping you would have seen that. All day, I've been hoping to see you wearing it. It would have told me that just maybe ..." Brace paused, gathering his courage to go on. "Just maybe you could be falling in love with me, the way I'm falling in love with you. Maybe ..."

As he looked into her eyes, he noticed a change in them, from bewilderment to understanding, and he saw as well when her eyes began to shine with pleasure.

"But I have been wearing it," she told him, loosening her hand from his grasp and pulling at the clasp on her cloak. Pushing it away from her shoulders, she reached into the top of her jerkin and pulled out the small leather star-flower, its long ties dangling.

"I've been wearing it over my heart," she explained. "From your heart to mine. I know what you meant by this gift, Brace. And it means more to me than you could ever guess."

"Why didn't you tell me?" Brace asked.

Tassie glanced away for only a moment. "Everything is so hard just now, for all of us. So many things ..."

"I thought the same, at first," Brace admitted. "But," he smirked, "a very wise man told me that relationships are too precious a thing to be put off until later."

Tassie smiled then. "Ovard," she guessed.

"Ovard," Brace replied with a grin.

"He is right. They are precious things."

"What should we do, then?" Brace asked, taking her hand once more. His fingers touched the leather flower, still warm from the heat of her body. "What do you want me to do?"

"Kiss me," Tassie whispered.

Brace swallowed, surprised. "Kiss you? Now?"

Tassie nodded. "Yes, now."

Brace felt a smile tugging at his lips. Why shouldn't he? No matter that they weren't alone. He leaned toward her, running his calloused hand over her soft brown curls as their lips met. It felt like the most natural thing on earth to him, as though he was meant to kiss her. The cold night air seemed to vanish as a comforting warmth spread through him. When he finally moved away, ever so slightly, he could see in Tassie's eyes that she felt the same.

"This is right, isn't it?" he asked her. "You and me?"

Tassie nodded, her face flushed. "I think it is, Brace."

Was this real? All those years, all those other girls, other women—it hadn't been real, had it? It had all felt exciting and worthwhile to Brace at the time, his sly ways of catching their attention, followed by the two of them sneaking around to be together. A game, hoping no one would notice them. But he'd never really known their hearts, not a single one of them. Not the way he knew Tassie: The way she cared about others, wanting to be a medic, to help and to heal. Her shy, demure side and her feisty side.

"Some day," Brace began, "when this is all over, when we find Haven, you and I—we could be one, the way Arden and Leandra are one. Would you like that? Would you want to spend the rest of your life with a rogue thief like me?"

Tassie smiled her wise smile. "You are no rogue thief," she told him. "And yes. Yes, I think I would."

When Brace turned in for some much-needed rest, his heart felt light. He was sure that the gleam in his eyes or the smile that he couldn't seem to get off of his face would give Jair reason to question him, but fortunately, the boy was sleeping deeply.

Tassie truly cared for him! Brace wondered if this could be a dream. If he was asleep, he wanted to stay that way. If he was really awake, he knew he would dream as if sleeping on a cloud! If he could only get to sleep! His mind and heart were full of thoughts and emotions he'd assumed he would never need to deal with. When he pictured Tassie's face behind his closed eyes, his heart skipped a beat. She'd said yes! She said she could see herself spending the rest of her life with him! Continuing on as a thief, Brace knew, would be out of the question now. How could he, if he stayed with Tassie? She had goals, she had dreams, and she had convictions. Brace's life would belong to her, as much as she would belong to him.

He let out a sigh, trying to slow his thoughts. *There will be time to consider all of this*, he told himself. *It doesn't need to be now.* He did need to get some sleep.

She'd told him not to say a word about their conversation, but when Brace told her that Arden and Ovard both knew of his feelings for her, she'd blushed a little, nodding. She said she was aware of that, but with the added concerns of Leandra's pregnancy and Zorix's injury, they all needed to focus on working together to find Haven as quickly as they could. If the night screamers really were trying to stop them, then they could expect the attacks to get worse as they got closer to their goal.

She was right, of course. *There will be time for all of that later,* Brace told himself again. *Sleep now! You won't be any help to anyone if you're walking around in a half-sleep all day tomorrow.*

Aside from Tassie and Brace, the rest of them went off to sleep with heavy hearts. The gray half-light of daybreak did little to warm the weary travelers when morning came, nor did it do much to lift their spirits. Zorix had not improved. When Leandra gave him small pieces of dried meat, he ate them, but very slowly. Concerned, Ovard asked whether Leandra thought he could go on.

"I'll have to carry him," she replied.

The sack of black beans was nearly empty, so Arden poured what was left in with the remaining barley. Using the bean sack and strips of leather, he made a sling for Leandra to carry Zorix in, so she could keep her hands free.

Packing the tents away was an especially slow and laborious task, with their tired and aching arms and legs, and the constant wind blowing cold over the flat area of rock. Brace allowed himself to steal a few sideways glances at Tassie. Once or twice he caught her eye, and he winked at her, making her blush and shake her head at him, a tiny smile on her lips. *Get back to work, you silly thing*, she seemed to be telling him.

The mountain cliff, as rugged as ever, rose ahead of them as they continued westward. Several times, their boots knocked stones loose as they picked their way upward, and once, a large section of rock slid out from underneath Tassie's feet, causing her to throw herself sideways against the rock to keep from sliding down with it. Fortunately, the pack she was wearing broke her fall.

Unfortunately, she carried her medical supplies inside the pack, along with the jar of honey, which had broken wide open. Its contents oozed all over everything else in the leather bag—wooden bowls, rags for bandages, and jars of powders, large and small. Balanced precariously among the rocks, the rest of them did what they could to help Tassie clean up the sticky mess. They were not about to waste any of their precious supply of drinking water, so they made use of the already sullied rags to wipe away the remaining traces of honey from Tassie's supplies. Jair sucked every bit of honey from his fingers, knowing it would be the last time he would be able to enjoy the taste of it; for how long a time, no one knew. Tassie seemed to be near tears the entire time.

"Are you hurt?" Brace asked her, leaning in close. "When you fell, did you scrape something?"

"No," she told him. "I'm not hurt."

"What's wrong, then?"

"We could have used that honey."

Brace shook his head. "It's just honey. We have other food. We'll be fine."

"I know that," she replied. "But not Zorix. He doesn't want to eat. The honey would have at least given him a bit of nourishment to keep his strength up." She wiped at her eyes. "But now it's gone."

Brace looked up the side of the mountain, where Arden and Leandra were ascending once again, followed by Jair and Ovard, who was looking back at them.

"Please don't worry," Brace said, trying to comfort her. "Try not to let it upset you. Zorix will eat when he's hungry. He's just hurting, that's all." He offered Tassie his hand, helping her along. He honestly hoped that he was not lying to her.

"Try and keep going," Ovard called to everyone over the noise of the wind. "We have gone over so many peaks now, it could be that this will be the last."

"I certainly hope so," Brace muttered to himself, but he was not about to place any bets on the matter. Unfortunately, his thoughts proved true. When they finally reached the crest of the peak, before them stretched yet another rough, stony mountain.

"This isn't the end?" Jair cried out. "Do these mountains go on forever?"

Arden stood, his feet wide, breathing hard as he looked out across the windswept landscape. "Keep your chin up, lad," he said, running his fingers through his hair. "One step at a time."

"But we've crossed so many mountains already! What if they *do* go on forever?"

"Nothing goes on forever," Ovard told him. "We'll just keep on as well we can, one step at a time."

"I don't want to do this anymore!" Jair shouted. "I'm so cold. It's so dark. Everything is going wrong. Look what happened to Zorix. Look what happened to Arden. Look what happened to my face. I'm tired of people getting hurt. And I'm so tired of being afraid!"

Ovard went to Jair and firmly took hold of his shoulders as the boy started to cry.

"I'm afraid too, Jair. We all are. We're all cold, and hungry, and tired. But we can't give up." Ovard wrapped his arms tightly around him. "*You* can't give up, Jair. Please don't give up."

"I can't do it," Jair sobbed. "I just can't."

"You can. If we stop now, we'll just be stuck in these mountains. We'll stay cold and hungry. If we give up now, we'll never find out how amazing Haven is. You know it's out there, don't you? It's waiting for us."

"Yes," Jair answered through his tears. "I know it is. There are just so many mountains."

"I know, son," Ovard told him gently. "Don't let the hardships weigh you down. Do you remember why we started out? It seems so long ago, but do you remember?"

"Yes," Jair answered. "I do. Your books—the prophecies about the times changing. Men's hearts growing hard, the skies growing dark, all of it. It's happening now."

"It is," Ovard agreed, looking up to face each of them as they gathered in closer. "And it's up to us to try to do something to stop it. We *cannot* give up now."

Jair pulled himself free of Ovard's embrace and wiped his face on the sleeve of his roughspun shirt. "I'm sorry."

Arden cleared his throat, and Jair turned toward him.

"We are all in this together," the archer told him. "*Harbrost—* honor and courage. We need it now more than ever, don't we?"

Jair nodded. "I'll try and do better. I'm just so *tired.*"

"Let's take a rest now, shall we?" Ovard suggested. "We can gather our strength for the climb down."

"Yes," Tassie spoke up. "Everyone drink some water. But not too much. We need to make it last as long as we can."

Brace found a place flat enough to sit and lowered his aching body onto the rock with a groan. He watched as Leandra tried to encourage Zorix to eat more of the dried meat, but he turned his face away, never opening his eyes. The end of his long, thin tail hung limply out the side of the sling, and his fur was losing its sheen, fading to a pale yellow-gray.

"He isn't doing well, is he?" he asked Ovard quietly, when Jair was out of range of hearing. The older man shook his head.

"No, I'm afraid he is not."

"What can be done for him?"

"None of us knows. Tassie says she knows nothing about this type of wound."

"She was mourning the loss of the honey," Brace told him. "She said it would have helped, at least a little."

"That's true enough, it would have. He needs to eat to stay strong, and so do the rest of us."

There was very little left for any of them to eat, the truth be told. Bits of dried meat and a handful or two of Milena's vine peas was all they had that did not require water and a hot fire for cooking.

They'd been stopping so much more frequently now than they did at the beginning. Brace remembered the days when they were just south of Lidden and Bale, when they stopped only at midday to eat, and in the evening to make camp. Now, it seemed that they stopped every hour, though with the sky as gray and hazy as it was, a person needed to look that much harder to make out the position of the sun.

Somehow, they managed to make their way down the side of the last peak they'd climbed, and were now nearing the top of the next. What they would see once they reached the windy summit, none of them could guess. No one dared speak any words of hope either, knowing it would be that much harder if—or when—more mountains appeared, stretching out endlessly before them. Too many things had been dashed against the rocks already—elbows, knees, the last of their honey—they did not need to dash their hopes as well.

Brace pulled himself along one step at a time, using his hands nearly as much as his feet. When his head cleared the top of the rise, a strong, cold gust of wind pushed his hair across his face, blocking his view. Brushing it away with one of his gloved hands, he held his breath as he gazed ahead. A damp fog moved quickly across the land, carried along by the strong, steady wind. Arden came up beside him before Brace could determine what lay in front of them.

"More mountains?" he asked, breathing hard.

"I can't tell," Brace replied. "I can't see through the fog."

At least this time, it was a natural fog, not created by night screamers flying wingless through the night air. In a moment, Brace felt a hand grasp his shoulder, and he looked back to see Jair peering over the side of the mountain beside him, while Leandra, Ovard, and Tassie joined him.

"Let's all catch our breath," Arden told them, running his sleeve across his forehead.

"What's out there?" Jair asked.

"Can't see it," Brace replied. "We'll have to wait for the fog to clear a bit."

The cold wind drove at them, like so many knives of ice. Waiting was hard, but wait they did, taking time for another mouthful of water and a chance for their hard breathing to ease up.

After some time, when the fog still had not cleared away, Brace grew weary of staring at it and turned away, catching Tassie's eye. He smiled at her, and she smiled back, placing her hand over her heart, over the leather star-flower that Brace knew was hidden inside her jerkin.

"What is that?" Jair's voice drew Brace's attention, and he turned to look out over the precipice.

"Out there," Jair continued. "That's not another mountain, is it?"

The fog had finally begun to clear and was trailing along in thin, curling wisps. The land below them was wide and flat, covered with a blanket of high evergreens. Along the horizon towered what appeared at first glance to be another row of mountains. It was high, almost as high as the peak where they all stood, looking down. Very high, and very wide, and very smooth. A mass of solid gray.

"No mountain I've seen has ever looked quite like that," Leandra spoke up, cradling Zorix in her arms.

"Do you see that?" Ovard added, pointing. "Do you see how the far sides seem darker than it does in the center?"

"I do," Brace replied. "What are you getting at?"

"It seems higher in the center as well," Ovard went on, undeterred.

"What does that mean?" Jair asked.

"The shape," Ovard said, grinning widely through his beard. He pressed his fingertips together, curving his hands inward. "Do you see what shape it has?"

"It's a crescent moon," Tassie spoke up.

"It is," Ovard told her. Pointing his finger straight at Jair's surprised face, he added, "Just like *that* one!"

~ 26 ~

Climbing down the last of the rocky cliffs, they made it a point to go slowly. Seeing the high, gray, crescent-shaped wall of stone gave them a sudden renewal of energy, brought on by a surge of hope. The words went unspoken, but the thoughts on every mind were the same—could this be the end of their long journey? Could they be on the brink of finding Haven at last? Gladly leaving the mountains behind them, they edged their way into the level, wooded valley. The entire stretch of land was in shadow, and though the strong winds could not reach them through the limbs of the trees covering their heads, it was damp and cool. Brace was glad to be draped in his long wool cloak, and for the use of Arden's leather gloves.

Enormous trees surrounded them on all sides. Fearing there may be wild animals as well—the natural sort—Arden drew his bow, clutching it tightly in his fist as he walked on at the head of the procession.

"We must be cautious," Arden spoke, finally breaking the silence. "If something is trying to stop us from finding Haven, entering it may not be an easy thing."

Entering Haven! Could it possibly happen, really and truly? Tassie came up beside Brace, took his hand, and squeezed it tightly.

"Is this really happening?" she asked quietly. Brace opened his mouth to speak, but couldn't find the right words.

"It seems to be." He shrugged his shoulders, then squeezed her hand in return.

The blanket of fallen needles from the towering evergreens crunched beneath Brace's boots as he followed Arden toward *something*. Wonders, miracles, Ovard had said. Everything the world so desperately needed to put an end to the darkness. *Somehow.*

The sudden twittering of startled birds overhead made Arden jump, and he glared up at them. Jair continued forward, slowly, but with a look of determination in his eyes.

"This is it," Jair said, staring ahead at the high wall of curved stone. "This is the place." He sounded as though he knew beyond any doubt that they had found the way into Haven at last.

"This," Brace thought aloud, "is just a wall. A very high wall, yes, but still just a wall. It isn't a city. If this is the gate into a city, where is the door?"

"We found the pass through the mountains," Ovard spoke up. "We can find the way into Haven. We just need to look for it."

"Right," Arden agreed with a nod. He turned and cautiously approached the enormous wall of stone. Leandra, cradling her arms around the sling where Zorix huddled against her, lowered herself to the ground. Unstopping her flask, she tried to pour a bit of water for Zorix to drink, but he did not open his mouth.

He looks positively gray, Brace thought. How much longer could he hang on? Leandra looked up at him, tears glistening in her eyes. Brace felt his heart miss a beat.

"Is he all right?" he asked in alarm. "Zorix—he isn't ..."

Leandra shook her head. "He is alive. For the moment." She closed her eyes, looking as though her heart might break in two.

Brace took a step toward her. "Miracles, Leandra," he said. "Haven is supposed to be a place of miracles. Maybe there will be something inside that can help him."

She nodded, her face grim.

"I think I see something!" Arden called out. Brace cast another glance at Zorix and Leandra, then hurried off to join the others while Tassie remained, kneeling at Leandra's side.

"What have you found?" Brace asked when he saw Arden, Ovard, and Jair gathered together, close to the base of the wall.

"A crack," Ovard replied. "It runs all the way to the top, from the look of things."

"Straight and smooth as an arrow," Arden added.

"A crack?" Brace asked. "What good does that do us?"

"There is more," Jair told him. "Down here." He motioned for Brace to follow him as he made his way along the wall toward the left. Ovard followed, but Arden hung back.

"Where are Leandra and Tassie?" he asked.

"Back there a bit," Brace replied, nodding in their direction. "Zorix." He shrugged helplessly.

Arden understood. He took a breath, gathering his strength, then walked toward them, where they sat among the trees.

"Over here," Brace heard Jair call out. When he reached the place where the boy stood waiting, he could easily see what had caught his attention. Strange shapes protruded from the rock wall, in three straight, even rows.

"What is this?" he asked, as Arden stepped up to join them, gently leading Leandra along, with Tassie beside them.

"Some kind of writing, I think," Ovard answered, running his hand along the top row of carved figures—letters, perhaps—which jutted out peculiarly.

"Writing?" Arden asked. "If this marks the entrance into Haven, this could be some kind of message. A welcome, I wonder? Or a warning to keep away?"

Brace slowly shook his head. "I've never seen any writing that looks like any of these shapes."

"Oh, but you have," Ovard told him, gently laying his hands on Jair's thin shoulders and turning him so Brace could see.

"Just there," Ovard continued. "In the crescent moon. The markings on his face, don't you see? They are letters. I've studied them so many times, they are all but burned into my memory. Some of these stone characters seem to match."

"Do they?" Jair asked. "So, what people have been saying is right? I am the key into Haven?"

"It seems you are," Ovard told him.

"But what can we do?" Tassie asked. "We can see the marks on Jair's face, and we can see these stone letters here, but how does that help us? We don't know what the writing tells us."

"No," Jair agreed, running his hand along the stone letters. "This one seems loose."

A creaking sound filled the air, startling all of them, as the letter slowly sank into the stone wall.

"What just happened?" Leandra asked in alarm.

"It disappeared," Jair said in amazement.

Ovard stood staring at the wall, stroking his gray beard, deep in thought. "Could it be?" he muttered under his breath.

"What?" Brace prodded. "What do you think this is all about?" The remaining pale gray light of day was fading quickly. "If you've got something in mind that we should be doing, let's do it!"

"What is it?" Arden added. "Do you think you've deciphered this?" The archer still had his bow ready, and he eyed the woods behind them apprehensively.

"I am thinking," Ovard began, "that the writing on Jair's face is a word, or words. If we match the letters in the correct order ..."

"The door may open?" Leandra finished.

"That's what I'm thinking," Ovard told her.

"That sounds wise to me," Brace spoke up, stepping closer to the wall. Was that the wind he'd heard, high up in the mountains, or were the screamers coming out again? He did not want to wait to find out. "Let's do this."

"All right," Ovard replied. He studied Jair's face a moment, then turned toward the wall, his eyes scanning the carved stone shapes. "This one."

He pressed it gently, and it sunk into the wall with a loud grinding noise.

"It worked!" Jair exclaimed, but in the next moment, each of the stone letters that had sunk into the wall returned to their original positions, flush with the others.

"That wasn't right," Ovard thought aloud. "That first letter, that isn't part of Jair's markings." He pressed the second figure once again, and, as expected, it sunk into the wall once more.

"The next one." Again and again, Ovard studied Jair's face, then cautiously proceeded to gently press each letter in order. He'd gotten nearly halfway through when the next letter that he pressed caused each of them to come rumbling back into place.

"What happened!?" Jair exclaimed in dismay.

"I don't know," Ovard replied, surprised.

"Let me have a look," Arden suggested. He looked intently at the markings on Jair's face, causing the boy to blush under the scrutiny. Then he looked closely at the wall. "What was the last one that you touched?" he asked.

"This one," Ovard told him, pointing, being careful not to brush his fingers against it.

Arden studied the rows of strange-looking stone figures in silence. "I think I see," he finally spoke up. "These two, they look almost exactly the same. Do you see as well? This one, the only difference is this small curve added on the end of it."

"I do see it!" Ovard replied. "Good eye, my friend."

Brace felt the hairs on the back of his neck stand up when a loud, familiar screech echoed through the trees behind him. Screamers— and they were close. Brace turned to Ovard, whose wide eyes revealed he'd heard the sound as well.

"Go faster," Brace managed, his voice tight with fear.

Starting once again from the beginning, Ovard went through each letter quickly but with extreme care. The screeching grew louder and more frantic as he went on. Arden looked in every direction, his face grim. Brace could see puffs of gray smoke drifting through the trees, getting closer. When Ovard finally reached for the last letter, he hesitated. "This must be the one," he addressed the group. "Everyone look at it. Is this right?"

Brace leaned close, peering at Jair's markings, then the wall, back to Jair. "It is," he answered. "Arden? Leandra, Tassie? What do you say?"

They all quickly reached an agreement, and Ovard took a breath. "Now we see what will happen."

As the last stone shape sunk into the wall, a moment passed in silence, while everyone held their breath. The screamers were suddenly silent as well. Without warning, a loud *boom* reverberated through the air. Jair startled and leapt closer to Ovard.

"What is that?" he asked loudly.

A creaking and groaning echoed around them, the sound of stone against stone.

"It's the wall," Arden announced in surprise, stepping away from it. "It's *moving.*"

"It's a door!" Tassie exclaimed.

"Everyone—get back," Brace advised. "It's moving this way."

As everyone moved away quickly, a large section of the high stone wall began to swing slowly outward, scraping along the ground. The night screamers began wailing in loud, shrill voices as they burst out through the trees, barreling toward them. Brace readied himself, his muscles tight, ready for an attack. It never reached him, though. Several yards away from where the group stood, the screamers stopped and turned back the way they'd come, as though they'd hit an unseen wall as high and solid as Haven's gate itself. Frantic now, the strange creatures darted back and forth, desperate to get at the ones who'd managed to open the door, but powerless against some unseen force.

Farther and farther the wall came as it opened, and Brace retreated away from it along with the others, their hearts pounding. When finally it came to a stop, they gathered close, staring through the wide gap that now lay open before them. It was all Brace could do to gaze inward, past the high, gray walls, at what must have been the most brilliant white light that he had ever seen in his life.

~ 21 ~

Come on!" Jair shouted. "They can't get us in there!"

Hurrying through the wide open door in the high stone wall felt to Brace very much like stepping into another world. All he and the others could do was stare in amazement at what lay before them.

Arden kept his head better than any of them. His first thought was to get the door shut behind them. Though it appeared that there was no way for the night screamers to enter, their very presence was unnerving, to say the least. Fortunately, closing the immense stone door was an easy task. A large square plate extended from the wall just beside the opening, and when it was pressed, the door began to swing back slowly, creaking and groaning, drowning out the night screamers until, when it was at last fully shut, their eerie sounds could not be heard at all. Once Arden was satisfied that they were all quite safe, he at last joined the others and began to look around him.

Yes, another world! Brace thought. The forested stretch of land at their backs was cool and shadowy, but the open area before them shone brightly, and emanated a strange warmth. The light was near blinding at first, but as his eyes adjusted to the change, Brace could just make out the walls of a wide, sprawling city spreading out before them, seemingly endless.

As he walked by, Jair let his fingers trail the stone walls lightly, then gazed at his fingertips. "They are warm," he said, in a quiet, almost reverent voice. Ovard simply stood, looking over it all. How many years, Brace wondered, had he dreamed of this moment? And here it was. All of that time, all of the secrets, the sacrifices he had made, for himself, and for Tassie and Jair as well, it was all proving to be worth it at last.

Several narrow streets lay stretched out before them, running at angles to one another toward a common point some distance away, like beams of light emanating from a bright, full sun. The pale, warm stone walls stood quite taller than their heads, and the roads between them were so wide and flat that Brace did not feel at all closed in by them.

"Is this all a dream?" Tassie whispered. Then, raising her voice for the others to hear, she asked, "What is that sweet smell?"

Brace breathed in the scented air. "Flowers?" he guessed.

Jair turned away from the wall and looked in every direction. "This way," he said, quickly choosing one of the pathways and hurrying down it, farther into the brightly-lit city.

"Wait a moment now," Ovard called after him, but Jair paid him no mind. They had no choice but to follow him down the smooth, stone-paved road. The boy stopped suddenly when the street opened up into a wide circle, large enough to hold several hundred people at once. All along the walls grew leafy vines, heavy with some sort of fruit that Brace was sure he'd never before seen, even with all his moving around from place to place.

"That's what we were smelling," Jair announced.

"How ... How did you know this was here?" Leandra asked.

Jair turned to face her. "I don't know," he said with a shrug. "I just *knew*, I think."

"What is this?" Brace asked, stepping toward the nearest wall and running his hand along one of the large red pieces of fruit.

"We can eat it," Jair told him.

"How can you be sure of that?" Arden questioned.

Jair dipped his head. "I don't know," he replied in a small voice. "Doesn't it *look* like we can eat it?"

Tassie examined one of the round fruits growing beside her

before pulling it from the vine. "It feels soft," she said, "and ripe." She looked around at them, expectantly. "There is no way to know whether or not it is safe to eat," she said. "But this is Haven, is it not? A safe place, a place of wonders and miracles. If we can't eat what grows here, it would not seem right, would it?"

"It wouldn't," Brace agreed. He slid his dagger out of his boot, and held a hand out to Tassie. "Let's open it."

With a tiny smile, Tassie placed the fruit in Brace's hand, and he sliced it down the middle, while everyone gathered close to see. The inside of the fruit was very dense and very red, dripping thick, syrupy juice into Brace's palm.

"It smells all right," Tassie commented.

"Well," Arden said, "let's try it." He reached up to take one of the halves.

"Arden," Leandra began, an edge of worry in her voice. "How can you be sure?"

He hesitated a moment. "It's fine, Leandra," he said gently. "It's *fruit*. I'll be all right." He picked up one piece, pulled away the firm outer skin, and took a small bite.

"Very sweet," he said, wiping the juice from his lips with the back of his hand. "It's good. *Very* good." He turned and offered the rest to Ovard, who accepted it. Without further hesitation, Brace ate part of what he still had in his hand, then gave the rest to Tassie. Smiling, Jair ran to the vine growing up the wall nearby and pulled two more pieces free.

They walked as they ate, soaking in the sight of Haven's inner walls. They seemed to be made of glass, over two feet thick, but clear as water in a wash basin. And the light! Each brick glowed, a light source of its own.

Their joyous wonder at discovering what had to be Haven was dampened only by Zorix's worsening condition. By now, his slow breathing had become quite labored. At the far side of the open circle, a row of crumbling stone benches lined one of the walls, near what remained of an ancient fountain. Leandra sat, gingerly at first, until she was certain that the cracked stone would be able to hold her weight.

"Help me get him out of this," she said, tugging at the leather sling. Brace pulled his dagger and carefully cut away two of the leather ties. It felt strange, being close enough to touch her. The last time he'd been so close, she'd had him pinned to the ground with a knife at his throat. She was not quite so bold at the moment, nor did she seem as strong as she had. Gently holding Zorix in her arms, Leandra pulled the wide piece of leather away until it fell in a heap on the ground. She lifted Zorix until his head rested on her shoulder.

"Zorix," she said aloud. "Speak to me, please. Don't let go, do you hear me? Don't you let go. We're *here*, Zorix. We have found Haven, and there is hope here, you must try to find it. Please."

For a moment, Brace thought that Zorix would open his eyes, but they only fluttered momentarily.

"Does he hear you?" Ovard asked gently.

Leandra nodded. "He does. He tries to speak to me, but all I get are feelings. He hurts, all over his body. It hurts to move, even to breathe. And he is weakening."

She tenderly ran her hand over the gray fur on Zorix's head, then looked up, slowly shaking her head. Arden took a few steps away, then abruptly turned back.

"I feel so much stronger now," he blurted out. "When we first came in through the outer wall, I was so tired, all over my body. My legs ached, and my back. But now I feel refreshed. My muscles feel renewed, and I'm no longer exhausted. Do any of you feel the same?"

"You know," Ovard commented, "I think I do. I hadn't thought about it."

"I do as well," Brace agreed, realizing for the first time that the bruise on his right leg had finally stopped throbbing.

"There is something about this place," Arden continued. "Something healing. I was thinking," he said, coming close to Leandra and lowering himself onto the bench beside her, "that it could be the air here, or the heat, or the light. But, if that were the case, *he* would be improving as well."

"What, then?' Leandra asked him.

"It must be the one thing we've had that Zorix hasn't. It must be the fruit."

Leandra's eyes widened, filled with a hint of hope. "Zorix won't eat anything at all, though, not even meat."

"We'll try and make him," Tassie said as she came close, pulling the leathery skin off another piece of the large, juicy red fruit. "Tell him how important it is. Tell him he needs to eat this, no matter how bad he feels."

Leandra nodded, then closed her eyes. She sat quietly for a long moment before looking up.

"I tried to tell him," she said, sounding defeated. "I don't know if he understands."

"Open his mouth," Tassie instructed her, tearing off a piece of fruit slightly larger than her thumb.

Leandra obeyed, gently pressing her fingers between Zorix's teeth until his mouth opened just enough for Tassie to slip in the fruit.

"Eat it, Zorix," Leandra told him. "You *must* eat it." Her words did no good, however. Zorix turned his head aside and let the fruit drop to the ground. Leandra shook her head, but Tassie was determined, tearing off another piece.

"Open his mouth again."

Leandra followed her direction, and this time, Tassie held the fruit over Zorix's mouth and squeezed it, letting the juice run onto his tongue, then sat back to watch him swallow.

"That's something, at least," she said. "We'll keep doing that. It should help him, Leandra. It really should."

Leandra nodded. "Thank you."

Tassie turned, attempting to wipe the sticky juice from her hands. Brace noticed when she tilted her head slightly, as though she'd seen something that puzzled her.

"Jair?" she asked. "What are you looking at?"

Brace turned to see Jair facing a nearby wall, his eyes locked onto its surface.

"This writing," he answered. "I can read it."

Ovard made his way over to stand behind Jair, resting his hands on the boy's shoulders.

"You can read this?" he asked, incredulous. "I can't even read it, with all of the studies I've done. What does it say?"

"'The city of Haven,'" he read. "'This city of refuge is open in welcome to all who will enter it with pure hearts. May all who find themselves within these sacred walls find peace and safety, for years upon years upon years, even until the end of all time.'"

Brace let his mouth fall open in awe. "How did you know how to read that?" he asked.

"I don't know," Jair told him, absently rubbing at the markings on his face. "I think it's the same as how I knew where to find the fruit. Something inside me just told me."

Ovard gently mussed Jair's hair. "I think you're more than a key, my boy," he told him. "I think you have found your true home here. This is where you belong."

"Where we all belong," Jair said firmly. "We all belong here, and so do a lot of other people. Good people, like it says here. People with pure hearts who need a safe place to live, where they won't have to be afraid, or sick, or hungry. We have to help them get here."

"We will, son, we surely will. But in the meantime, I think we should see what remains to be seen. Jair, will you lead us to somewhere with a roof overhead, where we can unload our things?"

Jair smiled. "Follow me."

The boy led them down several streets to a large dwelling built out of stone that glowed a bright light all around its frame. The peak of the roof towered over the high walls nearby. Two large doors revealed the main entrance, one of them slightly open.

"What is this place?" Ovard asked.

"I'm not exactly sure," Jair replied, but he showed no hesitation in pulling the heavy door open wide enough for them to enter.

"Come on," Jair encouraged. "This isn't Bramson. This is Haven! Nothing here will hurt us. Didn't you see? The screamers couldn't even get near the gate."

Brace noticed Ovard's smile as he led the way on, following Jair in through the large open door. Brace followed, taking Tassie's hand as she looked around, her eyes taking everything in. Inside the glowing stone building was one large, open room, with shelves lining the far wall.

"Books!" Jair called out, turning toward Ovard with a smile. "Haven's books! You can learn everything you've ever wanted to know about it!"

Ovard crossed the room and slowly, reverently ran his hand along the dusty leather-bound volumes. He gently pulled one from the shelf and opened it. "But I can't read any of this," he said, his voice heavy with disappointment.

Jair stepped up beside him and peered over his shoulder. "I can," he said quietly. "I can teach you."

Ovard smiled at him. "What does this one say?" he asked.

Jair tilted the book so that he could see the page more closely. "'The keepers of remembrance,'" he read aloud, "'the ones entrusted to keep the knowledge of Haven alive in their hearts and minds, and to pass down this remembrance from generation to generation.'"

Jair paused and looked up at Ovard, who nodded for him to continue.

"'So many are departing,'" Jair went on with ease. "'An age of abandon has begun, the hearts of many growing cold toward their home within Haven's walls, yearning for what may lie beyond, for what the world may have to offer them. Lest Haven be forgotten, the Sent Ones go out among the people, the keepers of remembrance. With every hundred, two are sent. They travel west, they travel east, and north and south. May the keepers be true to their task, may they never forget their home of old. Should the departed wish to return, the keepers will know the way, for they have been given the key.'"

"The key," Ovard whispered.

"I thought I was the key," Jair remarked in awe.

"You *have* the key," Arden spoke up. "There must be others who have it as well."

"My parents must have been descendants of keepers," Jair thought aloud. "But the book says that for every hundred people who left Haven, two keepers were sent. My parents couldn't have been the only ones who remembered the way back. Could there be more people out there who know the way back in? Do they know it's time to come home?"

Ovard let the pages of the ancient text slide closed.

"There's no way of knowing," he replied. "I suppose all we can do is wait and see."

One hour, two ... how much longer they wandered Haven's streets, Brace wasn't certain, but now he felt as though he were being gnawed at from the inside as he lay on his back, staring up at the low, pale stone ceiling of the small dwelling he'd taken as his own. Jair found, some time after leaving the ancient library, an area of Haven that had evidently been housing for the townsfolk, judging from the remains of cookstoves and stone supports for bed mattresses. They found water as well, cool, running water in a stream as clear as crystal. They folded the hide tents and stuffed them with leaves and grasses, making for very comfortable and fragrant bedding.

The relief in Leandra's eyes had been more than visible, showing her gratitude at being led to a place where she could lie down, and at the effect that the red fruit juice was having on Zorix. His breathing was coming more easily, and he finally opened his eyes to look up at her face. They were open for only a moment, but it was enough.

They unloaded all of their possessions—extra clothing, blankets, food, and Tassie's medical supplies—and arranged them along various shelves. They chose four of the homes for the time being, one for Arden and Leandra, one for Tassie, which was a bit larger and could double as a clinic, one for Ovard and Jair, and one for Brace. It was a strange feeling, once again having a roof over their heads and protective walls around them.

In addition to the smaller homes, they found long, common halls and other large, high-ceilinged rooms whose purposes were still a mystery to them. Here, they may not have every convenience of life within a city's walls, but it was a far cry from fighting to survive through scorching deserts and windy mountain passes. What weighed on Brace's mind now were the words that Jair had read from the wall in the circular courtyard: "A refuge, open in welcome to all who will enter it with pure hearts."

It was the *pure hearts* that troubled him. Ovard had long been searching for Haven because he felt that doing so was a responsibility that had been laid upon his shoulders. Jair was all but placed into his arms when the boy had been small, and with him came the knowledge of the long-lost city. Arden and Leandra had joined the search in order to provide protection for the travelers; they had no ulterior motives. And Tassie ... Brace was certain that Tassie, of all people, hid no guile within her heart.

But *he*—so many years, so much deceit, so many times his hands had been soiled by the things he had stolen, from the wealthy and cottagers alike, it made no difference. He had cared only for himself. *A pure heart?* When had he ever had a pure heart? His feelings for Tassie had not even been pure—not completely, not at first. No. He didn't belong here. The creators of Haven would surely not have welcomed him here.

"Brace?" Tassie's voice came to him through the open doorway. He turned to see the outline of her figure, with the bright light of Haven filling in the area around her.

"Yes?" he asked, sitting up on the bed. "What is it?"

Tassie came into the room, slowly, and sat beside him.

"Are you settled in?" he asked her, and she nodded, smiling.

"I am."

Ovard and Jair had gone off again for the moment, a fact for which Brace was grateful. It gave him a bit of time to speak with Tassie alone.

Tassie's smile faded. "Is something troubling you?" she asked.

"Zorix is getting better by the moment. He will come through all right."

"Well, that's good to hear," he told her, "but that's not what has got me thinking."

"What is it then?"

Brace let out a sigh, and rubbed at his freshly washed hair, still slightly damp. "It's this place," he began.

"Haven?" Tassie asked, surprised. "What could possibly be wrong? Isn't it everything you had imagined it would be?"

"No, it is," Brace told her. "Well, nothing is wrong with Haven."

"What, then?"

Brace looked down at the cobbled floor. "It's me," he said, but Tassie put her hand on his face and made him look up at her.

"It's me," he repeated. "I don't think I belong here."

"Why not?" Tassie asked firmly.

"This is a perfect place," he replied. "A place where people can come and have freedom, a place meant for ... well, for people who deserve to be here. And I don't."

"You don't? And who has decided this?"

"I have," he told her abruptly. "The words on that courtyard wall, they said Haven was a place for pure hearts. You know what I've been, Tassie. You know I've been a thief and a liar all my life. I don't have a pure heart. I don't deserve this place."

Tassie's lips pressed together, they way they always did when something displeased her.

"But you are someone who helped us get here," she argued. "You've given of yourself, Brace. You gave up your plans to escape to Danferron. You helped provide for us. You even risked your life to save Jair from that angry dragon."

Brace grinned sarcastically. "You make it sound like I pulled him right out of the dragon's jaws."

Tassie shook her head. "You know what I'm trying to tell you. This place may be perfect, but that does not mean that *you* need to be. Your heart is not perfect, no, but neither is mine, or Leandra's, or Ovard's, or even Jair's. And, if you left, where would you go? You can't stay in Dunya, where you're a wanted man. Would you run to Danferron? Would you leave Jair behind? Would you leave *me*?"

Brace could hear the frustration rising in Tassie's voice.

"I didn't say I was going to leave," he told her. "I just … I don't know."

Tassie stood abruptly. "You may be used to running, Brace, when things get too difficult to face, but I thought you'd learned that was something you don't need to do." Her voice was accusatory. "I thought you'd grown past that."

Brace reached out and grabbed hold of her hand. "Hush, Tassie, calm down, please. I'm not going to run away."

"Can you promise me that, Brace? Can you? Because if we're going to be together, I don't want to have to be fearful that you'll leave if things get too hard."

"Hush, Tassie," Brace said again, rising to his feet beside her.

"No, I won't hush," she told him. "I want you to promise me." Her green eyes flashed.

"I promise." Gently but firmly, Brace pulled her toward him.

"That was too easy," she said, but her voice had begun to soften.

"I promise," he told her again, looking deep into her eyes.

Tassie nodded slowly, holding his gaze. "I believe you," she whispered.

"Good," he whispered back. "I wasn't lying."

"Then no more talk of leaving," she told him, stepping back. "At least not for good. There is so much that needs to be done here. Homes that have been empty for centuries need to be repaired, also things in the common areas. The fountain in the courtyard needs to be fixed. There is still so much of the city we haven't seen, things that have yet to be discovered. We've got to get Haven ready for what it's always meant to be, full of people. And you can't have forgotten: someone needs to go back for Kendie."

"Kendie. Yes. We promised her, didn't we?"

"We did."

Brace nodded. "I can go back for her."

"You'll go and bring her back," Tassie went on, her voice softening. "And Haven will be her home, and yours."

Brace nodded, then leaned forward until his lips met hers. She started to pull away, but soon gave herself over to his kisses.

"Stop now," she told him after a moment.

"Why?"

"This is your place," she replied. "But it isn't mine. Don't go too quickly. If you still want me, then we will have our own place, the two of us." She smiled a coy smile. "And then we won't have to stop."

"*If* I still want you?" Brace asked, running his hand along her hair. "You know I do."

The sound of someone clearing his throat caught Brace's attention, and he turned to look toward the doorway to see Arden leaning against one wall, smirking.

"I don't see any marriage symbols on those hands of yours just yet," he told them, and Tassie reddened. "Besides," Arden continued, "Jair has found something else that you might find interesting."

"What is it?" Brace asked.

"You'll have to come and see," Arden replied, waving them on.

Outside, the light of day was beginning to fade into evening. It all seemed so much more natural, though, not at all like the way it had been, so early, and the sky was not at all hazy. No strange fog hung around the horizons, ready to pour in on them. The light radiating from Haven's city walls was beginning to dim as well. Apparently, the stones seemed to know when it should be daylight, and when it needed to be dark, when the people living here needed to sleep.

Arden led Tassie and Brace past the curving streets lined with homes of varying sizes, on past another courtyard, this one very square, and into one of the large structures with the high ceilings.

"What is this?" Brace asked as they stepped in through the high, wide doorway.

"I'm not certain," Arden replied. "Some kind of meeting hall, maybe?"

Jair and Ovard stood along the far wall, looking at it closely.

"What have you found?" Brace asked as he approached them, holding Tassie by the hand. "More writing?"

"No," Jair told him. "Look and see."

Stepping closer, Brace could see that an image of sorts had been carved into the stones. It was quite large, as though meant to be visible all throughout the room. It appeared to be a deer of some sort, frolicking through leaves or flowers, its head turned so that it faced the crescent moon above its back.

"I think this is Haven's crest," Jair voiced his opinion. "I think we need to get some cloth and make a banner. Every city needs a banner. Meriton had one; even Bale has a banner, and Bale is just a villa, not a city. When people come here to be safe from the darkness, wouldn't it be perfect for them to see Haven's banner flying from a high tower in the circle courtyard? It would welcome them home."

"That is a fine idea, Jair," Tassie said, beaming.

"Haven is our home now," Jair added, turning toward Ovard. "Isn't it?"

"It certainly is, and I hope it will be for a very long time."

Jair nodded, looking around at each of them as he spoke, his voice full of excitement. "It is our home, and Tassie, you can be our medic here. And Ovard, you can teach people about art and music and history, and Arden, you can show people how to use a bow, and shoot arrows. And Leandra—"

"Leandra is going to be busy for a time," Arden interrupted. "Zorix is still healing; she'll be looking after him. And then, she is going to be a mother. Don't forget that. She'll have a little one to watch over."

"Right," Jair replied, grinning. "She is going to have a baby. And I'll be one of the good-uncles. And Brace, so will you."

Brace smiled. "I will."

"You are Haven's key, Jair," Leandra told him, wrapping her arms around him from behind. "This place is in good hands with you looking over it."

"Me?" he asked, his eyes wide. "You think I can look over *all* of Haven?"

"You are already doing it, young man," Ovard told him proudly. "I think we would all do well to have you in charge of things."

"I don't know if I can do it alone."

"You won't be alone," Ovard encouraged. "We're all here to help you."

Brace wrapped his arms around Tassie's shoulders, no longer caring who took notice or what they might be thinking.

"Well, Haven's Key," Ovard continued, patting Jair on the back, "what is our main priority for the time being?"

Jair smiled. "Getting everything ready to welcome everyone here, starting with Kendie." He turned, fixing his eyes on Brace. "And then, we'll have a *wedding*."

About the Author

Tia Austin lives in Northwest Washington, where she enjoys spending time outside, walking the forest trails and along the rocky beaches. She has been writing fiction and poetry ever since she was a child. Her favorite genres to write (and read!) are fantasy and historical fiction.

CPSIA information can be obtained at www.ICGtesting.com
Printed in the USA
LVOW12s0545260314

378795LV00003B/8/P